THE
LAST
WILD
HORSES

THE
LAST
WILD
HORSES

A NOVEL

MAJA LUNDE

Translated from the Norwegian by Diane Oatley

SCRIBNER

LONDON NEW YORK SYDNEY TORONTO NEW DELHI

First published in the United States by Harpervia,
an imprint of HarperCollins Publishers, 2022
First published in Great Britain by Scribner,
an imprint of Simon & Schuster UK Ltd, 2022

Copyright © Maja Lunde, 2019
English translation copyright © 2021 by Diane Oatley.

Originally published as *Przewalskis hest* in Norway in 2019 by Aschehoug.

The right of Maja Lunde to be identified as the author of
this work has been asserted in accordance with the
Copyright, Designs and Patents Act, 1988.

SCRIBNER and design are registered trademarks of The Gale Group, Inc.,
used under licence by Simon & Schuster Inc.

1 3 5 7 9 10 8 6 4 2

Simon & Schuster UK Ltd
1st Floor
222 Gray's Inn Road
London WC1X 8HB

www.simonandschuster.co.uk
www.simonandschuster.com.au
www.simonandschuster.co.in

Simon & Schuster Australia, Sydney
Simon & Schuster India, New Delhi

A CIP catalogue record for this book
is available from the British Library

Hardback ISBN: 978-1-4711-7564-0
Trade Paperback ISBN: 978-1-4711-7565-7
eBook ISBN: 978-1-4711-7566-4

Designed by SBI Book Arts, LLC

Printed and bound by CPI Group (UK) Ltd, Croydon, CR0 4YY

MIX
Paper from
responsible sources
FSC
www.fsc.org
FSC® C171272

EVA

Heiane, Viken, Norway, 2064

The stallion's attraction to the mare verged on euphoria. The instinct was all-consuming, making him delirious, unpredictable. As a human being, I will never understand such an intense, physical craving. Well, there was a period of my life when I'd allowed myself to be pulled under the surface, where I'd let go, but only for a few minutes and that was long ago. I could no longer afford such a luxury. The only drive propelling my actions now was hunger. Hunger can make a person behave irrationally, too, in a manner resembling madness. Hunger can compel us to do just about anything.

There's no arguing with an animal's drives, so I had to protect Nike, my mare. Rimfaxe was relentless, although the fences around Nike and her foal Puma should have been enough to keep him at a safe distance. Nike was in heat and this lured him to the paddock no matter how much I yelled and gesticulated. She'd lost her partner, Hummel the stallion, last autumn. He'd been old and tired; I took pity on him. And now Nike was alone. I knew she would not find peace until she conceived. But she couldn't have what she wanted because she was a takhi, one of the few remaining wild horses in the world, and Rimfaxe was just a wholly ordinary, tame horse Richard had freed before his departure from the neighboring farm one year ago. The foal of a wild horse and a tame horse would inherit predominantly the characteristics of the tame horse; the bloodline would die out after just two generations, and all our efforts to bring her here, the work invested to ensure the continued survival of her breed, would have been in vain.

"Get out of here, Rimfaxe!"

The stallion rubbed against the fence, thrust his muzzle toward Nike trying to reach her, and the mare encouraged him, lifting her tail and turning her hindquarters in his direction.

I ran closer waving my arms.

"Get out of here! Shoo!"

Rimfaxe whinnied at me, twisting and side-stepping a bit, before trotting away, his haunches expressing his indignation.

"Forget about it!" I shouted after him. "Go find a horse of your own kind!"

Soon, I would no longer need to guard them like this. It was September. Nike was about to commence her six-month anestrus period, six months of peace and quiet for both of us. During the winter, I had control over the animals' behavior and my own situation. As long as the larder was full, as long as the winter storms kept their distance, as long as the power didn't go out, life was manageable in the winter.

I walked all the way over to the fence, leaned against a pole, and reached my hands out to the wild horses.

"Good morning, Nike. Hi, Puma."

They turned their heads toward me, recognizing my voice. Puma came over first, his skinny legs nimble against the ground. He was still new to the world, a little unsteady, and his movements had a kind of hesitancy. He poked his muzzle through the fence and snuffled softly.

"Do I have something for you?" I asked and smiled. "You think I have something for the two of you?"

I stuck my hand in my pocket.

"Okay, but just for today."

Nike came over as well. Her nostrils flared when she discovered the carrots I'd taken out of my pocket.

"There you go, little one." I gave the first carrot to Puma. A small carrot, because he was still too young to digest much of anything except the mare's milk.

Nike stomped one hoof.

"Take it easy. There's one for you, too."

I gave her the biggest one. It vanished into her mouth in a flash and she crunched on it loudly.

"Don't tell Isa," I said.

Nike snorted, waving her tail.

"Isa's strict? Yes, my daughter is strict."

I stood there just watching them for a little while though they paid me no further attention, and then I turned and hurried back to the farm. It was Friday, shopping day, and I had to go down to the quay. Sometimes fishermen or hunters would still show up down there. The hens had laid many eggs in the past week and maybe somebody would come who'd be interested in them.

I hurried past the abandoned newsstand, where the windows were broken and the advertising posters bleached pale from the sun, walked up the hill around the enclosure that had sheltered cat species of all kinds, passed by the small wetland area that Grandfather had created as a refuge for endangered amphibians at the start of the new millennium, and the fenced-in grove where the wolves had hidden, the shyest species we'd had.

For all three generations during which my family ran the park, the animals had thrived in our care. They had demonstrated as much by giving us offspring. The public came to be entertained and to learn, and the highlight was the chance to see the baby animals. Then visitors would laugh and point and say look, look, how cute, how incredibly cute! Once the snow leopard had triplets; it caused a sensation. We never had as many visitors as we did that summer. But for us, new life was always a serious matter. I remember the other children at school thought we were strange, that it was embarrassing to have friends over. Breeding and impregnation were topics of conversation around the dinner table in our house. And when new, small creatures came into the world, we cared for them as if they were our own children. No, they're not ours, they're theirs, Daddy always said, and our job is to make sure they have the best possible living conditions so they will want to reproduce.

Now the snow leopards were gone, most of the other animals, too; only a few remained in my care. A small herd of Finnish forest reindeer lived in the large area previously inhabited by the wolves. The species was not endangered, but they managed more or less on their own down there, which was why I hadn't yet released them. Two mangy peregrine falcons, both females, I still kept in a cage. They didn't require much care, but I feared they would die if the day should come when I could no longer look after them. A single Scottish wildcat lived alone in the area of the park furthest west. I couldn't bring myself to set him free; then he would just mate with a tame cat and his bloodline would die out. And of course, Nike and Puma—my most cherished animals. I protected them fiercely.

It was Anne, my sister, who'd taken on the responsibility of bringing wild horses here to Heiane. She'd been talking about them ever since she was a little girl. I remember how she watched the same films on YouTube over and over again, sat by herself with her iPad in her lap and headphones over her ears while the horses galloped across the screen in front of her. She worked for several years to buy a stallion and a mare from a sanctuary in France and finally she got Heiane accepted into an international breeding program. Nike and Hummel were some of the very last horses to be sold between parks. Horses like Rimfaxe would always survive, but there were far too few wild horses left in the world. I hoped that when all of this was over, when life had stabilized and it was possible to contact potential partners out there, it would be possible to acquire a new stallion for Nike. Because in Mongolia there might still be wild horses. They'd had so many. Some of them must still be alive?

4

Nike and Puma were named after running shoes. Anne came up with their names; she'd named all our animals. She named them after things that no longer existed: clothing, electric gadgets, watches, and cars. Isa thought it was funny; she still laughed at the names from time to time. Personally, they reminded me a little too much of Anne. Not just of her sense of humor, but of her drive. And her presence; those two things were perhaps connected. She was formidable and she was a person who got things done.

But Anne was gone—her strong voice, her body that never sat still. She'd left Heiane, she'd left us and the horses, said it was just for a few months, but she never came back. The last time I spoke to her she'd made it as far north as Trøndelag. That was almost one year ago. Then our telephone stopped working. The signals vanished and we were really alone. Isa started locking the door every night. We're safe here, I said, and installed a dead bolt on the inside of the door.

"When will you be back?" Isa asked.

I was standing beside the pickup, ready to drive down to the quay.

"You know that I don't know. Maybe nobody will be there today. Maybe nobody has anything to sell. The last time I had to wait for several hours."

"Can't I come with you? We can do the cows together when we come back."

"It's best if you stay here."

"Alone." She hunched her shoulders apprehensively. "Can't you teach me to drive soon?"

"You're only fourteen."

"It's not exactly like we're going to be stopped."

I took a chance and reached out my hand to ruffle her hair.

"I'll be as quick as I can."

She didn't twist away, let me pat her on the head.

"If any strangers should come, lock the door," I said. "Remember the dead bolt, too."

"I will."

"And pretend you're not home."

"I know, Mother."

"And by the way, can you check and see if the cellar door is closed? I don't want the rain to get inside."

"Yes."

"Bye now, sweetie."

I gave her a quick hug. Isa hugged me back. Friday was the only day she would actually hug me back. She was as tall as me now and had pimples on her forehead, but her cheeks were still as smooth as a child's. When I thought about Isa, it was a child I pictured, so every time I saw her now, it startled me. She was tall, thin, and gangly, had small breasts under her T-shirt and high, chiseled cheekbones. Just one year ago she was a child; now she swayed her hips a bit when she walked, her movements self-aware and studied, as if she were putting herself on display all the time, as if there were anyone here to show herself to. I wondered if, from now on, I would always be startled. If I would always be surprised at the sight of my child, and whether all parents had the same reaction.

Isa released me abruptly, realized that she was too old to hug me in this way. We fell silent; she looked away, embarrassed.

"You won't forget the cellar door, will you?" I said to help her.

"No," she said. "Go on, then."

I got into the pickup, started the engine. The sky darkened and the first raindrops splattered loudly against the windshield. Isa was still waiting in the yard; I could see her in the rearview mirror. If I squinted, she still looked like she was seven or eight. She stood the way she's always done, with her feet slightly turned out and one of her arms around the other, as if she were hugging herself. I swallowed and focused on the road.

I'd driven a couple of kilometers without seeing a soul when a small group suddenly appeared on the left side of the road. A mother, a father, two daughters. Each of them had a knapsack on their back and they were pushing a neon-yellow bicycle cart full of possessions in front of them. The rain poured off them, their faces hidden beneath large hoods, their clothing so wet it was dark. Only the bicycle cart's letters shone undaunted: *Sports Extreme.* The father held out his thumb when he saw me, a lone, white finger, sticking up from a skinny hand, the universal sign that you were one of them, a wanderer.

I stomped on the gas pedal, sped past them as fast as I could, avoiding the rearview mirror so I'd be spared the sight of their reaction.

Isa wanted us to leave, to be like them, live on the road. Abandon Heiane and head north the way all the others had done in search of the small villages that still existed, in search of a human society where life resembled the life we'd had before. All of Europe was *walking*, in a state of disorientation, without a destination. For many years people had been displaced; the drought drove them into exile. The borders were closed in the north when I was still a child. Then The Collapse came. And the war. For seven years, they kept at it—the war over food, over water. Instead of investing their energy in preparations for what we knew was coming, they invested everything in winning. But nobody won; only losers remained.

Now nobody went to war any longer and everything we'd fought for was gone. Even the borders had disappeared.

We were lucky to live here. We were lucky never to have had the battlefields in our backyard, to have a well full of water. A farm, a home, something to cultivate, animals to breed. As long as we had the farm, we wouldn't be forced to migrate. There should be no question about it. But something or other changed when Anne left us. And when Richard and his family also left immediately afterward, and Isa lost Agnes and Lars, her only friends, she started pestering me. She didn't understand why we still lived here. She brought it up all the time, worried about it, claimed that the animals gave us less than before, that they were starting to get old, the cows and the hens and Boeing, the pig, who actually should have been slaughtered for Christmas last year. Richard and his family had gone in the direction of Nordland. They had family near Bodø, and they still lived well up there, they claimed. There were enough fish in the ocean for them to manage and the society still resembled a small city. It was to Nordland that Isa sometimes said she wanted to go when I asked what her plan was. As if we would manage to make it all the way up there; as if the little community still existed when all the others had disappeared. If we left, the highway would become our home.

Besides, Isa forgot about the animals. They weren't here for us, after all; it was more that we were here for them. The few wild animals that remained in the park needed me. Especially Puma. We couldn't leave him, particularly not now that the grass was withering and a whiff of decay hung in the air.

When I left the farm, the rain had been merely a drizzle, but as I approached the harbor the sky turned a dark gray, almost black. Several weeks had passed since the last heavy downpour, but the ground was still saturated with moisture. The water would have nowhere to go and I thought about the cellar, envisioned how the rain would leak through, cover the floor, and rise.

Hopefully, Isa had remembered to close the cellar door. The outside stairway turned into a brook in a downpour and if the door was open, the damage would be even greater. We kept our flour down there— last summer I'd bartered my way to two hundred kilos of wholemeal flour—and the vegetables, even though there were less than I'd hoped after the wet summer, and ten kilos of rice I'd been fortunate enough to get hold of a few weeks ago. The last time there was a downpour, I'd moved the sacks onto shelves higher up. But maybe not high enough.

It was raining harder and harder, the sky coming closer, an enormous, threatening body that descended upon the landscape. The drops pounded against the roof of the cab and flatbed. While last summer was so dry and hot that nothing would grow and I went around with a constant fear of a fire outbreak, we'd hardly seen the sun this year. I was wearing a rain jacket, rain pants, and boots, but was clammy through and through, even inside the pickup. The damp permeated everything. When I was a little girl we distinguished between rainy spells and dry spells. Now we distinguished between the many different kinds of precipitation. The lightest kind that hung like mist in the air, so you didn't notice it was raining until you saw the water beading on your jacket. Drizzle and light rain, in my opinion, were the same thing, but Isa insisted that drizzle was finer than light rain. Then there was heavy rainfall, this despondent precipitation that fell straight down on windless days. Squalls of rain stirred up by the wind. And the most intense downpours, when the sluices of the heavens opened, the world became an ocean, and I couldn't help but think of Noah.

I drove all the way down to the water and parked just a few meters from the quay. Heiane had been a trading post for fifteen hundred years. We used to be proud of our history, even had a small museum where visitors could see old jewelry and tools from the time when the Vikings met here and traded their wares. The jewelry was stolen a long time ago, and otherwise, there were no visible traces of the past in the village. Heiane was but a collection of houses and summer cabins around the quay; the settlement spread upward across gently rolling hillsides. The houses that had once had uniform red and white surfaces were now full of nuances, like tie-dye. People still lived in some of them, but fewer and fewer all the time. Everyone I'd had contact with had long since moved away. Everyone except Einar. He lived with his buddies in one of the village's most beautiful cabins, an old sea captain's dwelling with a huge annex, the paint peeling off the walls, and punctured glass in the picture windows. The cabin's waterfront location would have once been worth millions, but, in recent years, the water's edge had crept steadily closer as the ocean rose indiscernibly, a few millimeters annually. I couldn't see anyone outside, nor any lights in the windows. As long as I didn't run into Einar, everything would be fine. I was afraid of the wanderers, too, the hungry desperation that drove them, but still nobody had found our farm. Nobody could imagine that the almost overgrown gravel road actually led somewhere, to someone. Nobody except Einar. So it was his tired, rough face I saw when I turned the key in the lock and threw the dead bolt every evening.

9

I didn't get out of the pickup right away, but, instead, sat for a moment surveying my surroundings. The harbor was quiet. It's been several years since the stores closed. Several years since I stopped using money. I paid mostly with milk and eggs, which we had enough of year-round. In the summer and autumn, we also often had corn and some vegetables and fruit, but this season a lot had been washed away by the rain. The vegetables and fruit we harvested we always kept for ourselves. They were precious; the blossoms had to be fertilized by hand. There were still some wild insects that helped out, but I had long since given up on the beehives. The bee boxes were in the barn now. The sweet aroma of honey and beeswax still clung to them, a faint presence that inhabited the entire huge interior, and sometimes I would go over to the corner where the hives were, inhale deeply, feel how the scent filled me, amazed at how long it lingered, the scent that was the memory of everything we'd lost.

I usually traded for meat or fish. Protein for Isa. Sometimes hunters came to the quay. They brought with them game from the forest: squirrel, wild boar, and fox, sometimes deer and wolves, but also farm animals that had escaped, wild dogs and cats. And magpies; you could always shoot magpies.

During the first years following The Collapse, people had talked about how all the animals would die because the ecosystem was in turmoil. When one thing came to a halt, everything came to a halt. But they forgot that there are always species that take over, that step in, that adapt. And they forgot that we human beings no longer occupied as much space.

The species that pulled through were better off than ever before. Not all species of birds could survive without insects, but the omnivores, like the crows and the magpies, continued to flourish in increasing numbers. They ate whatever they could find—nuts, compost, small birds, carcasses, Spanish slugs, worms, the eggs of other birds; they fed screaming offspring in full nests, reproduced again and again. They grew larger and larger, sliding across the sky with their screaming, hoarse cries, always hanging up there above us as if they owned the world.

During the past half year, the number of people who came here on Fridays declined steadily; now the quay was sometimes even deserted. Today a lone fisherman sat beside his boat. A man, they were always men, those who came alone. I couldn't see anyone but him and therefore chanced opening the door of the pickup, taking my basket with me, and walked over to him.

A codfish stared up at me out of a cracked Styrofoam crate. It couldn't have been larger than a couple of kilos, but that was enough for Isa and me. I said I wanted to buy it and offered him the three eggs I had with me.

"Four," he said.

"Three," I said. "That's all I have."

"The cod is worth more than three. You know that."

"I bet you're sick of fish," I said. "I bet you really have a craving for eggs."

He stared at me, his eyes narrowing.

"I have a couple of crows," he said. "You can have one of them in exchange for your eggs."

He pointed down at the deck. Two dead birds lay there, shot, both bloody. Some of their sisters and brothers sailed across the sky and swerved toward the boat as if insulted by the killings.

"We don't eat crows," I said. "There are too few of them. You have to stop shooting them. Besides, they taste awful."

"You just have to add a lot of spices, then you can't taste the cod liver oil."

"I'd rather have your fish."

"I get that. It's fresh. I caught it yesterday. Fresh and clean."

"It's not clean. You know that as well as I do. I'll give you three eggs."

"I want four."

"Listen here," I said. "I have a daughter. She's a growing girl. We need the eggs for ourselves."

"I have two sons," he said. "Eight-year-old twins. I don't see them often, am out fishing all week long . . . there's so little fish now that soon I'll have to go out on the weekends, too."

"I have a son, too," I said. "And a husband. There are four of us sharing our food supplies."

I noticed a few drops of moisture trickling down my neck. I just wanted to go home, peel off my rainwear, fry the fish, share it with Isa, feel properly full.

"Three eggs," I insisted, one last time. "Please, that's all I have with me."

I lifted my hand to my throat, tried to dry myself off and maybe it was the movement that caused his eyes to start wandering. Downward, toward my breasts, hips, everything hidden by the shapeless rain garments.

"How old are you?" he asked.

So, he was one of those. I regretted the hand movement, that I had failed to stand completely still.

"Too old for you," I said.

I tried to stand tall, straighten my back.

"You can have the fish for free," he said. "The cabin is warm."

He kept looking at me. I stared back at him, forcing him to meet my gaze. I'm not the one who's supposed to regret this, who's supposed to feel ashamed, you should. The drops continued downward, ran over my collar bone, and down between my breasts. The damp woolen undershirt irritated my skin and I stood completely still.

Suddenly he looked down and squirmed; maybe he was embarrassed. That gave me courage. I quickly took an old newspaper out of the basket, leaned down toward the fish, and lifted it onto the paper.

"I'll take the fish. Because you were a jerk."

I noticed his astonishment but didn't look at him, just wrapped up the cod as rapidly as I could; it was slippery against the paper, making it hard to hold it in place. I placed the fish in the basket, getting slime and blood on my fingers, and wiped my forehead with one hand, maybe leaving a bit behind there as well.

"Fine," he said. "Sorry."

"Drop it," I said.

"I don't know why I suggested it," he said. "I've heard that others do it . . . so I thought . . ."

"Don't do it again," I said. "Don't suggest it again, not to anyone."

"I won't," he mumbled. "Got it."

Where did he even find the desire? I knew how I looked. My damp hair was plastered against my skull, my skin had become coarse in recent years, my face was lined, my jaw protruded, giving me the look of an animal, a lynx, my chewing muscles the strongest in my body. An aging animal. It had been a long time since I'd dyed my hair, a long time since there was any hair dye to be had, strands of steely gray hair pushed their way through my scalp all the time. I probably looked older than my forty-three years.

I ran my fingers across my forehead again, wanted to wipe off the blood I didn't know for sure was there. Then I stepped away, about to leave.

"But I would like to have the eggs," he said.

"I'm sure you would."

I put my hand in the basket and took out three eggs, two brown and one white. I tried not to think about his eight-year-old boys, though I wasn't certain they existed; they were maybe just something he invented, the way I also lied about a husband and another child.

He accepted the eggs carefully. Three eggs for one fish. I'd won; the fish was worth four eggs, at least. He'd wanted to steal something from me, but I was the one who ended up stealing from him.

I turned away from him, a little ashamed, but still angry. I had to get home, away from him, home to Isa.

That was when I saw her.

A woman alone at the bus stop. A wanderer.

She had a small knapsack on her back, no other luggage. And she was holding an umbrella in her hand.

An umbrella. I couldn't remember the last time I'd seen somebody with an umbrella—a meaningless little roof that she tried to hold up against the wind so it wouldn't flip inside out. She was already soaking wet, her jeans dark with water, it was dripping from the straps on her backpack.

I started walking toward the pickup. The woman with the umbrella was not my responsibility; the fisherman's sons were not my responsibility.

But I was unable to refrain from turning around again, from looking at her one more time.

A moment of calm between gusts of wind allowed her to relax. She stood tall, waiting, although the timetable had been torn down long ago and it had to be obvious that no bus would be stopping there.

The fisherman was in the process of undoing the moorings. He wouldn't touch her. But there were others. Einar, his buddies, their filthy hands, and the aggression that arose when intoxication met with hunger. They were stupid and ridiculous, but they were stronger than her.

The rain intensified. The wind rushed across the landscape, driving the rain up underneath the umbrella.

I thought about the cellar door again; I bet Isa forgot about it. The rice could be ruined.

I took out the key, stuck it in the lock. The woman was maybe ten meters away from me and now her eyes met mine. Her face was in the shadow of the umbrella, but I could still see her clearly. Motionless, she didn't blink, it was a gaze from which I couldn't hide.

I could smell the stench of the fish in the basket. I had gotten it for three eggs; it was worth five.

I raised my hand. It stunk, too, of fish blood and slime, and I probably had flecks of blood on my face.

"Do you need help?"

"No," the woman said.

She answered so quickly that I didn't believe her.

"Where you headed?" I asked.

She shrugged. "North."

"The bus isn't running."

"I know."

"It hasn't run for several years."

"Yes."

"Where'd you come from?"

"The south."

"Did you hitch with a boat?"

"I hitched, yeah. With a car, a truck, another car, a boat, a car, then another boat. Maybe there were more. I can't remember."

"And now?"

She made a face. "Like I said, probably north. If I wait here, maybe somebody will stop and give me a ride."

"You should go onto the main road," I said. "More cars pass through there."

"Okay," she said. "Thanks."

I opened the door to the pickup. She stayed where she was. She was frail, shifted her weight a bit from side to side even when she was standing still. Not much taller than Isa but, although she was small, or maybe precisely because of that, her cheeks were round. She didn't have to eat much to maintain her weight, or perhaps she was better than most people at finding what she needed. Besides, she was apparently on her own; she didn't have to slide the best, most fatty morsels across the table to someone else. Her eyes were also round, a bit wide-eyed, vigilant, as if nothing escaped her notice.

I got into the pickup, started the engine, drove slowly forward. The power gauge was almost at zero, so I didn't switch on the fan or the windshield wipers, hoping the battery would last all the way home.

I peeked in the rearview mirror. She'd started walking. A slender female body on the road.

She's not your problem.

A whole fish for three eggs.

We needed the fish. Isa needed it. And besides . . . a wanderer.

But a woman alone, so easy to grab, restrain, force to the ground.

I stopped the pickup and opened the door.

"Hop in," I said. "It's warm and dry in here."

She glanced at the seat beside me, toward the warmth inside the pickup.

"No. I don't need any help," she said.

"Hop in anyway."

She hesitated. The rain fell even harder. The drops of water bounced against her umbrella, it looked like it would soon be destroyed by the weight of it, as if the seams in the thin fabric would tear. She was starting to shake from the cold.

"No. I'm moving on," she said. "I don't need any help."

Even though she held her head high and I saw that she was trying to come across as strong, the little crack in her voice gave her away.

"Maybe *I* need help," I said.

She squirmed, the umbrella trembled feebly in her hand, sending small waterfalls tumbling to the ground. She looked at me, at the pickup.

"Are you alone?" she asked.

"Just me and my daughter."

The woman nodded slightly, as if this reassured her.

"Maybe I could stay for one night," she said. "Just until my clothes are dry."

"We have an available bed for one night," I said. "We have eggs and milk, too."

"Thanks," she said softly and got into the pickup.

THE STORY OF MY VOYAGE TO MONGOLIA
AND WHAT I FOUND THERE

Written in St. Petersburg, September 1882

CHAPTER 1

AN EXTRAORDINARY
DISCOVERY

The house is silent except for the sound of the maid rummaging through the kitchen cabinets. I am sitting at my desk and have decided to write my story. I have been trying to put words down on paper for a long time, have written long letters, all of them to the same man, but every single one of them ended up like a hard-packed snowball in the wastepaper basket. Today, after a stroll through the Summer Garden, I finally understood that my attempts at correspondence are futile. I am not supposed to be writing letters; Wolff isn't supposed to be my reader. This story is not about him and me, it is about the wild horses. This is their story, and somebody has to tell it before too many of the details fade into oblivion.

Hopefully, my text will find its way to a reader or two, the story of our search for the wild horses and about the life lived by both animals and humans on the steppes. It should capture the interest of all those with even a modest interest in zoology and ethnography and, if you are one of these readers, I would request your forbearance with any superfluous details or tedious digressions. Out of respect for the actual events, I haven't dared omit much, because who knows what may prove to be of significance for posterity?

My tale begins on an ordinary Monday morning in May of 1880 with the sound of iron horseshoes clattering against cobblestones slick with rain on the street outside the apartment and the coachman's loud *ptro*. I then heard the sound of the carriage door being opened and footsteps against the ground and, in the next second, three loud raps of the front door knocker.

On that day, as now, I was at my desk in my study on the second floor. Mother had just gone out to do run some errands. I was alone and was intending to review the accounts one more time before leaving for work. I felt a slight irritation over the metallic pounding of the knocker against the front door, but also a certain sense of relief. The accounts for the zoological garden were anything but jolly reading. No matter how many times I examined them, the figures showed no signs of improvement. I caught myself hoping they might move around, change places, that plus might become minus and minus plus, that they could live, become equals, as spontaneous and warm-blooded as the animals they represented. The evening before, I had, in fact, studied the account books after four stiff drams in hopes that the inebriation might cause them to start dancing. But not this time, either. My field is the natural sciences and mathematics is considered a part of this, but the path from the living creatures to which I, as assistant director of Petersburg's zoological garden, had dedicated my life, to these blue lines of ink on grayish-white paper was as long as from here to Mercury.

The problem was Berta, a hippopotamus I had insisted we purchase from Germany a few months ago. The director left the acquisitions to me; he took care of operations and staff, while the animals were my affair, and Berta, therefore, my responsibility, including the challenges the acquisition entailed. She did indeed attract visitors; yes, in fact, the Petersburgians loved this colossal, slow-moving animal. There was always a small throng of people standing outside her cage and the public cheered every time she emitted the smallest snort or grunt. For my own part, it had been a long time since I had cheered about Berta. Yes, she was, what should one say, a striking animal—many even called her *magnificent*—but the cost of shipping her here from Hamburg had been even *more* magnificent.

Piotr, the houseboy, entered the room and placed a silver tray bearing a business card in front of me, while informing me in his aloof manner that I had a visitor.

I picked up the card and studied it. Ivan Poliakov, Zoological Institute.

"If sir permits," Piotr said, "I would like to mention that Poliakov was red in the face and out of breath, as if it were a matter of some urgency."

"Thank you, Piotr. Please show him in."

A minute later, the door opened and Poliakov, my closest colleague at the institute, stood before me. I did not see the biologist often. From time to time, he might contact me with news concerning large animal shipments to Europe with an eye to new acquisitions for the zoo but he had never come to see me at home before. He was, indeed, both red in the face and out of breath, but what Piotr had neglected to mention was that Poliakov was also smiling so broadly that his face was virtually straining at the seams, revealing two full rows of brown teeth.

"Welcome," I said.

"My dear Mikhail Alexandrovich," Poliakov said. "My good friend."

"Ivan Poliakov," I replied. "I hope all is well with you, with your wonderful family. Your lovely wife and beautiful children."

"Yes," he said. "Yes, indeed."

I had apparently overdone it. Situations such as this, where I found myself one-on-one with other men, often knocked me off balance. I took care not to appear arrogant and cool, but also feared that my behavior would be perceived as fawning.

Poliakov, however, did not seem to notice my uneasiness. Without waiting to be asked, he took a seat by the coffee table. Then he corrected himself, got to his feet again as if the chair had nipped him in the behind.

"My dear friend, have a seat, please," I said. "I apologize for my lack of manners. I am a bit distracted. It's the accounts. It's that time of year. You know how it is . . ."

I didn't finish the sentence. He knew absolutely nothing about the state of the finances, and I would presumably not meet with any understanding. As an employee of the Zoological Institute, his salary was paid with the same uniform precision as the stride of the emperor's marching soldiers.

"Be that as it may," I said. "I can see you have some news that you are eager to share with me. And here is Piotr with the samovar. Let us have some tea. Would you not like a glass?"

"Tea? That's not necessary, but since you offer . . ."

With a swift movement he grasped the glass held out to him, his hand trembling slightly. He put the glass down on the table with a light thump causing a few drops to spill over the lip. He picked up the sugar tongs and dropped no less than three clumps of sugar into the hot beverage, stirred five times with a spoon, and poured the entire contents of the glass down his throat in three large gulps.

"I would like you to accompany me to the institute," he said hurriedly. "I have something I must show you. A dispatch rider delivered it yesterday evening with a shipment from Mongolia."

"Mongolia? And you have come here personally to tell me this?"

"From Colonel Przewalsky. He is on his way home, but the package arrived before him. I would very much like you to take a look at the objects."

"And *what* exactly are these objects?"

"An animal hide and a skull."

"A dead animal? I prefer to have doings with the living."

"From a horse, a wild horse."

"Is that right?"

"I have never seen anything like it," he said and again his mouth opened into a broad, brown grin.

Before continuing my rendition of the events, I think it necessary to begin with some biographical information about the main character of this story, that is to say, the undersigned. Not to say that I am the most important personality in this peculiar tale. I would never make such a claim and I am quite certain that my name will be omitted from the history books when the official accounts are written in due course. But you might well remember me, at the very least.

My name is Mikhail Alexandrovich Kovrov. I was born in Petersburg in 1848. The same year as the Paris Uprising and subsequent abdication of the throne by Louis Philippe of France. Unrest spread through Europe; in Austria, the chancellor was obliged to step down, but our own emperor showed strength, as always. And when sparks of insubordination were ignited in Moldovia and Walkachia, he crushed every sign of rebellion. I, of course, knew nothing of these events. My life was about my mother's lap and my father's strict, but fair, form of justice. We lived in prosperity. My father, Aleksander Kovrov, enjoyed great respect as a captain in the cavalry. When he and my mother met, her most fertile years were already behind her and they conceived only one child. It was, nonetheless, my clear impression that their marriage and brief life together was both happy and satisfactory and that they held one another in the deepest regard.

When I was seven years old, however, our existence changed. The fatal event that would turn everything upside down occurred on an afternoon in January. It was already dark, as winter afternoons are up here in the north. My father was on his way home from work and about to cross the street. I don't know if he saw the horse-drawn carriage that came driving at a ludicrous speed or if he died instantaneously. But both the coachman and the pedestrians who happened to be standing in the vicinity spoke of the sound of the horses' hooves against my father's body on the cobblestones—hard iron horseshoes against a soft human body. I kept trying to imagine how that must have sounded; on one occasion, I even lay down on the floor of the library and dropped a rusty horseshoe onto my bare, little boy tummy, which did not produce any special kind of sound whatsoever.

This happened at the exact same time that Tsar Nicholas I contracted a horrible case of pneumonia, refused treatment, and regrettably passed away. While the nation was in mourning, we mourned as well. The tsar lay in *lit de parade* for two whole weeks, and my mother cloistered herself in her bedroom with her tears. When she finally emerged, it was to see the deceased emperor. I remember that we passed the bed where Nicholas I lay very slowly, that Mother pressed my face into her skirts and sobbed that she didn't know for whom she was crying the most, the nation's little father or my father, while I carefully tried to turn my head to catch a glimpse of the corpse. Since then, I have always associated significant life events with the tsar's family.

After this, Mother and I were alone. There was some comfort in the fact that we were not left destitute. My father's pension provided for us handsomely. Not that we could live as before, mind you, but we were able to keep our home, the spacious apartment on Grivtsova Lane, and had sufficient means to live a modest, but relatively comfortable, life.

I will always associate my childhood with the large, quiet rooms of our home and my mother's warm presence. She was truly a self-sacrificing mama. There were no compromises made when it came to my well-being. I received the best cuts of meat at the table and was sent to a good school.

School, yes . . . a brief and brutal part of my life. I remember the first day very well. My mother had followed me to the gate, kissed me goodbye three times, and waved when I took my place in line in the yard outside the large, dark building. I did not speak with any other children, was not acquainted with many of them, but I immediately liked the system. It was as if the school were organized in long rows, as if we weren't individual boys but merely a part of a formation. We stood in lines; we marched in step. At least until the school bell rang. Then, all of a sudden, I was alone.

The way the other children ignored me coldly during the first days was something I could live with but, eventually, as most of them found places in groups, a new dynamic emerged: the boys began searching for confirmation that these affiliations were precisely right. Such confirmations were often elicited through the incitement of conflicts with other herds, but even more so by humiliating those of us who were left out.

I remember my new slate. I had been so proud of it when I started school. I remember how it was smashed, how the boys made bets about what was the hardest, my skull or the slate.

My skull was the hardest.

When for the third time I came home to Mother with inexplicable injuries and refused to say how they had been inflicted, she told me that she had looked into hiring a private tutor.

"A private tutor?" These were the most beautiful words I had ever heard.

After that, most of my life transpired inside the apartment. In the company of the most proficient teachers Petersburg had to offer, with lessons in both Russian and French, I was spared having to move any further away from home than our front gate.

Three doors down vis-à-vis our building was the Geographic Society. Early on, I had noticed the different gentlemen entering and leaving the premises. They were often dusty and dirty, arrived almost always alone carrying canvas bags covered with stains and suitcases, the original colors of which had been virtually eroded away beneath nicks and scratches. Their skin was weathered, their hands tanned and powerful, every bit as worn and scraped up as their baggage. I listened eagerly to the gentlemen's conversations. I cocked my ears trying to catch all the details of where they had been, how the journey had been made, with whom they had traveled, and especially what kinds of animals they had seen or even captured. The fauna out in the world was entirely different from the animal life we were familiar with here in Russia, I heard them say. They spoke of how there were birds and animals so colorful and strange that it was virtually impossible to imagine them without having seen them. I begged my mother for books and, on every one of my days off, I dragged her with me to the Kunstkammer, Peter the Great's museum of natural science, where in addition to studying the collection of numerous monstrosities preserved in jars, one could see mounted animals from all corners of the earth.

That it was zoology that become my field hardly came as a surprise to my mother and she supported my choice. When I was awarded an auspicious post at Petersburg's zoological garden, we were both happy. The zoological garden is private. For that reason, I couldn't assume my father's rank, but I enjoyed the respect of the city's bourgeoisie and received a respectable wage. The zoological garden was a popular get-away for the many residents of Petersburg and contributed to both the entertainment and edification of the citizenry. The work was, thereby, meaningful. And at home, peace continued to prevail. Mother and I had our meals together in the morning and the evening. A pleasant, cozy warmth dominated the rooms, which always smelled clean and faintly of my mother's perfume. On rare occasions, we had guests for tea or dinner, but usually it was just the two of us and the servants. I was satisfied with my life. It did, of course, come to pass that Mother brought up this business of a *girl*. Sometimes she would speak warmly about a cousin or another suitable candidate, but I always talked my way out of the subject. The work at the zoo was my great passion . . . a bit too great, one might say. In the course of the five years since I started working as assistant director, I had been a strong catalyst for the initiative to acquire a large number of new species, among these the above-mentioned Berta. If it's possible to call a hippopotamus a cherry, Berta was definitely the cherry on top when it came to the zoo's financial challenges. When Poliakov sought me out on this May morning in 1880, it was not merely curiosity that motivated me, but equally so the prospect of new sources of revenue.

He had had the carriage wait. The coachman clung to the seat, shivering as the rain presumably did its best to soak through his leather coat, and he brightened when we came out.

"Take us back," Poliakov said, and gave the coachman a whole fistful of coins. "As quickly as you can."

The rain dripped against the roof. The water sprayed off the wheels and the underbody of the carriage creaked. The coachman whipped the horses, making it clear that he set out to give Poliakov full value for his kopeks, and I tried my best not to think about my poor father. Instead, I pumped Poliakov for information. I asked probing questions about the size of the hide, about the color, about the structure of the skull. But he asked me to wait.

"We'll look at it together when we get there," he said. "I need to hear your reflections about the species."

Then he fell silent.

A tarpan, it had to be a tarpan, the wild horses that formerly had lived freely on the steppes of Prussia and east of the Ural River. One specimen still existed in Moscow's zoological garden but, as far as I knew, there was uncertainty about the origin of the stallion, about whether it was a purebred or mixed breed. Anyway, the animal was old and without opportunity to produce progeny. Since I'd never traveled outside the city of my birth, I had never seen the horse, but I had seen a photograph of it and I could understand the doubts surrounding the specimen's origins. It was small, dark, and shaggy, heavy and lethargic, not at all the way I imagined wild horses—galloping across the steppes with the wind in their manes and tails.

Finally, we arrived. Poliakov hurried up the stairs ahead of me and into his office. There he went to stand beside the desk, which had been cleared of papers and books. In the center of the desk, lay a few pieces of bone, a skull, and an animal hide.

"Here we have it," Poliakov said and I detected the slightest tremble in his voice. "Killed by a hunter named Kirghiz, surname unknown, near Guchen. Don't ask me where it is. Given as a gift to Colonel Nikolay Mikhaylovich Przewalsky, who forthwith understood the significance of the find and had it sent home immediately."

At first, I was disappointed. The hide was smaller than I had envisioned, neither brown nor black, but a dun color, almost gray, and with a dark stripe from head to tail. Neither was there anything remarkable about the skull; it was like most skulls—hard bones, hollow eye sockets.

"Quite a find," I said and tried to mobilize a touch of enthusiasm.

"That's putting it mildly!" Poliakov said.

I walked over to the desk and lifted the skull. The bone was cold and dry. I slid my fingers over it, half closing my eyes, feeling my way forward like a blind man, trying to imagine the horse to which it had belonged. It was as if the physical encounter with this, which once had been an animal, did something to me. My fingers immediately recognized another living creature. I *saw* it.

"The bridge of the nose is broad. There is something almost Roman about it," I said.

"Good observation," Poliakov said. "I had the same impression."

"And the hide," I put down the skull and stroked the skin with my fingers. "The color is extremely pale. And large, isn't it?"

He nodded. His eyes sparkled. "But smaller than other horses."

"This confirms that the stallion in Moscow is not a true tarpan," I said.

"Does it?" Poliakov asked.

"Doesn't it? The so-called tarpan in Moscow is small, dark, and has a long, flat-lying mane. In this case, we are dealing with a larger animal."

I picked something up that I immediately recognized as a cannon bone from one of the animal's legs.

"The upper body is large and quite heavy, but the legs are surprisingly short. This is a horse that is quite different from the specimen in Moscow we've seen photographs of."

"You're right about that," Poliakov said. "This is truly a different horse. But your reasoning is still not correct."

"It's not?"

"I don't want to draw any conclusions about Moscow's stallion," Poliakov said, "as to whether it is a tarpan or a hybrid. . . . I have no grounds to make such claims. But this horse . . ." He paused and again he smiled so his face seemed about to split open. "I think we are dealing with the horse the Mongols have been telling legends about for centuries. A species that I, truth be told, believed was nothing but a myth. I feel reasonably certain that Colonel Przewalsky has discovered a new breed of the genus *Equus*. A species that is ancient, perhaps even the oldest existing horse breed."

"What?" I said. "Do you mean that this is really the original primordial horse?"

"Nothing less," he said.

"The horse we have seen in cave paintings?"

"The caveman's horse," he nodded and grinned. "The horse that came before all other horses."

"That can't be right," I said. "They were extinct thousands of years ago. Or not just extinct, they've evolved into the horses that now live in the world."

"That is what most people believed," he said. "But the Mongols have talked about this horse throughout the ages. You have certainly heard about the takhi?"

"But nobody has observed a takhi for at least a thousand years."

"Not until now," he said.

I had to restrain myself to keep from jumping for joy. I reached out my hand again and closed it around the skull. This is how it must have felt to have found the holy grail.

"A takhi . . . ," I said. "Przewalsky has found a takhi."

"He has found the last real wild horse," Poliakov said. "It must, of course, be given a proper name now, a Latin name, something that honors its discoverers."

"Indeed," I said. "Yes, clearly. *Equus takhi*, possibly?"

He snorted. "It must be given a name that honors its discoverers."

"Exactly. That's clear. So, what would that be?" I asked, although I already had my suspicions about the answer.

Poliakov smiled again, so broadly that I could see the entire inside of his mouth where his teeth were deteriorating rapidly. "The name of the species is to be *Equus przewalskii poliakov*."

KARIN

Mongolia, 1992

Mathias's chin dips toward his chest and his head rolls from side to side. I resist the impulse to poke him, try to wake him, check that he is fine, make contact, ensure he's alive. He is just sleeping. He has always been able to sleep anywhere and anytime, ever since he was a little boy. He was what they call an "easy baby." As long as he was nursed, he almost always fell asleep. There was no reason to complain about him, not back then.

There is little left of his soft baby cheeks. Now his face is full of beard stubble. He also smells faintly of sweat, like a strange man, and is grimy with fatigue after the journey. He has grown so old that the lines in his face are no longer erased when he sleeps. Or perhaps it's not age that makes him look so worn out already, but the life he has lived.

It is still inconceivable that he manages to sleep. My behind burns from the hard, wooden benches on the cargo plane. The noise of the engine is like the climax of a war and everything around me is shaking, as if every single screw on the airplane were loose. I squirm, searching for a bearable sitting position. Even just a few minutes of sleep would have helped, but that's impossible. I should have been a horse, able to sleep standing up, with all my weight resting on one of my hind legs. In many ways, it must be easy being a horse.

But they're not having such an easy time of it *now*, my horses.

The horseboxes are set up in two rows in front of us. I can't see a thing through the two small breathing holes. The airplane drowns out any sounds they make, but I think I can hear them all the same. As if I am inside there. As if I'm the one who is falling against the walls and hitting my head against the boards on all sides of me.

Seven hours by truck from the reserve in Thorenc, then ten hours in the air from Paris. I have never allowed a horse to travel so far before.

There is some consolation in the fact that I am also uncomfortable. The cargo plane is Russian and confirms all my prejudices against vehicles from the Soviet state. They are clunky and noisy. The smell of exhaust is intense. But this was the only plane I could get hold of that was big enough. And within my budget.

Budget. Tired of the word.
Just like I am tired of
Financial statement
Funding
Budgetary limits.

I didn't become a veterinarian because I love accounting, I said to Mathias a few weeks ago. He laughed at me. C'mon now, Karin, he said, because he never calls me Mom. Karin, you aren't a veterinarian any longer, you are a project manager.

Project manager.

Yet another term I'm sick of.

He called me a magician, too, by the way, because I can achieve the impossible. The greatest nature conservation project of all time,

Karin, and you are making it happen! He sometimes says that kind of thing to flatter me. And it happens that I allow myself to be flattered. I have to admit it.

Several hours later, the plane is finally preparing for landing in Ulan Bator. Mathias has woken up at last. The horses are whinnying so loudly that nobody can sleep.

"Easy, easy," I say softly, as if that could help.

The effect of the drug I have given them has long since worn off, but I can't give them more. They have to be awake when we arrive; I can't risk them stumbling. They must have control over their legs. Luckily, I hear no sounds from Sydney, the lead stallion. The others listen to him—if he is calm, they will stay calm as well. A herd is a herd is a herd. The hierarchy is always the same, with a lead stallion and a lead mare. I think of them more like guards than leaders. Sydney guards the herd. The harem's safety is all that matters to him.

The plane approaches the ground. Mathias shuts his eyes.

"Landing is the most dangerous part," he says. "People are afraid when the plane takes off, when you are in the air, but, statistically speaking, the landing is the riskiest part of it all."

"But flying is one of the safest things we do," I reply. "You're safer here than on the streets of Berlin."

He opens his eyes, grins suddenly.

"And that's twice as true for me."

"What?"

"Did you hear what you said? I am safer here than on the street in Berlin. Isn't that the whole point?"

"You know I didn't mean it that way."

"It was kind of funny though!" Mathias shouts to be heard over the sound of the plane.

"What?"

"Relax! IT WAS KIND OF FUNNY!"

And at exactly that moment, the wheels hit the runway. The brakes scream, the plane shudders.

"Sweet Jesus!" Mathias yells.

Then the fun starts. TV cameras, journalists carrying notebooks, and affiliated interpreters, bouquets of flowers pressed into my hands, a speech in Mongolian by a civil servant wearing a trilby hat.

I try smiling at him but can tell that my smile is not exactly convincing.

"Thank you," I say. "I would like to get the horses out of the airplane now. Can we get started?"

"Just a few questions first," Trilbyhat says.

I answer the journalists' questions as briefly as I can, my eyes fixed on the boxes inside the plane. Twenty-eight hours have passed since the mare Askania Nova was shut in. She is the calmest of them all, which is why I brought her first. But twenty-eight hours is far too long. It is so cramped inside the box. It must be difficult to breathe, the head constantly smashing against the wall, the small air holes through which it's hardly possible to get a whiff of fresh air. I can barely breathe myself. I light a cigarette, inhale. It doesn't help much.

The trucks are ready and waiting—eight identical vehicles, Soviet as well, apparently the way everything is here after many years of close collaboration with the communist Big Brother. But the country is a democracy now. Has turned toward the West and toward its own history. Toward Genghis Khan, the country's former autocratic ruler, toward events from hundreds of years back in time, the time when the Mongolian Empire was the largest in the world. That is, perhaps, one of the reasons why there is so much enthusiasm about getting the takhis back. Nothing is more historical than the horse from the cave paintings.

Yet another whinny can be heard from the boxes.

I throw the cigarette to the ground, crush it under my heel, turn to Trilbyhat, and wave my arms.

"We really must start now. We HAVE to start."

Finally, the crane gets to work. A mechanical creaking can be heard as it lifts the first box out of the plane. Hamburg is inside. He is only two years old and still the most peaceful of the two young stallions I have brought. Now, he neighs loudly. The box sways gently from the straps. I am afraid it will come loose, but the driver of the crane fortunately maintains control and lowers the box safely onto the truck.

I enter the airplane between the boxes, talking to my horses.

"Easy, easy, now, you'll be out soon, you'll be out soon."

I give them apples, their favorite treat, through the openings at the bottom near the ground. Only snouts and teeth can be seen. They snatch up the apples, crunching the fruity pulp between their teeth. It's a good sign that they're hungry. I peer through the airholes that are at my own eye level. Their coats shine; their large, moist eyes glitter. I can hear a snort here, a low whinny there, nothing to indicate that something is wrong. I light yet another cigarette, take a step back. The smoke tastes better now.

After an hour and a half, all the boxes are finally in place and secured on the flatbeds. The television cameras have been cleared away. One lone cable remains, forgotten and left behind on the ground. The public officials finally disappeared; even Trilbyhat has left. The boxes are in place on the trucks, an entire convoy is ready on the road, and the drivers are about to get in. There is room for only one passenger in each vehicle. I get into the one in front, Mathias the one behind. Just as well, perhaps it will be easier to sleep when I am alone, when I won't have to watch his large, heavy head drooping uncontrollably toward his chest.

The truck stinks of gasoline and sour milk, but the seat is soft. I lean back. The airport is located on the outskirts of the city. It is surrounded by felt tents called *gers*, the Mongolians' most common type of lodging. White, round, and all about the same size, with horizonal bands around the walls that hold the tent canvas in place and a hole for a chimney in the ceiling. The altar always faces north—the most holy cardinal point. The door faces south; around it, objects are stored that are used in daily life. Lambs and chicks are also kept inside in the spring until it becomes warm enough for them to be outdoors. All the tents are organized the same way. You can always determine the compass point when you see a tent. That's nice. Orderly. Practical.

As soon as we have the airport behind us, the Mongolian steppes spread out before us. Grass and sky, no trees. And after just a few hundred meters, we see the first animals. A flock of sheep and goats are grazing beside the road. They scurry away as our long convoy rumbles past.

A wind races across the landscape flattening the grass against the ground, stirring up clouds of dust.

Dust, dust from the steppes, the feeling of it on my tongue. It has only been a month since I was here last for the final preparations, but I have apparently managed to suppress the feeling.

Mongolia *is* dust and grass. Endless plains with tufts of thin straw, arid soil, and sand as far as the eye can see. And then the size—four times the size of Germany, but only two million people. Waves of grass are rippling as far as the eye can see and finally it lulls me to sleep. A dreamless sleep, the way all sleep should be.

I awake with a start. The driver turns the key in the ignition and the engine falls silent. Then the door to the truck opens and there is Mathias. He throws out his arms, smiles.

"You said it was big, but it's incomprehensible until you see it with your own eyes. Good God, what a waste of space. And the tents, they are fucking awesome!"

Tourist.

I get out, turn to face the camp. At least one hundred people have turned up here as well. They have gathered in front of the science building beside the paddock into which the horses will soon be released.

The building has been painted since the last time I was here. An intense shade of blue, perhaps not exactly the color I would have chosen, but sky blue is the preferred color here. Blue, orange, and pistachio green. Even the rooftops are bright colors. At first, I thought it was ugly. But I have grown accustomed to the carnival. When nature itself is so monotonous, it's nice to have something colorful to look at.

Everyone is silent, watching me. Watching the short, German, middle-aged lady who started this whole business. People come from the tent camps nearby; some are semi-nomadic, some probably more settled. And then the staff of the wildlife reserve. Young men, each of them mounted securely on horseback.

At that moment, Jochi comes walking toward me, his eyes hidden beneath an American baseball cap, but I can see he is smiling broadly.

"Karin. At last!"

I reach out my hand, but he doesn't take it; he hugs me instead. Well. I can't remember him ever having hugged me before. But I presume it is appropriate today and return the gesture quickly before releasing him and taking a step back.

"We did it," he says in his impeccable British English.

Jochi speaks much better English than I do. I always feel embarrassed when we attend meetings together. He has written to me that he is trying to teach the staff English. I picture all of them riding around and speaking with his perfect Oxford pronunciation. That would be something.

"Well, we haven't done it quite yet," I say. Bronx knocks his hooves against the walls of the box; Askania Nova whinnies. "And now we have to let the horses out."

"Soon," he says. "You're in Mongolia now."

A few drops of milk are sprinkled into the air with a *tsatsal*, a small spade wrapped in blue fabric, before the silver bowl of horse milk is offered to me. The wind blows creating tiny ripples on the white surface. I swallow it down and notice that it leaves a milk moustache behind, which I wipe off. Mathias wrinkles his nose slightly at the strange flavor but says nothing. We have talked about this ahead of time.

The rituals here are simple and down to earth. I like them. A sacrifice is made to the sky and to nature. The nomads are Buddhists, but they also worship the ground beneath their feet and the heavens above them. They believe that everything in nature has a soul. If, at all costs, one must worship something, this, at least, is a meaningful way.

The silver bowl is taken away and, finally, we can get to work. I signal to the man on the crane who has been waiting in his seat behind the gears.

Loud mechanical sounds can be heard as Sydney's box is lowered from the truck. It dangles in the air. Suddenly it looks so small against the big, wide sky and the endless plains. A couple of Jochi's men take hold of it and guide it into place in the paddock.

Then the next, Hamburg. Everything is moving quickly, a bit too quickly. The workers are too quick about fastening the straps. Imagine if one of them breaks, if the box falls off because the hooks aren't secured properly? A broken leg often means death. Or if the box is destroyed and the wooden splinters hit the horse? Just one tiny splinter can cause a reaction, inflammation, and infection. It has cost me thousands of marks to get them here; these animals are worth more than racehorses. I can't afford injuries, functional disabilities, impairments of any kind.

But the box is secured correctly and soon it is also on the ground. Jochi gives a thumbs up. Mathias of course responds immediately, as if the two of them are old friends. Jochi seems to like it because he smiles.

At last, the eight boxes are lined up side-by-side in the paddock, only a half meter of space between each of them. They are constructed of pine boards and sheets of black metal, the fronts covered with stickers.

Jochi says the word to four of his men and asks four young nomads to help out as well. They all jump up onto the roofs of the boxes and place their hands on the hatch.

"Ready?" Jochi asks me.

I nod. I can feel myself sweating.

When is a species extinct? When not a single live specimen is to be found? Or when the last *free* specimen has disappeared? I have always thought that a species that is no longer found wild in nature actually no longer exists. The wild horses haven't *lived*—not the way it is in their nature to live—for more than one hundred years. They have survived in zoos and reserves, dependent on human assistance. On hay, fortified feed, salt, and medicine. On people who cared about the herd, separating individual stallions from the harem, preventing aggression and fights. On help to prevent inbreeding. And the more time passed, the more the species adapted to receiving help from humans. The characteristics best suited to the life they have lived have endured. Survival of the fittest, even in captivity.

But now it's happening and I have no idea how it will turn out. The wildest qualities of the horses may have already disappeared; characteristics their forefathers had a hundred years ago may have been eroded out of them over the years in Europe. But the hereditary lineage is pure, I am, at least, sure of that. The horses I have with me are true takhis, primal horses, the only breed of horse on earth with sixty-six chromosomes. All the others have sixty-four.

And now, all traces of the years in captivity will disappear. Here in Hustai, they will first spend a few months fenced in until they become accustomed to the landscape. Then they will be released, left to manage on their own. These eight are the first; more will be brought next year. I have horses waiting at a farm in Thorenc, in France. When there are enough of them, they will be responsible for increasing their numbers. At some point, the species will again be strong enough so I can leave them. Five hundred horses, five hundred horses that breed, giving birth every year to new, strong foals; only then will I be able to relax.

Relax. I don't know what that is. *Madness* is the word I have heard used the most to describe my project. Hubris. Who do you think you are, what is it with you, why do you think you will be the one to succeed?

But this has nothing to do with me. This is about the horses. And I don't suffer from hubris. I just want to save the species.

On the signal, each of the eight men grasp the hatches on their respective boxes. They pull the hatches upward simultaneously and the doorways open.

Hamburg is the quickest. He runs, neighs, turns, and takes a lap around the paddock. No limping, no sign of exhaustion or tying up, no stiff muscles after being locked up for so many hours.

Sydney follows right behind him; he has always been quick and strong. He deserves to be a leader. The stallions look healthy, move without difficulty, toss their heads, neigh, snort.

How are they now? What is it like to be them? Finally, free. Finally allowed to run again. But they have no understanding of the word *finally*, of how long they have been in captivity, and they don't know that this was the very last time I will allow them to be imprisoned. For the rest of their lives, they will remain here.

Soon Bronx moves out of the box. Bronx the powerful. All the horses are named after the first zoos that bred the Przewalsky foal. I have always thought Bronx's name especially suited him. Tough and strong. I have never been to New York but have heard that the Bronx is a rough neighborhood. I see my stallion as the leader of a street gang. He was huge even at birth; I had never before seen such a large foal. I remember how the veterinarian from Thorenc and I had to help him out. For a while, we didn't know whether he would survive, but he proved to be a tough one. Nothing gets to Bronx. Now he gallops from one side of the paddock to the other. Simultaneously, the two mares, Askania Nova and Paris, trot out and the foals, Woburn and Halle.

Only Praha, my lead mare, stays inside.

The other horses have moved toward the fence at the far end of the corral. Some have started grazing. Bronx bares his teeth at Sydney, already challenging his position in the herd. At some point, Bronx will take over. He is the strongest of the young stallions and will one day be a leader. But until that time, I must protect them from their own aggression. I must isolate the independent stallions from the rest of the herd in a separate corral.

But first Praha. Her muzzle sticks out of the opening of the box; otherwise, she shows no inclination to move. She who is usually the first. A trickster, she always manages to get a few more apples, a few more carrots, the freshest, greenest grass.

Praha is the grandchild of Orlitsa, the last free takhi. Orlitsa had been a gift to Chairman Voroshilov in Mongolia in 1957. Out of the forty-one wild horses found in the world at that time, only twelve proved to be fertile. Voroshilov took Orlitsa with him back to the Soviet Union. She gave birth to four healthy takhi foals in captivity before she died in 1973 at twenty-six years of age. She provided sorely needed fresh blood—Orlitsa, *She Eagle,* the thirteenth horse.

From just thirteen horses, the species has been rebuilt foal by foal. Zoos all over the world have collaborated. Everything has been monitored and controlled to ensure the best possible distribution of the genetic material we've had available. The specimens I brought with me here are all descendants of different horses. And Praha descends from the strongest of them all. Powerful, alert Praha.

But she is not herself now. She doesn't want to come out.

Jochi looks at me.

"Is there something wrong with her?"

I shake my head.

"Probably a bit worn out from the journey," Mathias jokes. "Dissatisfied with Russian amenities."

I can't be bothered to reply. I walk toward Praha.

"Come on, Praha. Come," I call. "My mare. Come on out. Out."

If she is injured, the balance of the herd will be disrupted. That won't do. Everything is new for them here. For that reason, the herd must remain as it is. I can't have any power struggles. Such rivalries always lead to injuries. I can't afford injuries and need Praha.

"Do we have any more apples?" I ask Jochi.

He hands me a bag. I stick my hand into it, grab one, feeling the slippery peel against my sweaty fingers.

At the scent of the apple, Praha raises her head.

"It's me," I say. "Come on, now."

Then I put the apple down on the ground and step away. "You must come out and get it."

It is silent all around us. Everyone's attention is focused on the mare.

She snorts softly.

And finally, she starts to move. Stiffly, moving her hoofs tentatively in front of her, stretching her neck, she moves a few steps forward. Her hindquarters are still in the box, her nostrils flare.

Praha was one of the very first horses I got for the reserve. She adapted quickly and has given birth to healthy foals every single spring. She has always had quick deliveries without any complications. And she follows up on her foals, stays close to them, always knows where they are. A good mother. Sydney and Praha have been inseparable since he arrived in Thorenc. He mounted her immediately and from that moment they belonged to one another. Her last four foals have been his, including Woburn, who is just four months old.

Finally, Praha takes the final steps out of the box. She emerges at last from the darkness inside, from the trampled hay and dung she has been tramping around in. People clap.

"Hey!" Mathias calls.

Praha's muzzle moves toward the apple and she wolfs it down.

Then the mare takes a few steps away before breaking into a canter and joining the others. Her gait is nice and smooth; everything seems fine. To be on the safe side, I hurry into her box and check her stools. They are as they should be, no signs of constipation. She is probably just tired.

Now they are all grazing the way they always do no matter where they are, as long as there is grass to be eaten. Horses, simple horses.

Jochi smiles again under his cap.

Mathias pokes me in the ribs.

"You'll see. Your horses will be fine." *Your horses*, as if he were saying *your teddy bears* or *your dolls*.

"They aren't mine," I say.

"Yeah, right." He laughs.

"Why are you laughing?"

"They are yours, Karin."

"But you know why we're here," I say.

"So they can be their own masters?"

"Yes."

He becomes serious. "That's what you always said to me, too," he says. "You know, when I was little, that I had to become my own master. Do you remember?"

"No. No, I don't remember that."

He keeps looking at me. Okay, fine. I remember that I may have said something like that once. I was probably trying to express something or other about independence, using words a child would understand.

Maybe that was a mistake. I have made many mistakes, I guess.

But why is he bringing this up now, are we supposed to stand here talking about why he ended up the way he did?

No. He just says the first thing that comes into his head, pursuing all trains of thought. Poor impulse control. That's maybe my fault, too. Is impulse control genetic?

I turn to Jochi.

"We must give them all proper examinations. Now, right away. We must check to be sure they haven't been injured during the journey."

EVA

We drove in silence for a few minutes. I kept my eyes on the road but was aware of the presence of the woman beside me, the smell of her, of a wet human being, wet dust, wet, unwashed hair. Her hands rested quietly in her lap. She had grime under her fingernails, but not as dark and thick as mine, and no hangnails or small cuts indicating that she was accustomed to manual labor.

"My name is Eva," I said.

"My name is Louise," she said.

Her accent was hard to place; she rolled her r's.

"You're not from around here?"

"No."

"But you speak Norwegian well."

"I have spoken Norwegian since I was a child."

She gave no indication of having anything more to say, so we drove a few hundred meters in silence. I wished she would say something, something that confirmed she could be trusted.

"We live on a farm," I said. "Or it used to be a park. We took care of species in danger of extinction. And the public came to see the wild animals in a natural habitat."

Suddenly, I felt as if I were babbling.

But she turned her head and looked at me.

"Natural? What do you mean by natural habitat?"

"As natural as it can be behind a fence," I tried to explain. "We had a farm with domestic animals, too. Pigs, cows, goats for the children."

"Do you still have animals?"

There was eagerness in her voice.

"Do you like animals?" I asked.

"The ones I have known, I have liked."

"We have kept a few of the wild ones. And the domestic animals. Two cows, two calves, four goats, and six hens."

"No rooster?"

"He died last winter."

"No bull?"

The questions were coming quickly now.

"No. Not any longer."

"And all the others, those that were here before?"

"At first we just downsized. We sent animals to zoos in Europe that were still open. But when there were no longer any zoos to send them to, we had to set them free."

"Where?"

"In the forest."

I noticed that she was looking at me, waiting for me to continue. I became uncertain, unsure why she was asking questions and digging; was there something else she was trying to find out? How the farm was situated? How defenseless we actually were? Or was she actually interested?

I said nothing more. There was no point in explaining, anyway. She couldn't understand what it meant to release a rare creature, to set free a snow leopard. Free? We let the animals go, shrugged off responsibility, gave up; there was no freedom in that. I remember how we had drugged the snow leopards, Rolex and Longines, two of only three thousand snow leopards in the whole world, how they staggered around before lying down and falling asleep. We had asked the neighboring farms for help loading them into the truck. Then we drove them away, down a bumpy cart road as far into the forest as we could. There we lifted them out and left them behind. The male and the female in the same place. Even though they were solitary animals, only meeting during mating season and otherwise always alone, we let them start over together in the hope that they would at some point manage to mate, that they would have time to do so before something killed them. They'd been born in captivity, had always been fed by humans. But we had, at least, made sure they had to work for their food in the park, hung the prey high above them so they would have to exert themselves, given them entire carcasses, so their living situation resembled the conditions out in the wild. I consoled myself that they were perhaps, therefore, a bit better prepared. But they were actually doomed. Pale fur against a green forest, easy prey for hunters. They were the ones who would be hunted by hungry men with hunting rifles, who had no idea that these animals were precisely two of a handful of their kind, and who didn't care. Maybe hungry children were waiting at home; maybe they didn't have the luxury of leaving them alone.

We drove on. I swerved to avoid a bump in the road; the pavement had long since deteriorated.

"You said you need help on the farm?" Louise said after a while.

"Yes . . . yes. We need help."

"I am used to working for my keep."

She reached a hand toward the fan and tried to adjust it.

"You also said the car was warm and dry," she said, "but the windows are fogged up, the seats are damp."

She shot me a quick glance. Was she afraid? Trying to find out whether she could trust me?

"The heater uses a lot of electricity," I hastened to say. "I try not to use more than I have to. Never know when we will lose the power."

"But at least you have electricity. On borrowed time."

"An old man runs the power plant here. He has no intention of giving up yet."

"Everything is still on borrowed time," she said.

And then she fell silent again.

I glanced at her. She had light-brown eyes; her hair was dark. She was younger than me, maybe by as much as ten years. Her skin was still smooth. She looked unspoiled. Fresh.

I turned off the main road and stopped the car. Previously, there had been a sign at this intersection, large and shiny, informing visitors that they were now headed toward the Heiane animal park. The wind had blown it down two summers ago; now it lay in the ditch and you could no longer see what the road had once led to. I had also dragged a dead tree halfway out onto the road so it looked like the road was never used. No strangers would find us here; no wanderers would come calling, trying to steal our food or our animals.

But now I moved the tree, drove a few meters, put the tree back in place, and got in the car again. Louise saw all of it. I trust you, I thought, I can trust you, can't I?

Previously, the road had been open and daylit, but now it was submerged in semidarkness even in the middle of the day. The trees took over the world; the birch and Sitka spruce spread faster and faster the warmer and wetter it became suffocating the few flowers still to be found along the edge of the ditch. Only the damp moss thrived in the dim light.

We drove around a bend in the road and through the gate. At the entrance, we were welcomed by the sign bearing an image of the place's mascot, the wolverine Jens. Although the paint had worn off, you could still see his broad, cartoon-character smile.

Isa and I lived in the part of the park that had once been called The Farmstead. A white farmhouse, a red barn, and a small, red cowshed. The color had faded from the sun and wind and many of the boards should have been replaced; they had rotted in the rain. Fungi penetrated the wood and slowly invaded, the mold spread. The roof had also started to leak. The boards were disintegrating; the wind took hold and threatened to tear them away.

It was my father who had had The Farmstead built. It was his big project. Here city kids had come by the busload to see life on a farm.

Or how life on a farm should be. A farm paradise, an animal heaven, where everything was on the four-legged creatures' terms, designed to ensure their comfort. Now it was different. All the animals Isa and I had kept on the farm were here to help us, and I was no longer able to give them what they needed.

I drove into the yard, parked, and took out the basket holding the fish.

Louise got out of the car and looked around. She discovered the big map of the park that was hung up on the fence and walked over to it.

"Forest reindeer. Scottish wildcat. Wolverine," she read. "I don't even know what a wolverine looks like."

"Small and brown," I said. "As cute as a teddy bear. But they are strong, can down animals many times their size. I have even heard about a wolverine who took down a moose. Sat on it and bit down hard."

"Is it endangered?"

"It was made a protected species sometime in the 1980s and the species started to recover. But they don't thrive very well in the damp climate. There are probably more up north. Even though they are scarce, they are hunted. Maybe you have eaten wolverine meat without knowing it."

"Maybe."

She ran one finger across the map, stopping at some of the names.

"You had wolves?"

"Yes."

"And you released them? In the forest here?"

"We sent the wolf pair to a park in Sweden that managed to stay open for a while after we had to close."

"No longer here, then? Puh."

I understood that she was trying to be funny, but was unable to smile thinking about the two limp animal bodies in the trailer. It was the only time I'd seen them close up. They looked small and thin, innocent, while asleep. It was almost inconceivable that it was for these very animals that we'd had the park's strictest security measures.

"Anyway, there are so many wolves in the forest these days that a couple more or less doesn't really matter," I said.

Louise made a face. "I know. I have probably eaten wolf, as well, without knowing it."

"You would have noticed. The meat is very tough, sinewy."

At that moment, Isa came out of the farmhouse. Three different emotions slid across her face. First the fear she'd felt at discovering she was no longer alone, the relief over seeing that it was me, that I was back, and then curiosity about the stranger I had brought with me.

She pulled up the zipper on her rain jacket and came over to us while staring at Louise.

Louise offered my daughter her hand and smiled. Isa accepted her hand without returning the smile, but she was clearly conscious of her arm movement, the handshake. She remembered to squeeze the hand firmly, I noticed; she reminded herself of that, the way I had done so many times before and practiced with her: let me see a real handshake, there you go, like that and look the other person in the eyes when you say your name.

A year ago, Isa would have asked who are you, why are you here, where are you from; she had been a why-child, wearing me out with all her questions. Why can't we see the planets when they are so close to us, why is it only people who can talk, why are carrots orange, why does everything fall down except for birds, why is my father Einar? As a part of her new self-awareness, Isa now apparently also controlled her curiosity. She behaved as if it were the most natural thing in the world for us to have a visitor, as if we had people here all the time, as if strangers were nothing out of the ordinary for her.

I followed Louise into the farmhouse, leaving the fish in the kitchen. I could fry it for the evening meal—make something tasty, since we had a guest. But there wasn't enough for three. And it would also be better to save it for a day when we really needed it. After she had left.

We had plenty of room—five rooms plus the kitchen and two baths. Some of the rooms were outfitted with old, rustic furnishings. Rag rugs, lace curtains, pinewood tables and chairs, but only the two rooms that had been open to the public. The others were half empty with cold floors and echoes in the walls.

I showed Louise into the guest room. A bed and a chair. That was all. She looked around her but said nothing.

I reconsidered.

"We have another one that is nicer," I said.

I took her into Anne's room. The light filtered through my great-grandmother's crocheted curtains. On the wall hung an amateur painting depicting Heiane when the farm was first built. Our great-grandfather's brother had painted it and, when Daddy wanted to put it away in the attic, Anne rescued it and hung it in her room. I remember that she talked about taking it with her when she left, but it was too big. She hadn't taken much of anything else with her, either, no more than she could carry, and I had left the room as it had always been. Even her aroma still clung to the walls, the perfume she always wore until it was no longer possible to get hold of, a faint citrus scent. Once a week, I took care to dust and keep the room presentable. Everything was ready in case she should return.

"How nice," Louise said.

"No reason why you can't stay in here," I said, and didn't know which of us I was trying to convince.

I went into the kitchen so Louise could change out of her wet clothes. There stood Isa. She turned to face me. Her self-awareness had vanished and suddenly she was just a fearful child again. She spoke softly, suppressing her anger:

"Who is that?"

"She needed help," I said.

"But who is she? Have you met her before? Did somebody come with her? Do you know someone who knows her?"

I shook my head.

"Good God, Mom."

"Isa, it's just for one night."

"But why in the world . . ."

"We mustn't stop helping each other."

47

"You want to help everyone. Isn't what you're doing for the animals enough?"

"The animals do more for us than we do for them."

"Sure! Those crazy horses of yours do tons. That's right. Nike and Puma do all kinds of things to make themselves useful."

Her voice had become deeper in recent years, a little hoarse; I suspected she allowed it to crack on purpose, especially when she was being sarcastic. Like now. Her irony had slowly infiltrated her speech. I couldn't remember exactly when it started. But there had been more and more of these biting comments and now there was never a conversation in which she failed to emit some acidic observation or other. The discovery of irony as a tool had clearly been of great import for her and it seemed as if she took pleasure in tipping her head to one side, narrowing her eyes, and saying with calmness and composure the exact opposite of what she meant.

"We are still able to take care of them," I said. "We are able to take care of these two horses in particular. You know that."

"Good thing you live alone, then," she said. "That there's nobody else here you must take into consideration, that you can just decide everything by yourself, that you can drag whoever and whatever you want into the house without having to think about how it might be dangerous."

"She doesn't look very dangerous."

"It is also idiotic to bring people here when we are leaving anyway."

"You must stop saying that."

"And it's one more person to share the food with."

"She needs help."

"She needs help." She mimicked my words in a baby voice.

Spoiled brat, I thought, damned spoiled brat. But I didn't say it. On one rare occasion, I'd exploded, fired words at her, and it only made everything worse, because then she had an excuse to use the same type of words against me. A hundred times over. You said it, so I can, too. And it went on for months. You said it that time, you screamed it really loud, actually, so I can, too. I can say whatever the hell I want.

At that moment, Louise came back. She was wearing a dry T-shirt, but still the same wet jeans. Her feet were bare against the worn pine-wood floorboards. Maybe she just had the one pair of socks.

"You can borrow some dry clothes," I said. "Isa has some extra things."

Only a strange twitch of her mouth revealed Isa's dissatisfaction. She stood by the kitchen counter, I was by the window, Louise walked barefoot into the space between us. She looked first at my daughter, then at me, then back at Isa again.

"You look like your mother."

Isa made a face.

"It's true," Louise said. "There's a strong resemblance."

"Terrific," Isa said.

I tried to smile.

"Not exactly what you want to hear when you're fourteen," I said.

Louise looked confused.

"Really? No?"

Isa rolled her eyes the way only a fourteen-year-old can do, as if she didn't just roll her eyes but her entire body.

"But, why not?" Louise asked. "Why don't you want to hear that?"

Her bare feet against the floor were slightly pigeon-toed. Suddenly, I felt bad for her and sent Isa a severe look.

"Sorry," Isa mumbled. "I didn't mean it like that."

Then nobody said anything else. We just stood there, the three of us standing in the kitchen, Louise in the middle between Isa and me. Another body in this room where it had been just the two of us for so long.

I started setting the table. Pushed a chair from one side of the table over to the end so the chairs formed a triangle; so we could all see each other equally well.

But Isa wanted to move the chair back.

"We're going to trip over it."

"It will be fine."

I pushed it all the way under the table. "See, it doesn't take up any room at all."

"It's in the middle of the floor."

"It's better like this."

"Fine."

It wasn't fine, but she said nothing more, just threw the cups on the table. I already regretted it. Louise would be leaving tomorrow; there was no reason to change anything. No reason to make Isa angry.

Louise had been standing in the background watching us. Now she took a step forward.

"I can sit anywhere."

"Sit here," I said and placed my hand on the back of the chair.

Louise nodded uncertainly, came over and pulled out the chair.

Isa sent her a spiteful glare before walking over to the refrigerator. I took out the box of crispbread. I baked it myself. It was usually our evening meal—crispbread with butter. Sometimes with dried or smoked meat, on the rare occasion apple jam. When we ran out of the wholemeal flour in the cellar, I didn't know what we would eat. It had been a long time since I had seen somebody selling flour down on the quay.

Isa made tea. The homey smell of peppermint filled the room. The peppermint plants in the garden were hardy and spread quickly. Now that it was impossible to get hold of coffee, this was what we drank.

We ate in silence. The sound of the crispbread crunching loudly between our teeth was embarrassing. Isa did not deign to grace me with a single glance. She was an expert at using silence as a weapon. She knew the anxiety that came over me when nobody spoke. Mealtimes had always been important for me. Although there were only two of us, we were to sit down and eat breakfast, lunch, and dinner together like a proper family. At specific times and with fixed routines. And we were to talk to each other, tell each other about our day, plan the day to come.

I couldn't remember the last time somebody else ate with us. Richard and his family had been here from time to time, but the meals with them had been difficult. Richard paid far too much attention to me and Tina would get angry. And they argued incessantly with their son who was a year older than Isa, tall, well-developed, and in eternal opposition. I was always surprised when I remembered that there was only one year's difference between him and Isa. He looked like an adult, while she still played with dolls.

Their daughter Agnes was also a concern; she had fallen ill three years ago, an infection in a cut that wouldn't heal. There was no medicine to be found. They didn't know if she would survive but she came around finally although she was never really well again, picked at her food and said little. Richard thought he could find help for her up north. In the end, he seemed unable to think about anything else. If only they could leave, they would manage to find a doctor who could help Agnes. As if there were fully operational hospitals lined up all along the road.

We kept eating without saying anything. The loud crunching of crispbread was disconcerting.

"How long have you lived here?" Louise asked after a while.

"Our whole lives," I said, relieved that someone finally spoke. "The park is a family enterprise."

She looked at Isa and then at me.

"And now that's just the two of you?"

I nodded. "My parents died young. After that, my sister and I ran the place."

"And, where is she?"

A sudden, slight hammering in my temple. "She left."

"Where to?"

I shook my head, as if to deflect the discomfort.

"Don't ask about Anne," Isa said loudly.

"Now, Isa," I said.

I looked at Louise. "It's nothing dramatic. My sister left, but we believe she's coming back."

"*Believe* being a key word here," Isa said.

"Isa."

"And you're furious with her. That's why you never say a word about her." She turned to face Louise. "And don't ask about my father either, because one thing's for sure and that's that she can't bear to talk about him."

"That will do," I said.

I stared at her trying to harden my gaze, but Isa's was more teasing than confrontational.

Louise cleared her throat and looked down at her plate. "Tasty crispbread," she said softly.

"Isa and I have managed just fine," I said. "From the very beginning. Isn't that right, Isa?"

She nodded reluctantly. "Fine enough."

"And we have home schooling every evening," I said.

"Yeah, sure, it's great. Every evening." Isa said.

"School is important," Louise said.

"Even on Saturdays," Isa said.

"One day, you will thank your mother," Louise said.

"Did you hear that," I said and smiled.

Isa made a face in reply.

When bedtime came, Louise hesitated in the hallway.

"You sleep in there, then?" She pointed at the door to my bedroom.

I nodded.

"And Isa in there?"

"Yes, why do you ask?"

"It's not important."

"Good night, then."

"Good night. . . . And again, thank you."

I lay awake in the darkness. There was only a thin wall between Anne's room and my own and sound carried in the house. But I couldn't hear anything from the room.

In the past few years, I had begun appreciating sounds. As people disappeared from the farms around us, the silence grew more and more intense. Impenetrable, resilient, swallowing every noise. Only when it blew or rained was the silence drowned out by the sound of the wind through the spruce trees or raindrops on the roof.

Anne's bed creaked. I had never appreciated that sound—Anne tossing and turning in her sleep to the accompaniment of the loud whining of the wooden bedframe. And during the months before she left, the sounds continued almost without interruption throughout the night. My sister, who had never before worried about anything, was unable to sleep. One morning when I opened her bedroom door, I saw that she had taken the mattress off the bed and placed it on the floor out of consideration for me. I should have understood the decision she was on the verge of making, but it still came as a shock when she left—that she gave up.

Now I couldn't hear a sound. I couldn't hear Louise getting undressed, sitting on the bed, pulling the covers over her body, and settling in. I should have heard something, I thought, if only a faint cough.

Why was it so important for her to know where we slept?

I twisted and turned heavily, so the bedsprings creaked. I made noise to receive a reply, but there was none to be heard.

I didn't know who she was.

I had brought her home and I knew nothing about her. Her age, where she was from, if Louise was her real name or what her family name was. Had she been a man, I would never have done such a thing.

Isa shouldn't be sleeping alone. Louise could easily slip into her room, stand over the bed, over my sleeping daughter, pull out a pillow, place it over her face. Or maybe she had a knife or a firearm in her bag. Neither Isa nor I had locked our doors. I should have told her to lock her door. Her head against the pillow, my beautiful daughter, sleeping, her smooth skin, the long eyelashes against her cheek, the calmness of her breathing. And maybe Louise was standing over her at this very moment. Holding something in her hands.

There were so many stories. In recent years, there had been even more. Every single time I took a moment to talk to somebody in the area, I heard about something. Attacks, robberies, rape. The wanderers who broke into the homes of the few residents who remained, taking what little they had, family jewelry, potatoes, meat, eggs and milk; and if they didn't find anything, they perhaps took their self-respect, especially from the women, shoving them up against the wall, pounding against them, leaving them without the desire to go on living.

I myself had never been robbed by strangers. Only by Einar.

Once I bought an old hunting shotgun. It came with some ammunition and I had managed to get hold of some skeet ammo that could be used, even though the gunshot was small. I put the shotgun under my bed. A few weeks passed. I was so pleased with myself, I remember, during those weeks, almost hoped that Einar would come, so I could chase him away once and for all. And when he finally showed up again, I ran into the bedroom and got the gun. I took position in the doorway and aimed the shotgun at him. I thought that now I would finally see the same anxiety in his face that he had seen in mine so many times. But all he did was laugh. Then he took two quick strides toward me and, in one swift movement, without a word, tore the weapon out of my hands and aimed it at me.

He took the gun with him when he left. I never saw it again.

I later acquired a captive bolt pistol for slaughtering—didn't want to be dependent on Richard anymore when it came time to put the animals down. Unlike many other pistols used for stunning animals prior to slaughter, this one had a gun barrel and could be mistaken for an ordinary handgun. It would not kill an intruder, just knock him out. Still, I left the pistol in the outbuilding having learned my lesson. It would not have been much help to me now anyway.

I should have had a proper weapon. Louise wasn't stronger than me; she wouldn't have succeeded in tearing it out of my hands. I should have bartered for a new shotgun, not to defend myself against Einar, but against threats like her. But a weapon would be expensive and I no longer had anything to give away; our valuables had long since been used up, traded away—new winter boots for Isa, already worn out, a drum of fortified feedstock, long since empty, a salt block for the horses, soon licked away. And I didn't dare trade away our food; it was now the most valuable thing we had.

I turned over again, lifting the small of my back off the mattress and releasing it hard. The bed creaked loudly. I then coughed loudly and demonstratively.

One second passed. Two. Three.

Then a sound from the next room could be heard. The bed creaked. Louise was twisting and turning in there. She coughed gently, as if in reply. She's not dangerous, I thought, she's not dangerous.

CHAPTER 2

A MAN OF MANY TRADES

Equus przewalskii poliakov

Equus
Przewalsky
Poliakov.

The name was pounding through my head when I arrived far too late at the zoological garden due to my meeting with Poliakov. The primordial horses, in herds on the steppes, the wind in their manes and tails, running always running, the way they had been running for thousands of years. Imagine, they really exist.

Outside the entrance, the organ grinder was hard at work cranking out his creaky melodies, and at the ticket window several mothers stood in line with their children in their Sunday best for the occasion. It had rained during the night, but the sky was starting to clear; the wet ground shone and there were mud puddles everywhere. A little boy had found it fitting to bathe in one of them and mud was splattered all over his white sailor suit. It dripped off the hat's long, silk ribbon and his British nanny scolded him, mixing English phrases with broken Russian. Apparently, we should have put in another layer of gravel.

I hurried past the line and met an employee leading a pony by a rope on the way to the little riding ring. I exchanged a few pleasantries with the zookeeper while simultaneously my eyes took in his outfit. We had twelve keepers, all dressed in green uniforms with black trim and gold buttons, and I was extremely particular about their keeping the garments mended and clean, the shoes polished, and the gold buttons shiny. This employee had clearly not understood the required standard.

"You will find shoe polish in the shed," I said. "Please use it."

He nodded, leading the pony behind him. Over by the riding ring, a discernable line was already forming. The children were allowed to ride one lap each on the back of the small animal and many ran to the end of the line as soon as they had finished, as if the anticipation of riding in itself, the feeling they had while waiting in line, was as much a part of the experience as the actual ride—a pretty uneventful affair lasting about one minute at a walking pace. When a modest riding trip could incite such enthusiasm, just imagine the joy a Przewalsky horse might bring?

But the public could be difficult to understand. I could not fathom, for example, why they dedicated so little attention to our rare antelope. He could, in truth, have used a bit of company. His companion had died almost immediately after the two of them arrived at the zoo last year and now he just lay listlessly on the floor of the cage with little interest in anything we offered him in the way of food, not even showing enthusiasm for fresh spring grass. And his brown eyes became duller with every passing day.

But the public crowded around Berta. The big, heavy animal was allowed to be outside now in the summer. We had given her a proper, lovely, filthy area, particularly muddy today after the rain. Every time she rolled in the mud—making a mess of herself the way they weren't allowed to do—the children cheered.

A keeper opened the gate leading into her pen. I glanced at my watch; it was time for the first entertainment segment of the day. The keeper was one of our most experienced, because although hippopotamuses seem calm, almost lethargic, they can become quite violent should they feel threatened. That is why only a very few people were permitted to get close to Berta. The public was completely silent. The keeper approached the hippopotamus cautiously, slowly, then he took hold of her and hauled himself up onto her back.

I heard the crowd's applause and cheers behind me as I continued on toward my office. He had clearly managed it today, as well— standing on Berta's back with nothing to hold on to. It was a trick I knew visitors told others about when they came home after a day at the zoo and, therefore, an experience new guests expected to have. Both Berta and the keeper had to repeat the routine several times every single day now.

I kept walking in the direction of my office, passed the fountain that was babbling merrily, and made a mental note about how some weeds had invaded one of the flower beds. It was the growing season in June and unwanted plants popped up virtually everywhere the split second one turned one's back.

But otherwise, the park was at its most beautiful. The flower beds were in bloom, the wooden buildings were painted in cheerful colors, and, in the middle of the zoo, stood the radiant, recently constructed stage where we would provide entertainment every single evening in the coming weeks. All the same, suddenly I felt there was something missing.

I passed the pygmy chimpanzees, the brown bear, the big cage full of budgies and parrots. There were children and adults everywhere who clapped and squealed and talked about the animals. A mother and a little girl were looking at the brass plaque that was nailed onto the wall of the brown bear's pen, where they could read the animal's Russian name, its Latin name, and about its origins. The mother explained what she read to the child and I heard them talking about the bear and about Siberia. A surge of pride washed over me. The zoological garden offered entertainment perhaps, but a visit provided, first and foremost, new knowledge and engendered curiosity about the fantastic world we live in. Imagine the conversations the primordial horses would potentially inspire—about species, about evolution, yes, maybe even about Darwin.

"A horse! A horse! My kingdom for a horse!" The words suddenly slid through my mind as I strolled through my own little kingdom. Seldom had Shakespeare been more suitable.

There was a vacant pen beside the camel's cage. We still hadn't decided what we would put in there and the horses would thrive next door to other ruminants. *Equus przewalskii poliakov*, I thought. We can put you in there. I tried to picture it, the horse, a stallion, small, stout, how it would be to stand beside it, place one hand on the horse's forehead, pet it gently as children and adults gathered outside cheering and clapping louder than ever before. And a foal, I thought, tiny, fragile, and on shaky legs, the first wild horse foal ever in a zoological garden— the horse from the myths, from the caves, the origin of all other horses. The residents of Petersburg would love it; they would form lines so long that we would never have to worry about the budget again.

But who could procure a wild horse for me?

I hurried on to my office and closed the door. On the shelves, I had all the trade journals and magazines. I started leafing through one, read about expeditions to foreign countries—some dramatic, some fiascos, some so violent that I shuddered. I picked out a few names, considered their achievements. One name in particular stood out: Wilhelm Wolff. Although he could not be more than forty years old, he was already a wildlife capture legend. The stories about his exploits were many and incredible. He had acquired his interest in animals as early as the age of four in 1848. His father, who had been a fishmonger, was given six live seals, which some fishermen had found caught in their nets. Wolff's father was an imaginative and animal-loving man and he decided that he would put the seals on display by his house in Hamburg. The residents of the city quickly thronged around the seals' cage, and even paid to see them, which prompted

Wolff's father to take the animals to Berlin, where the enthusiasm of audiences was even greater.

This was the beginning of their business. The family started out on a modest scale with a cow, goats, geese, a monkey, and a parrot, but quickly expanded to include hyenas, birds, and a polar bear. The menagerie had acquired a permanent home on the family property, where eager spectators were charged an admission fee, but Wolff's father quickly understood that there were good commercial possibilities in the purchase and sale of these exotic animals to traveling menageries and circuses. Little Wilhelm grew up surrounded by wild creatures, learned to take care of them from an early age, and both respected and adored them. His father, however, was a man of great foresight and realized that the family enterprise might find itself in need of more than just knowledge about animals and animal husbandry. He therefore sent his son to school to learn both French and English.

By the time Wolff was an adult, the enterprise had grown from being a modest sideline to a thriving family business. Thanks to the many zoological gardens that opened in Europe and America in the 1860s, they were contacted by new clients all the time. One of Wolff's most loyal buyers was the world-famous Phineas T. Barnum. On one occasion in 1873, Barnum had supposedly purchased animals for an amount of no less than £3,000 and Indian elephants were said to have been included in the acquisition.

Over the years since then, Wolff had captured animals from all corners of the earth. He and his men had not only more experience but, I daresay, more passion for the field than anyone else on the planet.

I started digging eagerly through my business cards until finally I found his. I had never met Wolff personally, but we had corresponded on more than one occasion in conjunction with large-scale animal transactions. I sat holding the card in my hands, ran one finger over his name.

Wilhelm Wolff, I thought, could you be my man?

. . .

"You're quiet, Misha," Mother said.

"I apologize," I said and quickly shoveled hen with cream sauce, one of her favorite dishes, into my mouth.

I hadn't contributed to the conversation at the table, she was right about that. My thoughts were focused on the letter I would sit down and write after dinner.

"You're busy. No need to apologize for that," she said.

"Yes," I said. "Yes, indeed."

"Your father was the same way," she said. "He was often too consumed by his own affairs to have time for me and I knew better than to disturb him."

"You were always a good housewife for him," I said.

Oh, no, without realizing it, I had again said the h-word. *Housewife*. I hoped she hadn't noticed.

"An excellent *chef* as well," I said quickly. "This meal, did you plan it yourself? It's truly delicious, the sauce not too heavy, not too thin. I assume you have personally seasoned it to taste?"

I wanted to say more, but it was already too late. My mother's gaze was distant, as if she were staring at something a bit to my left, always to the left, beside the heart, and I knew what was coming now.

"I passed the Summer Garden today."

"I see," I said. "The trees are budding now, I presume. A beautiful time of year, don't you think?"

"The Summer Garden is a lovely place to walk, regardless," my mother said.

Regardless . . . a carefully chosen word, which implied that she would not be deterred.

"That may be," I said and dipped yet another piece of meat into the sauce, the second to last cut on the plate. Soon I would have been at table long enough to allow me to leave without incident.

"Already full of young, beautiful people," Mother continued. "I saw no less than three groups of girls pass by behind the fence. They were beautifully dressed in brightly colored frocks. And, imagine, I spotted Jelena among them."

"Did you now."

Jelena was the adoptive daughter of my mother's cousin Betsy. She and her brother Aleksej were two members of a flock of nine siblings. When both parents had died just a short time apart, the children were distributed among family members. Betsy was childless and allowed first pick, a choice that, according to her own words, had been almost impossible. The first time I had been introduced to the two siblings, Betsy had cried.

"Here they are," she said. "The two lucky ones. And the others— Lord knows what will happen to them, the poor children, poor, poor children."

Aleksej and Jelena both looked extremely uncomfortable, I remember, as if they were not pleased about being the chosen ones. There were no winners in this situation, according to my mother. They apparently never did become fully and wholly a family because cousin Betsy couldn't help but think about, and duly mention, that she perhaps should have chosen two of the other children instead, and perhaps she should have also spent more time on the decision. It was, after all, the most important of her life.

"When was the last time you saw your second cousins? It must have been at least one year ago?" Mother asked.

"It was on the date of your wedding anniversary."

Mother tended to surround herself with family members on this day, as if Father were still with us—and so he was, in a manner of speaking.

"No, Jelena didn't come. She was in bed with a cold. You remember that, certainly," she said sharply.

"Exactly. That's how it was," I replied, even though I had no recollection of Jelena's absence at this family gathering. She was just one of many distant female relatives, young girls who were introduced to me from time to time, pulled out of the group and led over to me, and who took my hand quickly, giggling, without looking me in the eyes.

"She has really grown into a beautiful girl."

One of Mother's favorite lines.

"I have no doubt."

One of mine.

"Did you speak to her, then?" I asked.

"She seemed so jolly—you know how young girls can be, full of laughter and joy—I didn't want to ruin the day for her, so I refrained from attracting any attention to myself."

"But the day would certainly not be ruined by a conversation with you."

Mother ignored my attempted flattery. "Can you believe she is already so grown up that she strolls with her girlfriends in the Summer Garden," she said, her voice expressive of something I could only interpret as false incredulity.

"It is also a lovely place for a stroll," I said. "If one has time for such things. Strolls, that is."

"It is a matter of priorities," my mother said.

"For some people, perhaps," I said.

She didn't respond. She chewed for a while in silence.

I guided the final piece of meat into my mouth, the sauce a touch too salty, the meat on the tough side; I had to chew thoroughly and at length before the bite could finally be swallowed. She clearly noticed it and left me in peace . . . or perhaps she was speculating about how she might choose her words in the future. If she could only come up with the magic words, I would give in. If she only mentioned something like baby shoes or a woman's dress or the name of the right romantic setting, then I would immediately go out into the world and find someone to marry.

The thought always made me dizzy. A woman . . . in here, in these rooms, in bed with me at night, another living creature who would occupy space, dresses, garters, and unfamiliar odors—no, no, no. But Mother never gave up, apparently. Of course, she simply wanted me to be happy and, since getting married was the norm, since *the good life* was defined by marriage, by a beautiful woman, another body in the marital bed and, subsequently, the laughter of children, the sound of footsteps tripping lightly across the floor, tall sons at a father's side, she thought that this was something that I too dreamt of deep down.

Often, I would resort to telling short anecdotes from the zoological garden to guide her thoughts onto something else, funny episodes that had happened in the course of the day, stories that could be embellished, exaggerated, or perhaps revised ever so slightly to make amusing points. Sometimes, if nothing special had happened, I would even pull out old stories, which I just updated a bit to fit the season and the age of the animals. But today, I needed not revise nor exaggerate in order to have something exciting to tell her.

"I have decided to see about the acquisition of a wild horse," I said.

"A wild horse?"

"Not just one, actually. I am thinking of an entire family. A stallion, a mare, and a foal."

It took a while for my mother to respond. I don't know whether it was due to a lack of interest or a particularly large bite she had just put into her mouth.

"Why wild horses, in particular?" she asked finally.

"These aren't ordinary horses, but none other than the veritable *primordial horse*. They have been recently rediscovered in Mongolia."

"Mongolia? That's far away."

She placed her fork down beside her plate and wiped her mouth painstakingly with the napkin.

"The discovery is a sensation," I said.

I put my hand in my pocket, pulled out the business card bearing Wolff's name, and fingered it a little bit.

"Then you should get yourself a horse like that, if it will make you happy," Mother said, and a tiny sigh escaped her lips.

"Yes. I am going to try," I said.

"Yes, Mikhail," she said. "Good."

She stood up and reached out with one hand, sort of automatically, to ruffle my hair.

She had been ruffling my hair like that for as long as I could remember. I couldn't bring myself to say that I found it a tad strange, now, at my age, that I, truth be told, was actually filled with a certain distaste when I felt her hand up there, and caught myself wondering if she would continue also after the hair on my head had fallen off—if she would ruffle my bare skull, when that day came—so I twisted deftly away, with a quick, practiced movement, while simultaneously I pushed the chair away from the table to signal that I was about to get to my feet.

"Two horses," I said and waved the business card in front of her nose. "Two horses are the minimum—a stallion and a mare. I am going to write to Wolff right away and inquire about an expedition."

KARIN

Sydney's harem gathered down below in one corner of the paddock and were grazing calmly. They had survived the trip well. No injuries. They are robust animals. Hamburg and Bronx are separated from the other horses in a separate corral a short distance away. As long as they aren't in the same area as Sydney, it will be like this. Few conflicts, a minimal risk of injuries. But the moment they are released, I know that everything will change. Fortunately, it will still be a long time before they're grazing in the wild.

I take my time unpacking. I have the largest room on the second floor. From here, I can see the paddock on one side and the ger tents—Mongolian yurts where the camp employees live—on the other. The tents are also fenced in. There are wolves in this area, dangerous for the horses, and potentially for us. But I don't fear the wolves. You can see them from far off; you see everything from far off on this landscape. We are thirteen hundred meters above sea level, but it doesn't feel like being in the mountains, not the mountains I am familiar with from Europe. These are steppes—grass-covered hills and valleys—at once both gentle and brutal. Not a tree in sight. I have always liked the open view offered by the ocean but feared the dark depths. On the steppes of Mongolia, I get the same feeling of space but without the uncanny depths, and you can move wherever you want, unimpeded, in all directions.

When it starts to get dark, I go outside to check on Mathias. He has been given his own ger. He requested it personally, said that if he was going to Mongolia, he wanted to "do it right."

I knock on the door. Wait. Waiting in front of a door, that is a feeling all its own. The closed door can be hiding anything.

No, not here. Not now. He is clean, detoxed. Has stayed clean for several months. And out here, he can't get hold of anything anyway.

There was a time when it was nice to wait outside his door. Once, he must have been four or five years old, I remember standing outside of his room and listening. I couldn't hear any sounds from inside. Had never before experienced that he locked himself in, but I liked it, liked that he wanted to be alone also. I raised my hand, knocked, and waited for an answer. None came. I knocked again and now suddenly the door opened.

"Why did you knock?" he asked.

"I wanted to respect your privacy," I said. I had always been careful to express myself properly when I spoke to him.

"What does that mean?" he asked.

"You have the right to decide when you want to be with other people and when you want to be alone."

"But I don't want to be alone."

"Why did you have the door closed, then?"

"It just happened. I didn't mean to."

After that, he started putting a big teddy bear in front of the door so it wouldn't lock. He called it the "bear watchman." The bear watchman sat there also at night, the only time Mathias was actually in his room. During the daytime, he preferred to stay in the living room or the kitchen where I was. He followed behind me talking and talking. Wanted me to pick him up, wanted to put his arms around me, kissed me on the cheeks all the time. It was nice; it was. But he was there constantly, always, like a kind of extension of me. Even though he was so small, there was so much of him. I needed air. Just a little air. I started smoking. Stood alone on the balcony in the cold and inhaled deeply. It helped a little. Karin is just going outside to smoke, I said, and went out alone. At least I didn't smoke inside.

And I still don't.

"Come in," Mathias replied to my knock on the ger door.

His voice is high. Happy. Sort of happy? Maybe he is just pretending to be happy to cover up the craving for a fix. I have tried to understand this craving, this drive, that overrides all others. I have thought that maybe it's a kind of invisible harness that steers him, dragging and pushing him. He has come here to be rid of the harness once and for all. At least, that's what he says he hopes for. I don't know what I hope. Hope is a meaningless emotion. Passive. I can't put my own hope to any good use whatsoever.

I open the door to the tent and walk in. The interior is in semi-darkness; it takes a moment for my eyes to adjust. Just a small oil lamp glows on the table. A faint light filters through the hole for the chimney in the middle of the ceiling.

Mathias stands in the center of the tent and throws out his arms.

"Look at this!"

Yes, he really is happy. Spins around and waves his arms. Points at the colorfully decorated cupboard. The chair, the table, heavy wood furniture, all of it hand painted. The bed full of soft, woven blankets. Thick wool threads spun, wound into balls, and threaded in and out of a loom. Every single centimeter of thread touched by human hands. The tiny iron stove in the middle of the room—a simple, black box that I know produces a surprising amount of heat. The floor is linoleum with an imitation pine pattern, the plastic an unexpected breach against the style of the furniture and blankets. In the wood basket lies dried cowpats ready for use; on the table are teabags, cups, and a thermos full of hot water.

"They are big tea drinkers," I say.

"I don't mean the tea, I mean everything!" Mathias says.

He walks toward me holding out his arms, ready for a hug, and embraces me. It is not just with me that he is a big hugger; he has

always been able to hug everyone without any inhibitions whatsoever.

"I'm so glad I came along, Karin. This is going to be great, really
great."

He holds me for a long time. His beard stubble tickles my cheek.
How quickly his beard grows. My grown-up, living boy. He is clean
and, out here, there is nothing to tempt him into deep water again.
Maybe this time it will actually work.

Maybe.

His beard prickles.

I wriggle free. "You've seen where the shower is?" I ask. "And the
bathroom? There's a septic tank; it works pretty well, and the ground-
water is relatively clean, but you should probably boil it for the first
week."

"Shower?"

He sniffs under his arm with an exaggerated movement. "Are you
saying that I need a shower?"

"Not at all. I didn't mean it like that."

"Take it easy, Karin, I was kidding."

He laughs, has always laughed. Sometimes it was the laughter I
listened for when I was out looking. Loud, raw. Increasingly hoarse as
the years passed. Life on the street changed his voice, as it changed the
rest of him. Hoarse from tobacco. Hoarse from all-nighters. Hoarse
from heroin.

He sits on the bed. Reaches for the thermos.

"Tea?"

"No, thank you. I just wanted to see how you were doing."

He pours himself a cup. The aroma of Earl Grey mingles with
the scent of cow dung from the basket and of the wool from all the
blankets.

"Terrific, as you can see. And you?"

I wait. Take a step toward the door. "Fine . . . fine."

He takes a sip of his tea. Looks at me with a tiny smile.

"Listen, about Joschi . . ."

"Jochi," I correct.

69

"Jochi. First name or last name? Should I call him Mister Jochi? Or Mister something else?"

"Mongols have only one name. They use the father's name for a surname but write it first. You can just call him Jochi."

"Just Jochi. Should be able to remember that. . . . Anyway. What's the deal there?"

"Deal? There's no deal."

He puts the cup down on the table in the middle of the bright-orange and blue-rose painted flowers. Drops a sugar cube into the tea, stirs, his smile unwavering.

"It's just kind of strange that you've never talked about him."

I feel that suddenly I'm blushing.

"I must have."

"No. You've mentioned that there's a leader here, not what his name is. Nothing about him. Kind of strange that you haven't talked about him more since the two of you know each other so well."

"We don't know each other so well."

"But it would have been nice."

"What's that?"

"If there had been something."

"I'm fifty-six years old, Mathias."

"And?"

He throws out his arms. "There are no limits for love!"

I rest my hand on the door handle. "I have a job to do here."

"Nobody's questioning that. But it's possible to have two thoughts in your head at the same time."

I open the door, notice that it's already cooler outside.

"No doubt. But for my own part, I only have one."

I leave Mathias. He is probably still grinning, but I don't turn around.

I walk away from the research station, move up the hillside. The terrain is easy going but, even so, I am soon short of breath. It must be the altitude. It is dusk; the temperature drops so quickly that I can feel the change as I walk.

Mathias's grinning face remains stuck on my retinas. I don't understand how he can grin. In his life, nothing is funny. That is why I brought him here. No, I haven't brought him, he asked to come along. Demanded it. My last chance, he called it. An unusually dramatic change of course for him. He came to Thorenc straight from rehab. There's nothing for me in Berlin but the street, he said, and he was right about that. He had messed up everything so many times that there was nothing left. Three years ago, he even lost the few hours of visitation he had with Sarah.

Sarah, a soft face, a nose she often crinkles just the way Mathias did when he was little. Thank goodness for Child Services. They stepped in and provided everything required when her mother died of an overdose and Mathias was unable to take care of his daughter. It is better for Sarah to be spared having anything to do with Mathias. And with me. I have read about it—how contact with the biological family makes everything more difficult, that it can confuse the child. And now that Sarah is well taken care of in a foster home, it is better that I stay away.

On the few occasions I saw her, it was her crying that made the strongest impression on me. There was a force to that crying. I remember that I was envious of it, how she cried until she was heard.

When I lost my mother, I didn't cry. Not a single tear. I just did what I was told. Now you must be a good girl, a big girl, I remember people said. So I tried to be big and good.

Madame Drouet said that I should cry more. Crying is semivoluntary behavior in humans. I could decide to cry; I could refrain. I never asked her whether she thought I would have managed better had I cried more because the crying would have aroused pity in others.

Maybe nobody felt truly sorry for me.

I didn't ask Madame Drouet about anything at all. She was the one who asked me questions, while I just sat there staring at the tips of my shoes.

A calm, friendly voice. You're sleeping poorly, she said. No, I said. I sleep. I am able to sleep. But you dream, she said.

Yes, I dreamed, dreamed until it was impossible to go to bed, impossible to get up in the morning as well. The nightmares held me back. It took me several hours to put my feet on the floor. My horses bore the brunt of it; the poor horses, I started slacking off. Put the entire project at risk. I was given sleeping pills, but they didn't stop the nightmares. Finally, the doctor in Thorenc sent me to Drouet.

Tell me about your son, she said. How is he doing? How do you feel when he goes off the rails?

Mathias cried as a baby. Often. I picked him up every single time.

There was a clock on Madame Drouet's wall. I stared at the tips of my shoes, at the clock, down at the tips of my shoes again. They were worn, caked in mud from the farm. Time passed too slowly and too quickly. It took half a day to meet with her. I had to drive halfway down to the coast on terrible roads, because there was nobody like Drouet to be found in Thorenc. The drives affected my work almost more than my sleeping problems. In the end, it didn't help. What works, is to pull yourself together. Set the alarm. Concentrate on something that matters. Work. After a few weeks I called and said I wasn't coming back. She said that was a shame. That she thought we "were in a good process." In her opinion.

The landscape spreads out below me with swaggering entitlement. No matter where I turn, there is more of the same. Nothing to fix my gaze on, nothing to be afraid of, either. And I can just walk, walk for an eternity, without meeting a single barrier for days, months.

Originally I wanted to reintroduce the horses in the Gobi Desert where the last free takhis were captured. That was where they came from; it was logical that they should return there. But nothing else was logical about putting them there. The landscape of the Gobi is brutal, barren, great distances between water sources, no roads, no infrastructure.

It was the Mongolian authorities who had suggested Hustai. Just a few hours' drive north of Ulaanbaatar on good roads, at least by Mongolian standards. When I came here, I understood immediately that they were right. This is a good place for the horses. Miles and miles of grass-covered steppes, many water sources, an area where protection from wolves is possible. And when I arrived at the valley, which in the end became the camp site, I had no doubts. A mild lowland plain shaped like an island, enclosed by steep hillsides offering protection from the wind and hard weather. Centrally located on the flatlands, like the pupil of an eye, with clear water flowing in from a watering hole.

There, by the water, lies the camp. And I have to go back now because I am losing visibility, the contours are disappearing suddenly—grass and stone, tufts, and uneven terrain becoming a dark mass. The darkness tumbles upon the landscape as if someone were pouring out a sack of coal from the sky.

The door to Jochi's room is open when I get back. He is sitting at the desk against the one long wall, notices me right away, stands up, and walks out into the hallway.

"I was looking for you."

"I just went for a walk."

"Mathias said as much. That maybe you wanted to stretch your legs."

Suddenly, I realize that my cheeks are warm. Pull yourself together, Karin. Nothing's going on here.

"There's a lot we need to talk about," Jochi said.

"Yes, we'll do it tomorrow."

"And the next day."

He smiles.

"Yes," I say. "Good night."

"Good night. . . . Karin?"

"Yes?"

"I'm glad you're here. That we managed it, at last."

"Yes. Me, too."

I am out of breath when I get back to my room. I sit on my bed. Leave the lights off. Just sit there in the darkness listening to my own breathing.

When did this happen?

I've thought about him, but not in that way.

Has it become a thing because Mathias said it's a thing?

No. It's not a thing.

I don't even know how old Jochi is. I know he isn't married, but not if he has someone. He was recommended by the authorities. A well-known biologist, they said, who speaks excellent English, fluent Russian.

But I remember that the first thing I noticed was his straight neck. It looked strong. Then his thick, black hair, just a few grey streaks. His face gave no hint of his age. He could be as old as me or fifteen years younger. I've never asked. His age has never mattered to me, not until now.

EVA

It was still dark when I woke up. I picked the alarm clock up from the nightstand. Pressed the button that lit up the display, remembered that I only had one remaining battery, that it was important not to press for too long. It was five minutes to five, ten minutes until the alarm; I might just as well get up.

I never woke Isa this early in the day. She was a child; she needed more sleep than I did, and maybe even more now than before. I remember how I had been at that age. I could sleep until one. Maybe she could, too, but I never gave her the opportunity; there was too much to do.

But she was spared having to help out with the milking.

I pulled on pants, a tank top, and a sweater. My overalls were hanging on the porch, the stench of them was too strong to keep them inside. Then I opened the door.

It was only then that I remembered that there was a stranger in the house and I stopped moving, listened. Not a sound from Anne's room. As I tiptoed across the floor toward the kitchen, the hallway felt longer than usual. In the kitchen, the furnishings were just black silhouettes. I strained to see clearly; it was as if the rooms were darker than they normally were, as if the house were not really mine.

I went to the sink, filled a glass. The water tasted different as well, sweeter.

Today she would have to leave. Today I would drive her up to the main road and make sure she got a ride heading up north.

At that moment, a door opened. I turned around. Louise was standing in the doorway.

"Sorry," I said. "I tried to be quiet."

"Couldn't you sleep?" she asked.

"I have to do the milking," I said. "I always get up at five."

"Oh," she said. And then, sort of casually, "Cows?"

I nodded. "They have to be milked morning and evening, but you can just go back to bed."

"But I can help you," she said.

"There's no need," I said. "I am used to doing it alone."

"I won't be able to sleep anyway. Besides, I would like to work to thank you for the food and the warm bed last night. That was the deal, right?"

There was something pleading in her eyes.

"Of course," I hastened to say. "You can borrow Isa's overalls."

I walked quickly across the yard. Heard her footsteps on the gravel just behind me. Then I opened the door to the cowshed. The goats turned to face me.

Here, there had been dozens of cows, hens, pigs, goats. The goats were especially popular with all the children who used to visit us. Tame and playful, willing to be petted by small, reckless children's hands. I had been unable to part with them and was even less able now. The winter before, I discovered that the ewe was expecting and, suddenly one day, two little bundles were there. White as snow, smiling, playful, tiny creatures. Isa spent hours with them; with the animals, she behaved as if she were eight years old again.

They should be put down. I didn't have enough hay for more animals and neither did I know where I would get hold of more now that

I no longer had Richard to help me. As long as there was fresh grass, we could keep them. But the winter would soon do away with every-thing green, and then I didn't know what I would do with the kids or the other animals. The extra haybales I had planned to take from Richard's barn would not be enough for all of them. We should have gathered more in the summer. We could have mowed the grass with a scythe, raked it together, and left it to dry on the ground. I could have had Isa turn it over every other day. But the summer had been too damp; it would never have dried properly.

We had two cows, Apple and Micro. They were both old. In our former life, they would have been shot a long time ago. Still, they had given us two calves that spring, Sam and Nok. I hoped that at least one of the calves would be a male, but both disappointed. Now I had two new cows. I should be grateful, but new dairy cows were not much help as long as I had no bull. I used to borrow Richard's for breeding, but the bull fell ill and died a short time before Richard and his family left. Perhaps yet another reason why they decided to run away.

The cows bellowed in our direction. Louise jumped.

"You okay?" I asked.

"Sure," she answered, but looked anxious.

I still used the milking machine even though I only had two cows and could have easily milked them by hand. But I liked the routines. First, wash the udders with lukewarm water, then take hold of them, warm and dry against my skin, squeeze a little milk out into a saucer, make sure there are no traces of blood or lumps in it. Then turn on the machine, the intense racket of the pump, connect the teat cups, watch the milk run through the plastic tubes and drip down into the pail I had placed below. Before we had a large tank; we milked liters a day, but now everything ran into the same pail. For good days, I kept an extra pail ready.

Once the udders were empty, they would detach themselves from the pump. After that, I cleaned the tubes, sending liters of water through them. I was particular about the cleaning, although nobody checked the milk any longer, and Isa and I were the only ones who drank it. The routines gave me the sensation that nothing had changed.

Louise watched everything I did, asked to be allowed to try, both the washing of the udders, the connection of the machine, and the subsequent cleaning. She learned quickly.

When we were finished, I found a cup and dipped it in the pail, filled it with milk, and handed it to her. She drank without asking any questions and swallowed it down in big gulps without reacting to the taste, temperature, or texture.

She drank until the cup was empty, then she wiped the milk off her upper lip and handed it to me.

"Have you ever tasted raw milk before?" I asked.

"No," she said.

"You didn't find it strange?"

I remembered how visitors used to wrinkle their noses at the warm, fatty milk straight from the cows. Louise was silent for a moment, considering.

"I don't know," she said. "I didn't think about whether it was strange. Only that it filled me up."

I did a round—checking in on all the animals, the pig, the hens, and the goats, making sure they had enough water and feed. We collected rainwater for them in huge tubs; the precipitation ensured that they never ran dry. Louise watched everything I did attentively, and as soon as she'd understood what I was doing, she wanted to try. I watched her thin back as she shoveled muck, the eagerness filling her movements.

By the time we came out of the cowshed, it was light. A lone bird was singing; it sounded like a blackbird. I remembered my childhood, how the mornings of the summer were associated with birdsong. Now we rarely heard any birds other than magpies and the song filtered through me like a soft light.

"What are we going to do now?" Louise asked.

"I have to look in on the other animals. But you can go inside if you like."

"No, I'll come with you," she said quickly.

"Are you sure?"

She nodded so firmly that I said no more.

We headed down the walkway toward the other part of the park. All the roads were paved. Once upon a time, someone had ensured that the entire farm was adapted for wheelchair users—*universal design* it was called. I would have liked to have seen a wheelchair here now. There were huge cracks everywhere gaping open to reveal the soil beneath, the sprouting weeds. With every passing winter, the cracks grew larger and larger. The water that settled into them expanded when the frost came; ice takes up more space than water. There's little that can stop ice and certainly not porous asphalt.

I showed Louise the forest reindeer, but he didn't approach the fence. The Peregrine falcons sat half concealed at the very top of their cage and the Scottish wildcat was hiding. She didn't look particularly impressed and I could understand why. She still attempted to ask questions, to show an interest, but it wasn't until she saw the wild horses that a huge smile opened up her face.

"You said you didn't have horses?"

She lay her hand on the gate to the enclosed pasture, about to open it.

"Can I pet them?"

"No," I said. "These are not ordinary horses. They're wild horses."

She looked at me quizzically.

"We never enter the paddock. There must always be a barrier between you and the horses."

"Why?"

"Do you have any experience with horses?"

"I have tried riding."

"These are different. Wild horses can't be tamed. You can never ride them."

"But," she said, thinking out loud. "You call them wild? They can't be really wild if they live in captivity."

Captivity. Some people used that word to describe zoos and animal parks. In the old days, zoological gardens were prisons for animals, but at Heiane, the animals were well taken care of. And without us they wouldn't have managed to survive. But I refrained from explaining all of this to Louise. It would sound as if I were defending myself from criticism and I didn't want to argue. I just wanted to talk to her and was pleased to see how she lit up when she saw the horses—Anne's horses.

"They're sensitive," I said. "They react to even the smallest of things. They can be calm one minute and start kicking their back legs the next."

She looked at Nike and Puma in astonishment. The munching jaws, the sluggish movements.

"Yes, it's hard to believe," I said.

"Have they ever kicked you before?"

"No, but I've never given them the opportunity, either."

We stood there watching them. Puma suddenly shook his head, whinnying softly before dashing away. A few meters forward, a little jump, then he pulled up short and turned toward his mother to see if she was coming, whether she wanted to come along and play. When she showed no sign of following him, he trotted back just as quickly, all the way over to stand by her side. Nike lifted her head slightly, sort of looking at the foal with indulgence, a gaze common to parents of all species, I thought, the blank fascination one feels over the antics of one's own children.

"Are they wise?" Louise asked.

"What do you mean?"

"Like, compared to a dog, how smart are they?"

"There's a difference between being smart and wise."

"But once I read about a horse that could count?"

"You mean Der Kluge Hans?"

"Yes, maybe?"

I became enthused.

"Hans communicated by knocking a hoof against the ground. He could count from one to a hundred, and he counted all kinds of objects and people, windows on buildings, boys in the street, and he could do mathematical calculations. When his owner, William von Osten, asked what three plus two was, the horse knocked the ground five times with his hoof."

Louise nodded. "But wasn't it true that he couldn't add, not really?"

"That's right. Von Osten showed him for many years, until a psychologist examined him. The psychologist discovered that the horse didn't actually answer the questions asked by the owner, but instead was responding to his behavior. When the owner asked a question, he unconsciously leaned his head and upper body forward and this was the sign for the animal to start knocking its hoof against the ground, and when the horse had knocked the correct number of times, the owner lifted his head and the animal understood that this meant he was supposed to stop. Hans was perhaps not a mathematical genius, but he was good at reading body language."

"More wise than smart, in other words."

I nodded. "I have a book. It's in the house. The author has written about him. I have many books about animals, if you are interested."

"Yes," she said. "I would like that."

Reading a book takes time, I thought.

We walked slowly back.

A book can be read in a day or a week.

"I read fast," she said.

"But there's no hurry."

She stared at the ground. "I really hadn't planned on staying for more than one night," she said softly. "You don't have enough food for one more person."

"You don't eat very much."

She laughed a little. "I eat what I am given."

We continued walking in silence.

Finally, she stopped. "Fine. If you're sure. I would very much like to read that book."

CHAPTER 3

A FINANCIAL CHALLENGE

I will not tire the reader with the contents of all the letters exchanged between Wolff and the undersigned, but, with time, they constituted a bundle so thick that I had to give them a drawer of their own in the secretary.

Wolff had already heard about *Equus przewalskii poliakov* when I contacted him, but he disputed my claim that the horses Przewalsky had discovered were true wild horses and believed the finding of bone fragments and hide must have come from a mule.

Przewalsky quickly returned to Gobi and claimed to have seen the animals again with his own eyes, but did not succeed in capturing them. Wolff, however, was not convinced.

I dug out all the details I could find about the wild horses and filled my letters with them. A number of traces of the horses had been found, the oldest from 900 BC, where the monk Bodowa wrote about the species in his notes. Another account stemmed from the year 1630: the honorable Chechen-Khansoloj reportedly gave a wild horse to the Emperor of Manchuria, which indicates that the horse at that time was already viewed as being both rare and valuable. I even

82

found stories about how the great Genghis Khan himself reportedly saw wild horses on his way to Tangut, and that they frightened his own horse to such an extent that it reared up and the autocratic ruler was thrown to the ground.

Wolff made the argument that we could not trust these old sources, but I responded that there were also more recent accounts. The Scottish doctor John Bell, who was on the service staff of Peter the Great, was extremely certain about his sightings of takhis when he visited Gobi in the last century.

Wolff, however, was not convinced. Independent of whether the horses, in fact, did exist, there were other challenges, he wrote. In one of his very first letters he mentioned *funding*. A dry and dull little word, perhaps, but of great significance. Such an expedition would cost far more than I had imagined, and I understood that it was expected that I would sponsor the better part of the escapade.

I spent many evenings poring over both the accounts and budgets into the early hours and I discussed the matter with the director of the zoo, who fortunately responded with enthusiasm to the idea of wild horses. Cases were forwarded for different types of sales, but I wanted at all costs to avoid sacrificing any of our animals, especially Berta, who was the most valuable creature we owned. Instead, I solicited the help of the zoo's many patrons.

A number of them were willing to donate, though none of them in amounts that made any significant difference. Even after I had been begging for a long time, more than half of the items in the budget remained unsettled. I was, however, certain that I knew how I would manage to raise the money. I had every confidence that I would receive all the required assistance from a specific individual, a gentleman of high rank, whose name there is no cause to reveal.

This was a gentleman with whom I coincidentally fell into conversation with several years back at one of the city's baths. He visited the place *incognito*, and it was, therefore, a while before I understood his social standing. He was about twenty years older than me but, in spite of this, the conversation between us flowed quite effortlessly. When speaking with him one-on-one, my usual insecurity vanished. In our conversations there were no elusive rules that I sought to understand, no customs that I struggled to comprehend.

On a few, rare, former occasions in my life, I have encountered people with whom I experienced this same absence of restraint. A simplicity, as if we, independent of rank and age, inhabited the same sphere. I would hold that I've experienced that such a special rapport can arise between men, a contact wholly different from that between men and women, where the oppositions create an attraction. In this case, the attraction arises precisely because the two of you are essentially the same, because you are both wandering around the earth in the same type of body. Maybe because one, in purely physical terms, meets one's surroundings with the same *conditio sine qua non* whether one is fat, thin, tall, or short. Or maybe it has nothing to do with physical constitution. Maybe it's about what is between the ears—that the masculine mindset is, quite simply, different from the feminine. Whatever the case may be, with this gentleman, I immediately felt this type of connection—a strong mutual understanding.

He invited me to his home the following Thursday and I remember it was exactly a Thursday because, over time, that became *our day*. Every single Thursday I called on him; apparently it was convenient as his wife had her own program on this day.

I began looking forward to the fourth day of the week, to our conversations. He was extremely interested in my work and never tired of listening to me talk about the zoological garden. On several occasions, he also offered to cover the cost of small-scale repairs in the park. He never felt the need to receive any form of credit for these donations; contributing was pleasure enough in its own right, he said, as was seeing the results of his donations. That he and I alone knew that he had been responsible for procuring the beautiful, wrought iron gate for the brown bear's pen, or for the repairs on the arctic foxes' cage, filled him with a warmth that could not be replaced by public announcements and brass plaques.

When my idea for an expedition to Mongolia arose, I understood that he was immediately enthusiastic and supported my plans wholeheartedly. Several Thursdays passed and I permitted myself to bring up the matter more often, yet never with any results. Then, the summer came and he left the city to be with his family at their summer residence in the countryside until September. In the middle of August, however, I received a letter from him. He wrote that he had returned and requested that I come to call as soon as possible.

It was a hot afternoon, a Tuesday. The heat hung heavily over the city. It is in the summer months that one is really reminded that Petersburg was built on a swamp. The dampness from the canals and the surrounding lakes and bogs never rises into the sky—it lies like a lid on top of the city. The stillness of summer prevailed as the city's festivities were on hiatus. Most people with the means were still to be found in the countryside.

A Tuesday, I thought, as I was driven up the avenue toward his white, stone mansion; never before had I been to visit him on a Tuesday. I liked it, that he had summoned me as soon as he returned, that he hadn't even wanted to wait for two days.

When I arrived, I found him in the library between prodigious three-meter-high shelves full of Russian and European classics. He sat in a large armchair by the window. The heavy curtains were half drawn, as if he were shielding himself from the summer day outside, and his face was turned away from the light such that half of it was in shadow. I was on the verge of embracing him, had already stretched out my arms, ready to kiss him on both cheeks, but when he merely sat without moving, my hands dropped and I suddenly didn't know what I should do.

He must have noticed my confusion because then he got to his feet.

"My apologies," he said.

My benefactor held out his arms to me and greeted me, but the vigorous embrace I had anticipated was not forthcoming. His gestures were heavy and indifferent.

He sat down again and now I saw that something was, in fact, wrong. He moved in the way one does when trying to avoid pain—stiffly and in jerks.

"Have a seat, my dear friend." My benefactor nodded toward the armchair opposite.

A servant entered with a fruit platter, but I didn't eat anything, waiting for my benefactor to say something more, offer an explanation.

After my eyes grew accustomed to the darkness, I also noticed that it was more than a shadow that darkened his face, that his left check and eye cavity were discolored by bruises and extravasations. I leaned forward, trying to see more clearly, but the sharp contrast between light and shadow on his face confused me.

"Is everything all right?" I asked.

"It is just very hot," he said.

"But I can see that something has happened?"

I lifted my hand to indicate the bruises.

He twisted away. "It's fine."

"You came home earlier than planned?" I asked.

"I have been here for a week and a half already," he said.

At home for a week and a half without even sending word? He fell silent again, sat motionless; the dust particles danced in the air in front of him. The room was hot, as if heat emanated from the dark green silk wallpaper. I wanted to ask more questions about the bruises, about the injury he so clearly had suffered, but suddenly didn't dare.

"I am well underway with funding for the expedition," I said instead.

"The expedition?"

"To Mongolia. I have been corresponding with Wolff. You remember, the wildlife capture specialist."

He lifted his hand and stroked his discolored left cheek.

"Yes, I remember him."

"He still hasn't said yes," I hastened to add, "but I am hopeful that I will succeed in eliciting his enthusiasm."

"I am sure you will," my benefactor said.

There was, however, no enthusiasm to be detected in him. He kept his eyes fixed on the bookshelves behind me, as if he were afraid to look me in the eyes. Tolstoy, Homer, Dickens, Darwin—all of a sudden, I felt that they were all of far greater interest to him than I, the man who was not an avid reader.

"Now I am working on the funding," I said. "As I mentioned before the summer, the amount I need to raise is considerable."

"Yes," he said. "It will be costly. I can imagine."

I expected him to say something more, mention the donation he would make personally, but he was silent.

I squirmed, my shirt sticking to my body. I could feel my forehead glistening with perspiration.

"I came as soon as I could," I said finally. "The minute I received your message. I had the impression that there was some urgency?"

He turned his face toward me. Finally, he looked me in the eyes. He stood up and moaned softly.

"Are you in pain?" I asked and stood up with him.

He walked over to the window, where the light falling on his left cheek disclosed the full extent of his injuries. He said nothing about his face but placed one hand against his side.

"A broken rib," he said. "I fell off my horse last week."

"My dear friend," I said. "Why didn't you say so? You could have called me, with your wife in the country and you here all alone, I could have helped you."

He raised his hand abruptly to silence me.

"Misha . . . hush."

I fell silent. I was hot, but not from the summer heat. A flush rose in my cheeks, confusion, anger. I wanted to ask, but I didn't dare. I wanted to leave but could not.

And then it came: "I am unfortunately obliged to cancel our Thursday meetings in the future," he said.

"Oh? You are?"

I concentrated on staying calm, not wanting to reveal any agitation.

"It is due to factors that are beyond my control," he continued.

"Of course," I said. "That's how it is sometimes."

I pressed my lips together to keep them from trembling.

"I appreciate the weekly visits, but no longer have occasion to receive you," he said.

"I see." I took a breath. "Then I wish you a swift recovery."

I wanted to leave before he could say anything else, leave before I expressed my feelings. But he lay his hand on my arm and held me back.

"Mikhail, I adore our friendship. You know that."

I didn't look at him, didn't want to risk it, and slipped adroitly out of his grasp.

"If you would permit me, I hope you don't mind if I don't see you to the door," he said. "The stairs are especially painful."

"I can certainly manage to ask the servant to call a carriage without your help," I said and walked toward the door.

I could hear how sharp my voice sounded, like a cutlass, but I was unable to restrain myself. Love appears to be an emotional condition, friendship a disposition, Aristoteles wrote. But some friendships are so strong that they are reminiscent of love, and the emotional condition that is prompted when they come to an end is equally strong.

I placed my hand on the door handle and turned toward him, one final hope leaping through me.

"How long . . . ," I said and was unable to finish.

"I will be in touch," he said.

"Yes," I said. "Of course."

"I will be in touch," he repeated. "You needn't waste your precious time on contacting me."

"No."

He never wrote to me again. I filled many pages with my thoughts to him, but didn't send them. I caught myself wandering through the area close to his residence in hopes that I would run into him, in truth, a hopeless endeavor, in that he never ventured outside except in a closed carriage.

One day in late September, when everyone had returned from their summer homes and the life of society recommenced as usual, my mother returned from a reception and repeated a rumor she had overheard about my benefactor concerning an incident at one of the city's public baths. It had occurred the week before I visited him, and it was this incident that was the cause of all his injuries. My mother spoke about it with shock and disbelief, claiming that he got what he deserved. I refused to believe that what she told me was true and asked her to stop spreading lies.

It was a difficult winter. I had lost my closest friend and, simultaneously, my hope of funding an expedition to Mongolia was dwindling. Finally, I saw no other recourse but to sell Berta. It was with a deep sense of grief that I waved goodbye as she was led into the cramped trailer of a traveling menagerie. It seemed that she stared at me sadly, almost accusingly, when the door closed behind her and she was locked into the dark trailer where she would soon begin a life of jolting and bouncing down the highway. I tried to console myself with the thought that she was an animal, that she didn't have the predisposition to be *accusatory*. Besides, as a traveling artist, she would have the chance to bring joy to far more people than in the zoo. The circus was one of the largest in the country. Every single evening, they welcomed many hundreds of people into the tent: both children and adults would have the chance to see a real live hippopotamus and a magnificent specimen to boot. But the thought did not warm my heart.

The only thing that added a touch of lightness to these heavy months were the letters from Wolff. I waited for every single one with excitement. The tone of the letters was slowly changing, I thought. While the first letter had been an unequivocal no, he was gradually softening. That I had managed to raise my share of the required funds was a strong argument, but both his unreserved commitment and full funding were still missing.

The sale of Berta caused a reduction in ticket revenues. It became all the more important for me to convince Wolff without delay. In an effort to understand how the wildlife capture specialist thought, and with an eye to the formulation of convincing and clarifying arguments, I tried learning more about his endeavors. The more I read, the more curious I became about his character. What a man! I could have written an entire book about all of Wolff's fantastic exploits. I will therefore permit myself to relate one of his ventures, the one that, by many, is considered the most impressive: The Nubian Caravans.

In 1870, Wolff sent one of his most trusted men, Lorenzo Cassanova, to Nubia. The hunt was carried out as planned, but Cassanova had not made it any further than to Suez with the animals before he became seriously ill and Wolff had to travel south personally to lead the expedition on to Europe. The caravan contained the most fantastic African animals imaginable: giraffes, elephants, buffalos, lions, ostriches, panthers, jackals, and monkeys, and the animals' young and fragile offspring: zebra foals, rhino calves, and lionets. Wolff was faced with an almost impossible task. The amount of food alone that had to be procured was of astronomical proportions: vegetables, bread, hay, fruit, meat for the carnivores, not to mention milk for the youngest animals obtained from one hundred accompanying goats. There was also a long list of additional challenges. During the first trip to the station, nine of the sixteen ostriches escaped; they ran as if possessed through the streets of Suez. The ostrich can reach speeds of up to seventy kilometers per hour, so even the fastest of stallions cannot overtake them. The enormous birds scared the wits out of man and beast, and the entire city was mobilized in the attempt to capture them. Thanks to the buildings of the city, which slowed the ostriches down, it was finally possible to contain them. Had they been running in open fields, the people of the city wouldn't have stood a chance.

The freedom-craving ostriches created an unfortunate delay in the expedition, but finally they managed to reach the station. However, once there, one of the train cars caught fire and the entire menagerie was suddenly in danger. The animals were kept at a safe distance while the flames were extinguished and, at long last, were loaded onto the remaining cars of the train. The conditions were, of course, far more cramped than originally planned. The lions had to share a car with the hyenas, the giraffes with the zebras, and, between their legs, small goats bleated, at every moment in danger of being crushed between huge animal bodies on sudden turns.

Wolff asked the engineer to drive as fast as he could and he, in turn, asked the stoker to fire the boiler as much as *he* could. Both the engineer and the stoker were heavy drinkers and Wolff's anxiety was compounded. It was no longer the well-being of the animals he was worried about; he also feared for his own life. The stoker did nothing but shovel in coal and Wolff was terrified the boiler would explode.

I can only imagine how relieved he must have been when he finally arrived in Alexandria. The first day was spent tending to the poor creatures, all of whom had suffered during the horrible train journey. At the same time, however, Cassanova lay on his deathbed and Wolff ran from his bedside to the suffering animals and back again.

In the course of the night, poor Cassanova died and Wolff grieved mightily for an hour or so, until it was time to take care of the animals again. At that time, Migoletti, one of Wolff's colleagues, also died and Wolff inherited his animals further expanding the size of the herd.

The next morning, all the animals were loaded onto a ship headed for Italy. With a pounding heart, Wolff stood on the quay and watched as his beloved creatures were hoisted up by crane, swinging through the air between the ocean and the sky. Finally, they were all on board and what a sight it must have been; what I would have given to have been there. The ship was a veritable Noah's ark!

The crossing to the Italian coast transpired without incident of note, but when the ship finally arrived in Trieste, all the residents of the city were waiting on the quay, which was not hard to understand in that this type of cargo had never, before or since, sailed into the ports of Europe. The combined catch of Cassanova and Migoletti was gigantic and included, in addition to all the small animals, four Nubian buffalos, a rhinoceros, twelve antelopes and gazelles, five elephants, fourteen giraffes, seven lions, eight panthers, thirteen hyenas, and twenty-six ostriches, one of which was the largest specimen of the species that world had ever seen.

While Wolff and his men unloaded, curious locals stood on the quay watching every single movement. Every time an animal created a fuss or moved too much while it was dangling from the crane, they gasped loudly in unison.

The journey continued by train to Vienna, Dresden, and Berlin, and, with every stop, the group was depleted as individual animals were sold to zoological gardens in the different cities, where they were immediately bred. Their descendants are still living in zoological gardens all over Europe.

I tried to imagine the excitement Wolff must have experienced during the journey. He could not have felt properly secure until every single little antelope calf found a home in one of the continent's zoological gardens. But the losses were, as far as I know, few. A large percentage of the menagerie actually reached its destination.

Wolff was the best in his field. My respect for him increased with every story I read and now I was corresponding with him . . . with *him*.

And then, six months after I first saw the skull in Poliakov's office and when I had almost given up hope, I received a letter, the contents of which were better than I could have conceived of in my wildest of dreams.

Wolff had not only been convinced, he wrote, he had actually raised the money. The Duke of Bedford, a passionate collector of animals, had gotten wind of the wild horses and become virtually obsessed with acquiring several grazing pairs for his property.

I had already read about Bedford's animal reserve in several different journals. In recent years, such sanctuaries had become fashionable. Wolff was among those who spoke warmly about placing the animals in more "natural" habitats, allowing them to graze freely rather than placing them in cages, and giving them larger, free-range areas of land. Personally, I wondered about this way of thinking. The purpose of keeping animals in captivity was, after all, to use them for observation. Imagine what a child or an ignorant adult, for that matter, can learn by witnessing an animal at close range. When, to the contrary, the animals were allowed to run wild and move about large land areas as they saw fit, it would be impossible for the public to study them in close proximity and, obviously, then the whole point of keeping them in captivity disappeared.

Amongst the upper class of many European countries, the current craze was to allow the strangest animals to wander about freely in large garden facilities, and the more animals one had, the higher one's social status. The Duke of Bedford was one of the most avid animal collectors and had apparently long shown a fervent interest in Przewalsky's horses. Now he wanted to be the first to bring the animals to Europe. He wanted to purchase no less than six horses for a handsome price and had even put a solid advance on the table, which gave us all we needed to get the expedition on its feet.

I laughed as I sat reading the letter inside my office, then got to my feet and shouted loudly.

"Yes! YES!"

I continued to read the letter as I stood there, gulping down every word, because Wolff had not only raised the requisite funding, he had also decided that he wanted to lead the expedition *himself.* His zeal for this idea, for the horses, had grown, he wrote; my enthusiasm had been infectious, and, as if this weren't enough—and I gasped as I read the final sentences—as if this weren't enough, he, Wolff, was already on his way here, to Petersburg. I could expect him any day now.

KARIN

U tter darkness, the darkness of war, black-out curtain darkness. A huge ball falls toward the red sand on the tennis court.

Mother shakes me and, as I slowly awaken, I hear a deep rumble in the distance.

"We must go to the cellar," Mother says.

I am warm and sleepy. "I don't want to get up. I don't want to get up."

"You must," Mother says. "You must wake up."

The bed I am lying in still feels alien, as unfamiliar as everything else at Carin Hall, such as the rooms and the people.

I wake up and I'm in that alien bed, hear my mother's voice and can't get away.

Mommy. Mommy.

We left our whole world behind in Berlin. The stairwell that smelled of boiled cabbage. The walk to school that I could do in my sleep. The dark backyard where my friends and I played ghosts in the evening. The neighbor's wife who always slipped me something to eat because she thought I was too thin. The teacher at school, Fraulein Kammerer, who often smiled at me extra long and called me clever. I have left my family, my aunts, uncles, cousins, grandmother, and grandfather, all of whom lived nearby and whom I saw almost every single day.

The huge flock I had has been reduced to a single person: Mother.

Every night I lie down close to her, even though I am far too old. I press my nose in between her shoulder blades, inhale the scent of her. It is warm and soft, but not like before. The smell of cabbage is gone. Mother smells of cleaning products now. Always cleaning products. Sharp soft soap, peppery evergreens, like an artificial forest.

In Berlin, Mother made her living by sewing and ironing, but in the past few years there was no longer enough to do. Nobody paid for such services. A second cousin found her a job in Schorfheide in the home of Hermann Goering, the *Reichsmarschall*. He had ten cleaning ladies already, but still he needed an eleventh.

Mother says she is fortunate, that we are fortunate, both because we need the money and because Carin Hall is located in the countryside. We're safe here, she says. And then the name is so nice, Carin Hall, after you, Karin.

Yes, I like the name. And even though it is written with a C, it feels like this place is my own. The forest, the meadows, all of it is mine.

The first days following our arrival, I stay in the servants' quarters. Then I start to miss Mother and go looking for her in what they all call the hunting lodge. There's nothing lodgelike about it; it resembles a castle. I sneak through the large rooms, drawing rooms, and salons. The dark wood paneling, huge chandeliers, antlers upon antlers upon antlers. And hunting trophies, stuffed animals with staring eyes, walls covered with landscape paintings, and hand-embroidered antique tapestries depicting medieval people in stiff poses. I understand that Goering is a collector. He collects objects, chandeliers, rooms, heads.

He also collects live animals. He has two lion cubs in the cellar, people say, two lovely lionets. They are growing quickly and will apparently be replaced by new cubs when they get too big. I look for them but never manage to find them.

On the third day when I am walking around the hunting lodge like this, I am discovered. A man in a uniform with a stiff collar screams at me. What are you doing here, ragamuffin, get out of here. In the evening Mother talks to me gravely and for a long time. I must never enter the estate again. Mother works for Goering; she is his now. He apparently collects people, too.

After that, I start wandering around outside. Walk quietly out of the servants' quarters and past the main entrance where two stags cast in bronze wish me good day. I continue across the courtyard, past the gardens. Past the entrance to the bunkers in the ground. I trot across the shooting range. Past the tennis court where the red sand is always freshly raked. Finally, I enter the dense, green forest.

Into the forest. To the wild horses.

Sometimes I just stay there with them. The soft buzzing of insects, bird song. The light from the sun shining through leaves and branches, creating a lace pattern on the ground. And the horses' familiar whinnying.

But then the booming starts up again and I am no longer able to stay there. I am pulled away. To my bed, to the darkness of war. Mother wakes me. Hurry, hurry, Karin, wake up. Quickly. Quickly.

I sit up with a start, breathing hard.

Mommy?

Mommy!

But she isn't here.

And it isn't nighttime, it's morning.

The sun shines directly into the room, making the lamp light invisible.

I try to breathe calmly.

Here. Now. 1992. Hustai. I am fifty-six years old. No bombs, just the penetrating silence of the steppes and the air I pull in and push out.

In and out.

My breath is making too much noise.

I should quit smoking.

. . .

I smoke the first cigarette of the day outdoors with the horses.

Praha is in heat; she stays close to Sydney at all times. Turns her rear toward him, lifts her tail, whinnies, and squirts urine. I have kept them separated since March, not wanting to risk any of them being in foal on the journey here. Now they are ready, all of them. Long overdue, I hope. Because now they must start breeding.

I don't miss the work of breeding sporting horses. A shit job. A *dangerous* shit job. You have to put breeding hobbles on the rutting mare to prevent her from kicking the stallion to pieces. The stallion kicks his forelegs in all directions, kicks the sides of the mare. He often struggles to hit the target. It's a three-person job: one person to control the mare, one for the stallion, and the third as a mediator, who makes sure the mare is properly penetrated. A faulty penetration can, in the worst-case scenario, kill the mare. A rectal tear. Peritonitis. Inflammation of the peritoneum. I once lost a mare this way. I have seldom felt like such a failure, even though it wasn't my fault, not really. It was nature's fault. Nature has failed horses when it comes to impregnation. It is, I guess, like humans and childbirth. Something that should be simple is almost impossible.

With the wild horses, it's easier. They just get on with it. They would never let me come close to them anyway. And I still haven't lost any. It makes me think that the takhis are actually better equipped for this.

Sydney sticks his muzzle up against Praha's rear end; she lifts her tail even higher, then she pulls away suddenly. He just stands there, as if he's waiting. She squirts out a bit of urine. A half-hearted signal.

Come on, now.

But Praha flings one of her back legs in his direction, neighs. And Sydney turns away.

I breathe heavily. Wait, just wait.

I wish there were something I could do. Praha, Askania Nova, and Paris must become impregnated soon. I need three new foals next spring. Then the herd will have eleven animals. And when the new foals are born, I will return to Thorenc to pick up more. Twelve horses are waiting there; three of the mares are already in foal. My European herd is growing steadily. I have hired a French veterinarian to take care of the horses while I am here.

Investors and patrons will receive what they have been promised. They have given me two years. Only the landowner in Thorenc has expressed willingness to make any further investment, but that's because he wants a nature park in the region. An "amusement farm" where visitors can see wild horses, buffalos, and farm animals. The first time I met him, I thought he was an enthusiast like me. But then I understood that he is actually only in it for the money. The land he owns has little value as arable land. Neither is it spectacular enough to attract tourists for the nature alone. But in his opinion, if you give visitors something more, the feeling of something special, they will come. The agreement is that I will return to Thorenc once the Hustai operation has been set up. Then the idea is that I will start up the operation he envisions as a "picturesque farmstead hotel," while I breed more horses for Mongolia. That's *his* plan. I don't know if it's mine; I know nothing about hotels. I have an idea that service and serving will constitute key operational components. And cleaning and bedding with overlapping folds. On those occasions when I have stayed at a hotel, I have noticed that it's handy to have a kettle in the room. Sometimes the cleaner laid a flower on the bedspread or towel. It is presumably such details that some guests appreciate. But beyond that, I have no idea of what is needed to satisfy customers. It should be obvious to everyone that a person who always wears hiking boots, a fleece jacket, and military pants, who chain smokes, and doesn't exactly have a liking for small talk will be a mediocre fit for the service industry. But I have never questioned the landowner's plans. I'll address problems as they arise.

There are several problems I must address as they arise. That I have no further savings, for example, because everything has been invested in the horses. That I sold the apartment in Berlin at too much of a loss—nothing is worth anything in Berlin right now—and, therefore, no longer have anything that can be called a home.

If I don't succeed in two years, I will be left high and dry. I will probably not find another job. I'll be almost sixty years old. Outdated. Broke, homeless, and unemployed.

Yes, indeed.

You sure know how to set yourself up, Karin.

I walk the short distance back to the camp quickly following the tire ruts. I stub out my cigarette. My stomach is growling; nicotine makes me hungry.

A marmot darts across the road. Yellowish fur, black snout and eyes, and long whiskers. Another one follows close behind. They are just babies. Playing. They tumble down into a hole in the ground and disappear. Luckily, there are many of them here; you can barely walk one meter without running into one. They are cute in the way that makes many people squeal, especially women and children. Pointy black noses and buckteeth. Quick, funny. They often stand on their hind legs and scan their surroundings. They look like serious, chubby, little men. But it is not because they are cute that I am happy to see them. It is because they are wolf fodder. As long as the wolf is full, my foals will be left in peace.

The first time I came to visit this area, I had read about the animal life ahead of time. I still hadn't been able to grasp how rich it is. That the completely uniform, almost barren grassy landscape could be the home of so many different species. And how the shortage of trees allows you to spot them easily. It's teeming with wildlife. Roe deer, wild sheep, wild boar, lynx, foxes, hare, hedgehogs, hamsters, mice. And birds, there are birds everywhere. Eagles, falcons, owls, and vultures. The vultures— the carrion birds—the most useful animal on the steppes.

The nature here can frighten people. Some speak of the loneliness of the steppes. But I never feel alone. I know that I am seen at all times. Observed. Every single step I take is noticed by hundreds of other individuals. Insects on the ground and in the soil hear the sound of me like a deep rumble and crawl away; flying bees, bumblebees, and flies swerve abruptly away; birds slide across the sky with their eyes fixed on every single movement I make, at every moment prepared to flee; and the marmot scurries across the path in front of me, at a safe distance from that which might constitute a danger.

In Thorenc, I was often alone on the disused mountain farm. People in the village asked if I was lonely. If I didn't become afraid in the darkness. The first couple of times I was asked, I explained to them about the animals. I had the horses, after all. But relatively quickly, I realized they didn't understand. Or didn't want to understand. They thought I was strange, a freak. A hermit.

Fine. Perhaps I am a freak.

I liked those years. I liked Thorenc. Far away from the big city. Far from the streets of Berlin. I liked France. The small wine shops, the boulangeries. Even the flower shops. And I never bought flowers. Plants belong in the ground, not with the stems cut off for decoration. I can't for the life of me understand why people buy cut flowers. Putting flowers in a vase is nothing short of murder in slow motion.

I visited France often, even before I found Thorenc. That was where my father fell to the ground, the same soil that I walked on.

But I haven't traveled much in my own country, Germany, and I have never gone back to Carin Hall. Why should I?

When I open the gate to the camp, Mathias emerges from his tent. His hair is disheveled and he squints against the light. Wrinkles his nose, the way he has done ever since he was little. It's as if his little boy face is hidden beneath the rough features.

He notices me and smiles.

"Good morning, Karin."

I remember that he said *Mommy* a few times when he was in kindergarten, had heard the other children say it and wanted to try it for himself. But I thought it sounded strange. Karin, I said to him, my name is Karin.

"Hi," I say.

"You wouldn't believe how well I slept in that tent. Like a baby."

"Good."

He stretches, looks around.

"I've never understood that expression before, about the vaulted sky above. Not before now."

"I see. . . . Breakfast?" I try to return his smile.

"Yup."

Inside, Jochi is awake. The three of us sit down at the table in the big kitchen. Mathias is burning the toast. The smell of singed bread stings my nose. He scrapes off the blackened crusts, spreads on thick layers of butter, chatting with Jochi the entire time. Asks questions and digs. Doesn't let himself be hindered by the language.

"I didn't know your English was so good," I say when there is a pause in the flow of conversation.

"No?"

"He speaks English really well," Jochi says and smiles. "Better than you."

"Yes, perhaps."

"I've read books in the original language," Mathias says.

"Smart," Jochi says.

When did you do that? I want to ask. But I stop myself. I suddenly remember him in the living room, during a period of sobriety, with *The Lord of the Rings* in his lap. He read from the moment he got up until he went to bed at night. When he had reached the final page, he disappeared again.

"There's a lot you don't know about me, Mother," Mathias says.

Jochi chuckles. I laugh too. It sounds false. I quickly get to my feet.

"We have work waiting," I say.

I regret it immediately. The words sound stilted.

"That's what's great about work," says Mathias. "That it actually waits. Doesn't go away, I mean."

Jochi laughs again. Louder now.

"He's funny," he says to me.

"Yes," I say. "I guess he is."

The laughter continues when I leave. They keep laughing until I have shut the door behind me. There's no end to how much time they have.

I pull my windbreak tightly around me. Stick my hands in my pockets and quickly walk the hundred meters over to the horses. Right away, I can see that something has changed. Praha is more agitated. Jumping about nervously. Lifting her tail. She allows Sydney to sniff. And this time she stands still.

He rears up slightly.

Come on. Come on, Sydney.

His member grows, snaking out of his body like a thick worm. Then he mounts her. Lays his forelegs on top of her. He stands on his hind legs, his entire weight on the mare. There is something foolish and clumsy about the movements. A male mounting a female can appear pathetic. The struggle to be on top, the uncomfortable, moaning exertion.

All she can do is stand there and let him carry on. He emits a few strangled, squeaking sounds as he plunges inside her. His tail whips up and down. Is he enjoying it? Instinct drives him to do it; he mounts her to procreate, but he doesn't know that. It's just something he does. Something he will continue to do in the coming days. Until Praha is no longer interested, until she is impregnated.

Then three final, hard jabs, and he stops moving. He pulls back and turns away. She waves her tail gently. Praha's just as calm now as she was throughout the entire session, as if she hadn't noticed what had taken place.

"Good," I say and notice that I'm smiling. "Good, Sydney. Good, Praha."

I turn and walk over to find an apple for each of them.

CHAPTER 4

AN UNEXPECTED TRAVELING COMPANION

It was early February in 1881. I was sitting in my office in the zoological garden's administration building looking at the figures for our feed supplies. I had to order more hay immediately. My usual supplier, a farmer whose farm was just a few kilometers away, had run out due to an unusually hard, snowy winter and I would be obliged to find another. I scribbled a hasty letter to inquire as to whether there was anyone he could recommend, pulled on my winter coat, and went out to find a messenger. I hadn't walked many meters before a watchman—a young, recently hired oaf some twenty years of age—came trotting toward me. He said that I had to report to the entrance immediately. There was a man there, a foreigner, who absolutely did not want to pay for admission to the zoological garden but, on the other hand, claimed he had an appointment with me.

The watchman talked a steady stream as we hurried toward the gate and he told me that the stranger had a large suitcase with him that he dragged through the slush on the ground, that he had spoken to him in Russian with a heavy accent. I understood straight away that it was him.

Wilhelm Wolff was leaning against the wall by one of our two ticket windows. Under the shelter of the broad awning, he was completely dry despite the falling sleet. His suitcase was indeed of impressive dimensions. It would, in fact, be more accurate to call it a travel trunk and it made me immediately envious. It was battered and marked with traces of countless expeditions and covered with stickers from places I knew of only as names on a globe.

I had seen several photographs of Wolff, but they were always taken from a distance, blurry and grainy, and I had therefore formed my own images of him; in these he had been tall and heavyset. The man who stood before me, however, was quite short. He was wiry, and the muscles flexed in his throat as he restlessly shifted his weight from one foot to the other. This uneasiness was something I would later discover was a part of him. He had a body that withstood nights without sleep, days on horseback or the back of a camel, for that matter, a body strong enough to respond in kind to one or more blows, and quick enough to be able to run away should this prove to be the only option.

His face was not much to look at. Scarred and rough, with shaggy eyebrows that hid his eyes and made him appear fierce.

I must admit that I was a bit frightened.

When he saw me, his eyes lit up and I immediately liked him better.

I apologized for his having been kept waiting, said that I'd had no idea he would be arriving today, that the journey would be made so quickly.

"It's not *that* far from Hamburg to Petersburg," he said with a crooked smile.

His Russian was melodious and his vocabulary sizeable. His French as well, as it would turn out; he switched effortlessly back and forth between the two—as did many of the well-to-do of my city—and our conversations were always in both languages.

I invited him to my office, and we left the travel trunk inside the ticket office. He strolled nimbly down the footpaths, apparently unaffected by the huge, wet pellets of sleet plummeting out of the sky.

He looked around him constantly. All the buildings in the garden were of wood, all in a traditional building style, and it struck me how pitiful they must appear to him—how tiny the garden was, far smaller than its corresponding big brothers in Berlin or London.

It had been unusually mild during the past couple of weeks. The snow was reduced to slush on the ground, and the park was colored with different shades of brown and gray. Further, there was an intense stench of animal excrement coming from all the open cages we passed. The primates were creating an uproar; it sounded as if they were in the process of murdering one another inside. Our big brown bear wandered restlessly back and forth, scowling grimly and hungrily at everyone who passed by. Every single watchman we saw was mud-stained and unkempt and none of them directed so much as a smile in the newcomer's direction.

He did not, however, seem to be affected by any of it, although he commented constantly on everything he saw.

"Pygmy chimpanzees."

"We have only two, unfortunately. But the children love them."

"And this is the parrot house?"

"Yes, yes, exactly."

"More Budgerigars . . . a Gray parrot . . . look at that beautiful red tail. And is that really a Carolina Parakeet?"

"Yes, we are proud of it."

"You must be sure to take good care of it."

"We are doing the best we can."

We sat down in my office. I offered him something to drink—tea, vodka, wine, hot chocolate—but he declined, accepting only a glass of water.

He lit his pipe and stared at me with those deep-set eyes of his. My hands began to sweat and I didn't know where to rest my gaze.

"I discussed the matter with my men before I left Germany," he said. "We concluded that the best time to arrive in Mongolia would be in the spring. That will give us plenty of time—the entire summer— for the capture. We won't have to worry about the cold."

"Exactly," I said. "The spring. Excellent."

"And further," he continued, "the mares will have just foaled, so we can bring back both mother and offspring."

"Excellent," I repeated. At the same time, I glanced at my almanac. "The spring . . . which month are we thinking about then?"

"April," he said and sucked on his pipe. "Possibly May."

Blue clouds rose into the air; the smoke settled around him erasing the sharpest contours of his face, as if he weren't wholly real.

"The spring months," I said.

"I said the spring, yes."

I fumbled with the almanac, unable to refrain from looking at it, at the number of weeks, days.

"That doesn't give us much time . . ."

Then he laughed suddenly, a short, loud guffaw.

"For this spring, yes. But not for next spring."

I exhaled, noticing that I had been holding a large quantity of air in my lungs.

"Next spring? So, you're saying not now . . . but a whole year from now?"

He took the pipe out of his mouth and pointed at me with the stem.

"Tell me," he said. "How long do you think it actually takes to travel to Mongolia?"

My cheeks grew hot, of course.

"It's nothing to be ashamed of," he said. "You have never done this before."

"No, I haven't," I said. "But I apologize all the same. I have read countless travelogues. I know, of course, that this will take a long time—both the planning and the journey itself."

He didn't smile, but I could see in his eyes, which were sparkling below his heavy brows, that he found me and my inexperience entertaining. He put the pipe down in the ashtray, unbuttoned his coat, and took three envelopes out of the inside pocket.

"I have acquired a letter of introduction and accreditations from the Chinese Embassy in Berlin and Prince Alexander of Oldenburg.

The latter will hopefully ensure us a warm welcome from the Buddhist Lama Dr. Radmai, who resides here in Petersburg. According to
what I have been told, Radmai can offer us information about both
the country and the people of Mongolia so we will be prepared for the
journey. The equipment must, of course, be acquired, but it is even
more important that we gain an understanding of the country we will
be visiting."

"Great," I stammered. "Truly splendid."

"Further, I presume you have a number of preparations to carry
out yourself," Wolff continued. "My impression is that this is the first
time you will be taking part in an expedition of this nature. I assume
this will have practical consequences for your work and also your
personal life. You have, perhaps, a family?"

"Uh . . . yes," I said.

And then I was unable to speak another word. He took for granted
that I would be accompanying him. To Mongolia. Me. To Mongolia.

I thought of our correspondence, all the letters I had received, all
the letters I had sent. My own words . . . what had I written? Never
had I formulated the sentence: *Unfortunately, I am unable to take
part . . .* or *Regretfully, I have obligations here at home that prevent me
from . . .* if anything, I had referred to the expedition as *ours*.

The truth was that I had allowed myself to get carried away. As
I was writing my letters, I had actually imagined myself out there
riding on a camel across the steppes or through the Gobi Desert,
meeting people from foreign cultures—valiant descendants of Genghis Khan with dark eyes and golden skin.

I had never believed that the expedition would come to pass. I
had, if only subconsciously, thought that the letters were the closest
I would come; that the entire undertaking was, and would continue
to be, a pipe dream. When I read Wolff's letters and plans, I wasn't
really doing anything other than what I had done as a child when I
eavesdropped on the stories of the adventurous travelers who walked
in and out of the Geographic Society. I had made the stories of others
my own.

But now Wolff was sitting here having organized both the funding and accreditations.

I thought about my mother, I thought about our comfortable apartment on Grivtsova Lane . . . and, for some reason or other, I thought of chicken in cream sauce.

The devil you say. Really, what the devil.

EVA

Louise spoke French with the animals—long, undulating sentences in this language I didn't understand. They liked it, were calm when she was around. It seemed as if Isa also liked Louise and her French because, more and more often, she followed behind her and tried to pick up words and expressions.

Louise took over the care of the hens for Isa and the cows for me. She had nothing against getting up before we did, she said, neither did she mind going to bed as early as this required. Every evening, she turned in by nine o'clock and Isa and I sat up for a while, devoting the time to her schooling. I had the impression that Louise thought she should give us this short period of time to be alone. For my own part, I actually wished that she would stay up with us. Isa was often angry and dismissive. It was easier when Louise was with us—then, for the most part, Isa behaved. Regardless, I could put up with more now. I exploded less frequently, screamed less frequently. I could feel it in my body, in my back, that I no longer had to do all the work alone.

We never talked about when she would leave, but every morning I woke and felt a flicker of relief over her still being here now that all the others had disappeared. Even my animals were leaving little by little.

The forest reindeer had calved in the spring. They ate up everything in their area and I had no hay to give them. Finally, I set them free in the forest.

Now the only animals I had left were the Scottish wildcat and the two falcons. The wildcat hid every time I showed up and one of the falcons seemed sickly and lethargic; I never saw her fly. I made my visits as short as I could, doing only the most necessary tasks before leaving again. It was too painful to be near them.

I could only bear being with the horses. Puma ran back and forth around the mare—playing with her, sort of blocking the way—while Nike remained calm, a patient mother who never became angry. There was still enough grass for them in the enclosed pasture; the frost had still not come, but the grass grew more slowly than before, and they grazed their way farther and farther down toward the stubble field. Autumn was coming quickly now; soon the stable growth of plant life would be replaced by winter's brutal dormancy when there would be little for my horses to eat. Then, I would have to supply them with food. There were still a few haybales left at Richard's farm. I hadn't known how to retrieve them with just Isa to help me, but now that Louise was here, it would, perhaps, be possible. I began making plans both for that and for the winter with Louise as part of the household.

We were in the process of clearing up after the evening meal. Louise taught Isa a few French words—told her the words for plate, cup, and glass, how to say here's the cup, you can have the glass, we are doing the dishes. The old dishes with the buttercup pattern that had almost disappeared clattered as they stacked them in the corner wood-carved cupboard, where they had been stored for three generations.

I said nothing, was just happy—about Nike and Puma, Isa and Louise, about the candle burning in Great-Grandmother's old candlestick on the counter, the fire burning in the stove, and the haybales at Richard's farm that we would now be able to retrieve.

But just when I had removed the last plate and wiped off the table, the lights went out.

"Shit," Isa said.

"*Isa*," I said.

"'Isa,'" she mimicked.

Louise laughed, halting my next unpleasant remark.

"It's been a long time," I said. "It's been a long time since the power went out."

"You have a bad memory," Isa said. "It's only been five weeks, right before Louise came. A power cable broke."

"Luckily, we have Henrik," I said.

"Henrik?" Louise asked.

"The man who runs the power plant."

"He's ninety years old," Isa said.

"He's no more than seventy," I said.

"He may have died, for all we know," Isa said.

"Isa, now," I said.

"Sorry," Isa said.

"Wow," I said. "Not often I hear that word coming out of your mouth."

"Wonder where I learned it. Not from you, that's for sure," Isa fired back.

I opened my mouth, closed it again, didn't know how to respond. The blood rushed to my face. I knew that we were headed into one of our arguments. They could be long and tenacious. And with each new argument, Isa's replies were tougher, faster. It was more and more difficult to put her in her place. She always wanted to have the last word.

"Anyway," Louise said calmly.

I turned toward her. For a moment I had forgotten that she was there.

"Maybe we should go to bed," she said, looking at me and then at Isa.

Isa nodded, sent me one final glare, but luckily said nothing more.

"The power always comes on again in the course of the night," I said and got to my feet.

I found a flashlight in a bowl on the kitchen counter and handed it to Louise.

"Look, you can use this when you go to your room. But save the batteries."

I lit tealights for Isa and me, placing them in old jam jars.

Louise said good night and went into her room. We could see the light from the flashlight glowing through the crack under the door.

"So, she got the flashlight?" Isa said.

I could tell from her voice that she was still on the warpath.

"She's a guest," I said.

"I thought she lived here now."

"She's still a guest."

"She should turn it off soon. She's finished undressing for sure. She still has it on, look."

"Give her a little time."

"Do we have any more batteries? I thought you said those were the last of the batteries?"

"We have a couple more."

I hoped that would do it, but Isa just kept going.

"Good grief, why is she taking so long," she hissed. "Is she, like, removing makeup or something?"

"Worry about your own light," I said in exasperation. "We don't have very many of those left, either."

I handed her the jar containing the tealight.

"I'm not tired," she said. "It's far too early to sleep."

"Then you'll just have to sit up in the dark!"

She made a sound, the kind of sound I think only teenagers can make; she sputtered and sighed at the same time. And, of course, rolled her eyes. Sometimes she can be quite predictable.

"You should tell her," Isa said, and nodded toward Louise's door. "Maybe she didn't understand."

"I think she understands that we don't have many batteries."

"But just to be sure."

"It's not necessary."

"Just to be sure!"

"Night, Isa."

"Night!" she said, tossed her hair and flounced into her room.

At that moment, the light went out in Louise's room as well.

The next morning, the lights were still not on. The kitchen was silent without the humming of the refrigerator. I didn't open it, not wanting to release what cold air remained inside.

I had to carry water in from the well; the water pump didn't work without electricity. I lit a fire in the old woodstove to boil water for tea. The stove was tricky until you learned how to use it, but with enough kindling and a precise opening of the door of the stove with the window ajar, it burned merrily. And once the fire was going properly, it emanated enough heat to keep the whole house warm for hours.

It wasn't the first time we'd had to use it and I was grateful to my father who, once upon a time, had installed it when he built The Farmstead.

All the farms had solar cells, ours too, but the battery had been destroyed in an autumn storm two years ago and, since nobody charged anything for our power consumption any longer, I had never gone to the trouble of having it repaired. It was only when the power went out that I regretted it. There were many things on the farm I managed to repair myself; as long as it required a hammer, nails, screws, and a drill, I could fix it, for the most part. Or standard couplings. But the battery was another story.

Louise came in. She stood for a moment in the doorway, looking at me in confusion. In her hand, she was holding an empty pail.

"I went to milk but forgot that the milking machine runs on electricity."

I stood up quickly. It was already six o'clock. The cows' udders would be about to burst out in the cowshed.

The two of us hurried out.

They were restless, mooing. I took the milking stool and squatted down beside Micro. The heat from her body engulfed me. The udder was dry and almost hot to the touch. The spray squirted loudly against the bottom of the pail the minute I took hold of the teats.

"Can you take Apple?" I said.

"But I can't," Louise said. "I don't know how to milk by hand."

"Watch me."

She came over and stood next to me.

"Sit down."

I gave her my seat.

"You must hold on at the top and squeeze at the very bottom."

She tried, but only a tiny stream came out.

"Harder," I said. "Squeeze harder at the top."

I wedged myself in beside her; the stool was wide enough for both of us. Then I placed my hands around hers and squeezed together with her. Now the milk squirted down into the pail.

Her underarms slid toward mine. Her fingers were warm. I could feel how she squeezed them eagerly around the teats.

"Careful," I said. "Not too fast. Try to find a rhythm."

I squeezed along with her, released along with her, and could feel that she had gotten the hang of it. Soon, she managed it alone. I stayed put there a bit longer anyway; it felt good to be physically close to another human being.

When I got up, I could still feel the impression of her hands in mine, the skin on her arms against my skin.

I was alone here with Isa, and even more alone now than before because Isa had left me. The child's body was gone and, with it, closeness to another person. I no longer had physical contact with anyone except when Isa gave me one of her brief hugs. I never had a back against mine, a cheek against my own, a hand to hold. The physical loneliness became stronger as Isa set increasingly clearer boundaries for herself. Richard hadn't helped. He had just made it worse.

When we went inside again, the refrigerator was still silent and the lamps dark. A power failure didn't normally last so long. I should try to find out if something had happened.

I got in the car and started the engine. Checked the power gauge. It was almost half full.

I drove slowly all the way up to the power plant. But on the last hill, I had to apply pressure to the throttle, and the further I drove, the worse the road was, making me force the car over large mounds of soil and stones from a landslide.

Finally, I could drive no further. I opened the door and got out. In front of me, the road was covered with dirt, mud, stones, and uprooted plants. I continued on foot, climbing over big boulders, pebbles sliding into my shoe. Around me was a low-growing forest but the mossy ground cover was gone.

I stopped, stared upward.

Where the power plant had been. Where the dam had been.

The wooden poles that had once been solidly planted in the ground were now lying scattered across the hillside like matchsticks.

The heavy, low concrete building that had housed the power station and Henrik's apartment was no longer there.

The endless rain of the summer had seeped into the foundation causing it to dissolve and finally mobilized all the soil on the hillside. The landslide had taken everything with it.

He could be there. He could be lying buried underneath masses of soil and debris, still breathing. Not that many hours had passed since the power went out, thirteen, no, fourteen. He could still be alive.

I started running up the hill, sinking into the ground, my shoes filling up with dirt. I fell, got dirt on my trousers, my jacket, could taste soil in my mouth. I stood up again, tried to keep walking upward. I thought I saw something up there, something blue, a color so bright it was out of place in the natural landscape, maybe the corner of a garment, a sleeve, a trouser leg.

I made it all the way up, threw myself down, dug it out.

It was a cap. His cap.

"Henrik?"

He could be lying here anywhere.

"Henrik!"

I bent over again, started digging with my hands, throwing aside large stones. I stopped to listen, called his name, listened again.

Nothing. No birds, no animals, no electricity buzzing.

. . .

I drove into the yard, remained in the car.

For sure he had gotten away. He had probably left a long time ago, charged the car one last time and drove away. He had a brother in Gudbrandsdalen, had talked about going there for a long time. He wasn't here any longer, wasn't lying beneath a ton of earth, suffocated, his mouth full of dirt and wide-open eyes staring at nothing.

I couldn't think about him and shouldn't say anything to the others. No reason to worry Isa.

At that moment, she came around the corner of the house. I struggled to breathe calmly, opened the door, and went out to join her.

She stopped suddenly, just stared at me.

"You look a fright!" she said, an echo of all the times *she* had been out playing in the dirt and mud.

"Hi, sweetie," I said. "Are you ready for a feast?"

"But, mum, what happened?"

"It's nothing," I said, hastening to explain. "Henrik has left. You remember he talked about leaving? And we don't have electricity anymore. Let's see what we can do about food."

I closed the door to the bathroom behind me, grabbed a washcloth, and filled the sink with cold water. Pulled off my filthy clothing, stood there in my underwear. Put a washcloth in the water, but suddenly I was unable to wring it out, just stood there feeling the sensation of the damp terrycloth between my fingers. The taste of dirt was still on my lips and in my throat, the smell in my nose. I dropped the washcloth, sat down on the toilet lid, closed my eyes, was so tired, so weary, slumped down onto the floor, pulled my legs under me, felt my cold, wet fingers against my shins, pulled my knees all the way up to my chin, rested my head against them.

At that moment there was a knock on the door.

"Eva?"

It was Louise. She opened the door carefully. I tried to get up, but my legs wouldn't support me. She came over to me, sat down on the floor beside me, laid one hand on my arm.

I tried to tell her what had happened, whispered, so Isa wouldn't hear, or perhaps I whispered because my voice wouldn't carry either.

Louise nodded slowly as I explained. Asked no questions.

When I had finished, she stroked my hair gently. Some lumps of soil shook loose and dropped to the floor.

Then she stood up and found the washcloth in the sink. With resolute movements, she wrung it out. I closed my eyes as she stroked my face with the damp fabric.

KARIN

D on't you get tired of it?" Mathias asks me one day.

We are standing by the paddock watching the horses graze. They eat partly from the ground, partly from the extra feed we put out for them; the paddock no longer has enough to offer. Praha lays back her ears in warning when Askia Nova tries to eat right beside her. She wants the best blades of grass for herself.

The mares still circle the foals constantly; even though they are a year old, they are still monitored. Sydney walks a bit on the fringes, is calm, but always vigilant. It's been a long time since he had a go at any of the mares. I hope they are all in foal. I think I can already detect a downward bulge in Praha's tummy, even though I know it's too early for her to be showing.

A short distance away, in a separate paddock, are Hamburg and Bronx. They are grazing close to each other. Suddenly Bronx bares his teeth at Hamburg, neighs softly, wants to show his strength. That is as it should be. Everything is as it should be. Now all I can do is let time work for me.

I turn toward Mathias.

"Sometimes I get tired of waiting."

"Waiting?"

"Like now. Waiting for them to be ready. Wondering whether we can open the gate."

"Jochi says you should keep them fenced in until next year."

"Maybe that's what Jochi says. But I say that they're ready this year."

"It won't hurt certainly to wait and see a bit?"

I don't like that he has started using Jochi's arguments.

"They've been waiting for hundreds of years."

"Exactly. So, what's one year more or less?"

He has a little grin in the corner of his mouth, as if this were amusing. As if he wants to foster a conflict between Jochi and me. Create tension. *That* is something he has already managed just fine as it is. I don't need even more.

I turn away from him, hoping that will stop him. Grab a pitchfork and start shoveling more feed over the fence. Mathias stands there smoking.

"There's something I've never asked you, Karin."

I don't reply.

"Karin."

". . . Yes."

"Why horses, exactly?"

I continue pitching. Deep movements, bending, lifting, releasing the hay so it tumbles over on the other side of the fence.

"Dogs are boring," I say. "Cows are just livestock. Pigs stink."

"But what is it about horses, then?"

What is it about horses?

I say nothing about Carin Hall.

Neither do I say that horses are honest. That once you've understood how they react, everything is simple. That when you know what makes them aggressive, what makes them kick, what makes them bite, it's like arithmetic. You know what you will get.

Horses don't lie. They don't betray you.

Horses can be trusted. It can be hard to predict what will cause them to react, because their senses are sharper than ours, but the reactions are always reliable.

MAJA LUNDE

They don't bear a grudge or stay angry and bitter. You may be obliged to hurt them and they act in self-defense there and then. But afterward, when the pain has passed, they will accept the carrot you are holding in your hand.

It is easy to know what makes a horse content. Their needs are transparent. Their behavior, as well.

And the horse comes back to you again and again. At least, as long as they associate your voice with something positive. If they associate you with something good, like carrots, apples, or pellets. Or grooming.

Also, horses don't disappear into the streets in the middle of the night. Horses don't take overdoses. Horses do not lose custody of their own children. I don't say any of this.

"Everyone thinks cats are so cuddly," I say, "but they are in fact only interested in mating. Did you know that? That's why they rub against your legs the way they do."

"I'm not surprised," Mathias smiles and it looks like he actually appreciates the answer.

I put down the pitchfork. We stand together in silence. Mathias takes a hit of the cigarette. The smoke hangs in a gray veil around him, subduing the colors of the landscape. Then he coughs loudly and resoundingly, the kind of cough that comes from the depths of the lungs, the sound of raw dampness. Something about it reminds me of the ocean. Of large ocean creatures fat with lard.

"You should quit," I say.

"What?"

"You should quit smoking."

"And what about you?"

"I am not coughing the way you are."

"Maybe I'll quit," he says.

Maybe I'll quit. Trustworthy. I am going to quit. I am going to quit. I am going to quit. I never could have imagined how important those words would become for me: *to quit.*

"The climate up here has probably helped your cough anyway," I say quickly. "The dry air."

120

"That's possible," he says.

He takes a step toward me, lifts one hand, and pats me on the shoulder.

"Nice that you care, Karin."

"Yes," I say. "I really think you should quit smoking."

"I'll quit if you quit." He says it like a conclusion and takes a deep drag on the cigarette.

"Why exactly Przewalsky's horses then?" he asks then.

"I call them *takhis*."

"But why exactly them?"

I picture the mare at Carin Hall that watched over her foal. I sat on the other side of the fence. I was wearing a light-colored summer dress that was now too short. I folded my thin legs beneath me in the grass—long and city-girl pale and covered with mosquito bites.

"They must be rescued," I say. "The species is unique."

"Yes, I know, sixty-six chromosomes and all that. But why are you the one who is supposed to do it? And why not another species? Tigers? Polar bears?"

"If every person chose one species to save, the earth would have looked completely different."

"Sure, sure. But why did *you* choose the wild horses?"

"You make it sound like they were something I picked up in a toy shop," I say, and hear how my tone of voice becomes sharper than I'd intended.

"No," he says, suddenly serious. "That's exactly what I mean. It wasn't exactly like it was a random choice for you?"

I don't reply.

Can't tell him about Carin Hall. Cannot envision what such a conversation would be like. Am I supposed to stand here sobbing in his arms?

Perhaps others do such things.

He is watching me, waiting for an answer, but when he understands no answer is coming, he shrugs.

"Good thing you have Jochi," he says.

"For the horses?" I say.

"For you," he says. "It's nice listening to you two. You never stop talking. Not just about the horses, by the way, but about the grass. Oh, my God, you two talk about grass so much. Where it is nutritious, the color, the types. I had no idea it was possible to talk so much about something so boring."

"You've never been to Mongolia before, either."

Where other people see grass, I see *stipa* and *festuca*. I see myriad types of stalks, in all shades, from verdigris green to bluish-green. I see ears of grain being twisted and turned by the wind, some filmy and soft as cotton, others hard and rigid. And I see everything else that grows between the stalks. Now in the short growing season, there is life in every single, tiny spot. The valleys become meadows of flowers—bright yellow bedstraws and buttercups against mauve meadow geraniums. And edelweiss—small white stars growing from nothing on stone-covered hillsides.

"Is everyone here like you and Jochi?" Mathias asks. "Is everyone just as hung up on grass?" He chuckles suddenly. "But perhaps I'm not exactly the person to criticize you about *that*."

I ignore the joke. "They live on grass," I say. "Without grass, no animals."

"But still."

"Yeah, still."

"It's good for you then, that you have him."

"He's clever."

"He's just as nerdy as you are."

"Don't start that again."

I turn away. Jesus, I'm blushing. I notice that actually I *want* him to start *that* again. That maybe he will mention something he's seen that I haven't noticed, that he has picked up on some hints from Jochi.

Jochi and I have had so many meetings, so many phone calls, written so many letters to each other, and the communication has always had the same tone—neutral, clear, without sentiment. If I were to give it a color, subject it to a litmus test, it would be the color of paper. But now, the tone has acquired a color. I don't know which— neither red, acidic, nor blue, alkaline. It doesn't make any difference; I just know that the color is intense.

Jochi notices it, too; I am sure that he notices it. He has developed a habit of scratching the closed-cropped hair on his neck as if he had an insect bite there. Scratching and scratching in the same place. I can't remember him ever doing that before.

Every time the three of us are together, it all becomes even worse. Having grown-up children is exhausting. They pick up on a lot. Too much. Mathias looks at me when I look at Jochi, and Mathias looks at Jochi when Jochi looks at me. And if we should happen to be standing close together, Mathias watches both of us and raises an eyebrow, always the left one. His eyebrow says *what did I say*, even though he is silent. But silent. . . . He is never actually quiet. He is always kidding around with Jochi; they have apparently become good friends, those two.

There is so much I wonder about. So many questions have suddenly begun to pop up. Things I never thought about before.

Where did Jochi grow up? How many siblings does he have? Is he the oldest or the youngest? What kind of child was he, a quiet book-worm or someone happiest on the back of a horse? How and why did he decide to study biology? Why horses? Does he miss teaching? The students? Did they like him? Was he popular? I am sure he was popular.

But I haven't asked a single question. Instead, I have picked up fragments and details from random by-the-way snatches of Jochi's conversations with Mathias. He has a sister, I've learned. The sister will turn sixty this year. She is eight years older than Jochi, so I un-derstand that Jochi is fifty-two. Fifty-two, fortunately, so the age dif-ference is not a problem. And he has said that his mother is older than his father. I wonder if that was a hint. He spent most of his childhood in a tent—they were semi-nomads—but he has said he prefers living in a house. When he told me this, that he prefers houses, I remember that I wondered whether what he was really trying to say was that he prefers a more Western lifestyle. That someone like me is not alien to him. But I dismissed it. I realized that it is not typically Western or Eastern to build houses, just that it is typically *Mongolian* to live in a tent.

When the three of us are together, I often sit hoping that Mathias will ask about everything I am wondering about. But he seldom does. Mathias is concrete; he is here and now. He asks questions about the reserve, about the animals, about the work. He tries to make himself useful. Jochi is good at finding work tasks for him to do. Praises him, says that Mathias is *handy*.

And Mathias is right; Jochi and I talk about the horses. About grass, a lot about grass. That's how it has been each of the four times I visited the country, but it is only now that I notice it.

Mathias draws a breath, is about to ask about something else, or perhaps say something, maybe something about Jochi. But nothing comes. Instead he takes a final drag on his cigarette before extinguishing it on the ground.

"Be a little careful," I say. "It's dry."

"I'm always careful," he says. And then suddenly he laughs. "*Careful* is my middle name."

"Ha, ha."

He grins so I can glimpse several fillings. "At least I can laugh at myself."

"Yes, you can."

He leaves me. I turn back to the horses.

It is July 31. They have been here for many months now. Everything has gone well, very well. The foals are playing the way foals do. The dynamic in the harem is as it should be. Sydney and Praha have kept their positions in the hierarchy. The others don't challenge them; they are team players. Bronx and Hamburg are young and strong, but neither of them wants to challenge Sydney yet. The teamwork is a part of their survival. It is inherent. And the mares are in foal.

I know how quickly winter will come. August and September always go by surprisingly fast. I want to have the horses out before the snow comes. They must manage on their own well before the frost sets in. There's no more time. I must set them free.

The time has come to open the gate.

CHAPTER 5

AN ILLUMINATING CONVERSATION

I didn't feel I had any choice but to invite Wolff home with me. I was convinced that he would decline, but he accepted my invitation without hesitation.

"Then we will save money on both room and board," he said, "and there will be even more for the expedition."

When I think back on this, I understand that this attitude is typical of Wolff. He doesn't care about his own comfort or well-being, only about the expedition, the capture. It is impressive, but also lamentable. Wolff is a man who no longer knows how to live an ordinary life. The capture of wild animals has become his life.

As we sat in the closed carriage and clattered across ice patches and through mud and sleet toward Grivtsova Lane, worry and enthusiasm were battling it out inside me. In Wolff's mind, I was already part of the expedition. He had no idea how ill-prepared I was for something of this nature, what an amateur I actually was. Simultaneously . . . how many times as a child had I stood by the entrance to the Geographic

Society and watched them walk by, the weathered travelers? How many times had I hoped for a word with one of them, but never dared to take the leap? And now Wilhelm Wolff himself was to stay in my home— sleep there, eat there, live there, and converse with me as much as I might desire, and perhaps he would also take me with him into the rooms restricted to members only because he must certainly be allowed access?

But I didn't dare ask. I didn't dare speak at all. The number of words I spoke during the entire long way home could be counted on one hand.

Wolff didn't seem to notice my silence; he remained steadily focused on the urban landscape as we trundled through it, apparently without fixing his gaze on anything in particular.

Darkness was falling when we arrived. Together, we carried his travel trunk to the front door. I wondered whether its heaviness was due to money—that he had basically brought the entire amount with him in cash—but dismissed the idea. Presumably, it was full of paraphernalia for the expedition. I knocked on the door and Piotr opened immediately.

He looked inquisitively at Wolff, then at me, and then back again.

"This is Mr. Wolff," I said. "He will be staying the night."

"Staying the night?"

"And possibly a little longer."

"Is that right?"

Piotr appeared dumfounded. Overnight guests were not a daily occurrence in our home.

"Kindly prepare the guest room right away," I said.

Piotr nodded and opened the door for us, and I started dreading my mother's reaction.

She was sitting in the parlor. Wolff, who had taken off his coat and turned out to be wearing a simple, dark brown suit, courteously took her hand and kissed it.

I had mumbled something about how I lived with my elderly mother, that it was just the two of us, otherwise he knew nothing about her, but it seemed he wanted to make a good first impression.

"Your son has told me many nice things about you," he said. "I am so incredibly grateful for the invitation to stay here."

Mother stared at him, taking stock of him with her eyes.

"You will be staying here?"

"Piotr is already making up the bed," I hastened to say.

"I see," she said.

There were no signs of the surprise she must have felt, and I was impressed by the stoicism with which she received this news.

It was not that I had sought to hide from her what I was doing. I had shared both my fervent wish to obtain Przewalsky's horses for the zoological garden and passages from my correspondence with Wolff. But I will be the first to admit that I hadn't, perhaps, talked *a lot* about the German wildlife capture specialist. And that he was on his way to Petersburg? Well, I had apparently neglected to mention that.

It was a strange evening. Mother said little, but the look in her eyes spoke volumes. It wasn't until late in the evening, following a supper during which the conversation had dragged and after the newcomer had said good night and gone to bed, that Mother began asking questions.

"Misha, this was truly a surprise."

"Yes. He showed up quite out of the blue."

"Did he, now. I see."

She leaned over the silk rose centerpiece on the dining room table and adjusted a few of the flowers.

"I'd received a letter that he was on his way, but had no idea he would arrive so soon," I said.

"No."

She lifted one of the roses, blew on it. A tiny cloud of dust billowed into the air.

"How long were you thinking that he would stay?"

"I appreciate your hospitality tremendously, Mother. I know that he does too."

"So, we now have a lodger?"

Her voice betrayed hard-won composure.

"I wouldn't necessarily call him that," I replied. "We have a guest."

"Because he is not paying for lodging."

Mother could become angry, but she was seldom sarcastic like this . . . a bad sign.

"Everything is being saved for the expedition," I said softly.

"Which, I am to understand, you will also be taking part in."

"On that particular point, there has been a tiny misunderstanding that I will clear up as soon as the opportunity arises."

"I think it arose many times during supper."

She lifted another rose, blew the dust off this one as well.

"Wolff has had a long trip. I didn't want to trouble him with anything further today."

"He didn't talk about anything but when the *two of you* would be leaving for Mongolia."

The rose was placed resolutely back in the vase.

"As stated," I stammered. "I didn't want . . . It would have been rude . . . on the very first day."

"I can't help but wonder where he got this idea from. You. Mikhail Alexandrovich. To Mongolia."

"Who knows."

"You know."

Her eyes bored into me and all I could do was stare at the floor. I could practically feel her fingers take hold of my left ear—dragging me through the apartment and into my room—the way she always did when I was a child. There, she used to give me a spanking with a belt, but mostly for the visual effect, I believe, because she never pulled down my trousers or applied force. It was her fingers clutching my ear that I remember as the strongest humiliation, and it was into the grip of the thumb behind my ear, the index finger squeezing from the front, that she channeled all her frustration.

The last time she dragged me behind her by the ear, I was twelve years old. I had committed the crime of breaking a porcelain figurine of a young maiden. I was the same height as Mother and I think she must have had a sudden realization of how big I had become in the midst of the moment of punishment, because halfway to my room she released me abruptly, stared at me for a moment in wonder, murmured that I could forget about supper, and left me there.

I tried to rein in my childish exuberance. I seldom gave her cause to be angry; on the contrary, I tried at all times to preserve the harmony of our home. I can barely remember the time when there were three of us. Throughout my entire conscious childhood, it had been just Mother and me, and being just two does something to a family. If one of the two experiences a day or a week of dejection, it is unavoidable that the other will also notice a certain contamination. I imagine that in ordinary families with many members, there are more people to lean on, to converse with if someone should become taciturn—other family members with whom to seek refuge should one member become angry. That's not how it was in our home, so I learned at an early age to proceed with caution, both literally and in a figurative sense.

But now I had, for the first time in many years, incited my mother's wrath and it was a justifiable wrath; that I must admit. Poor Mother. Here I came dragging a complete stranger home with me, demanding that he dine with us, demanding even that we make up the guest room for him. And as if that weren't enough, he spoke about how I would be leaving her.

"I am so sorry, Mother," I said. "I am really sorry."

"You know what I want for you, Mikhail," she said and got to her feet.

"I just don't enjoy being sociable."

She inhaled. She seemed about to speak but stopped herself and shrugged. "I will inform Piotr that they are to prepare meals for three people from now on," she said.

"Thank you," I said. "Thank you very much."

"And when it comes to the expedition . . ."

"Yes?"

"Since you have initiated the entire venture, the die has perhaps been cast by your own hand."

"What?"

She opened the door to her own room. "It seems that you must go, Misha."

"No, of course I'm not going. Why would you say something like that?"

She sighed softly. "I think you understand."

"I'm not going anywhere," I said firmly. "Of course I'm not."

EVA

The freezer in the larder was my safety net. There I had meat and fish for the weeks when I couldn't get hold of anything on the quay. The food still didn't smell bad, but it didn't smell good, either. I breathed through my nose. No, I still couldn't detect the odor of anything spoiled.

On top, lay the cod I had bartered for in my most recent trade. I had thought it ought to be saved for a day when we really needed it. I poked the flesh of the fish with my finger. It had thawed, was soft, and I put the fish to one side.

I retrieved a couple of shopping nets and started filling them. Every time I bent over the freezer, my back protested. It was already so old, my entire body was old; I had worked enough for two lifetimes.

Louise helped me carry the nets full of food up to the kitchen. I noticed that I became short of breath on the stairs. Twice I twisted my foot, almost stumbled. It was as if my feet were tired, tired of the same steps every single day, the same movements, in and out, up and down.

Louise turned around and scrutinized me.

"It's fine," I murmured.

In the kitchen, we spread all the food out across the table and then sorted out fish and meat. The fish would not hold for long. We would have to eat as much as we could in the next few days. For the rest of it, we would have to come up with another solution—salt it or preserve it. I had built a food smoker out in the yard, but it didn't work the way it should.

I picked up one piece of meat—veal. The last we had from the calf Philip, who'd been slaughtered last year. Had I known that Richard's bull was going to die, I would have let Philip live. We still hadn't touched the meat. Now I lifted a piece up to my nose, felt uncertain—didn't it smell a little rancid already, was the meat already inedible?

"Is it okay?" Louise asked.

"Yes," I said.

I sat down, my heart immediately pounding with anger directed at myself. The freezer was an invention that belonged to the past, electricity from a cable. I should have known that this could happen; I should have fixed the battery.

At that moment, Isa came in with two buckets of water.

"It stinks," she said and picked up the half-frozen cod I had put to one side. I could smell the odor of fish as she moved it.

"It smells the way it should," I said.

I held one hand over my forehead, didn't want her to see that I had tears in my eyes. "We will have to try and salvage as much as we can."

"I'm not eating food that's gone bad," she said.

"It hasn't gone bad yet."

I took the cod away from her and placed it on the counter again.

She made a face.

I stood up and started packing up the meat. Noticed both of them watching me.

"I'll do it," I said. "Find something else to do, you two. This is a one-person job."

Soon the freezer was empty. It yawned toward me. I shoved the lid down; it slammed with a hollow thud. Then I kicked the side of the freezer, as if that would get it running. I almost expected to hear the humming sound commence, see the orange bulb on the side start blinking, but it was dead. I missed it. Who would have thought it possible to miss a freezer so deeply, as if it were a live human being?

Then the work started. I picked up every single piece of fish and sniffed it. Most of the pieces went into the garbage pail. I stood for a long time holding the cod in my hands. Sniffed it several times. Finally, I had to throw it out too. The meat, on the other hand, I would try to salvage. I still had a large bag of sea salt I had bought from a fisherman last year. I went to find it. I spread the pieces of meat out across the kitchen counter, cutting some of the largest into smaller pieces. It had all thawed already but was still cold. That was good; the meat should be cold when I salted it. I dried off all the pieces with a clean dishtowel.

Then I took out the biggest saucepan we had and sprinkled salt across the bottom. I placed the meat on top of it, one piece at a time, kneading salt into them, packing the pieces in like sardines in a can. Then I covered the saucepan and carried it down to the cellar, which was the coldest room in the house. It should actually have been put in the refrigerator—impossible not to see the irony in *that*. In three weeks, I would rinse the meat, hang it up to dry, and then smoke it. Hours of work just to preserve a few pieces of meat.

As I worked, my hands were so heavy that they almost didn't function, and my eyes so tired that they kept falling shut. I was so fed up. Ever since Isa was born, I had been hoarding. I was like a squirrel, had food in all the cupboards, saved everything I found. I held back all the time; when Isa wanted to eat something right away, my first impulse was to put it away, even though it maybe wouldn't be as good in the morning. When Isa asked if we could have a treat, the answer was no, always no.

I was so tired of food, our dependence on food. So tired of thinking about food, about food here and now from the moment I woke up in the morning—*do we have enough breakfast for today*—until I went to bed in the evening—*did Isa have enough to eat at supper.*

I spent the whole day finding food, preparing food, salting, pickling, preserving, and taking care of the animals who gave us food, on sowing, pollinating, weeding, and harvesting. The work took its toll on my body, became like an illness, making my arms and legs ache. Everything was painful—bending over, lifting, straightening up. I was so exhausted, worn, used up, lived out. But I had to continue, keep going, keep finding food for us, food for the animals.

"Jump in," I said to Isa and Louise. "You can share the seat."

Louise sat, while Isa stood where she was.

"Why do we have to pick up all the hay today?" she asked.

"We should have picked it up a long time ago," I said. "While we still had power for the car. Now we'll just have to hope that it will do." I pointed at the power gauge, which was down to two lines.

"Geez, just asking. There's no need to get so cross."

"I'm not cross. Jump in now."

She stood looking at the pickup's two lone seats. "There's not enough room."

"Maybe you can sit on my lap?" Louise said.

Isa just stared at her, then suddenly she smiled. "Fine."

She crawled onto Louise's lap, banged her head against the ceiling, and laughed loudly. "Ouch!"

Louise laughed as well, "You're heavier than you look."

"Thanks," Isa said. "But my head, seriously . . ."

"Can't you sit side-by-side instead?" I asked.

"Okay, okay." Isa squeezed herself in beside Louise. "You're fatter than you look."

"And you're nicer than you look," Louise said. "Can you manage the door?"

"Maybe," Isa said.

She pulled it shut with a muffled thud. "Ow, it is *too* crowded. Can you move further in?"

"No," Louise said.

And then they laughed even more. They kept it up, giggling, and joking throughout the whole bumpy ride out of the park. Their bubbling laughter and joyful voices relieved some of the pressure in my chest.

We pulled out onto the main road and drove the hundred meters over to the driveway of Richard's farm. I suddenly saw him on the side of the road, holding a scythe, his shirt off, impossible to keep my eyes off him. Or on the tractor driving toward me. The face that opened into a large smile when he saw that the visitor was me. Nobody else smiled like that when they saw me, as if he had awakened from hibernation to a bright, clear summer day.

The road was empty; we met no wanderers today. It was good to be spared the sight of them, to be spared having to turn them away and, not least, spared the conversations they could provoke when Isa would start pestering me.

I parked in the yard, backing up as close to the barn bridge as I could get. I hadn't been here since Richard and Tina left a year ago. Richard had struggled to hide his tears and hugged me a bit too long, so tightly that my breasts were squeezed up against his ribs. Tina's sharp cheekbones had collided with my own, her arms releasing me from her embrace right away. Why don't you come with us, Richard said, set the animals free and come along? Tina stared at him, now suddenly her eyes were shiny, too. Simultaneously, she handed me the set of keys without a word. I didn't answer either—acted as if I hadn't heard him—and merely accepted the keys.

Richard and Tina were competent and collaborated well, at least on practical matters. The farm had been a model homestead that produced good crops and was also beautiful and well maintained. But in the mere course of the year that had passed since they left, everything had changed. The wind had loosened the roof shingles. Visible rot and fungi were eating their way into the cladding on the farmhouse. Seeds had been sown by the wind penetrating the soil beneath the gravel in the yard, in the gutters, between the pavement stones of the front walk. All the flower beds that had once been so beautiful were now overgrown with weeds, which had spread like a green veneer across the property. I swallowed. So much work, so much effort, and, in just one year, everything was ruined.

I hurried over to the barn and unlocked the door. A strange odor had invaded the building—something rotten—and I could hear dripping somewhere inside. I walked over to the haybales; they were farthest inside in a corner where, luckily, it was dry.

"Come on!" I nodded at the other two.

We took hold of the first bale together, tipped it over onto one side and started rolling it toward the barn bridge. It was not like the old-fashioned, round bales weighing more than a ton. It weighed just around three hundred kilos. Still, it was completely unwieldy and far too heavy to lift.

"Don't let go," I said as it started moving downward.

"Ugh," Isa said.

"Help," Louise said.

And the bale kept rolling.

"Let go," I shouted suddenly.

The bale rolled heavily and slowly away, straight toward the car. I thought it would hit it, but then a board on the barn bridge caused it to wobble and veer to one side. There, it finally stopped and tipped over.

"That was how we weren't supposed to do it," I said.

The girls laughed.

We could only take two bales per trip, so we kept at it for several hours. On the last trip, the power gauge in the car was close to zero. But we managed it. Finally, all the haybales were stacked in a dry corner of our own barn. I didn't have many animals, so they would survive on this for a long time, for many months. And it should be enough for all of them—for Nike and Puma, too.

That evening was sunny. We ate dinner out in the garden. Isa lay a tablecloth across the rotting garden table, which had once been painted white. All the food that had to be eaten amounted to three courses. Afterward, we were so full, we each had to lie down in our respective sun loungers and stretch out.

Isa laughed. "I feel like a stuffed sausage. Look here, look how big my stomach is."

She pulled up her T-shirt and showed us. Her skin was taut as a drum over all the food inside, but big was an overstatement.

"I look like I'm pregnant."

"I bet it's been a long time since you've met someone pregnant," Louise said.

I turned my face toward the sky; it was turning pale. The sun hung low, the rays carrying the last of the summer heat. I closed my eyes, clinging to the warmth, trying to save it. Tomorrow it would rain again, for sure, but the hay was in. We could do it, I thought, we could actually live without electricity as long as we and the animals had enough to eat.

KARIN

A quiet night. I sleep heavily in the lamplight. No visit to Carin Hall.

When I awaken and draw the curtains to one side, the horses are the first thing I see. They are grazing just a couple hundred meters from the paddock. The harem is in a group; the two stallions are a short distance away. Their heads are facing the harem, but they don't move any closer. It doesn't seem as if any of them have understood that they are free to go wherever they please.

Every evening, the horses return. Every single evening, of their own volition, they walk back in through the gate. They know there are treats here. They know that I am here—the mistress of the house—with the gentle voice, apples, and carrots, even though I have long since stopped giving them anything extra.

But sooner or later, the grass will certainly draw them away. They will discover new grass, fresh supplies, bend, chew, digest, and then move on. An adult takhi needs three-and-a-half kilograms of food a day. That's many blades of grass. They are efficient lawnmowers. Sooner or later, they must certainly understand that they can manage without me, that the paddock is no longer their home. Only then will they be properly wild.

Jochi has hired a ranger, Agi, who will drive out every day and record the location of the horses. He will make sure they graze near the station and that they don't approach the border of the national park. Agi is also supposed to make sure that nomads don't bring large herds into the park. That the nomads' animals stay away from the grass intended for the horses. That tame horses don't mate with ours. And, above all, he is supposed to look out for wolves. The only good wolf is a dead wolf, the Mongols say. The wolves are the horses' biggest enemy out here, yet we still aren't allowed to kill them. Agi is equipped with a rifle; it is only to frighten off predators, Jochi said. Agi shrugged his shoulders at this. Made no promises. I can understand him. The wolf is cunning, hideous. As a veterinarian, I shouldn't think that one animal is uglier than another. The animal's body is designed for a function; it has nothing to do with esthetics. The wolf is highly functional—the sharp teeth, the large mouth, the flexible body—but I still think it is hideous. My opinion of the wolf is based on my own biology. I am predisposed to like animals with big eyes, soft fur, animals that resemble humans. But it's also a matter of knowledge. I know what the wolf can do. The harm it can inflict on other animals, my animals.

Fortunately, Agi has had little to do, so far, with or without the rifle. We haven't yet seen a wolf in the area. He passes the time tinkering on his moped. Most of the rangers have usually carried out their job on horseback, but, in recent years, increasingly more have started using motorized vehicles. I find it a nuisance. The motor disturbs animal life, scares the birds, the vehicles make ugly ruts in the grass. But Jochi said that if we wanted to get a really qualified guy like Agi, we would have to accept gasoline and exhaust.

I get dressed, go out into the kitchen, put the kettle on. It would actually have been nice to have a kettle in my room. I put two teaspoons of instant coffee into the cup and stir. Then I take the coffee, hang my binoculars around my neck, and go out onto the stairs. Look around me. The ruts on the main road are already so entrenched that we can soon call it a road—dry and red. The wind lifts a little sand up out of the ruts creating pink clouds just above the ground. At the other end of the plain, the tire ruts run toward the steppes. The ruts are not yet as entrenched here, but they change with every trip inland I take. I should start riding again. I used to ride. You can't be a horse veterinarian if you don't ride. But I did it because I felt it was something I had to do, never because I liked it. Driving a car, on the other hand, I love driving a car. And I am an expert driver, parallel park better than anyone I know. That skill, in particular, is not one I have much use for here.

It is hot and sticky. I associate two colors with Mongolia: blue and green. Royal blue sky, bright green grass. Vast, monotone surfaces with clear colors. But today the world is gray. Clouds are banking up above me in various mixtures of white and black. And the color of the grass is muted, like in a photograph with reduced chroma noise, especially on the slope facing south near the camp where the sun beats down all day long. There the grass is more yellowish-brown than green. It resembles dried hay more than nutritious summer grass.

Jochi says that the country has become drier, less green. He believes the dry weather is caused by pollution in China and says it is going to get worse. He likes to blame China, I've noticed.

He must have seen me go outside because now he comes and sits down beside me. He also holds a cup in his hand. I recognize the scent of milk tea. Black tea with lots of milk and salt. I still haven't become accustomed to the drink. It tastes like a strange mixture of ocean and whey. Always makes me a bit queasy and very thirsty.

I nod at his cup.

"Do you think I'll have to start drinking that in order to be accepted?"

I immediately regret the question. Perhaps he doesn't understand that I was trying to be funny? Perhaps he thinks that I dislike the tea and, thereby, everything having to do with him?

But he answers in kind.

"Definitely. You will definitely not be accepted until you start drinking milk tea."

I try to think of a quick comeback. Keep this going, whatever it is. But I fail. He looks at the teacup, not at me. Stone faced. The Mongols are good at that. I stare at my own cup. Try producing a stone face as well.

Jochi moves a bit. Closer to me? No, just a movement.

Maybe his answer means that he thinks it would be easy for me to be accepted. That he would *definitely* acknowledge me? That one sip of tea is all that would be required for me to achieve acceptance? Or, maybe he means that it will be impossible for me to become a part of—or at least a small part of—his culture without embracing wholeheartedly all of his traditions. And what actually does the word acceptance mean? How has he interpreted it? As love, as respect, as a platonic friendship?

Karin, God help me, stop.

"I was wondering whether there is anything we can do to keep the horses from returning every night," I say.

He stirs the tea; the spoon knocks lightly against the cup. "They just need time."

"They should be more independent before winter comes."

"Or they shouldn't be out there when winter comes."

"Are you saying it was wrong to open the gate?"

"I'm saying we have to be patient. And if they still don't move away in the course of the coming weeks, if they keep coming back every evening, I think we should bring them in again."

I don't answer. Don't want to argue with him. We sit in silence. The sunlight hits us from one side, warming nicely already. It makes me comfortably relaxed.

"How is Mathias doing?" Jochi asks after a while.

I tighten my grip around the cup.

"Mathias? He's fine, I guess."

"He is?"

"Yes."

Jochi has turned and is looking at me. Suddenly I feel that he's sitting very close to me on the stairs. I can see the pores in the skin on his forehead and the close-cropped hair of his hairline by his cheekbones.

"What do you mean?" I ask.

"Are you sure he's happy here?" Jochi asks.

Am I sure?

"You've seen how enthusiastic he is about the country," I say. "He doesn't talk about anything else."

"Yes," Jochi says.

Has he noticed something I should have seen? Mathias is fine.

He is doing fine here.

"How is Agi doing?" I ask. "Is he getting restless?"

Jochi has fortunately no intention of pursuing the subject further because he answers right away. "He's still so happy about the new moped that he hasn't had time to get bored."

The sound of whinnying interrupts the conversation. I raise the binoculars to my eyes.

Bronx is approaching the harem. Hamburg is still keeping his distance. Bronx goes at Sydney, both rear up on their hind legs, attacking each other while standing.

"Bronx and Sydney?" Jochi asks since he doesn't have binoculars.

I nod. This is yet another challenge about their being set free—the danger they represent to one another.

The horses start yet another tussle. Sydney emits a loud and threatening neigh, flattens his ears back against his head. Bronx gives up and moves away.

Jochi gets ups. Takes his cup with him and goes inside.

"Shall we get to work?" he asks.

I nod. "I'll be there soon."

I lift the binoculars to my eyes again. Stare at them. The stallions are far apart now. No sign of conflict. No sign of any movement whatsoever.

Everything is progressing too slowly. The horses are far too close to us. They should move further away. I want them to be able to manage all on their own before winter comes, but as long as they keep showing up at the paddock every single evening, they aren't free.

I put down my cup and stand. Then I walk up to them.

I shouldn't come closer than fifty meters away from the horses, but now I break the rule and approach them. Twenty meters, ten. I wave my arms.

"Come on, now, get out of here!"

They are startled, move a few meters. Then they stop again, continue grazing.

I turn toward the camp. Down below is the row of round, white tents by the research station. With the exception of smoke coming out of the chimney of one tent, I see no signs of life. Still I am afraid someone is going to catch me. That Jochi will peek out of the window at this exact moment. But everything is calm.

Instead of going back, I continue walking across the hill. I can no longer see the horses or the research station.

I believe I am going to be met by a silent valley—by green grass, birds, and marmots darting between the holes in the ground—but a wall of sound comes toward me. Mooing, bleating, neighing.

The valley is full of animals. Cows, sheep, and horses—large, beautiful, semidomesticated Mongolian horses. They come straight toward me in a cloud of dust.

They are on the way to my valley, to the brook where my horses get water. But nomads are no longer allowed here. The nature here belongs to the wild animals; the grass belongs to them. The domesticated animals can both obliterate the ecological basis for their survival and upset the balance we are trying to achieve between the species.

I turn around quickly to go find Agi. I can't bring myself to try and communicate with the nomads myself. He'll have to chase them away; that's his job. It might not be simple. It could be that they will protest, perhaps view the valley as their own, have surely been here many times before.

I must hurry. Stop them even before they make it over the hill.

But then I stop. Because what will happen if I *don't* stop them? If I allow them to invade the reserve. What happens if the nomads' horses encounter my own?

I walk back calmly. Stand outside the station. Say nothing to anyone. Wait.

A few minutes later, the cloud of dust can be discerned above the hill. I turn away, pretending not to see them. But Agi discovers it quickly; he shouts something, then he gets on his motorcycle and drives up, followed by a running Jochi.

I take my binoculars and walk slowly after them. Agi is gesturing—unusual movements for him—and I understand that the nomads are clearly not giving in, that they don't want to turn around. Now Jochi has stepped forward. He also tries to explain.

Don't give in, I think, don't give in.

The nomads are mounted on horses—large, magnificent animals. Jochi has to look up at them like a little boy.

The discussion continues; the voices grow louder. I walk closer, can hear better even though I don't understand the words.

"What are they doing?" I call to Jochi. He turns around.

"I think they accept that they can't set up camp here, but they refuse to turn back."

I rush to his side. Maybe this is exactly what is needed.

"Let them pass through," I say.

"What?"

"Let them pass! It will be fine."

Regardless, it is already too late to stop them. The animals move like a single enormous and powerful body. The nomads are no longer listening to Agi because they are busy herding the animals. I see that they are trying to steer them around the harem, but three of the nomads' horses break away, making a beeline straight for mine.

Sydney rears up and neighs.

Jochi runs up, shouts something to the nomads, but they don't do anything. The nomads' horses are perhaps not fully tame yet. Maybe they don't have control. Or maybe they don't want to.

One of the horses—a big, black stallion—heads straight for Sydney. Challenges him.

Both rear up. I can see how the nomads' horse snaps and bites, trying to reach Sydney's neck.

Then one of the nomads is there; he moves in between them, seated on the back of his own horse. With great skill, he succeeds in separating them.

The other stallion holds his ground. Sydney slinks away, apparently vanquished. But the harem follows him and he quickly recovers—the winner after all, because the mares are still his.

One hour later, the cloud of dust has settled. Only the tracks left by the huge herd remain.

That evening, the harem doesn't appear at the paddock. They stay up there on the hill, still grazing when I go to bed, showing no sign of returning.

CHAPTER 6

A DRAMATIC INCIDENT
BY THE CANAL

On March 1, 1881, scarcely a month after Wolff's arrival, I was strolling along the Katarina Canal with my mother as was our custom on Sundays. The weather had grown colder. It was snowing; icy crystals crept in between my neck and my collar. I took my mother's arm, fearful that she would slip on the ice beneath the thin layer of new snow. She was over sixty years old. Her body had always been strong and quick, but, recently, I had been repeatedly surprised by how little energy she had, how physically weak and shaky she had become.

"I am able to walk without support," she said and pulled her arm away.

"There's no harm in a little support," I said. "It's so nice walking like this with you."

"Every single Sunday, in summer as well as winter," she said and there was something in her voice that I couldn't put my finger on. Was she distressed?

"It is always a pleasure," I hastened to say.

"But you will be leaving now."

"I told you that it's all a misunderstanding."

"Which you have yet to clear up."

We walked on in silence. On the street beside us, the carriages creaked as they drove past, a horse whinnied in the distance, and a butcher scolded a young assistant who dutifully pleaded for forgiveness.

"He spoke as if it would only be the two of you," Mother said thoughtfully. "As if nobody else would be joining the expedition."

"It is usual to ally oneself with the natives," I said.

"But it will still be only the two of you, if you go?"

She slipped on a patch of ice. I tightened my grip on her arm and she remained on her feet.

"I am not going to leave you, Mother."

"But I believe you *must* leave, Mikhail. I think you have already committed yourself."

"No, I have not, certainly."

At that moment, a bang sounded that caused the earth to tremble.

Mother collapsed. I pulled her close to me and, in the silence following the noise, I heard her terrified whisper: "Now they have him!" Now they have him!"

Him was the tsar. Alexander II had ruled Russia since I was seven years old with what, I would maintain, was a secure and stable hand. His flexibility with regard to change was, in my eyes, greater than that of any former tsar. In particular, his reforms for the serfs in 1861 stood out as a wise move. He gave twenty-two million poor farmers the right to marry and own land. For people living in the country-side, the reform must have entailed a radical transformation. The city people did not suffer as a result of the freedoms granted the serfs and we, therefore, ought not to have had much to complain about. How-ever, some factions held that everything the tsar did stemmed from an underlying wish to preserve a deep conservatism rather than a desire for change. One of the results of the land reform was that many of the former serfs actually *stayed* in the countryside instead of moving to the cities and becoming laborers and, potentially, also mortally dangerous revolutionaries. The same factions had also recently been fervently denouncing the tsar's cautious regulation of journalists, as if it were impossible to understand the necessity of keeping the most extreme voices in society under a certain degree of surveillance.

Despite Tsar Alexander II's will for reforms or, perhaps—and this is the most regretful of all—precisely *because of* it, there were certain nihilistic elements who felt things were not evolving quickly enough. More always demands more, it is said, and now, after the fact, when we see how brutal Alexander III has become as emperor, there is reason to ask whether the nihilists wouldn't have come closer to their ideal Russia had they allowed Alexander II to live.

Be that as it may: the tsar had, by the end of February 1881, survived so many assassination attempts that many people began to believe he was immortal or, at the very least, was like a cat whose nine lives had not yet been exhausted. During the past months, scarcely a week went by without our hearing rumors of dramatic events on the tsar's way to or from the Winter Palace. We had almost begun to view the assassination attempts as ordinary occurrences, like news about the price of potatoes or wheat.

Perhaps the tsar also viewed himself as immortal. There was, at any rate, no doubt about his vitality. He still loved his Katia with a passion and there were even rumors of his planning to marry her now that Tsarina Marie no longer stood in the way of the escapade. Evil tongues even held that they already *had been* wed in secret, and that Katia had been crowned. My mother loved the tsar deeply, but was shaken by the situation, and every time we heard about another assassination attempt, she blamed it on this: that his dissolute lifestyle stoked the rage of his opponents.

"Now they got him," Mother sobbed.

We stood still for a few seconds, but no further explosions were heard. I had time to notice how tiny she was in my arms and how vulnerable out here on the streets. Imagine if we had been even closer. Imagine if she had been alone.

Suddenly, Mother disentangled herself from my embrace. "We must go and see," she said.

"No," I said. "No, absolutely not."

But she walked on ahead. Her back was erect on the road in front of me. She was remarkably quick on her feet, her heels clicking against the cobblestones. I had no choice but to follow behind her.

We trotted along beside the canal for a minute or two. An errand boy came running in the opposite direction, his eyes wild.

"Mother, we're turning around," I said.

"It came from there," she pointed ahead of her. "My hearing is still good, you know."

"I know that."

Several carriages passed us on the street, all of them headed away. Two gentlemen wearing top hats shouted to one another that they had to take another route. A little girl was crying as her nanny dragged her along.

But Mother and I continued. She led the way; I trailed behind her.

Then another bang sounded.

At first Mother cowered. I tried putting my arms around her, but she lifted her skirts and started running toward the noise, placing her feet with remarkable stability on the slippery ground. I followed on her heels.

As we ran, I could smell the unmistakable scent of gunpowder, gunpowder and something else, which I would only later understand was flesh and blood.

When we reached the Konyushenny Bridge—Mother leading the way with me on her heels—this is the sight that greeted us: the armored carriage the tsar had received as a gift from Napoleon was completely destroyed. Smoke rose from the scene. On the ground were two large craters and people were lying everywhere—gendarmes, Cossacks, civilians—some were crawling, others trying to get onto their feet, still others lay motionless in the snow surrounded by epaulets, sabers, and chunks of something red I couldn't bear to try to identify, while the dust from the explosion snowed down upon them.

"No," Mother shouted. "No!"

I followed her gaze. A short distance away from us, right beside the canal, a man was trying to help another person up. He received assistance from an uninjured Cossack and several others came running. The man they were holding between them was bareheaded; perhaps his hat had fallen off. His coat was in tatters and blood was gushing out from where his legs should have been. It was the tsar.

Mother screamed and ran toward him wanting to help, but I restrained her.

"No," I said. "I forbid it. There is nothing we can do. We are going home."

She trembled all the way, sobbing and crying, wanting to return. I tried in vain to hail a carriage. Again and again, I lifted my hand in the air, but none stopped. They rumbled past us, forcing us far out onto the side of the road, as if we weren't even there.

When we finally reached the door to the apartment, Mother collapsed on the chaise lounge in the parlor without even taking off her coat.

I waved at the maidservant, asked that they immediately bring us a hot beverage and a few drops of fortifying tonic.

"I don't want to drink anything," Mother said. "I want to go back. I must learn what has happened."

"See here," I said and handed her a glass. "This will do you good."

She snorted grudgingly but swallowed the drink in three greedy gulps all the same.

Only the maidservant was at work in the house that day, the others had the day off. And it wasn't until dusk that Piotr came home. He brought news. Already the entire city was talking about what had happened.

The tsar had been transported to the Winter Palace. No attempt had been made to stop the bleeding; everyone saw immediately that it would be futile. Alexander was on his deathbed surrounded by his

family and closest friends. Katia had also entered the room screaming, only half dressed, wearing nothing but a pink negligee ("harlot,"
Mother mumbled). Father Bazjenov gave the tsar last rites and at exactly
3:30 p.m. he passed away. Everyone wept. Katia howled, her negligee
splattered with bloodstains.

Then they turned, one by one, to face Alexander III, the large,
simple, eldest son. They fell to their knees before him.

"A new tsar," Piotr concluded. "It would appear that we have a new
tsar."

"God help us," Mother said.

The entire evening passed and Wolff did not come home. It was not
until almost midnight that he knocked on the door.

Piotr and the maidservant had retired, but Mother was still sitting
up in the parlor, red-eyed and exhausted but, nonetheless, claimed she
could not rest.

When I opened the door, the sight of him gave me a start. Wolff was
filthy, his face covered with brown streaks, and a few seconds passed
before I understood that the streaks were blood. I said nothing, just
showed him into the parlor. Mother stood up and took his hand.

"I saw you," he said. "I was standing on the other side of the canal,
lifted my hand to wave, but the two of you had enough on your
hands." He looked at Mother compassionately. "How are you feeling?"

"I am fine," Mother said. "I was not the victim."

Wolff removed his coat; it was covered with plaster dust, wet with
melted snow, bloodstained. His eyes were even wilder than usual.
Death shone in them.

"So, you've been by the canal all day?" I asked, feeling a ripple of
irritation. He came here like a tourist. Knew nothing about us, about
the tsar, but was enthusiastically reveling in our disaster.

"All day and all evening as well," he said. "The tsar was driven
away. All the others were left behind. I couldn't leave a scene like
that. . . . At least twenty people must have lost their lives."

My irritation abated and suddenly I felt ashamed. He had stayed there to help, lend a hand, while we, on the contrary, had run away.

"Are you hungry?" Mother asked. "Thirsty?"

"Both," he said, and then I could see how tired and pale he was.

He got cleaned up while Mother brought in some food. Then we ate, facing one another at the big table in the dining room. He swallowed the wine as if he had never tasted wine before, chewed the bread as if it were the first time he'd ever eaten. He must not have had anything to eat since breakfast. His hand shook, his lower lip, too; he was unable to say much about what he had experienced.

"I thought I would meet with danger in Mongolia," he said. "I thought it would be memories from there that would be embedded in me. But this will, perhaps, be the strongest. The worst."

"I am sorry that I left," I said. "Had I known you were there . . ."

Mother gave me a sharp look, but said nothing.

"You were with your mother," he said, "and, fortunately, many people came to help. A giant coachman lifted the wounded onto his shoulders and loaded them into his carriage to take them to a doctor. Two young girls ran back and forth with water. A priest was there, too. He sat with the dying. And the neighbors opened their doors, brought blankets, tore up bedsheets for bandages."

"And you?" Mother asked.

"It has been my experience that in such situations people are often grateful for leadership. And that with good organization, unbelievable achievements are possible, even by the simplest of means. Besides . . ." He wiped his face with his hand, rubbing some rusty-red splotches with his fingers that the washcloth had failed to remove. "Besides, we act without thinking, I believe, when we see someone of our own species in danger."

"Perhaps we do," I said, and felt even more ashamed about having simply gone home.

He fell silent, shaking so hard that he could barely hold the glass in his hand.

I stood up, went to find a blanket.

"Are you cold?"

He shook his head.

"No . . . but give it to me anyway."

I walked over to him, stood behind him, unfolded the blanket, and laid it over his shoulders. As he pulled it snugly around him, I remained standing with my hands on his shoulders. I could feel his shoulder blades through his shirt, jacket, and the blanket—surprisingly narrow, but still broad enough to carry far more than his own weight, to carry me, as well.

Mother's eyes met mine across the table and I understood that she was right. The die was cast.

EVA

I was awakened by the sound of someone pounding on the front door.

"Eva? Are you there? Eva!"

I sat up. Was it locked? We had come in from the garden when the sun disappeared. We'd been laughing, I remember, all three of us, laughing at something Louise had said, or maybe it had been Isa. But had I locked up?

The answer came immediately in the form of footsteps clumping across the floor of the hallway and into the kitchen; the footsteps of more than one man.

It was daybreak and the faint morning light filtered through the curtains. I got out of bed, threw on my dressing gown, and hurried out into the kitchen.

Einar was already in the process of ransacking the kitchen cupboards. Sitting at the table was a man I had never seen before—big, heavy, and dirty. I tried to discern whether they stunk of anything, liquor or beer, but could only detect the stench of two filthy, sweaty men. Einar turned toward me.

"Not a drop in the house."

He was thinner than before, even thinner than his companion and just as dirty. A cut on his arm was open and undressed. The boots he had stomped in with were covered with congealed mud.

"That's right," I said. "Not a drop."

Not a drop, as usual, I wanted to say, but stopped myself. Communicating with Einar was like moving through low tide across wet stones covered with slick algae. Every single step had to be taken with caution. I could slip at any moment and, even when I felt I was in control, a wave could suddenly wash up and knock me over.

He slammed a cupboard door shut and nodded toward the man at the table.

"Peter. Eva. Eva. Peter."

Peter raised one hand in greeting.

I raised my own and thought simultaneously that I shouldn't bother, should have just stood motionless as a stone.

Einar sniffed. "You've become polite lately?"

"I try," I say.

I could pretend to play along to avoid provoking him. It could, perhaps, at least work on Peter, whoever he was. Not everyone Einar hung out with was as bad as he was and if they were sober, there was some hope. Although . . . I noticed their movements; both of them moved slowly, their speech slurred. Einar turned his head slightly, the gray light from the window hit him. I could see his eyes, the pupils . . . he had taken something, was on something. I thought all the old doctors' offices and pharmacies in the county had long since been gutted.

I knew that Isa was awake, that she was lying in her bed listening, picking up on everything that was said. Louise must also be able to hear us, but, luckily, neither of them came out. It was best if I dealt with this alone.

I looked at Einar, tried to meet his gaze, which slid away, not because he was high, but because he never looked at me—not properly. Maybe it was easier for him to be the way he was if he never looked me in the eyes.

He snorted again, exhaling through his nostrils. It made him look idiotic, like an oaf.

Then it was quiet. I wavered, uncertain as to whether the silence was a good thing.

"Did you drive here?" I asked.

"Fuck do you think? That I walked all this way?"

I hadn't heard the car. Why hadn't I heard it? Had I been awakened by the soft, humming engine, the sound of tires in the yard, I might have had time to lock the door.

But locking didn't help, not really. It would only make him angrier. Give him a purpose. Then he would be determined to enter the house no matter what. Then he would be capable of smashing windows, kicking holes through doors, screaming, bellowing. He loved that kind of thing, this stupid, stupid man.

It could keep me awake at night, the rage I felt about never being rid of him and the physical power he had over me quite simply because he was stronger—the strongest. There was nothing mediocre about him. I used to imagine that he was a descendent of one of the five types of humans that lived parallel with *Homo sapiens* before we took over the world, a Neanderthal, perhaps, who in its simplicity had been incapable of competing with the *sapiens*, or perhaps of some nameless howling monkey forgotten by history. He wanted to be a man's man and he managed it quite well, too. He was not feminine at any rate. I had never seen a woman behave in a similar fashion.

We had only been together for four months. He had been new in town, so nobody knew much about him. I liked that he was tall, liked that his hands were full of scars from working. I liked everything his hands had done with me. Anne had been against our involvement. She said it right away—that guy there isn't quite right—but I thought I saw something else in Einar. I guess I had the idea that I could save him. Besides, I was unable to let go of his hands.

Perhaps it wasn't so strange that he became angry when I left. He felt I had used him, I thought afterward, even though he never managed to say as much, in so many words. He was right. I ended it without giving him a reason. When a few months later he saw that I was with child, he was furious. Anne was also furious about my being with child, actually. She thought that nobody should bring children into the world anymore. And, at the very least, not when the father was Einar.

I had never seen him read. His vocabulary was limited to what was absolutely necessary. The only thing robust about his speech were the expletives. He was wicked and he was wicked stupid. And yet, I couldn't free myself of him. It made me want to weep with frustration, which I did, in fact, quite often.

His visits usually transpired in the same manner. He arrived late in the evening or at night. Isa stayed in her room when this happened; she had been ordered to do so in no uncertain terms. I often started by asking him what he wanted, even though I knew the answer. He wanted something—food, alcohol, something or other he could sell. He swore, shouted, knocked things over. Sometimes he tried pressing himself up against me—wanted *me* as well. It ended the same way every time. I managed to find something or other to keep him at bay, something that satisfied him, made him leave. It was a strange game with two players, and the only thing that kept me from surrendering completely to my fear was the knowledge that he always, always disappeared in the end, and he never asked to meet Isa.

I walked over to the cupboard containing dry goods.

"There's unfortunately not much here."

He moved close to me.

"You always think I want food, you know that, Eva? You think I just want to be fed, like your animals. You know that?"

"No . . . I just thought."

"Fuck!"

He slammed the cupboard door shut. Then he pounded his fist against it as well for good measure. I watched him as if from a great distance—he was nothing but an idiot—while simultaneously my heart hammered fearfully and I could feel the tears welling up. I was so tired, so tired of him, of never being free of him, of how he came back again and again, and every time I thought that he had finally ended up somewhere else, had finally left Heiane, he showed up again. And I was so tired of the balancing act, of trying to figure out what I should say and do, or not say and not do, to keep him calm, get him out, into the car or onto the road, just away from here, away from me and away from Isa.

At that moment, the door to Louise's room opened and she came into the kitchen. I tried shaking my head at her, signaling that she should leave, that I would handle this, but she didn't look at me, only at the two men.

I had thought of her as delicate, like gossamer, and her round eyes as a little childish, but now everything about her was different. While I had no plan while I stood there, at a loss, just as caught off guard as ever, she seemed to know what she was doing. Every single movement was assured and certain, calculated; there was a clarity about her.

"Look at that," Einar said. "Company?"

He turned to Peter. "There's one for each of us."

Peter didn't react; his head dipped toward the table. He was even more stoned than I'd realized.

"You don't need to play that game," Louise said.

She stared at Einar.

"What?" he said.

"You don't need to play that game where you use sex to frighten us."

"Uh . . . and you are . . . ?"

"You have to leave now. We don't have anything. Not for you and not for him," she nodded toward Peter.

"Who the hell are you?" Einar asked.

"You have to leave," Louise said.

She moved her hand suddenly then and something came into view. The bolt gun. She must have found it in the outbuilding, taken it with her, had it in her room.

Einar saw it, too, took a step backward. In the semidarkness of the kitchen it was impossible to tell that it wasn't a real firearm.

"Eva is my girlfriend. Did you know that?" he said.

Louise raised the gun a few centimeters. Held her finger against the trigger.

"I can come here whenever I damn well please," Einar said.

He always said that, but I wasn't his, had never been his.

"You have to leave."

She was expressionless and I didn't understand whether it was the weapon or her words that made such an impression on Einar. I had never seen him like this before. He made a noise as if he were about to say something, but nothing came out.

They stood facing each other in the middle of the kitchen. Peter was still sitting at the table, but now he lifted his head and registered what was happening. For my own part, I stood by the kitchen cupboards, sort of on the outside of it all.

"You have to leave," Louise said.

"Yeah, I damn well heard you!" Einar roared.

Then he nodded toward Peter, who stood up swaying, and Einar pulled him along toward the front door, all the while reeling off a series of uninspired expletives: *fucking cows, damn whores, bleeding cunts.*

The door slammed shut behind them, the car doors opened and closed, the motor started and then the car drove away.

Louise held her ground, motionless, in the middle of the kitchen, her face still expressionless. Only when the sound of the motor faded away did she lay the gun down on the kitchen table and turn toward me. I noticed that my cheeks were wet. She came over to me and put her arms around me.

"It's not a real pistol," I said.

"I knew that," she said.

I released all my weight against her and she held me.

We were the same height, just as thin; being held by Louise was like holding myself.

Then the door to Isa's room opened. We released one another and I quickly wiped away my tears. Isa padded barefoot across the floor, wide-eyed, pale, and disheveled.

"Did he just leave?"

I nodded.

"But usually he . . ."

I tried to smile at her. "We may as well get up, don't you think? It's late."

"Yes . . . but do you think he will come back?"

"I don't know. I never know."

"I don't think so," Louise said.

She smiled at Isa. Then she turned toward the woodstove and started building a fire. When it was lit, she filled the kettle with water. But she didn't include water for herself.

"Have a seat," she said. "I'll go out and take care of the cows."

KARIN

U tter darkness, the darkness of war, blackout curtain darkness.
Deep booms in the distance.

Mommy shakes me.

"You have to wake up," she says.

I resist, just wanting to sleep.

"You must," Mommy says. "They're bombing. It's coming closer."

Bombing—a jolting word. It jerks me awake, fills my body with a sharp feeling, a combination of concentration and fear.

But still I protest.

"You said there weren't any bombs here," I say. "I want to sleep."

Mommy drags me out of bed.

She tugs a wool jacket onto me. Ties a scarf around my neck. It's pink. She crocheted it for me. A Christmas present.

Another boom, closer now, makes me put my feet into my shoes.

"Hurry," Mommy says.

"Yeah, yeah," I sulk.

But I am not quick enough. I wasn't quick enough.

. . .

Goering loves animals, everyone says. That is why he has lionets in the cellar of Carin Hall. But not just lions; he takes care of the many species of the forest. Bison, moose, eagles, foxes. He also loves hunting animals. He invites guests to huge hunting parties. I have trouble making sense out of this. That he wants to shoot something he loves.

We have been at Carin Hall a few days when I discover the horses. There are three of them. They are kept in a large fenced-in meadow on the far edge of the property. They walk alone, their muzzles against the ground. A stallion, a mare, and a foal. Their coats are sandy-yellow, the color of wheat ready for harvest. The foal stands beside the mare. The stallion stays at a bit of a distance, glancing from time to time in the direction of mother and child, now and then toward the dark forest. The mother is taking care of the child, I think, and the father, in turn, is taking care of the two of them.

I knew of several horses in Berlin, city horses; the beer wagon was drawn by a horse, a weary old nag. She was large and heavy and did as she was told. These horses are different. Smaller, broader over the bridge of their noses, their manes are short and stand erect.

I walk over to them.

"Hello," I say. "Hello, horses. Are you all by yourself here?"

I pick a little grass and stick it between the fenceposts.

"Come on," I say. "Look, grass."

But they barely react.

The foal walks over to the mare on spindly legs, stretches toward her teats, and nudges them a bit in search of milk.

"You don't want grass? No, I understand you. You have enough already."

I speak to them softly, thinking that perhaps they like it. But they don't listen to me. They don't care. Still, I stand there for a long time. Here nobody chases me away.

The next day, I bring some apples with me because I know that horses like them. I tiptoed into the pantry in the servants' quarters and took them. I don't really feel like I have stolen the apples. It's Goering's food and Goering's horses. I think he would like my feeding them.

I hold the fruit out to them. "One apple for the mare, one for the stallion, and none for the foal. You just drink milk."

This time the horses lift their heads and prick up their ears. It is clear that fruit is something they recognize. I smile as I stick an apple through the bars and lift it toward the mare's muzzle. It disappears immediately. The stallion is there, too, extending his snout and I feed him in the same manner.

As soon as the apples are gone, the horses leave me again. The stallion walks alone, the mare stands beside the foal who has lain down to sleep. Horses can sleep standing up—I know that—but the foal apparently rests lying down. It looks almost lifeless on the ground, completely limp. Suddenly I feel worried. Is there something wrong? Is the foal sick?

But the mare seems calm, just continues grazing, and now I discover that the foal's sides are moving up and down. It's breathing.

After this, I go to see them every day. And the horses start to remember me. They lift their heads when I come. Twitch their ears, respond to my voice. I can't come up with any names for them, so I just call them *Mommy, Daddy,* and *Child. Come, Mommy, hi, Daddy, there you are, Child.* And the horses respond to their names. Especially the foal; when I say *Child* it lifts its head.

Sometimes I bring apples or carrots. Sometimes I am unable to steal anything. But the horses recognize me and come over to the fence anyway. They nudge my pocket with their muzzles and wait for me to take something out, and they don't get angry even if I don't have anything. Then they just walk a few meters away from me. But never far.

I am always alone here. I never see anyone ride the horses. And it doesn't seem as if anyone really cares about them besides me.

The mare and the foal stay together all the time. The stallion walks a short distance away from the mother and child. At first, I think that the foal is not really important to him, but since I have been sitting there every single day, I've come to understand that it's not because he doesn't care that he keeps his distance, but because he's standing guard. He is a father taking care of his family. I wonder how it feels to be taken care of by a father.

Three years have passed since *my* father fell, a fallen soldier in France. During the period immediately following his death, Mommy's face was wet all the time. She didn't have time to stop and cry, so she cried while she worked, ironed while the tears fell. Large white bedsheets. Always large, white bedsheets made damp by her tears.

A fallen soldier. They always use those words. And I pictured him, *how* he fell. That he tripped over something. I tried to imagine what that something could have been. A tree root, I thought, on the ground. I thought that he was running through a forest of tall trees, down a kind of path, and that he tripped over a root.

I couldn't understand why that killed him. Why he didn't just break his leg.

A lot of time passed before I understood that Daddy had been shot. That all the fallen soldiers had been shot, or bombed, or blown to pieces by a grenade.

But even long after I understood this, even though I knew he'd died from a bullet, it was still *the fall* I pictured. Again and again, I imagined how he ran. And then suddenly dove forward. And then fell.

The fall was death itself.

That was how I made sense of it anyway, that Daddy was gone.

"They're gone."

I open my eyes.

"They are gone," Jochi says, who is standing beside my bed.

I roll over, the taste of sleep in my mouth. I can feel the indentation of the pillow on my cheek.

"Sorry," he said. "I shouldn't have woken you up . . . but they're gone."

I wanted to run to the window. Considered for a moment wrapping the duvet around me like a dress. But I was only wearing underpants under my T-shirt. Can't show myself to him like that, to anyone.

He clearly sees that I am embarrassed because he is walking toward the door.

"Sorry," he says again. "I shouldn't have woken you up, but I wanted you to know right away."

He leaves. I call to him in a voice hoarse with sleep, "I'll be right out."

The plains are deserted, the hillside where they were yesterday empty.

Just sky and grass. Jochi and I.

"I'll send Agi out to look for them," he says.

"They've probably just walked over the ridge," I say.

"He'll locate them quickly," Jochi says.

"Yes."

"Yes . . ."

I don't know what Sydney and Praha thought when they saw me, whether they had a kind of system for definitions. That one, the one with the apples and the fortified feed, she is one of us, that's why we are staying close by. They haven't thought about the fact that they're horses or that I am human. But the nomads' horses have disturbed this balance. Awakened the instincts of Sydney and Praha. The definitions have changed. And because of that, the grassy plains have opened up for them. The ridge is no longer an unsurmountable barrier. They have understood that they can go wherever they want. Horses don't need nursemaids. Horses need a leader stallion and a leader mare. Sydney and Praha have finally started to lead.

"That didn't take long," Jochi says.

"That's good," I say.

"What should we do now?"

"Work."

Jochi and I are in the process of mapping out the animal and birdlife of the region. This is part of the long-term project, something we owe the Mongolian authorities. Somebody always wants something. Both here and in Thorenc, I have ended up making more promises to the landowners than I can keep. The difference is that I see the inherent value of this work. And I won't have to deal with teakettles in hotel rooms.

Not much happens, but enough. I fall into a rhythm following the diurnal cycle. Every day is the same; there is no difference between a Friday and a Sunday and this calms me.

Agi soon finds the horses in a valley a few kilometers away. They are happy there, out of sight of us humans, with an abundance of green grass and water. Agi gives daily reports of their location. Jochi and I also go out there every single morning to make sure everything is fine.

We get up at 4:30 a.m. The horses always move down to the watering holes at dawn and as the temperature rises, they move back up into the mountains. The Land Cruiser—which was actually far too expensive, but which I bought because I was sick to death of the Soviet crates they call cars in this country—bounces over tussocks and dry, sandy soil. Every day, the trip is a little easier. Soon, pronounced tire ruts have been worn into the ground—almost a road—between the watering holes and the station.

We can't stay with the horses for more than a couple of hours. After, I spend part of the day indoors. I sit in the office doing all the things I dislike—budgets, accounting, reporting, purchasing, and follow-up of personnel—to the extent that they can be followed up on when I don't speak the language. And part of the day outdoors. This is the best time of day—registering species, mapping out the entire reserve. I also write. Research reports, articles, applications, applications, applications.

Then the evening comes. Night falls; it quickly becomes chillier. I go to bed early every night. Fall asleep almost the moment I climb into bed. The manual labor makes me tired in a good way. I lie down and sink into the blackest, darkest sleep, where the dreams can't enter.

Mathias follows the same daily rhythm, but is rarely in the office. He stays outside, finds work, helps out where he can. I don't understand where Jochi got the idea that he is not doing well. My son has color in his cheeks, eats with a ravenous appetite. I had no idea he was so good at carpentry. He and Agi are repairing the entire fence around the paddock. They are also building a winter stable for the horses. It seems they communicate well in a mixture of English and Mongolian, from which Mathias has picked up many words, many more than I have learned. It suits him—holding a hammer, a nail in the corner of his mouth and the overalls. The first time I see him striking nails precisely on the head with a hammer, I am surprised. Then I remember where he learned carpentry. One of the rehab places he stayed in was a farm.

He came home from there with chubby cheeks and a healthy complexion. He wanted to live there forever, he said, or he wanted to find a place like that for himself. That was where he met Martina, Sarah's mother. They didn't talk about anything else but the farm. About the one they'd been on and the one they were going to find for themselves. They started searching. And I quickly made their project my own.

Mathias and I would sit at the kitchen table until late at night and go through the adverts together while Martina slept. Chatting, both of us. Farm operations, animals, equipment. This was something I knew about. I caught myself hoping.

But they didn't qualify for a mortgage. The banks don't trust recovering drug addicts. The farm became just one of the many things Mathias talked about, yet another thing he obsessed about, only to forget all about it with the first fix.

There was always a first fix. And the first fix was always the last, he claimed.

Just this once.
Just today.
Just one more time.
Just now.
Just because.
Just. Like that.
Quit.
Quit.
Quit.

When I caught him in the act, smoking heroin in front of the open bathroom window, I screamed. I can't do this anymore. I can't do it, you have to get out. Out. Now!

The next day I regretted it and asked them to stay. But by then, he had already found something, he said, he had found a nice place and it was probably better for me if he had his own place; he was an adult, after all.

He gave me a quick hug and went down the stairs to Martina, who was waiting outside.

Perhaps she was already pregnant. Perhaps Sarah was already a tiny bud in that skinny body.

Bronx is becoming more aggressive all the time. More and more often, we see him approaching the harem, challenging Sydney.

"He's grown stronger," Jochi says.

It is morning. We've parked a hundred meters away from the horses and are studying them through binoculars.

Bronx bares his teeth at Sydney, a provocation.

"It's good that he's getting stronger," I say.

"It's too soon."

The two horses circle one another. Then, suddenly, as if on command, Bronx lunges at Sydney. They neigh in chorus, their bodies forming a heart. They hold each other up, as if supporting each other, even though they are doing the opposite.

They are testing each other's strength. One second, two, three.

Then Bronx falls to the ground. Beaten yet again by Sydney. The young stallion struggles with his balance and Sydney exploits it, biting at his hock joints, one of the most vulnerable spots on a horse's body.

"Give it a rest, Sydney," I say softly. "Leave him alone."

But Sydney is relentless. He attacks Bronx. Over and over again, snapping, kicking, stomping his forelegs. Bronx twists away, but Sydney continues.

Now he's gotten hold of the tip of Bronx's right hock. He bites down hard into tendons and ligaments.

I walk toward them.

"Let go now, Sydney, let go."

Bronx tries to kick, but Sydney is stronger, has him.

Bronx emits a painful moan.

Jochi says something under his breath in Mongolian. I think he is cursing, but don't know, have never heard him curse before.

"Let him go!" I shout.

And finally, Sydney releases his grip on the leg. He neighs loudly, a warning sound, then trots away.

Bronx takes a few quick steps. I can see that the leg doesn't hold his weight.

"Is he bleeding?" Jochi asks. "Is the flesh broken? Can you see whether he's bleeding?"

"Yes. Yes, he's bleeding. Isn't he?"

"Yes."

"Doesn't look like it's from an artery though. It will coagulate soon enough."

"Let's hope so."

But Bronx is barely able to rest his foot on the ground.

"Shit." I lower the binoculars and turn toward Jochi. His mouth is drawn.

"What do you think?" he asks.

"I don't know. We must wait and see. There's no point in trying to examine him now. He is far too agitated."

We walk back to the car.

My heart is pounding hard, angrily. They are ruining things for themselves. The eternal rivalry. The injuries they inflict on each other is actually a kind of damage to their own species. Had it not been for the competition, the battles, this would have been easy.

I put the key in the ignition. Glance at Jochi before I start the engine.

"Horses . . . ," he sighs.

"Stallions . . . ," I say. "Not horses."

"Fine. Stallions . . . they apparently never learn."

"Maybe in the end. If we just wait long enough."

"A couple million years, you think?" He smiles.

"Something like that."

"What about Darwin?" he asks.

"What about him?"

"Survival of the fittest."

"Of the wisest, too. I hope the wisest will prevail in the end," I say.

"No signs of that yet," he says.

"No. Not yet."

The first day, the second, and the third, I think that it will be all right. Bronx is limping but seems to be doing better. I stand holding the binoculars against my eyes and try to study the wound on his leg. The edges of the wound are stuck together. There's little swelling.

"Is it healing?" I ask Jochi.

He raises his own binoculars and looks.

"I don't know. It's still pretty red."

"I think it looks better."

But on the fourth day, the leg has swollen up. He is no longer able to set it down. Bacteria must have found its way in. It takes no more than a tiny bacterium.

Jochi and I have agreed that we are not going to disturb the horses now. That we don't want to move closer, the way we dared before. If they are going to become wild, we must behave as if they were exactly that. I must encourage them to be shy. But now I violate that principle.

I don't say anything to Jochi and walk out to them.

Bronx is grazing far from the harem. He stands with his muzzle against the ground and moves as little as possible.

I move closer, thirty meters, twenty, ten.

He doesn't move.

"Easy boy . . . it's just me . . . take it easy now . . . easy."

I stop five meters away from him. Wait, notice that he is calm. Then I walk straight over to him.

His leg has swollen up like a balloon. The wound is open, big, ugly, and red. Fluid is oozing out of it. A subcutaneous infection.

Had he been a domesticated horse, I would have tried giving him antibiotics. He could recover. But I can't bring myself to give him an injection, not a wild horse and not every day for many days, which is what he actually needs. Maybe I can hide the medicine in apples or carrots. But the medicine wouldn't be strong enough. Besides, I have nothing here. The medicine must be ordered from Europe and there's no guarantee we would manage to get hold of the right type. Jochi and I have talked about how something like this could happen and what we would do. We have both known and agreed that if a wild horse should get an infection, we must let nature take its course.

I regret this. We could have tried, at least. We could have tried.

I keep hoping all evening, all night, that his wound will heal on its own. At first light, we go back to them, all of us, Jochi, Mathias, Agi, and I.

Bronx is now lying on the ground. We walk all the way up to him. The wound stinks and throbs. Flies are landing in the pus, are probably already laying eggs.

The stallion looks up at me, breathes, whinnies. His eyes are glassy with fever, but at the same time dull with exhaustion.

I turn away. My big, beautiful horse, I think, lovely Bronx. You were meant to be here; your foals were supposed to run around here for many, many years.

A shot. Then he's gone. I check his blink reflex, check the pulse on his jawline. Put the stethoscope against his heart just to be sure, even though I know he is gone.

Afterward, when I am alone, I lay my head against his big body. Inhale the scent of him. His hair tickles my nose.

Then suddenly I start to cry.

You must cry, Madame Drouet said. Why is that, I asked.

A semi-voluntary response. I must be able to control this. Stop the tears and control my breathing, which is coming in bursts. Pull my face away from Bronx's coat.

My cheeks become cold from tears; my breathing is jagged in my chest. It sounds like laughter but is horribly painful.

I don't arouse anyone's pity and I am incapable of stopping.

Bronx lies motionless in the grass. All life disappeared from his eyes the moment we shot him and just a short time later the birds are busy pecking at them. Luckily, the wolf leaves him alone. But the flies have laid eggs; the eggs become larvae. They swarm over him. Soon his dun-colored coat is full of life again.

Then the vultures come. They make impressive inroads.

I go out to see him often, always alone. Force myself to watch how the many species of the steppes do away with the body. He is only flesh now anyway—just flesh, gristly bone, and fur. Just food, quite simply.

The horse he once was has long since disappeared, and I no longer know who will be Sydney's natural heir. At all times, Hamburg is holding vigil close to the harem. Sometimes I see him lunge at Sydney. But there is something half-hearted about it; he is not as powerful as Bronx. The solitary stallion who is always alone pains me. I must re-mind myself of what I know only too well—that he is a horse, that for him this is different. He doesn't become consumed by loneliness. He doesn't reflect over how he doesn't have anyone, not a single individual who is *his*. That he is in isolation. A wild, free, and beautiful isolation. He can't feel the heaviness of the days passing without the company of others. Every time he sees Sydney, sees the harem, the instinct to change the situation takes over, but he is not strong enough, and neither do I know if he ever will be.

EVA

An autumn day of unstable weather, a gentle wind that came in gusts only to vanish again, a powerful hail shower, but also flashes of sunlight. In the evening, we could hear thunder in the distance, but fortunately it never reached us. When we went to bed, the clouds had departed and the autumn sky was a clear starry cupola above the farm. Einar and Peter didn't return.

For once, Louise stayed up with Isa and me. Isa appeared to like it, laughed at the things she said, asking Louise more questions than she had ever asked me. She is like an adult, I thought, conversing like an adult. It made me proud; she was grown up and lovely, a complete human being already. And I was proud of myself, that I had managed to raise a creature like her, even under these circumstances, all alone. It would appear that I have done something right, I thought, I have done something right.

I sat watching them, sitting and listening. Isa's questions were direct and intrepid and Louise replied slowly, with some hesitation.

"Why did you come here?" Isa asked. "Why to Heiane in particular?"

"Because I wanted to be by the ocean," Louise said.

"But we don't live by the ocean."

"I didn't know I would be stopping with you."

Stopping . . . it was a little word with great significance. We were just a stop for her. I wanted to ask what she really meant, but didn't dare.

"Why the ocean?" I asked instead.

"Everywhere else, you're locked in," Louise said.

"Are you?"

"Besides . . . I lived on a boat, once, when I was little."

"And you liked it?"

"I loved that boat."

"Where did you sail to?"

"Nowhere. The boat was on land."

"Huh?" Isa said.

"In a garden," Louise said. "Far from the ocean . . . but ever since then, I've always wanted to live close to the sea."

"And then you ended up here," Isa said, "in the middle of the woods."

I liked that she used the word *end*.

"But we can smell the ocean," Louise said. "Even if we can't see it, we can smell it."

Isa nodded.

"Do you have any family?" she asked then.

"No."

"Nobody?"

"Nope."

"But you must have had family?"

"They died."

"Did they get sick?"

"They died of thirst."

"What?"

Louise bowed her head. Her hair fell in front of her face, hiding it in darkness.

"They died of thirst when I was a little girl."

She said it slowly, as if summoning her strength, wanting to tell us more. But then she said nothing more.

Both Isa and I sat completely still. Isa stared at Louise, her eyes as round as saucers, her mouth half open. There was something about the expression on that young face that was hungry for scandal. Close your mouth, I thought suddenly.

"She doesn't have to tell us if she doesn't want to," I said to Isa.

"No, she doesn't."

But Isa just kept staring at Louise.

I stood up and started clearing the table, drank the rest of the tea in Isa's cup, brushed the crumbs off the plates into my palm and ate them, blew out the candle on the table. It had almost burned all the way down, one of the last ones we had.

"Can you tell us why you came here, then?" Isa said cautiously. "Why you came to Norway?"

Louise lifted her head slightly and answered, her voice faltering, without looking at Isa or me. "I was here once as a child. And I wanted to come back. But perhaps even further north. My mother always thought we should head north."

"Why was that?" Isa asked.

Then Louise got to her feet as well and started clearing with me.

"When I was a child," she said in a lighter tone of voice, "I always thought I wanted to get as far north as possible. How far north do you think it's possible to go?"

"The North Pole," Isa said, taking the question seriously. "Svalbard used to be on the sea ice edge. Before you could walk all the way to the pole point in the wintertime. If you were an arctic explorer, that is."

"And when you get there?"

"Then you've arrived."

"Or you can keep going," Louise said. "South again. On the other side of the earth."

"Walking all the time?"

"Yes. Always walking. Always in movement."

Isa nodded. "That sounds nice."

"It sounds tiring," I said to Isa and opened the door to the refrigerator so hard that the jars inside rattled. "You get tired if you just have to walk to the end of the park."

. . .

When I went into my room, I just stood there.

They died of thirst when I was a little girl.

I pictured Mommy, Daddy, and Anne. My own childhood, how we had run around the farm with all the animals. Mother who helped me put on my pajamas and tucked the duvet around my tired body, Daddy who loaded the dishwasher, Mommy who said that was enough screen time and come out and sit on the porch, all four of us, together. It was nice and it was ordinary; it was how children were supposed to grow up.

And now, I had Isa, I had the farm, I had the animals. Louise had only herself and she bore a pervasive loneliness.

I took a step toward the bed, but, all of a sudden, I was unable to make the movements necessary to undress, grasp the hem of my T-shirt, pull it over my head, undo the button above the fly of my trousers, pull them down over my thighs. My fingers refused to obey.

That they died of thirst; what did that entail? Was she there when it happened? Did she see it?

There was not a sound from her room, just like on the first night. I opened my own door quickly and knocked on hers.

At first, she didn't answer.

"It's me," I said cautiously. "Are you asleep?"

"Come in," she said softly.

She was sitting on the bed; she had not yet undressed.

"Can't you sleep?" she asked.

I shook my head.

She looked at me, her eyes dark. "Can you lie in bed with me a little while?"

Her voice was faint, plaintive, wholly unlike how it usually was.

"Yes," I said. "Of course."

She lay down on the bed and I crept in beside her. We pulled the eiderdown over us.

I hadn't slept with anyone else since Isa was small, when she would come into my room crying over nightmares. It was cramped and hot;

I didn't know exactly what to do with my arms. I could smell her breath, the scent of another adult.

"I would like to tell you," she said. "But I don't know how to do it."

"No," I said.

I didn't know what else I could say.

"People haven't asked me all that often," she said. "You are the first person to ask in many years."

"Maybe you just need to practice," I said.

I could feel her nodding.

One of my arms was wedged underneath my body, so I pulled it out. There was nowhere else to put it except around her, my hand on her upper arm. I squeezed it gently.

"You're there," she said, and her voice sounded a little more like her own.

"Yes," I said. "I'm always here."

CHAPTER 7

A LABORIOUS START

The distance between Petersburg and Kobdo is 5,000 kilometers. Our plan was to take the train to Moscow and, subsequently, on to Ob, where the railroad crossed the river of the same name. From there, the remainder of the long journey would be made by sled. It would be 273 kilometers to Biysk, which is about eighty kilometers from the Altai mountains.

The first few days after the incident by the canal, I worked with forced enthusiasm. I sat bent over maps and planned the itinerary with Wolff. Further, I cleared the expedition quickly with the director of the zoological garden. He was willing to give me the time off that would be required, and also invested a tidy sum in the journey. I honestly believe that he was pleased to be rid of the cost of my payroll for a time—he was every bit as worried about the accounts as I was, if not more so. My promises that I would personally procure these extremely rare horses for him and that the capture would create a global sensation made his eyes light up with all the radiance of a child's. The story he could tell the newspapers would be even better if one of his own employees was responsible for the acquisition.

A similar radiance could not however be detected in my eyes. The anxiety arrived the morning after I had made my decision. It began as a mild discomfort but intensified quickly. I felt dizzy every time I thought about the journey, nauseated, unwell; I had a kind of pressure in my diaphragm, a grip squeezing my bowels. I felt this way more and more often, and the closer we came to the autumn and our departure date, the worse it was—virtually chronic.

Wolff did not appear to notice my anguish. He whistled as he worked and became increasingly talkative with every passing day. I don't know if it was conscious, but it seemed as if he set out to compensate for my morose silence with enthusiasm, eagerness, and, not least, with uniquely bustling industry. During the past few months, he had been in regular contact with Dr. Radmai, the Buddhist lama, who had diligently shared both his experiences and good advice. Radmai spoke about culture, habits, and customs, but was less concerned about the purely practical aspects of the journey, and it wasn't until August that he remembered to mention Mongolian currency. We had planned to bring the entirety of our travel funds in cash in that we assumed that securities would be of little use in the Mongolian desert. We had, however, faith in our marks and rubles. Now it turned out, to our great surprise, that our money was not worth much more than horse dung in Mongolia.

The existing currency, if one can use that word, was a flat silver coin that weighed around half a pound. It turned out to be impossible to have these made in Petersburg; they had to be ordered from a particular smith in Hamburg. We waited for weeks and Wolff paced restlessly around the apartment worrying, first about whether the smith would be able to produce the silver coins, then about whether the valuables, in effect precious cargo that would be transported by train, would make it from Hamburg to Petersburg without incident.

He laughed in relief when the chest of silver was finally resting safely on the floor of the living room on Grivtsova Lane.

Personally, I felt anything but amused. I picked up a coin and weighed it in my hand.

The coin was thin, the color a pale silver, and not heavy. It felt cheap, almost worthless.

"So, our lives depend on this now," I said and could feel the grip around my bowels tightening.

"Or parts of it," Wolff said breezily and broke the coin in two. "You pay for goods using only the portion of the coin you think the purchase is worth."

"Like a cookie," I said.

What this amounted to was little more than a natural economy.

I immediately envisioned the cookies my mother broke into pieces and gave me as a child, and the crumbs that were left behind on the table. I used to lick my index finger and run it across the table to capture every tiny piece, quickly, when her back was turned. Once she caught me in the act and my ear stung for a long time afterward.

As if the cookies weren't enough, Dr. Radmai claimed that it would be wise to bring along several pounds of tea and a special type of multicolored wool ribbon, which the Mongolians, especially the women, were mad about, apparently. It appeared that our lives depended on the quantity of colored wool ribbons we brought with us. It was not strange that I woke up more and more often in the middle of the night with stomach cramps.

Autumn came; the rain poured down for days on end. I spent the evenings in front of the fireplace with my mother relishing the warmth, greedily eating the food the maidservant brought us, and sleeping in a bed that had been turned down for me every night. That I should leave appeared increasingly incomprehensible to me, why I had to abandon my soft bed, the warm fireplace, in exchange for an ice-cold tent and a winter so harsh that I would risk freezing off critical body parts.

However, I did not dare share my concerns with my mother. I presumed that my departure would be hard enough for her; I couldn't cause her further worry. Her affection for Wolff was also strong. Since his heroic performance following the assassination of the tsar, she had shown him deep respect. She even went as far as to have the walls of the guest room repapered and to ensure that every day there were fresh flowers on the bureau in the room. He was, for his part, exceptionally courteous and caring with her and made it understood how grateful he was that he would be permitted to "borrow me," as he put it, for such a long time.

I attempted to conceal my feelings from both Mother and Wolff, but they must have forced their way to the surface all the same. One evening when Wolff and I sat facing one another at my desk going through the baggage list, he suddenly lifted his head and looked at me. The flames from the fireplace filled his eyes with warmth.

"You are quiet?" He said it in French, and it struck me immediately that the French *vous* form sounded softer than the Russian.

"I'm sorry," I said.

"You're nervous about the journey?"

"Aren't you?"

He laid down his pen and ran a hand through his hair, which remained disheveled, sticking up in all directions.

"I remember the first time I left my home city, the first trip away, I was beside myself with worry—unable to sleep, unable to eat."

I squirmed, assuming that he wanted to reassure me, but I found no consolation in his words; if anything, I was embarrassed that I had not done a better job at concealing my feelings.

"My first trip was to the Egyptian Sudan," he continued, and leaned toward me. "The animal life of this region is almost inconceivable until you see it with your own eyes. The fauna is enormously rich. In the course of just a few days, we had observed elephants, rhinoceroses, hippopotamuses, giraffes, jackals, antelopes, ostriches. There were also crocodiles, snakes, baboons . . . I could continue indefinitely. But while we were riding across the savannas, I was altogether incapable of taking pleasure in the unique fauna. To be perfectly honest, I just wanted to go home."

I lifted my head and looked at him. His eyes met mine; they were warm. His tousled hair made him appear younger, less frightening.

"Why did you continue?" I asked.

"The African wildlife has, as you know, long attracted hunters from Europe," he said. "They arrive in large hunting parties, shoot to kill, to collect trophies, tear the tusks off the elephants leaving those magnificent creatures lying on the ground like carrion. On the fourth day of the expedition, we met such a party. They thundered across the landscape stirring up clouds of dust. They shouted at each other, hollered, had with them all the spoils from their hunt, and were now on their way back to Europe. We camped with them one night. The members of the hunting party carried hip flasks full of liquor; they ended the day with drinking, started the next by drinking even more. They called the hunt a sport, but I think they viewed it as a party—a backchannel where no holds were barred and where animal carcass after animal carcass was dragged to the party's altar. The half day we spent with them made me understand the difference between us. They were playing; we were working. They sacrificed; we preserved. Because behind all our work lay the motivation not just to capture an animal alive, but to keep it that way. Everything we did was about ensuring the individual specimens' well-being. In our caravan, it was not we, the human beings, who were the most important, but the animals."

He stood up, took a couple of steps across the floor.

"I have thought a great deal about the twelve hours we spent in the company of the hunting party. I think it represented a kind of . . . turning point. I realized that I hadn't made the journey with the same motivation as they had. I had wanted the excitement, the thrill of the sport, but that wasn't what was meaningful. . . . After that, I calmed down, I stopped yearning for home. Instead, I started longing to travel away."

He stretched, twisting his torso back and forth.

"I get restless working at a desk, you see. I need to move. All these preparations," he pointed at the lists on the table, "the time they take, I can feel my body fading away. After having lived such a large part of my life in movement, it's as if I have contracted a state of eternal unrest, as if the rocking motion of a camel or the shaking of a horse have become my body's true state and only in these movements do I find true repose."

I glanced quickly at my own body, the small paunch that had begun to emerge under my vest, my pale, soft hands. I could feel how the cushion on the chair comfortably embraced my behind and how tired I was. Already I was being drawn in the direction of my bed's down-filled pillows and freshly ironed sheets.

But maybe, I thought, maybe I would also experience a *turning point*; maybe I would also experience an almost physical transformative event, which would turn my psyche and physique upside down causing me to yearn to travel instead of for home, to wish for movement instead of sitting still.

The thought was vaguely consoling, a consolation that paled with each passing day. The truth was, I longed for home long even before I had left, and the homesickness, or actually a fear of this, a kind of prehomesickness, was soon all I could think about. I felt ashamed of the feeling. I had instigated an entire expedition. Wolff, the duke of Bedford, the director of the zoological garden, and the honorable Dr. Radmai were working and investing in my project, while I went around fearing that I would miss my mother's freshly ironed bedding. Yes, it was in truth shameful.

I had imagined the morning of our departure so many times, when the sky would be a rosy-pink full of promise. Mother would embrace me, sobbing in my arms, while I would absorb her grief with stoicism. I had even imagined that she would run after me, trying to hold me back, and that I would talk to her gently for a long time, comfort her like a child, until she finally released me.

I had also pictured how I would pass by the Geographic Society at the same moment that one or two of the most renowned geographers were on their way in and that they would notice me, perhaps ask where we were headed, and that I would say very little, but let it shine through that I was on an assignment, the details of which could not be made public knowledge, and that I was counting on a wildlife capture of sensational proportions.

A child's fantasies, I see now, and feel nothing other than shame as I write them down. I feel like crumpling up the paper or spilling ink all over the words.

The departure was quite different than I had imagined. First of all, we weren't leaving in the morning, but on the night train to Moscow at 10 p.m. Second, the weather was absolutely miserable. We had long since finished packing and sent our baggage to the station. In addition to the previously mentioned silver coins, the tea, and the wool ribbons, we were bringing a tent, clothing, firearms, ammunition, and provisions. Wolff had also decided that it would be wise to bring along fifty cans of evaporated milk that could be used to feed the foals of the wild horses, along with suitable bottles and nozzles for feeding purposes. Our packing was, therefore, not of the lighter variety.

The day of our departure, we had no plans beyond waiting. I woke at the crack of dawn, long before first light, and got out of bed right away. It was snowing sideways, the wind racing around the corners of the buildings and whining in the chimney. There was no reason to step outdoors unless it was absolutely necessary. I ended up walking from room to room and took no pleasure in food or drink. Mother asked me to sit down many times, but I was unable to comply. Finally, it seemed she could no longer bear to be in the same room with me and disappeared into the kitchen where I heard her speaking loudly and punitively to the cook.

It was not grief that informed her face when we finally left the apartment that night, but relief. And the wind was blowing so hard that there was no question of her accompanying us out onto the street, much less running after me in the snow. Wolff had retreated discreetly from the hallway and waited a few steps down the stairs where he stood staring out the window while Mother and I said farewell although, strictly speaking, it wasn't necessary as there was nothing dramatic about our parting.

When I had finally put on my coat, we sat down for a moment in silence together, as was the custom. We then embraced at the front door. Mother resorted to neither tears nor wailing; she kissed me on both cheeks and then stood on tiptoe to reach my forehead. Then she held my hands and said, "Now you go find these horses of yours. Then all will not have been in vain."

"I'll do my best," I said.

"No," she said. "You will do more than that. You are going to find them."

She subsequently released my hands and her gaze virtually shoved me toward the front door.

"Adieu, Mother," I said.

"Adieu, Mikhail Alexandrovich."

The wind shook the carriage as we passed the Geographic Society and not a single geographer was in sight. The city was almost deserted, covered with a thick blanket of snow, small flakes flew through the air, too light to settle. The snow imbued the landscape with a numbness that entered me directly so I no longer felt anything— not even the pain in my diaphragm.

I caught myself hoping that our train would be cancelled due to the weather, but it left as reliably as always. The station was bustling; laborers in felt boots and thick fur jackets crossed the rails, gendarmes and policemen patrolled, porters ran back and forth, there were travelers everywhere and their companions, people hugging each other goodbye. The steam rising from the locomotive crystallized quickly in the icy air. The locomotive engineer shouted loudly to the fireman who was still on the platform.

The noise, the movements, all the lights, the voices, none of this had anything to do with me. Without saying a word, we found our berths and installed our belongings in our compartment. Wolff then went to check that all of our baggage had been properly secured for the journey.

I lay down on the berth and stared at the dark, wooden ceiling.

Now it's happening, I thought, now I am finally leaving. But all I could feel was emptiness.

Then I heard Wolff's steps in the passageway. I had long since learned to recognize them, light and energetic; usually the sound of them made me content. But now I turned away quickly so I lay facing the wall. I didn't want him to see me. If he saw me, if I met his open gaze under the bushy eyebrows, I was afraid I would start crying like a child.

I heard him open the door to the compartment, then it was quiet for a moment; perhaps he was standing there considering my dismissive back.

"Are you asleep?" he asked.

"No," I said hoarsely.

"Everything is fine," he said. "The cargo is in place. The train is on time."

"Good," I said.

But I didn't close my eyes. I just lay there staring into the darkness. The train started moving, the whistle howled, the rhythmic pounding of the pistons bending and unfolding accelerated, while I lay there so quietly, so quiet.

KARIN

I cannot rid myself of the image of Bronx in the grass. The maggots, the bird beaks pecking his eyes. I have lost so many animals before. But never like this.

I am restless, incapable of concentrating on work indoors. Often, I end up going outside, interrupting my writing. Surfacing, sort of, from the office, going to see the horses, returning. Smoking cigarette after cigarette. Many more than I want. I notice that Mathias is watching me, observing my movements.

"You know what I think," he says one day when I am standing outside watching him and Agi doing carpentry work. "I think you need a break."

I look at him inquisitively. "A break?"

"A foreign concept. Let me explain. It usually means to sit down, take it easy. Or it can mean to get away."

"I'm taking a break now."

"I mean it. Take a trip to Ulaanbaatar. I am sure you can come up with an excuse for going there. Something you can organize. Something for the horses. Stay the night."

"I can't leave here."

"Yes, you can. And take Jochi with you."

"Why?"

Suddenly, I feel myself blushing.

Mathias grins.

"Because I think he needs it, too."

"Stop it."

"I don't mean it like that. I really think he looks pretty tired. . . . Agi and I will hold down the fort here. Okay?"

He turns to Agi and explains in simple English mixed with a few Mongolian words that I don't understand.

"Yes," Agi replies without blinking an eye. "Yes, sure."

Ulaanbaatar is a shock. All big cities are a shock, but Ulaanbaatar more than most, and each time I return, I think the place has gotten a little bit worse. Tent camps make up the outskirts of the city. Ger after ger, as far as the eye can see. In the wintertime, they all light their woodstoves. The city becomes an ashtray, the air almost unbearable. But now, in August, the city is still full of sunshine.

We drive downtown. The traffic becomes congested. Jochi's hand is on the stick shift ten centimeters from mine. He keeps it there at all times, as he must change gears often. Mongolia allows vehicles with the steering wheel on both the right and the left and it confuses me. It appears to confuse other drivers as well, because we pass two accidents in the course of our short journey.

Jochi parks the car outside Hotel Bayangol. I made reservations here out of habit. Foreigners always stay at this hotel.

When we check in and learn the price of two single rooms, I am startled.

"That's far too much," I murmur.

"The hotel? Or that we each have our own room?" Jochi says.

I am unable to reply. The joke catches me by surprise. It is so unlike him. And still, it's as if I can feel the proximity of his hand on the stick shift, right next to mine.

"We should have gone somewhere less expensive," is all I say. "I don't have to stay here every time."

"You made the reservation," he says. "I could have slept in a ger."

"I know."

It hits me suddenly that he may know someone he could have stayed with. That I have reserved a hotel room for him without asking. That maybe he has someone to visit—family, old colleagues, friends, a woman.

Sometimes he mentions other people. He has a huge network of contacts at the university, both here and in Moscow, but he has never spoken about anyone in a way that would imply the intimacy of people he could stay with, wake up with, eat breakfast with. Still, I am sure he has someone in his life, someone here in the city, with whom he has this type of relationship, this intimacy. But he is not planning to meet them now. He is here with me, at the hotel where I made reservations.

It seems I am blushing again.

We walk north toward Sükhbaatar Square. A short distance away, I can see the rooftops of some Buddhist temples. They reach for the sky, steadfast and unbending, having survived the years of Communism. But Buddhist tranquility does not fill the city. The bustle of traffic thunders in our ears. There are people everywhere, some nomads, but mostly they are city people. Men wearing suits, women in skirts. Something explodes somewhere. I spin around, feeling how the rapid pace of the city settles into my muscles causing them to clench.

Jochi also looks uncomfortable, scratches his neck again. A Lada with a broken muffler whizzes past. The sound grates in my ears.

I make a face. "What are we doing here again? I don't really like this."

"Europeans," Jochi says. "You miss your latté and French baguettes."

"It's not Asian cities that I dislike," I say. "It's cities in general."

"I know," he says. "That much I have understood."

We get our respective errands out of the way. He has a meeting at the university. I have purchases to make. In the evening we go out to eat. There's not much to choose from. Finally, we end up at a Chinese restaurant. I am served something with sweet and sour sauce. He orders beer for both of us. We eat our meal. He orders two more beers. It's been a long time since I last drank alcohol. My head becomes muddled; everything feels lighter. We sit facing each other and soon I can feel his leg under the table. His thigh. He shifts his position slightly until his thigh is up against my own.

There is skin beneath his trousers. Skin, skin, it's been so long since I have felt somebody else's skin.

We talk. About the usual things, the horses, Agi, the other employees. But we could have talked about other things, if we'd wanted to. The conversation flows so easily, everything is easy.

Hands, another person's hands. Stroking and brushing against my body, caressing and holding.

"I've never seen you drink before," I say, and am pleased that I manage to maintain a neutral tone of voice.

"Nor I you," he says.

"Agi drinks."

"Everyone drinks. Me, too. Just not when I'm working. And I work a lot."

"Vodka and airag. It seems like they subsist on it. Really healthy."

"Not *just* unhealthy. The alcohol scares the cold out of the body."

"And in the summertime, then?"

"In the summertime there's always a reason to celebrate."

"The summer *is* a reason to celebrate."

The spring is the toughest time for wild animals—for all kinds of animals living off nature. The toughest time in Mongolia. The winter reserves of fat have long since been depleted. The animals are waiting for rain, waiting for sunshine, for warmth, waiting for grass. And sometimes nature can trick us—give us the spring and then take it back again. I had been dreading the spring. Imagined that I might lose a horse, but I had factored in that possibility. I could withstand losing one. But that was before I lost Bronx. Now I am no longer dreading it. Instead, I try to avoid thinking about the future as much as possible.

"There is perhaps another reason why you haven't been drinking in Hustai?" Jochi asks suddenly.

He doesn't look at me, raises his glass and waits, holding it in his hand.

"Oh?"

"Mathias," he says.

"What about Mathias?" I can hear how my voice suddenly becomes sharp.

Jochi raises his eyes from the glass.

"I've understood why he's here," he says calmly. "I've seen his arms."

"I see," I say curtly.

He leans forward. Lays his hands on the table, palms upward.

"When did it start?" he asks.

I can feel my jaws tensing. "When he was fifteen."

"Pot?"

I can choose to cry. I can abstain. Crying can arouse pity in the person witnessing the behavior. I don't need pity.

"Weed and alcohol," I say and draw a breath, still trying to maintain an indifferent tone of voice. "It always starts with marijuana and alcohol. In the beginning, I didn't make a big deal out of it. I'm not uptight. I didn't care about any of it. Not until he moved on."

"And so . . . it has continued all this time, up to now?"

Jochi's voice is gentle but insistent. His gaze open and penetrating. He wants to dig into me, cut his shovel deep into my inner clay. And he thinks that by turning me over in this way, like soil in the springtime, he will be able to sow something new.

I squeeze the napkin in my hand. The paper melts into the sweat.

"Karin?"

I don't reply.

Why don't people talk about such things?

For all kinds of reasons.

The shame, the loss, the denial, degradation, despair, irritation, anger, discouragement, resignation, boredom. Yes, the boredom.

The first time I understood that what Mathias was doing was more than experimentation, I was filled with desperation and drive. We can solve this, I thought. We can stop this. He needs to be in treatment; there's help available. I have resources, I can talk people into accepting my son at the best places. I viewed his substance abuse as a slip, a mistake any young person could make.

Following his first relapse, it was the despair that overshadowed all other emotions. But after a few days had passed, the shame came creeping in because the relapse bore witness to the fact that this was more than a slip and that it was due to an error *inside* him.

With each subsequent relapse came new shades of despair and my shame grew. The degradation. Denial mixed with anger, desperation with hope.

I went in circles and every feeling had its place in the circle. I knew at all times where I was, what would happen.

Boredom was the very last of the emotions, a deep-running boredom that was accompanied by an inability to act. Apathy. The claws of boredom were so fierce it hurt. I scratched myself till I bled. Now it's happening again, I thought, it always happens again; there is no end to this.

There was no end until we came here, to Mongolia.

And I don't want to sit here fretting about Mathias. About all the nights when I went looking for him out on the streets of Berlin. All the time I spent listening. Trying to hear his hoarse laughter because he virtually never stopped laughing. Trying to catch sight of that forward-leaning, increasingly stoop-shouldered silhouette in the crowd of other stoop-shouldered silhouettes. Stumbling through deserted buildings, kicking used needles, tinfoil with brown, burned stains. The places got worse and worse up until the last time I went looking for him.

I don't want to be dug up, my insides turned over by Jochi, don't want to go into those nights again. Especially not the last night.

I release my hold on the napkin, lift my hand, take a long swallow of beer, and stare at the tabletop.

Skin, it's been so long since I have felt someone else's skin.

Mathias sent me here with the best intentions in the world. He wanted me to sit here at a restaurant with Jochi. He really wanted something to happen.

But my son has forced his way in between us. With his dirt, the filthy fingernails, the stench of the abandoned buildings, the smell of plaster, of crumbling brick. The disgusting, slumped body stands between us like a black shadow.

"Sorry," I mumble. "I don't want to talk about it."

"No," Jochi says. "I'm the one who should apologize. I shouldn't have asked."

I draw a breath. Finally dare to look at him. His eyebrows are raised. He is still waiting. There is still an opening for me to explain if I can just figure out how.

"Shall we pay," I say. It isn't a question. "Where is the waiter. Can you ask for the check?"

EVA

The nights and the days passed, the weeks, we found a rhythm. The power didn't come back, and I was unable to repair the battery. But it helped to have another adult to pitch in. I had the chance to do things I'd been putting off—repaired the fence to the goats' paddock, fixed the roof on the cowshed, searched the nearby farms for a working battery. Unfortunately, someone had beaten me to it.

One day, when I went to check on the Scottish wildcat, he wasn't there. The branches of a tree had grown far into the fenced-in area this summer. He must have climbed onto one of them and taken off. That night I opened the falcons' cage.

"Fly away," I said. "Fly."

But they just stared at me stupidly. I left and didn't come back until several days later. By then, they had finally disappeared.

Isa seemed happy about there being three of us. It had been several weeks since she'd pestered me about leaving. Neither did Louise say anything about the future or anything more about her past. I tried asking several times, but she always dodged the question.

She drank buttermilk greedily every morning, ate all the eggs she was given. Her cheeks filled out and she developed callouses on her hands. Every day, she was the first to get up and she would go out to the cowshed to do the milking. I think she liked it, that she liked sitting alone there leaning her forehead against the flanks of the huge animals, liked the rhythmic movements, the sound of milk squirting into the pail.

One morning, I was awakened by light shining in my face. I'd forgotten to close the curtains properly the night before and a sharp ray of light stole its way through the gap in the fabric. I lay in bed for a while, heard Louise get up and go out. It felt too late to go back to sleep, so I swung my feet onto the floor, got up, and got dressed.

I strolled across the yard, passed a couple of puddles left by the rain of the night before, kept walking toward the cowshed thinking maybe she needed help.

But she wasn't inside. The milking stool was beside Apple. The pail was under the cow, the udders dripped into a dash of milk on the bottom, and Louise was gone.

Then I heard a sound outside—a strange combination of barking and coughing as if someone were retching. The backdoor was ajar. I hurried out to the back. I hadn't been there in a long time. And there she was, standing in the tall grass. She didn't hear me, had her back to me, was leaning over. The grass concealed what she had left there.

"Louise!" I hurried over to her.

I wanted to touch her, comfort her, but she pushed me away with an expression that resembled shame. "Don't."

She turned, straightened, spat, long strands of mucus stuck to her mouth. On the ground, I saw the vomit—a modest yellow pool, half-digested food from the day before. Beside it was another pool with a dried crust on top. And another pool already in the process of rotting.

It wasn't the first time she'd been out here throwing up in the morning and it wasn't a tummy bug or food poisoning she was suffering from.

"Louise," I said. "You're pregnant."

She inhaled shakily and stared at the ground.

"Sorry," she said. "Sorry I didn't say anything. I just wasn't sure at first. I thought that my cycle was just off. It often is. But then I understood, felt it . . . I am eating for two and won't be able to help out. Sorry."

Then she finally looked up and at me, her eyes pleading.

I didn't reply.

My heart was pounding. I couldn't reply.

"Who was it?" I finally managed to ask. "Who did this?"

The thin body of hers under a large, heavy man. Because she felt she had to, because she needed food or a bed?

"What?" she looked at me in surprise. "Nobody *did* it. It wasn't like that. I wanted it. It was a man I met on the road. Just one night. But it was nice."

"Are you sure?"

"Yes. Of course, I'm sure. I know what it means to do something willingly."

Suddenly she laughed. And I felt myself smiling as well.

I took a step toward her. "So, you're really going to have a baby?"

She nodded, suddenly resembling a child herself, simultaneously embarrassed and proud.

"Do you know how far along you are?"

"I think my due date is in May."

A newborn in May. A May child.

"It's the very best month," I said. "Giving birth in the spring."

"And you're not angry?"

"Angry?"

Now it was my turn to laugh.

An infant, a human baby, here at Heiane. There had been two of us, now there would soon be four.

"Come with me," I said.

I pulled her along with me into the farmhouse, up to the second floor, found a flashlight, pulled down the ladder to the attic and climbed up.

"Come on." I waved at her.

She climbed up behind me.

In the attic, we were greeted by a wall of dusty, stale air. I lit the flashlight and shined the beam on stacks of old crates and furniture we no longer used.

"There they are."

In the corner were two cardboard boxes. I hurried over and opened one of them.

"Look, Isa's baby clothes. This is size 56. I remember it was a little too big for her at first."

"Was *that* too big?"

"But this one is a size 50. It will most likely fit if the baby comes when it's supposed to."

She took the garment in her hands.

"Goodness, how tiny."

"You should be happy it's not bigger. The baby has to come out."

"Ugh."

"And here," I turned around. "Here I have a baby carriage and a cradle. We'll have to air out the duvet," I said, sniffing it. "But everything has been all packed up, nothing has been ruined."

She nodded.

I couldn't help myself. I walked over to her and put my arms around her.

"We have everything we need here."

CHAPTER 8

AN EVEN MORE
LABORIOUS SEQUEL

My memories from the weeks that followed are as if covered with frost that hides all the colors and erases details. I can see myself from the outside, hunched over, uncommunicative, trembling, afraid of opening my mouth for fear I would burst into loud sobs. I can't have been much of a traveling companion.

From Moscow, the train voyage continued to the Ob River. All the trains adhered to the timetable; our baggage was at all times as securely and duly transported as we were. At the Ob River, we easily found (or *Wolff* easily found) four strong men who were willing to escort us on the next leg of the journey and had all the gear we required for the sled trip.

The sled trip south toward Biysk was a nightmare I would prefer to forget, although Wolff frequently claimed that the entire undertaking went "smoothly and was, under the circumstances, comfortable. Yes, I must say, *extremely* comfortable."

He whistled constantly, even though the wind threatened to swallow the sound of it, and he smiled far more often than I'd seen him do in Petersburg. His beard grew long and shaggy and was always full of ice crystals, as was the brim of his fur hat beneath which his eyes sparkled.

There was nothing sparkling about me. Although I had spent every single winter in the freezing, raw Petersburg air, I wasn't prepared for winter and cold like this. Soon the numbness I felt was not merely emotional; it was real. The frost crept into my body; I froze while I was sleeping, when I awoke, all day long. It was only when I was half asleep that I found a kind of peace. I would sometimes lie with my eyes shut and picture the light from the hearth in the parlor, hear my mother puttering around with something or other in the background, feel an ottoman beneath my feet, and the warmth of a soft blanket. Then I would wake with a gasp and it all disappeared.

After Biysk, the conditions of our trip became even more rugged. We rode horses and camels through the deep snow, moving more and more slowly. Every night we pitched the tents, but neither tent canvas, nor the small stoves we had and stoked as much as we could, nor thick fur pelts could chase away the cold.

Under these conditions, we traveled 965 kilometers. I had been long since convinced that I was in the midst of a bad dream, that nothing else but this existed—the snow, the back of the horse, the freezing tent at night, my fingers numb with cold in my gloves, and my toes, which I believed were about to fall off—and when we finally reached Kobdo in the Gobi Desert after forty-five days in these conditions, I was certain it wasn't true, that this trip would never end.

Every time Wolff had described Kobdo, I had pictured a city, but the place disappointed me deeply because this did not resemble any city I had ever seen.

We arrived nine whole days earlier than scheduled because the trip had been, according to Wolff, "uncommonly painless." We were, of course, far too early. It was just early March; now we would have to kill many weeks of time until spring arrived, when we could start the hunt as we had planned.

We had chosen Kobdo as the headquarters for our expeditions for the simple reason that there were no other alternatives. The city, if one can call a collection of single-story primitive stone buildings a city, was the home of fifteen hundred poor souls, of which three-quarters were Tatars and Mohammedans and one-quarter Chinese merchants. Kobdo is the starting point for the great caravan route to Peking; a trip that usually takes two and a half months on the back of a camel. The residents of the city therefore lived well off visitors like us and were happily at our service to procure whatever we needed as long as we were able to pay. Both the silver coins and the wool ribbons proved (to my surprise) to be satisfactory currency and we easily got hold of both food and equipment. We bought a Mongolian tent and purchased two stallions—magnificent Mongolian animals, more beautiful tame horses probably do not exist—but even they failed to coax me out of my despondency.

We pitched the tent on the outskirts of the city on a flat plain with an unobstructed view of the massive Altai Mountains—an ominous, oppressive wall in the distance. Personally, I wanted only to crawl into my bed and stay there. I had completely lost sight of the purpose of the trip; now the only thing I wanted was to sleep away the time until I could go home again.

When I look back on these months, I feel ashamed of my dark mood and my paralysis. What kind of man was I, anyway, to allow myself to be so consumed by such destructive feelings? Here I sit now in my study a year and a half later, and when I look back on my behavior during this initial period in Kobdo, it is like thinking about another person—a man who wasted his time.

But Wolff, as usual, paid no attention to my dejected spirits. He started exploring the areas surrounding Kobdo right away. Four different Mongol nomad tribes were living along the bank of the Zedzik-Noor River, each of which were led by a chief. Wolff apparently had a unique ability to come into contact with people. Using a mixture of sign language and Mongolian, which he appeared to learn in record time, he quickly made the acquaintance of these leaders and even claimed he found them to be extremely friendly.

I forced myself to accompany him on several of the outings but didn't understand how he could call them his friends. The Mongols' faces were impassive, as if carved in stone. Only their mouths moved when they spoke, they gestured little, and their eyes remained expressionless, so it was completely impossible to read their feelings.

A typical conversation between Wolff and a Mongol would proceed as follows:

Mongol: Mendi. (God be with you.)
Wolff: Mendi.
Mongol: Malzuruk mendi baina? (Is everything well in your home?)
Wolff: Mendi baina.
Mongol: Tana del chabana? (What are you doing here?)
Wolff: Manna chuduludu gores. (I've come to buy wild animals.)
Mongol: Mendi.

These conversations would often continue like this for a long time with a great number of repetitions. It was as if communicating in Mongolian was based on these repetitions, like a kind of poem or nursery rhyme. I made a couple of attempts at Wolff's urging, but always fell short. First of all, I failed to learn the language as quickly as he had. Secondly, I did not master the repetitions or manage to keep my face as expressionless as was clearly required. The Russian in me always emerged; one eyebrow would arch on my forehead or a smile would pass over my lips and the expression of my feelings seemed to confuse the Mongols; as soon as my inner life became visible, they would turn to face Wolff and continue the conversation with him alone.

Despite my communication difficulties, these trips and the acquaintances were very useful, and Wolff had soon made connections with three different groups who were more than willing, for a generous fee, to assist us with whatever we needed.

When I wasn't pining for home, I longed for spring. Every day the sun shined a bit longer, a few more minutes every day, but that was also the only sign that a new season was approaching; the cold was just as intense as ever. And then, one afternoon in the middle of March, the winds picked up.

I was sitting by myself beside the stove while Wolff was out searching for fuel for the fire. We used the same thing as the Mongols—dried manure. When we rubbed it to a powder between our hands, it caught fire immediately, but the small stove we had in the tent burned up everything we had in a few minutes, and we had constant difficulties purchasing what we needed. Now I lay the final cowpat in the stove, closed the door, and sat curled up as close to the fire as I could get.

I looked around me. This was now my home. Two folding beds, two travel trunks. A pot, a frying pan, a few tools, walls of canvas. No, not walls—a single large wall because the tent was round. I caught myself missing corners, somewhere to rest my gaze. The canvas was every bit as empty and sad as the unending whiteness outdoors. And so fragile, the tent could, without doubt, be overturned by the wind at any moment. The only thing that felt a tiny bit stable in the tent was the door. We had acquired a proper wooden door with a frame and handle and now it opened. Wolff entered in a cloud of snow with a fully loaded bag of dung on his back.

He hurried over to me and quickly fed the fire in the stove. I had long since become immune to the smell of the dried animal excrement and, if I had any reaction whatsoever, it was a kind of nascent fondness for the odor, presumably because I associated it with heat.

When the fire was burning steadily, we each fried our own cut of beef. Meat, always meat—it was virtually the only thing we ate, the only thing available, often frozen from being stored out in the cold. We thawed it slowly in the tent before frying it in the pan or boiling it in water. Despite my hunger, the shreds of red meat swelled in my mouth. I thought about the animal, about which body part I was now consuming, unable to refrain from picturing the powerful thigh muscles of the ox, how they flexed and rippled under its smooth coat as it moved.

I ate until I was scarcely half full, unable to eat anymore, and realized that it wasn't just the meat's sinewy texture that had prevented me from swallowing, but also a childish lump in my throat. Outside, the wind force was intensifying. Although we put more dung in the stove, it didn't seem to help. The wind took hold of the tent walls, shook it, and a chill crept in, penetrating the canvas.

"Shall I make some tea?" Wolff asked.

I nodded and, a short time later, gratefully accepted the hot cup he handed to me, took off my gloves, and warmed my hands on the steam. The water collected in small drops on my palm and quickly became freezing cold. I hastened to dry them off on the leg of my trousers and made do with holding my fingers around the cup and, in this way, attempted to thaw my frozen digits. I closed my eyes halfway, while I inhaled through my nose and reveled in the homey scent of tea.

I sat like that for a long time, motionless, sort of paralyzed by the cold, and, at the same time, terrified of moving because it felt as if the smallest of movements would potentially cause me to wail like a child, fling the tea to the ground, or perhaps scream in sheer lunacy.

"Is everything okay?"

Wolff's voice, gentle and warm, seemed to come from a distance.

I opened my eyes, stared directly into his and noticed, simultaneously, that tears were streaming from mine. I hastened to dry my cheeks.

"I apologize," I murmured.

"Nothing to apologize for," he said.

I took a sip of the tea; it was almost cold already, so I gulped down the rest before it lost what little warmth remained.

"Spring should have been here by now," Wolff said. "This wind, this winter—this isn't how it was supposed to be."

"No, perhaps not," I said.

"I am sorry for bringing you here far too early," he said, "that we had this long waiting period, which I assume for you feels meaningless."

"Not at all," I said. "No, not at all, I understand that the work we are doing now with the nomads will be useful, that when spring finally comes, we will be sufficiently prepared."

"Exactly," he said. "That is my thinking exactly . . . and tomorrow the wind will have calmed down."

I nodded.

"You're shivering," he said.

"Sorry," I said.

"It's really cold. An even harsher cold than before."

He stood up, pulled his hat down over his ears, stuck his hands into thick gloves, and then he went outside.

When he came back a few minutes later, his beard and his hat were covered with snow. In one hand, he held something I couldn't identify at first—a deformed tin can, the contents of which had exploded.

"The milk," he said. "The evaporated milk. The cans have frozen and exploded."

My heart sank; the milk was for the foals and now the cold had taken them instead.

"And the temperature is dropping," he said. "It's going to be the coldest night we've experienced so far. I think we should go to bed. We must sleep through the night, through the cold. Tomorrow will be better. And we can start the day with milk for breakfast."

We each crept into our respective beds, piling all the fur bedcovers we had on top of us.

"I'll watch the stove," he said. "Try to rest now."

I closed my eyes and almost immediately disappeared into a light sleep, where a stream of incoherent dreams disturbed me. I was at home in the apartment, Mother was trudging around, the heels of her shoes banging against the floor, she walked from room to room, in a circle from the dining room to the study, to the kitchen and back again, in her hands she held a cup of steaming tea, it was for me, but she never gave it to me, instead, she opened the windows, white snowflakes poured in, settling on the furniture and on all of Mother's knick-knacks, it's cold, I said, please close them, it's cold, but she just opened even more windows and the snow drifted like ghosts through the air.

Then I woke up. Wolff was still sitting beside the stove. The oil lamp was burning. He pushed dung through the stove's tiny hatch, but it didn't seem to help. The temperature in the tent was even lower than before.

Wolff closed the door of the stove, then he started doing a series of jumping squats in the middle of the tent where the ceiling was the highest, ten jumping squats with his arms at his sides and his head knocking the tent canvas with every jump.

It was so cold that sleep was no longer possible. I was shivering even more than before, trembling beneath the fur bedcovers.

He turned in the middle of a jumping squat and realized I was watching him.

"Are you awake? I'm sorry if I woke you. I hoped to avoid it, but I could no longer refrain from moving around."

I didn't reply, noticed how my teeth were chattering in my mouth, that the words would not obey me. He came over to me, sat on the edge of my bed like a mother. His breath steamed in frosty clouds from his mouth.

He hesitated a bit, then he reached out his hand, and stroked my cheek with his fingers.

He was startled by how cold I was.

"You have to get up," he said. "Get out of bed."

"No, no, then it will only get worse," I said. "Please."

But he took hold of me.

"You must move. You shall."

He said the first phrase in Russian, the second in German; both sounded severe. Then he pulled me onto my feet, standing directly before me.

"Just follow me, don't think, just follow me."

He started jumping, at first quite slowly.

"Come on."

I also jumped, but my body was stiff, as if my circulation had stopped, my blood frozen stiff in my arteries, like a pattern within thin ice on a mud puddle.

"Come on!"

I jumped again. Up and down. Up and down.

Then he started running in place.

"We'll run, we'll run, we'll run," he said. "Run, run, run, come on," almost shouting.

Two sprinting men, running in place, in a Mongolian tent on the coldest night I have ever experienced.

We ran as if our lives depended on it, and maybe they did. As we were running, I could feel how my blood slowly started circulating again, how the numbness left my fingers and toes and was replaced by an intense, prickling pain.

I whimpered.

"Keep going," Wolff said.

"It burns," I said.

"It's supposed to burn," he said.

We ran until our hearts pounded and our breath hung suspended in white clouds around us; we ran until we couldn't run anymore and collapsed on our beds.

Wolff's hat had slid down onto his forehead; he resembled a deflated sack. Suddenly I was struck by how comical he looked and an unfamiliar sensation bubbled up in my chest. A few hoarse croaks sounded from my chest. Wolff straightened his hat and looked at me in astonishment.

"Are you laughing?"

I responded with more croaking, odd regurgitations—I couldn't recall my laughter ever having sounded like this.

He responded by laughing as well; his laughter I recognized, he laughed often, but now it was more ebullient than ever before, almost childlike.

We lay on our beds and laughed until we were sobbing, but when our laughter finally ebbed away, we heard the wind again. The howling was even louder than before, the wind even more lethal.

Wolff got to his feet, considered for a moment, then he dragged his bed all the way over to the stove. He took all the bedding and fur pelts from my bed and laid them on top of his own.

"Come on," he said and nodded toward the bed.

I remained were I was, not understanding what he meant.

"Get under the pelts before we lose our body heat again."

"But . . ."

"Come on, Mikhail. Trust me."

He used my given name. Never before had he called me by my given name, and he looked at me with grave concern.

I crawled into his bed like an obedient little boy.

He threw even more dried dung into the stove, then he lay down beside me. The bed was narrow; we were lying as close together as two people can get. The heat of his body penetrated my clothes.

He grasped my hands. "You're still cold."

He guided my hands beneath the many layers of his clothing and pressed them against his own stomach. He did not make a sound, even though I was freezing.

I know that writing this is risky. I should tear these pages up into little pieces—they aren't suited for the eyes of others—because as I lay there in the bed, closer to another human being than I had ever lain, it wasn't the horses I was thinking about, nor the milk that would thaw and be ruined. It wasn't all the worries about the hunt or my intense hope that we would actually manage to find the horses, capture them, and transport them safely back to Petersburg, where we would be welcomed as heroes. All I could think of was him—his body, which was so close to mine, stomach against stomach, arms around arms. We were folded around each other like a closed jackknife; his body was my body, and all I could think about was him as I slowly grew warm.

A turning point. I had been waiting for the moment when everything would make sense, when I would understand why I was out here.

Two men alone in a Mongolian tent. This is how men sleep on expeditions like this; if it gets cold, they must seek warmth and consolation in one another. But the heat between us was not gentle and reassuring. It was burning.

EVA

The cradle was in the living room. I glanced at the bedding; there were holes in it, but nothing that couldn't be mended. I had already begun sorting the baby clothes into piles according to size. Pink dresses, light blue rompers, tights, and thin, white wool onesies—my favorites, as I recalled. Many of the garments had already been worn by several children, but babies grow so quickly that they were almost as good as new. Later, I would get Isa to help me bring down the baby carriage. Maybe the wheels needed to be oiled, air pumped into the tires; so many years had passed since it had been used.

It was half past five, but I had awakened early, feeling giddy and with a lightness in my body. I went out into the kitchen and started making breakfast, set the table. Boiled water for tea, put the butter, soft for lack of refrigeration, on the table. Isa came out of her room.

"Good morning."

For once there was nothing dutiful about the way she said it.

She stepped lightly across the living room to the baby things. Rocked the carriage a bit, ran her hand over a baby blanket and smiled.

We waited awhile before sitting down at the table, but Louise did not return from milking.

"Maybe something's wrong?" Isa said, half statement, half question.

I nodded and pulled on a jacket and rubber boots. Then I went out to the cowshed.

Even before I turned the corner, I heard the lowing sound.

The door was closed, but Apple and Micro were waiting outside. They had come back from the night pasture to be milked. I opened the door to the cowshed and let them in. Apple mooed again, tormented. I hurried to find the stool, milking her first, resting my forehead against her side as the milk squirted into the pail, talking to her calmly.

"There, there, have you been waiting a long time, poor thing, there, there, you'll be fine now, you'll be fine."

Micro was the calmest of the two, but she turned toward me when she heard the sound of the milk hitting the pail.

"It's almost your turn, almost your turn," I said to her.

She stomped the floor in response.

Finally, Apple was done, and I hurried over to Micro. I could feel how the huge animal calmed down as her udders were slowly emptied.

My hands were shaking and my fingers numb when I walked out of the cowshed again. In the kitchen, Isa was heating water for the dishes. She looked at me quizzically when I walked in.

"She wasn't there," I said.

"She's not in her room, either," Isa said, and her lower lip trembled.

I hurried into Louise's room. The bed was made, her bag was gone, but some of her clothing still lay thrown on a chair.

"Maybe something happened," I said. "Maybe she went for a walk on the property and fell or something. Maybe she's lying on the ground somewhere."

Isa nodded. "Maybe."

We split up, making sure to cover every inch of the huge, fenced-in grounds, even though I knew she hadn't gone for a *morning stroll*. She'd taken her bag.

When I reached the horses, I had to sit down. I was dizzy with hunger, dizzy with anger and confusion. She was pregnant. What was she thinking? What about the child?

I got to my feet. The water trough was empty; usually it was filled with rainwater, but there hadn't been much precipitation in the past few days. We had a huge water vat just outside the fence. I walked over and found a bucket, dipped it in the water, waiting as it grew heavy, just stood there like that holding the bucket because I didn't have the strength to lift it out again. A few straws of hay bobbed on the surface of the water.

Finally, I managed to pull up the bucket and picked the straws out of the water. I emptied the bucket into the trough, walked back to the vat, filled another bucket, poured it into the trough.

The horses came over and started drinking. They stuck their large muzzles under the water and slurped as they drank, their eyes half shut.

You're thirsty, I thought, sorry, and went to get yet another bucket.

When it, too, was empty, the horses were apparently satisfied because then they moved away. Puma walked by himself beside the fence while Nike followed behind him, watching over him.

I dropped the bucket onto the ground with a hollow metal thud.

I should have realized it, should have known. Anne would have seen it, she was like that, but I was hopeful, naïve, ignorant. I gave the bucket an angry kick.

"Mom?"

Isa was standing right behind me.

"Mom, what are you doing?"

"Sorry."

I bent over quickly to pick it up and placed it neatly beside the water trough.

"Did you find anything?" Isa asked.

"No."

"Me, neither."

I could tell that Isa was on the verge of tears.

"Why did she just leave? Didn't she like us, after all?"

"Of course, she liked us," I said and pulled her close to me. "Of course, she liked us. Especially you."

Isa allowed herself to be hugged and comforted. "Maybe there was something she had to take care of," I said. "I'm sure she'll be back."

"Do you think so?" Isa asked.

"Yes," I said. "For sure."

The day passed. We ate our evening meal in silence, went to bed in silence. Isa made a few feeble attempts at being obstinate, rude, her old self, but quickly relented. I didn't rise to the bait and she didn't have the energy.

Maybe Louise would come back during the night, I thought. I had left the door unlocked. She would sneak in and crawl into her own bed; the next morning, she would be there. I would hear the creaking of her bed when she got up at five o'clock, she would milk the cows, as usual, have breakfast with us, as usual.

A light drowsiness fell over me. I slipped in and out of sleep between a state of wakefulness and dreams. I mended baby clothes, darned holes, but the thread kept knotting, it was too long, I tried using a double thread, but that only made it worse, the thread tangled up, I put it in my mouth, cutting it with my teeth, pulled out the thread, held the needle up to the light, tried rethreading it but couldn't see properly, the light from the candle was far too dim.

KARIN

I lie awake in my bed. The bedding is itchy against my skin, the pillow too soft, the mattress too hard, and the entire room reeks of cigarette smoke.

Finally, I get out of bed and open the window to the night outside. The noise of the city hits me like a wall—motors and brakes, transformers, fans and sirens, voices, laughter, and shouting.

I stand by the open window, drawing the city air into my lungs. Inhaling deeply, exhaling. Deep breaths.

It doesn't help.

The city air, the city night, the way it had been the very last time I went looking.

The early evening light of spring almost three years ago. All of West Berlin was outdoors. Women in summer dresses, children on bicycles. But I didn't join in because the shadows of spring were found in another city. The city of the homeless, the city of addicts. Our city. Mine and his.

He came home in the morning. He no longer had a key, had fortunately lost it, and I hadn't wanted to get him a new one. He stole like a professional thief. I was tired of discovering that things I was fond of had disappeared.

I was working when he rang the bell, pouring over the takhis' genealogy. I didn't know which horses I wanted to breed, which genetic qualities I should cross. But I couldn't bring them here; I couldn't get started until I had a place to be. I had looked for places close to Berlin, close to Mathias. But now I had received a tip about a farm in Thorenc. The area resembled Mongolia. It would be ideal for the horses. I could get it for a good price. I was unable to get the idea out of my head, even though the place was too far away from Berlin, and from him.

The sound of the doorbell cut through the air. The voice over the entry phone was clear, the words distinct.

I let him in, heard his footsteps in the stairwell. Listened to hear whether he stumbled or dragged his feet. But the sound of his footsteps on the stairs revealed nothing.

Then he was standing before me. I could smell the scent of him—of the streets, of cigarettes, alcohol, plaster, and urine. Filth, always filth under his nails, in his hair. Here comes the hug, I thought, now he will reach out his arms the way he usually does and hug me for a long time. Until I carefully disentangle myself from his embrace.

But he didn't move.

"Hi," was all he said.

"Come in," I said. "Are you hungry?"

He was always hungry.

I put bread and sandwich things out for him. I never had much food in the house; when you shopped for just one person, you don't need much. But I found a TV dinner in the freezer. I had bought it with him in mind. I often kept a reserve of dinners like this so he could have something to eat even if he turned up in the middle of the night.

Today he just ate one slice of bread. He didn't want a hot meal.

Then he stood up. He brought the plate and glass over to the counter, shaking the crumbs into the sink. Usually he didn't bother with such things.

"Thanks," he said.

"You're welcome," I said.

It had been a long time since I'd asked how he was doing. I knew that he wasn't doing well. Besides, usually he would tell me without my asking.

He often talked at length about plans he had. A new program he'd heard of, a clinic, someone who could help him. Or he talked loud and fast about a new job opportunity. *Opportunity,* he liked that word. He sometimes came home freshly showered and brought flowers. In clean clothes, sort of sober. But often it didn't take more than a few minutes for me to see that he was on something, that the heroin had been replaced by something else. That his joy was just an added ingredient, external, and would fade along with the high. Many years had passed since I'd stopped believing in the word *opportunity.*

And today he didn't use the word. He had nothing to tell me.

"I guess I'll go," he said and went out into the hallway.

"Where are you going?"

Why did I ask about that? I didn't really want to hear the answer, did I?

"Just out," he said.

He took his anorak down from the hook on the wall, a frayed jacket; I could smell how it stunk of the street.

My heart wrenched. *Just out.* I should ask a follow-up question. I should keep him here. Ask him to spend the night. That's what a proper mother would do.

But I just stood there. Taking in the smell of him without doing anything. This was how he smelled now. There was no longer anything I could do.

Nobody should smell like that. Like a creature that lived in the sewer.

"I just wanted to say hello," he said, and pulled his anorak over his head.

"Sure," I said.

"What are you going to do today?" he asked.

"Go for a walk, maybe," I said. "It's a nice day."

"Yes," he said. "It's a nice day."

I should have asked him to go with me. I should have tried to keep him here. But I said nothing.

He opened the door.

"Have a nice walk then."

"Thanks," I said. "Bye."

"Bye," he said.

Then he stopped.

"Just one thing."

"Yes?"

"I won't be seeing Sarah anymore."

"No? But, why not?"

He grimaced. "You know why."

"That . . . that's too bad."

"Too bad? Is that all you have to say?"

He grinned. A quick little grin, mirthless.

And then he left.

He would not be seeing Sarah anymore. He had lost the few hours of visitation he'd had. Even that one small thing he had managed to destroy.

"Too bad." I should have said something more. Should I have comforted him? Or exploded and yelled?

But he was already gone and, anyway, it made no difference what I said or did.

It wasn't until a few minutes later, when I went into the bathroom, washed my hands, and smelled the scent of soap, that it hit me that today's visit had been different from all the previous visits. Not because of the news about Sarah. I had received bad news like that many times before.

But because he hadn't taken a shower.

I had put out a towel for him. Checked that there was enough soap and shampoo in the shower. Reminded him not to stay in there too long because the hot water would quickly run out. But he hadn't showered.

He'd left me just as dirty and stinking as when he'd come. That had never happened before.

I ended up pacing from room to room, never making it out into the sunshine. Drank cups of coffee that burned my tongue. Sat down to work. Got up again. Picked up a baby picture of Sarah that was on the bureau. The only photograph I had. The child was sitting on Mathias's lap. He smiled at the camera; Sarah's eyes were red from the flash.

Around seven, I went out, noticing how the key trembled in my hand as I locked the door.

There were plenty of places to hide in the city, especially along The Wall. There were abandoned buildings everywhere. They were covered with graffiti, slogans, and rats crept in the corners.

I followed The Wall. Walked through the old apartment buildings that I knew were empty. Often, it was easy to find him, as if he wanted to be found. The more recent the relapse, the easier it was to figure out where to find him. But now, it had been a long time since he'd been clean, and he wasn't in any of the usual buildings where people like him tended to hide.

I kept walking in a haphazard way. The hours slid by.

Finally, I reached a four-story, gray, isolated building. The buildings on both sides had been torn down. A green, surprisingly shiny gate was ajar. I opened it and walked in.

The courtyard smelled like urine. Courtyards like this always smelled of urine.

I squinted as my eyes adjusted to the darkness. A switch was connected to a light on the wall. I tried it, but knew, actually, ahead of time that it wouldn't work. There was never electricity in these buildings. The dust of plaster and decay crunched between my teeth and tickled my nose reminding me of the years just after the war.

Mailboxes on the wall, many still with names. One was open, gaping, at the bottom. I glimpsed a yellowed advertising brochure. One door on the right wall of the courtyard, one on the left, both leading into stairwells marked A and B.

I tried A. It was locked. I grasped the door handle to B, which slid open.

There was nothing to suggest that people were living here. Most of the occupied buildings bore signs of the inhabitants—graffiti, sleeping bags thrown into corners, empty tin cans left behind after a meal.

But still I went inside. It was a house on the street, one of many; I had to try every single one.

He should have showered. Why hadn't he showered?

There were three entrance doors on every floor. I tried all those on the first floor; none of them opened. All the doors on the second floor were also locked.

It wasn't until the third floor that I found an open door. It slid open silently, as if someone had just oiled the hinges.

I walked into the apartment.

"Hello?"

Nobody responded.

A hallway, an opening to a living room, brown, flowered wallpaper on the walls, a faint scent of perfume, old ladyish.

I went into the living room. It was empty. A door inside led to another room. I opened it.

"Mathias."

Someone was sitting there. Slumped over. A syringe in the arm. Blue lips. Scarcely audible breathing.

He was wearing an anorak just like Mathias's.

That smelly anorak.

Afterward . . . I remember the paper cup of cold coffee in my hand. I clung to it tightly. A nurse came and went. We still don't know anything, she said all the time; unfortunately, we don't know anything more. I remember the numbness that spread from my toes, up my legs, out into my fingers, into my face, mouth, eyes, made it impossible to speak, impossible to close my eyes, impossible to cry throughout the entire night.

But all nights come to an end. He will survive, the nurse said, and has suffered no permanent injury.

It was only when I received word of this that the paralysis released its hold. The nurse looked at me, asked if I wanted to see him. Yes, I said, I guess I must. But I didn't go in, not right away. I just stood there and could feel how I was trembling.

I had searched so many times.

A mother searches. It's what one does.

The next day I called the landowner in Thorenc. I'm coming, I said. How soon can I take possession of the property?

I have never searched again.

Have never seen Sarah again, either.

But I called Child Services. After a couple of weeks, I called. Just to confirm that what Mathias had said was actually the truth. They told me that Sarah was doing well now. That she'd been placed in a permanent home. They used that word, *permanent*. That she was in very good hands. Fine, I said. Fine, that was all I wanted to know. I hung up and thought about good hands. All hands were better than Mathias's hands. Many were better than mine, too, probably.

My hands were best suited for work.

EVA

I took the chance of using the car one final time to drive down to the harbor. It was Friday but there was but a single, solitary fishboat alongside the quay. This is how it had been the past few times I'd come here. Nobody came here any longer, to buy or sell.

The owner of the boat was the same fisherman who had sold me the cod the day I picked up Louise. He was in the process of packing up, stacking empty Styrofoam boxes on top of each other, securing them with a rope. I went over to him. When he noticed me, he looked down at the ground.

"Caught them this morning," he mumbled and nodded toward three small saithe in a lone crate on the dock.

"I didn't come to buy fish," I said. "I have nothing to trade."

He turned back to his work tightening the final loose end and coiling up the remainder of the rope.

"I'm looking for someone," I said. "Her name is Louise, she has auburn hair, is my height. I ran into her the last time I was here trading with you. Her Norwegian's a bit broken."

"A foreigner?" he said. "Refugee."

"She's French."

"Illegal," he said.

This startled me. The distinction between legal and illegal . . . it had been several years since I'd heard anyone mention it. The borders had fallen; everyone came now, or left, nobody was legal, everyone was illegal, me, him, it no longer made any difference.

"She was staying with me," I said. "She was my guest."

"I haven't seen anyone," he said. "There's nobody down here anymore. The fish is rotting, as you can see."

Then I noticed that his fish was dull and the color a bit off. He'd lied about when it had been caught.

"You'll have to eat it yourself," I said.

"I'm sick of fish."

"I can bring milk one day," I said. "Later."

Then I quickly walked toward the car.

"Hey," he shouted after me. "Things might have been fine, you know, things might have been fine had it not been for your kind."

"What?" I turned around.

"We would have managed to secure the borders. We could have protected what is ours. We still would've had . . . everything we had before."

Milk. Why had I promised him milk?

I opened the car, did not dignify the fisherman with even a glance. At that moment, I noticed smoke rising out of the chimney of Einar's house.

She couldn't be there?

I stood beside the open door of the car. Why would she be there, with him?

Then I closed the door again and walked up the hill.

Long before I turned the corner, I heard the sound of wood chopping. He was standing in the yard, an axe in his hand, splitting log ends with a single stroke.

"Well, what do you know."

"Hello."

He was apparently a bit rattled by the sight of me here, that I had sought him out, because he dropped the axe on the ground.

For a moment, I considered the distance to it, three meters, perhaps, if I moved quickly, I could run over and snatch it away from him.

He grinned suddenly. "You're looking for her. That French bitch."

"Yes."

"Maybe I have her in there."

He nodded toward the house.

Rage flared up inside me. I pictured Louise, his large body on top of hers.

"No?"

"Relax. Do you think I'd want someone like her? Ornery polecat."

I exhaled. *Ornery polecat.* The choice of words was surprisingly creative coming from him.

"But you've seen her?" I asked.

"That night, yeah. At your place. Vilest lady I've met for some time."

"And here?"

He took his time. "Does it matter?"

"But you knew I was looking for her."

The corners of his mouth slid to the sides of his face in what, apparently, was supposed to resemble a smile.

"What'll you give me if I find her?"

"Einar, if you see her, please ask her to come back. Please."

Halfway back to the farm, the car stalled—out of power. I just left it there, drove out onto the shoulder of the road, locked up, and left without looking back. For the first time since I'd learned to drive, I was without a car.

I didn't dare walk along the highway, was afraid of meeting someone and, instead, took the path through the woods. It was raining, but not enough to make any noise. A crow sailed over my head cawing loudly. No other birds were singing.

Caw, caw, caw. Another joined in. They circled above me, watching my movements—large, black shadows in the sky; their cries filled the air. It was a noise like no other, *caw, caw, caw.*

I picked up the pace, keeping an eye on them, happy there was dense cover of tree branches between me and them.

Isa tipped the chair forward, planted her toes against the floor, placed her palms flat on the tabletop and tipped the chair backward, then rocked forward again, landing with a thump.

She hadn't drunk her milk and the cream had clotted into a crust on top.

"We have to leave now, you realize that, Mom."

She tipped the chair again, even further this time; the chair teetered.

"Isa," I said.

"*Isa*," she replied. "No Louise, no baby, that damn foal is almost big enough to manage on its own. You know it's time to get out of here."

She held on to the tabletop, her ponytail swinging through the air behind her, the chair balancing on two legs. Then she let go letting the chair drop to the floor with a loud bang.

"You're going to make gouge marks on the floor," I said.

"What a crisis," she said.

I didn't reply. The pine floorboards were full of scrapes and scratches and had been that way for as long as I could remember. A dent from the grown-up plate I was allowed to eat off when I was five and had dropped on the floor, another from the frying pan Anne had suddenly dropped once when she forgot to use a potholder, scratches from chair legs, from the entire family's chairs, which were dragged across the floor every time we sat down and every time we got up, meal after meal, year after year. I loved this floor.

Isa planted her toes against the floorboards again and tipped the chair backward one more time.

"I can't stand to be here any longer."

"You can't stand it." I had to laugh. "Have you seen the people out there? Have you really looked at the people walking down the roads? Do you think they are better off than you are?"

"Yes, Mom. I've seen them. And you know what I see? I see that at least they can breathe."

Further and further, then her toes lifted off the floor, her fingers turning white against the tabletop.

"Isa!"

She smiled at me. "But you just want to stay here at home and be all cozy. Right, Mom, it's so cozy here at our house when we tend all the animals together, milk the cows side-by-side. It's so cozy when it's just you and me, right."

The narrowed eyes, the damn brat, sitting there and tipping the chair, balancing.

And then . . . suddenly she lost her balance, fell backward; the chair hit the floor, her head knocked against the wood floorboards, a sound escaped her, a strangled scream.

I stood up while she remained on the floor, her eyes open, her back against the chair, head against the floor, legs pointing upwards at a ninety-degree angle.

"Are you okay?" I asked. "Are you okay?"

I reached out my hand to her. She just lay there at a bizarre angle and the laughter bubbled up in me. I couldn't hold it back; a few snorts forced their way out.

"Sorry," I said. "Sorry."

She slumped over onto her side, still lying on the floor. "It hurts, shit. It hurts like hell."

I sat down beside her; helped her up into a sitting position, giggling.

"Mom!"

"Yes . . . sorry."

She had tears in her eyes but couldn't help but smile.

"Mom!"

I could feel the laughter in my diaphragm, not unlike tears, laughter and tears are connected, the same muscles, the same gasps.

"You should have seen . . . you should have seen your face . . ." And then she laughed as well, unable stop herself. "It hurts so much. My whole back. It hurts like mad!"

We sat next to each other on the floor until our laughter faded away. Then I lifted my hand and stroked her head gently.

"Are you okay?" I asked.

"Okay? I don't know."

But then she nodded slowly. "But I *will* be okay, at least."

"Good," I said. "Fine. That's fine."

CHAPTER 9

A MUCH LONGED-FOR LIGHT

All ice-cold nights come to an end; all winters as well. And the spring arrived suddenly, clearly, without remorse. The snow melted, giving the ground moisture, and the ground showed its gratitude in the form of green wisps of grass in every single place there was the tiniest patch of soil between all the stones, and my homesickness had disappeared. I no longer lived in the memories of our cozy apartment, of Mother, and the warmth of the fireplace. I lived here and now, together with Wilhelm Wolff.

The Zedzik Noor River flowed freely. One afternoon, we went out and discovered that the currents were glittering with the glistening bodies of fish. That evening, we finally ate something other than meat and, after that, we often went fishing in the river. The Mongols regard fish with the same disgust we feel for snakes—as impure food they wouldn't eat even if you put a gun to their heads—so we had the delicious trout all to ourselves. Our meat, on the other hand, was a much-coveted foodstuff and we often found beggars hanging around outside our tent, ready to haggle for our latest take.

"That's enough, now," Wilhelm said one morning when three young men appeared.

He walked in circles, then grasped a large piece of meat that was hanging from the ceiling for drying and chopped it into pieces, which he placed on a plate. He walked over to the trunk of food provisions, took out the bag of pepper, and proceeded to sprinkle the spice liberally on the meat.

"So much?" I asked.

"Even more," he said and sprinkled on a bit more.

I followed him as he went out to the young beggars. He offered them the plate and they looked at it in surprise, unaccustomed as they were to being served so willingly. Then they quickly extended their tweezerlike fingers, snatching up the morsels, and shoving the meat into greedy mouths.

The reaction was almost immediate. The men, who had no knowledge of pepper, sneezed and screamed and shouted for water and departed almost immediately. The rumors about how the meat was inedible must have traveled fast because, after this, nobody ever bothered us again.

We spent both the days and the nights together. We rode across the steppes, went fishing, hunting, searched for wild onion we could use for cooking. We got up at the same time, ate at the same time, went to bed at the same time, and slept at the same time. It was no longer the cold that compelled us to share a bed, but his face was the last thing I saw before falling asleep and the first thing I saw when I awoke.

Here comes another of those paragraphs that I should perhaps refrain from writing. But it appears I feel obliged to express the yearning I felt during these weeks. "The art of writing is the art of discovering what you believe," Flaubert wrote, and perhaps by putting the words down on paper, I will gain a grasp of my yearning. Because in the same way that I longed for home while I was still in Petersburg, I now longed for Wilhelm, even though he was constantly at my side. I wanted to lie close to him the way I had done on the coldest night. I was, however, no longer satisfied with that; I longed to come even closer. I wanted to be as close to him as two people can be.

While my longing grew, I consoled myself with the thought that at least I was growing closer to him as a human being. The more I got to know him, the greater was my respect. He was wise, kind, considerate, bright; he had a solution for everything and a compassion for the world around him. His knowledge was immense, his ability to learn impressive; he quickly learned to speak Mongolian but also picked up some Chinese phrases that he used in his interactions with the merchants.

I had never been able to talk to anyone the way I talked to him. I was reminded of my benefactor in Petersburg, how easily our conversations had flowed, but now, when I compared him to Wilhelm, I realized that there had always been something that jarred. I had always sought out my benefactor's recognition and approval. That was not how it was with Wilhelm; between us, the words flowed as smoothly and rapidly as the water in the river.

We worked all the time. Wilhelm never took time off. We started preparations for the hunt and built a paddock for the wild horses close to the tent site.

"Here they'll have plenty of room to move around," Wilhelm said.

"Like being free," I said.

"Well, not quite," he said.

"But a good transition for the life ahead, don't you think?"

"Yes," he said. "That it will be, at least."

"And here they don't have to struggle to survive. We will give them everything they need. Food and protection."

Every time we were out riding, we scouted. Once, we were indeed convinced that we spotted something. It was in the late afternoon; the sun hung low in the sky. It was still warm, but I knew the temperature would drop quickly when it set, and there was no time to be lost in returning to the tent. All the same, we didn't ride quickly, but held the horses at a leisurely pace so it was possible for us to converse.

Suddenly, Wilhelm fell silent. He stopped his horse, squinted. Then he lifted a hand and pointed.

"What's that there?"

I turned around.

"You see it?" he said.

"I don't know."

"But look—really look."

"Yes, yes. It must be something."

"A cloud of dust," he said. "Aren't those animals? They must be animals."

On the steppes, on the horizon, right beside the point where the sun would soon set, we could see the contours of something.

"Give me the binoculars," Wilhelm said.

"Binoculars? I thought you brought them."

"Dammit!"

Wilhelm dug his heels into the flanks of his horse and rode straight toward the sun. I followed behind; he was a far better horseman. I struggled to keep up and soon he surged ahead of me.

I was out of breath, my eagerness driving me. Imagine if we found them; imagine if it could be that simple, could happen so quickly. Imagine if already this evening we would ride back to the camp with a stallion and a mare?

But when we reached the place where we had seen the cloud of dust, there was nothing there, nothing but grass and rocks.

"But I am certain there was something," Wilhelm said. "I am completely convinced. You saw it too, didn't you?"

"Yes," I said. "Yes, I did."

The truth was that I was not absolutely certain. The eye sees what the eye wants to see.

After this experience, we no longer allowed ourselves to get carried away at the mere sight of something unusual on the steppes. We tried to remain level-headed and always made sure to bring the binoculars so we could more quickly disprove our delusions.

Wilhelm invited three of the local chiefs with whom he'd formed an acquaintance to accompany us in our search. We bagged a particularly large and magnificent argali ram and drank together while the meat was grilling. The three chiefs were vastly different in both age and disposition. The youngest was quiet and careful, the second youngest the most talkative, while the eldest seldom opened his mouth, but when he did, everyone listened. Despite their differences, the similarities were greater. They were calm and proud in their conduct, friendly, but difficult to read. I thought I could detect the great Genghis Khan in all three of their faces.

The Mongol Empire was one of the largest empires ever to exist, second only to the British Empire. It extended from countries in Central Europe all the way to the Pacific Ocean, into India in the south and Siberia in the north. In the thirteenth century, we were all Russians and Mongols—an unfathomable thought when you consider how far behind our culture theirs is today. Genghis Khan and his men hadn't had sharp bullets, powerful cannons, or huge battleships. But, thanks to their horses, the Mongols conquered half the world. No humans or weapons could stop them or the furious pace of their powerful steeds. They stormed across the land like an irrepressible, dust-filled wind from the steppes. They did not stop until they reached the ocean. When they reached the shore, they were forced to halt. There the horses reared up, whinnied, could not be compelled to continue, and the Mongols' strength, their one great advantage, became their weakness. They knew no other means of subjugating other nations beyond storming the barricades on horseback. They didn't build fleets of ships, couldn't sail or navigate, couldn't even swim, and without the horse, the Mongol was just an ordinary human being with skinny stick legs and an average intellect. The Mongol leaders used this rather unexceptional intellect to discuss the right of succession of Genghis Khan and the empire crumbled away quickly, as an empire will do when a powerful leader disappears. But they upheld the legacy of this great ruler. Mongol children sit on the back of a horse from the age of four, they ride like jockeys from the age of five, the horse is an extension of them, virtually fused with the Mongol. They are like centaurs; they do not have two legs with ordinary, thin human thighs, but, rather, four powerful, muscular legs, and the pride over the empire they once had is something Mongols still carry with them.

The three chiefs listened attentively, while Wilhelm—communicating in part through his recently acquired Mongolian, in part through sign language—explained our errand here in the country: that we were searching for wild horses, an extremely rare breed, and that we had heard rumors that the horses had been sighted in this region.

The eldest and most reliable of them nodded slowly, takhi, of course, takhi. Yes, he had seen the wild horses several times in his life, but always from a very great distance, running away. And that had been many years ago. Besides, hunting them was impossible, he continued, capturing them was impossible; they were too shy, their sense of smell too acute—he touched his nose—their hearing too good—he held one finger beside his ear.

Wolff tried his best to explain the objective of the expedition, the reason why we were here, that we'd come because of the horses. The chief gazed at us in amazement. We wanted to capture live animals; but what would we do with them? We tried explaining about our zoological gardens and reserves and then both he and the others laughed.

But even though the chief thought our project was ridiculous, they nodded with something akin to enthusiasm when we asked if they would consider offering their assistance. They presumably sensed that their reward could include both silver coins and colored wool ribbons.

From that night on, hunting parties from the three different groups were out on the steppes all the time. Sometimes they came to us to inform us of their progress, but usually reported nothing of interest.

Then one morning, shortly after rising, we received a visit by the eldest chief, who came riding into the camp. They'd found them, he said. The horses were to be found further south, a half day's journey away, not far from the river. There they had observed no less than three different herds.

Wilhelm and I glanced at one another. He concealed his reaction from the chief, but there was no mistaking the delight in his eyes.

"Can it be true?" I mused.

"We must see them for ourselves," he said.

We quickly filled two simple packs, mounted our horses, and rode toward the sun. Wolff moved quickly, almost aggressive in his impatience, while I did my best to keep up. Now it's happening, I kept thinking as we rode, now we are making history.

We rode the whole way without stopping. Wolff spurred his stallion onward, obsessed with arriving that very afternoon. He wanted to get there before the horses moved down to the river to drink, which would be our best chance to see them. We rode until hunger growled through our stomachs and our throats were as parched as the ground beneath our horses' galloping hooves. Wolff stopped from time to time so I could catch up with him. I could see how he was trying to contain his zeal.

"Just keep riding," I said. "I'm coming."

"I will wait for you, Misha," he said and handed me the canteen.

Finally, we arrived at the river that flowed like a recently paved street of silver through sparkling green grass. Far in the distance, we could glimpse the Altai Mountains—a dark blue wall against the bright sky. Wolff stopped by the riverbank, jumped off his horse, and started lifting down the packs.

"We'll make camp here tonight," he said, "then we can keep searching on foot."

I tried to help out but was exhausted from the long ride. He smiled at me and spread a blanket on the ground.

"Go ahead and rest. I'll unpack."

I lay dozing on the blanket while Wilhelm puttered around me. When he had finished, we let our stallions graze in peace. I was stiff and sore but managed, nonetheless, to climb to my feet.

We started walking south along the river scouting constantly for the horses through our binoculars. We both tried to be quiet, didn't talk, walking softly across the ground.

Suddenly I noticed a movement on the west side of the river straight ahead of us.

I stopped.

"Do you see something?" Wilhelm whispered.

"There."

I pointed.

"Just the wind blowing through the grass," he said.

"Maybe," I said.

We pressed the binoculars against our eyes, adjusting the focus in an effort to distinguish the faint nuances of the oat-colored grass, to discern whether anything stood out.

We crept closer cautiously, our binoculars at the ready.

"There is something," Wilhelm whispered.

And he was right. Something stood out against the grass, not so much because of the color, because the horses naturally blended in with their surroundings, but because of the shape—the soft curve of their backs, their waving tails, erect, short manes.

"It's them," I gasped.

Wolff said nothing, but grabbed my arm, stopped me, and pulled me behind a mound.

We had the wind in our faces so they couldn't smell us, and here, partly concealed, we could observe them without their noticing our presence.

I pressed the binoculars against my eyes as if I were trying to push out my eyeballs, while the herd slowly descended from a summit and walked toward the river to drink.

The harem included four mares, three one-year-old foals, a lead stallion, and four newborns, the latter brand new and fresh in the world. Happy to be alive, they jumped about on thin legs that were too long for their bodies and had protruding, knobby joints. Their ears were also too big, as if they'd grown faster than their heads; they moved almost like baby goats and neighed in equally frail, thin voices.

Now and then, a newborn would stretch toward a mare, suck milk from her teats, while the one-year-old foals and the adults bowed their heads toward the river, slurping as they quenched their thirst, standing like that for a long time, just drinking. I kept adjusting the focus of my binoculars, wanting to look at each of them, take note of their different characteristics, familiarize myself with them properly.

My legs kept carrying me away; I wanted to move closer, but Wolff squeezed my upper arm gently and restrained me.

Then they had drunk their fill. The horse I presumed to be the lead mare started moving back in the same direction from which they'd come. The others followed behind her, the foals in the middle. The adult horses took care of them.

Silently, the wild horses disappeared behind a hill leaving behind the river, the landscape, deserted now, as if they had never existed.

I turned toward Wolff and now he no longer held back his joy; his elation spread in fine lines from his eyes and his mouth cracked open into the largest smile I had ever seen.

"Were they real?" I almost shouted. "Say that they were real!"

The evening cold arrived quickly. We lit a fire and lay down as close to the flames as we dared, face to face.

"Can you believe we've found them," I said. "That they actually exist."

"I've never told you this, but I never really believed in the horses," he said.

"And you came along anyway?"

He smiled suddenly. "You were the one who convinced me."

"When? In my letters?"

"I must confess that, with time, it was more *you* than the horses that brought me to Petersburg. Your pen, your voice. All the details you described from your own life. Like the friendly conversations you have with people around you. I quickly understood that you see the good in everyone and manage to find beauty in everyday things—a plant pressing its way up through a crack in the ground or a light filtering down through the leaves on the trees. Yes, I became interested in the expedition. I thought that, regardless, it wouldn't be in vain, that even if we didn't find the horses, we would, without doubt, discover something else in this wasteland. But first and foremost, I became interested in *you*."

I laughed softly.

"Are you laughing at me, Misha?"

"No, not *at* you."

He chuckled.

"Are you cold?" he asked and now his tone was more serious.

"I'm not going to lie," I said slowly. "I wish I was cold, but tonight I am warm."

"Come close to me anyway," he said.

"Are you sure?"

"No." He swallowed. "But I am sure that we can't restrain ourselves any longer."

I lay my fur bedcovers beside his, covered us both with my blanket. He did the same with his.

There, in the cavern of the blankets, my longing was finally satisfied. For the first time in my life, I really became one with another person, my flesh became his, his hands mine, there was nowhere in the landscape of my body that he wasn't permitted to explore.

Afterward we lay on our backs side-by-side. There was such a multitude of stars above us that it was as if they *were* heaven itself, as if the darkness between them was but a lace fabric made of thin, black threads.

We lay like this, holding each other tightly, hearts and minds burning, I was burning up despite the cold night, I felt an affiliation with him, with the ground beneath us, with the world, a feeling more intense than anything else I had ever experienced, my own body was erased, I was him, I was the firmament, I was the earth I was lying on, everything was connected, even the horses, they actually existed on this earth and were a part of me. Everything stops here, I thought, everything begins and everything stops here.

EVA

I remember a winter when there was a lot of snow. Isa was maybe five or six. The snow stayed for days. We made snowmen and a fort in the garden. Every morning, I woke her gently and brought her over to the window. Is the snowman there today, too, she asked. Yes, I said. She was so little that I could still hold her in my arms. We planned what we would make out of the snow. Then I carried her out into the kitchen where I had lit the stove. A candle was burning on the table.

Now Isa is the one who has to wipe off the counter in the kitchen and make our beds in the morning. Now Isa is the one that lights the candle. I can't seem to change it. I can't seem to do anything.

Two weeks and nothing has improved. Louise has certainly long since set out for the North Pole. The North Pole and beyond, over to the other side, perhaps heading south again; perhaps she will keep going like that, around and around the earth without ever stopping.

It would have been better if she had never turned up in the first place, if she'd never been here.

. . .

We are almost out of candles. And we only light the stove for cooking. The soot from the smoke settles on the windows and walls. My clothes always smell like wood smoke.

And it rains. Man-made rain. All this weather was created in just sixty years. Starting in 1980, that was when things really took off. Sixty years of emissions and that was it. Well done.

Why did she leave us?

The human being is a really stupid animal—it's as simple as that. We are unable to think beyond next spring or the next birth. That's why everything's going to hell. That's nature's way—sooner or later, everything goes to hell.

And perhaps it has gone to hell before. Here or other places, on planets that resemble our own. Maybe this isn't the first time people have driven themselves and a load of other species over the edge of a cliff. Maybe it's the second, or third, or tenth time. Every time we work our way up to a certain level, then we do things sort of a little *too* well, build and destroy too much. And then everything changes. Or not everything, but *we* change.

Everything ends. And begins. We start from scratch again and again, as apes. We produce tools, live in caves, discover fire, invent the wheel, cars, computers, and finally vehicles that will never make it outside of our own solar system before we yet again have taken our own lives.

Maybe it is the law of nature, that our species is condemned to go to hell every single time it appears, here or on other planets. That a species can essentially be too smart for its own good.

I don't know if that's a frightening or a wonderful thought.

KARIN

Wool undershirt
Long johns
Fleece jacket
Fleece trousers
Wool socks
Thick wool socks
Wool sweater
Quilted trousers
Quilted jacket
Hat
Scarf
Mittens
Hiking boots
I get dressed and undressed. Dressed and undressed.
Winter coat

Nature has planned better for some species than for others.
The falling snow is fine and stinging and is quickly blown away. The horses eat it. They are no longer dependent on the water

sources. They migrate across greater distances now in the winter. Are more flexible, harder to find. And they eat the grass beneath the snow, digging with their hooves until they find yellow grass dried from the winter. They stick their muzzles down into the hollow, chew quickly. Their metabolism slows down. They're almost like bears. The body goes into hibernation even though they are out and about.

They look stronger now than in the summertime, not just because of the thick coat they have in the wintertime, which gives them an almost teddy bear–like appearance, but also because of the layers of fat they have stored. They have a lot to go on. I try to tell myself this, that they have a lot to go on, that they will survive the winter without any help from me.

Then, one afternoon in January, the wind picks up.

Jochi and I are sitting in front of the stove in the common room. The sound of the wind intensifies. It is evening. Pitch black outside. Mathias has gone to bed in his ger. Jochi and I are talking about work. Always about work. It's just as well. The horses need our attention. We haven't been to see them today; the wind is too strong, and they are too far away, have found a valley and watering hole several kilometers away from us.

How are they now? I have seen them in the cold before, how they huddle together. The foals are placed in the middle of the herd, sheltered by the larger bodies. But the solitary stallions walk alone; even now, they have nobody with whom to seek refuge. Will Hamburg be all right on his own?

The entrance door opens; the wind howls more loudly for a moment until the door closes again. I hear Mathias's footsteps on the porch. Then he enters the common room. He is covered with white snow, all bundled up. Shivering.

"Can I sleep here?" he asks, his teeth chattering.

I recognize him. He is the same boy who came to me in the night complaining about a nightmare. It started when he was four. He stood trembling beside my bed, his eyes as dark as the night, and his body drenched with sweat. Can I sleep in your bed, Karin?

I made room for him. He curled up against my body. What did you dream? I asked. But he didn't want to say anything, just wanted to sleep. Lay pressed up against me. Breathing deeply, his mouth open. I would lie awake. His breathing was so loud. The bed was too narrow for two people. At least when he was one of them. He tossed and turned constantly, his arms and legs sprawling in all directions. Even though his body was small, he occupied the whole bed.

The next night, he came in again. Now he wasn't crying as loudly but claimed firmly that he had had a "mare." I didn't ask about the dream. Just made room for him.

The third night, he didn't say anything about a dream, just stood there.

On the fourth night, I couldn't take anymore. When I was sure he was asleep, I snuck out of bed and lay down on the couch in the living room. The wool upholstery irritated my skin, the couch was too hard, and I only had a stuffy, synthetic blanket to have over me. Still, I fell asleep right away. Finally, I slept. The next morning, I told him that he had to stop waking me up. I created a reward system with star stickers on a paper plate that I hung on his wall. The prize for ten nights in his own bed was a farm Playmo he had wanted for a long time. He received it as soon as the ten days had passed and never came into my bedroom again at night.

"Sleep here?" I say to Mathias now. "Yes, I guess you can. . . . But the tent is actually just as safe. If it's safety you're thinking about. It's round. There's nothing the wind can catch hold of."

"Fine," Mathias says and turns halfway away. "Okay. I will be fine in the tent, for sure."

"Or you can sleep on the couch," Jochi says.

"Can I?" Mathias asks.

"Take the couch."

We feed the fire and feed the fire, but nothing helps. I am wearing a quilted jacket indoors, trying to work, but my fingers are stiff with cold. We end up sitting in front of the stove in the common room, all three of us. No matter how loudly we talk, the sound of the wind is louder. No jokes, no stories, or arguments can drown out the storm.

Finally, we stop talking. It's as if the sound of the wind has become a part of me. Like an intense case of tinnitus. We can hear how it labors, wearing and tearing at the roof and walls. Jochi is pale. Every time a hard gust of wind hits us, he makes a face.

"I don't trust buildings," he mumbles. "Wonder if I should move out into a ger."

But he stays with us.

For three days, we sit like this. For three nights, we sleep on the floor in front of the stove, on mattresses we have dragged in there from the bedrooms.

On the fourth day, the sound of the wind has finally changed. The rough bass is gone. Over the course of the day, the sound occupies less and less space; at dusk it disappears altogether.

Finally, we venture outdoors. Agi and a couple of his people are already working. Mathias hurries over to them and picks up a hammer with practiced hands.

"The ger tents are intact," I tell Jochi.

"You think he should have slept out there?" Jochi asks, and nods toward Mathias.

"No," I say. "It wasn't what I meant."

Jochi shrugs. I watch him, waiting for him to continue, but he says nothing more.

Wasn't he the one who'd said he didn't trust houses?

But even though the tents are undamaged, everything else has been blown away. The paddock fence is a mangled mess, resembling needlework left in the hands of a child. The horses' shed, which Mathias helped build, is nothing but kindling.

I walk over to the wreckage of the paddock.

"They should have stayed here," I say to Jochi. "We should have kept them here for the first winter instead of sending them out alone."

He could have said "I told you so," but he just shrugs, smiling impassively.

"But we didn't," he says.

I don't move. I actually just want to get into the car and drive it as fast as I can through the thin, white snow cover. Find them, make sure they are okay.

"Tomorrow," Jochi says. "We'll head out tomorrow at first light."

I can't sleep. The temperature drops to forty below. I have all my clothes on, but am still freezing; can't sleep, but not because I'm cold. Not because I'm afraid of nightmares. It's the horses I am thinking about.

They need sixteen liters of water a day. They must eat an enormous amount of snow to consume that much liquid. The thirst is more dangerous than hunger. They have no liquid reserves to draw from. And the wolves are just as hungry as all the other winter animals. A foal that is unable to keep up with the herd in the snow will fall behind. Then a wolf will appear in a flash with its powerful jaws.

Maybe Hustai isn't the right place for the horses after all. Maybe they aren't really designed for this natural environment.

Maybe they should have just stayed in Thorenc, where they were safe. Frederic, the veterinarian, sends a report every single week that the twelve horses are doing well. The three pregnant mares are thriving. In the spring, there will be fifteen in the herd. Here, I have already lost one of mine and, now, after the storm, perhaps more.

CHAPTER 10

A DREADFUL OUTCOME

The first thing I did the next morning, still not fully awake but giddy with sleep and happiness, was to reach for the body that had been lying beside me. But Wilhelm was already packing.

"Come back to bed," I said.

"We must bring the nomads with us," he said without looking at me. "We must start the hunt immediately."

His tone of voice was so businesslike that I caught myself wondering whether the events of the night before had been a dream.

I climbed out of bed and reached for him with one hand, wanting to hold him close to me, confirm the fantastic night, confirm that which was us, but he was already busy pouring water over the fire, which sizzled grudgingly.

Then he turned to face me. "We must get to work, Mikhail," he said. "We must think about the horses."

There was a finality to his expression and manner of speaking, but I was too emboldened by the night before to relent.

"I will never forget yesterday," I said.

At first, he didn't reply. He squatted down and stirred the ashes for a while, before finally turning to face me.

"'One can be the master of what one does, but never of what one feels,'" he said.

"Flaubert?"

He nodded. "There are rules," he said softly. "There are unwritten rules for friendship. Sometimes something . . . sordid can develop in a friendship all the same. If one is not the master of one's feelings, one must at least be the master of what one does."

"No," I said.

I squatted down beside him, took his chin in my hand, and forced him to look at me.

"'Your heart is an inexhaustible spring. You let me drink deep, it floods me, penetrates me, I drown,'" I said.

He twisted out of my grasp.

"Maybe Flaubert did the right thing in comparing feelings to water," Wilhelm said and dragged a stick forcefully through the glowing embers such that the sparks flew up into the air. "Sordidness is never there in the beginning, but it insinuates itself, the way drops of water find their way through rotting boards. No matter how solidly a building is constructed, the water will always find a way in the end, squeeze its way through, at first in tiny, almost invisible drops, then larger and larger until water is dripping everywhere, until the floor and walls slowly break down, disintegrate, and collapse."

"Wilhelm," I said. "My dear friend . . ."

"My father died when I was ten, your father when you were even younger. Perhaps that is why we have never learned . . ."

"You must stop. I don't want to hear any more of this."

I leaned forward, put my arms around him, and could feel how he resisted me.

"Please," I said. "No more talk of rules. Not here, not now."

His body softened. He turned his face toward mine.

"Not here?" he said slowly.

"Not here and not now," I said.

Our faces were now almost touching. Finally, he nodded slowly, confirming my words, our agreement. "Not here, not in Mongolia."

A wave of relief washed through my body. I leaned forward quickly and gave him a kiss on his whiskered chin.

"And now we are going to capture our horses," I said. "By tomorrow."

He stood up and put his arms around me.

"Tomorrow we will capture them," he murmured into my ear as we embraced.

After yet another night spent with Wilhelm, my body felt light and refreshed. We had only slept a few hours, but the sleep in Wilhelm's arms was warm, deep, and fortifying.

The three chiefs and five of their best men accompanied us. In addition to the ten of us and the horses we were riding, we had brought four more horses. The wild horses were so fast that we expected we would need fresh, rested replacements for our own horses during the hunt.

We moved slowly along the river as the huge light-red disc that was the sun appeared in the eastern vault of the sky. Immediately, the eldest chief raised a hand and pointed. He spoke with soft detachment in Mongolian and then he picked up the pace. I tried in vain to discover what he had pointed at, but nothing of what I could see through my binoculars gave me an answer. I was also soon fully occupied with the task of keeping up with the others.

It is said of my father that he was a fantastic horseman. Every time I meet people who have known him, they say the same thing—your father was a wonderful person and, especially, a fantastic equestrian. He rode like a god since childhood, as if he were born on the back of a horse, as if he were Mongol, Genghis Khan himself. I have been told this so many times that I catch myself feeling irritated each time another person showers me with this type of praise. I know that he was a brilliant horseman; it goes without saying, considering his post. However, I have not been endowed with the same talent and, in meeting with the Mongols, descendants of Genghis Khan, my inadequacy was impossible to hide.

They rode ahead without me, all of them. Nobody seemed to have noticed that I fell behind; they were far too intent on reaching what I presumed had to be a herd of wild horses.

I clung to the reins, bouncing up and down in the saddle, advancing at a far from suitable pace. I couldn't connect with the horse's rhythm. My body tightened into a knot of fear. The horse galloped as fast as he could after the rest of the party, but we never reached the others, only the cloud of dust swirling in their wake. I could feel the sandy soil settling on my skin and in my hair, how it irritated my nose with an itchiness so intense that I almost sneezed.

On that day, we had a headwind, so both our scent and the noise we made were carried away from the wild horses, but still, when I was finally able to see the horses with my bare eyes, they were already fleeing.

They ran with all their might, small, compact, and fast. The Mongols followed in hot pursuit, urging their large, powerful stallions to canter at a furious pace.

Behind all the others, I bounced along.

The Mongols were kings on their horses. With one hand, they held the reins loosely, with the other, each held an *urga*, a long rod with a noose on the end that they used to capture wild horses. I saw how the five Mongol riders closed in on the takhis and tried to surround them. Not even Wilhelm was able to keep up any longer; he, too, fell behind, forming a kind of rear guard with me (although I couldn't, strictly speaking, be considered a member of the guard at all).

I heard him call out something to the chief but was unable to make out his words. I saw him waving his arms, but the Mongols paid him no heed.

They approached the horses, surrounding one of the year-old foals. The chief held out his *urga* trying to snare him but failed; the foal was too quick, too agile, slipping away and joining the herd.

Again, I saw the Mongol try. Again, he came close. Again, he failed.

Wilhelm called out to them. He must have seen something I hadn't.

"No stop, please, stop!"

The speed of our pursuit, even my own, accelerated and accelerated; the wild horses bolted away, but the Mongols were right on their heels. Now they must certainly succeed, I thought; on the third try they must succeed.

But then a sharp, strange sound rang out, a sound that found its way into the stomach, into the heart.

"No," Wilhelm cried. "No!"

I saw the wild horses running away in terror, but the Mongols stopped. Wilhelm rode at a frenzied gallop toward them, pulling up short when he reached them. They were all standing beside something on the ground.

I dug my heels into the flanks of my horse and, for once, I managed to find the rhythm as I rode. When at last I reached them, they had gathered in a circle, everyone except the youngest chief. He was one of those who had taken the lead; now he stood outside the circle, said something to the eldest submissively, his words fading away. The eldest suddenly shouted back at him and the youngest quickly put away a firearm.

The circle opened to admit me. Lying on the ground in the fresh spring grass was the one-year-old foal they had been trying to capture. It was no longer moving. A red pool was forming beneath the wheat-colored body, spreading and expanding in the sand-colored grass.

KARIN

I turn around, look behind me. The car leaves behind a solitary trail amidst all the whiteness. The wind blows and it disappears. White, white, white; the sky is also white, grayish-white, I can barely see where the ground ends and the sky begins. I grow dizzy with vertigo. I turn around. Look at the car instead. The interior. Jochi's hands on the wheel. It helps. He drives slowly, with concentration. The motor is making more noise than usual. The car struggles through the snow, even though it is supposed to be designed for such conditions. We have two cans of gasoline, just in case. We can drive for many, many miles. We can get lost, if we want. And the flatbed is full of hay. We will stay out here until we find them.

The hours pass. We see no signs of life, nothing but endless whiteness. Jochi is silent.

I suggest lunch. He nods and turns off the motor. We have soup in a thermos and eat in the car. The soup warms my stomach. Steam rises out of the cups.

Jochi slurps as he drinks.

"Excuse me," he says.

I thought he knew that I'm not the type who cares about things like slurping.

"Do you think this is unnecessary?" I ask after a while.

"Why do you ask?"

"You're quiet," I say.

"So are you."

"Yes . . ."

"Of course, I don't think this is unnecessary," he says, then. Suddenly his voice grows louder. "Why do you think I'm here? Do you think this is just a job for me? Do you think I've chosen to live out here, far away from everyone I know, from the university, for the fun of it. Do you think you're the only one who cares about this project?"

He speaks so loudly and quickly that the steam from the soup dances in the air.

"No," I say. "Of course, I don't think that."

"Do you think I'm here for other reasons?" he asks.

"What reasons would that be?" I ask.

"Exactly," he says. "What reasons would that be?"

I drink the rest of my soup.

"Do you mind if I smoke?"

"It makes no difference to me," he said.

The day passes without our finding them. A couple of times, we get stuck, have to get out of the car and dig our way out. My toes grow so cold that I have almost no feeling in them. The horses are outside all day long. But they are made for this, I try saying to myself. Their legs are made for this; they are made of tendons, bones, and ligaments. *Should* be made for this. This is where they come from, after all.

But, actually, they come from everywhere.

Once they were everywhere.

The first time I saw a wild horse as an adult, it was in a cave painting. I was a nanny for a French family who were on holiday near Labastide in 1956. While the children were having their afternoon nap, I had an hour off. The family had talked about the cave paintings, but nobody had wanted to accompany me to the cave.

In the end, I went alone.

A small sign on a narrow dirt road was the only thing that told me that I was in the right place.

I had to climb a ladder to reach the entrance to the cave. The worst of the afternoon heat had set in. I saw nobody else. Nobody else could bear to walk in this heat.

The path was narrow and full of loose stones. Some slid away as I stepped on them. In several places, a hemp rope was attached to the rock as a railing, but it had been worn thin by the wind and weather.

I had brought two bottles of water in my knapsack. I bent over. Poured half of one over my head, threw my hair back. The lukewarm water trickled down my back.

I reached the cave and was looking forward to the shady interior thinking that caves are always cool, but it was disappointingly hot.

It took time for my eyes to adjust to the darkness. The cave was large and dim. It continued inward and I couldn't see the end of it.

I started walking. My footsteps created echoes against the walls. The light from outdoors grew suddenly dimmer when I discovered something that caused me to squint. Brownish-red lines like dried blood on the gray stone walls. I walked closer.

On the walls were drawings of people hunting. All of them were of people hunting.

And the horses they were riding were primitive horses. Recognizable as a unique species and different from all others. The short, bristly mane. The broad bridge of the nose. The compact, powerful body. Impossible to tame.

I stood looking at the paintings for a long time. Were these the horses?

I stared at the running horses.

Yes, they had to be. The same horses I had fed. The same horses who had been my friends at Carin Hall.

I couldn't bring myself to leave. Couldn't stay either.

I remember I wanted to cry. And maybe I did cry.

I cried.

My tummy, my chest convulsed in spasms, followed by sounds in a pitch higher than my own voice—sounds I could not suppress, which increased in intensity and echoed off the walls of the cave.

Then I heard footsteps. Somebody entered, a shadow suddenly blocking the light. I tried to breathe normally, get control over my crying.

I heard the click of a flashlight being switched on and then a cone of light slid across the walls. A man came around the bend.

"Hello?"

The light blinded me; he shined it on me for a few seconds. Just long enough to see me, to see my red eyes, and my cheeks, which were still wet, and then he moved it away.

He was older than me, his hair thinning, and he wore a tweed jacket and heavyweight trousers. His forehead was sweaty from the walk up to the cave.

He put his hand in his pocket and pulled out a handkerchief.

"Here you are, mademoiselle," he said in broken French.

"Thanks."

I wiped my face with it, drying my tears.

"A powerful impression," he said.

"Yes?"

For a moment I thought he was referring to me, that I had made an impression. But then he nodded toward the paintings.

"Imagine that people could paint like that, even 10,000 years ago."

I didn't reply.

"We are, in truth, a unique species," he continued.

"I'm not crying because the images are beautiful," I said and was surprised by the conviction of my own voice.

"Then why?"

"Because I'm angry."

"Why is mademoiselle angry? Who are you angry with?"

"I'm angry with Hermann Goering."

"The Marshal of the Realm?"

"Yes. I am angry with Hermann Goering—marshal of the realm, hunter, and animal enthusiast."

The man said nothing but nodded in encouragement, wanting me to tell him more.

"He had horses like this," I said, "during the war. He collected animals on his own reserve. Did you know that?"

"Yes. Yes, I knew that."

I had never before met anyone who knew about Hermann Goering's horses.

"But are you angry because of the animals?" the man asked. "He worked to preserve the species. It is one of the few good things one can say about Hitler and his men, their engagement in species in danger of extinction."

"I know it," I said, and suddenly didn't like how he was lecturing me. "I know all that."

"Are you angry with all Nazis? You're not alone there."

"No. That's not why, either. I am angry because my mother worked for Hermann Goering."

We walked down from the cave together, the man and I, and continued our conversation. He told me that he worked with wild horses in the Prague zoo. That he loved his work but was deeply concerned about the fate of the species.

We talked until it was time for me to return to the children. And when the evening came and they were in bed, he asked me to go for a walk with him.

Five days later, I quit my job as a nanny and traveled away with the man—behind the iron curtain, to food lines, to surveillance, to him, to the horses.

The year 1956 was the worst year for the species; only forty-one horses existed in the whole world. But it was a good year for me. I started my veterinarian studies, spending my days with books, and visiting the horses in the zoo every single evening. I was content, almost happy. But as the years passed, it became clear that the man was not the reason for this. He loved the horses, but was happy to keep them fenced in—in captivity. When I talked about how I wished I could see them running through open country becoming wild again, he said it would be impossible.

My passion for the takhis did not diminish, but my passion for him fizzled out. Sleeping with him every single night and waking up beside him every single morning was not for me. I found him attractive from a distance, but close up, it was as if his features were too rough. I found him wise to begin with but, after a while, I knew how he thought and what he would say so well that he was unable to surprise me. I didn't understand what he constantly wanted from me. Why he always wanted to talk about things big and small. Why he always demanded that we went to bed at the same time even if we weren't going to make love. Why it seemed to be a matter of life or death that we ate all our meals together. He liked telling me things more than he liked to listen. But when I told him that I wanted to have my own career, he understood that. And when I asked him to stop giving me lectures, he changed his behavior. When I said I didn't want to have children, that I would never want to have children, he respected my decision.

Still, it wasn't enough. We loved the same things, but I didn't love him.

I lived in Prague until 1959, until the first international symposium on the Przewalsky horse. There I met professionals from all over Europe. I discussed my ideas with them. Several of them thought as I did— that the species should be rebuilt, that one day it would perhaps even be possible for the horses to live in the wild. Without saying anything to the man, I made a decision.

On the last night, I made him dinner. Then we slept together. It was probably ordinary intercourse on his part. He was older than me, always expressed joy over my youthful body. Described me as voluptuous and firm. On this final evening, I managed to avoid becoming irritated with him. *Last time*, I thought continuously, *the last time*. And I didn't want to ruin things by asking him to use contraception. So, I let him finish.

It wasn't until the next morning that I regretted it. And when I sat in the taxi at the crack of dawn, long before he awoke, with my suitcase beside me, I was certain that I could feel the impregnation take place. A tiny twinge inside me when one of the many millions reached its destination, merged with the egg, and started the division of cells that would one day be Mathias.

EVA

I crossed the yard carrying the pail in one hand. The milk sloshed against the plastic. The cows had provided generously today. Apple and Micro were thriving, but I knew it was only because I gave them lots of hay, and that if I kept this up, the barn would be empty long before the grass began sprouting again.

I had made it all the way to the back door and was about to open it when a voice stopped me.

"Eva?"

I turned around.

It was as if she'd shrunk. Her face was pale, her lips dry. The color of her skin was almost green against a yellow rain jacket I couldn't remember having seen before.

I stood there, at first unable to reply, just mumbled *hi*.

She approached me. Her old backpack was on her back. It looked full, sort of bulging, and a sleeping bag was secured beneath the flap on top. The rain jacket was far too large for her and hid her belly.

Where have you been, I wanted to ask, why didn't you come back before now, after almost two weeks and why, why did you leave us?

I've already forgotten you, I forgot about you a long time ago. I don't wonder about where you are, when I wake up and when I go to bed, what you're doing, if you are safe, who you are with, if the child you are carrying is well, and why you left, why you left us.

"Hi," she said.

I didn't answer. The handle on the pail dug into my hand—sweaty, hard plastic.

"So much milk," she said.

"Yes," I said. "There was a lot today."

"I've missed having milk for breakfast," she said.

"You just left." The words sounded like a slap in the quiet morning air.

Her face was motionless. She took a step toward me and then another.

"I've come back, now," she said quietly.

"I see that," I said.

"Is Isa up?"

"People don't do things like that. Don't just take off."

She made a face. "I'm not very good at this . . ."

"This? And what is this?"

"I'm sorry."

Her face sort of cracked before my eyes; she pinched her mouth, her cheeks trembled, she looked young and at the same time very old, the lines from her nose to the corners of her mouth were sharp creases, even though she wasn't smiling, dark circles under her eyes. Her hair was greasy, a few pine needles were entangled in it, and she smelled of sweat, dirt, the forest.

"You've been sleeping outdoors," I said.

She shrugged. "I found a sleeping bag."

"Have you been sleeping in the woods?"

I put down the milk pail, tried to understand. Had she been here all along, right nearby, between the spruces, during the daytime wandering between the heavy trees, at night sleeping on the mossy ground, just a few hundred meters away from us, alone?

"I sleep wherever," Louise said. "I've always slept wherever. I'm also a light sleeper."

"But now you need a bed again," I said.

"That's not why I've come back."

She bent over slightly, as if the backpack were heavy, adjusted the straps. One of them had been rubbing against her collarbone; the skin was red and chafed.

"We were frightened," I said.

"I know," she said. "It wasn't my intention."

"But you knew we would be frightened."

"Yes. Sorry. I hadn't planned on coming back."

"You think that makes it better?"

"I didn't mean it like that."

She stared at the milk in the pail. She was thinner; her round cheeks were almost gone.

"So much milk," she said again.

"Yes," I said. "Yes, they are well fed. Are you hungry?"

She nodded.

"Very," she said, and her voice shook.

The rage drained out of me. I gave her the pail. She drank directly from it. For a moment, the only sound was that of her swallowing heavily.

We went inside. Isa was up, was standing in the kitchen wearing only a T-shirt. It was one of my hand-me-downs, just barely covering her underpants. Her long, skinny legs still had a summer tan. She turned when we came in, forgot to be embarrassed, forgot to ask questions, just walked straight over to Louise, and put her arms around her.

"Louise!"

"Hi, Isa, hi."

Isa chattered all day long. She was so pleased, was herself again, on her face the same expression she'd had for as long as I can remember, the way she raised her eyebrows when something surprised her, the irrepressible laughter. She was almost grown up, Isa, but simultaneously the same as she had always been, the child inside her play-fighting all the time for a seat at the table with the adults.

She dominated the conversation during the evening meal as well, bubbling over. But then she started yawning again and again; her eyes became shiny, narrower, even though she kept trying to hold them wide open, as if forcing herself awake. This is exactly how she has always yawned, exactly how she has always looked when she is tired.

"Go to bed, Isa."

I could see her forming a sentence that started with *but*, until her mouth opened wide with yet another yawn.

"Okay, then."

She filled a glass from the bucket of well water, took it with her, and went into the bathroom. I could picture her, how she lifted the toothbrush out of the glass and poured water on it, turned the hourglass upside down, the one I had bought for her when she was a child, and brushed her teeth the way I had taught her, for exactly two minutes, dividing the time between the teeth on top and on bottom until all the sand in the hourglass had run down.

"Good night," Isa said to us from the hallway before disappearing into her room.

Then it was quiet, both in the house and between Louise and me.

She got up and went into her room but came back quickly holding something in her hands.

She lay a stack of papers covered with handwriting in front of me on the table. The paper was lined. It looked as if it had been torn out of a notebook, maybe one of Isa's, but the handwriting took no notice of lines or margins; the pages were full of words.

"I didn't have enough paper. It's all for you," she said.

The ink had been smeared a bit in some places, but it was still possible to read what she had written.

"When I started, I thought that since I couldn't bring myself to tell you, then I could try to write it. I thought that I was just writing to myself. But after a while, I understood that I was also writing to you."

I scanned the pages. I registered a few words here and there.

"Read it," Louise said, "before I change my mind."

LOUISE

We lived in a house by a canal. We had a boat but there was no water in the canal. Daddy said that when the rain came, we would sail away. If only the rain would come, we would travel away from here to the ocean and from there, head north.

We had huge containers of water, blue on the outside, white on the inside. Water was the most precious thing we owned. We didn't consume any more than we absolutely had to. It was a game every day, to measure it out in precise amounts for each of us.

With every passing day, there was a little less in the containers; with every passing day, they reduced the amount of water they took for themselves. But never for me.

There were no other people there. Just me, Daddy, and a woman named Marguerite. They were lovers, the two of them, but I didn't think about who he was for her, just who she was for me, that she was a lap to sit on, a high voice that sang to me, that she was something of what I had been missing since Mommy disappeared.

Mommy always carried water with her, a bottle in her bag; she always made sure to have enough both for me and for August, my little brother.

It was as if the water disappeared with her, with them.

But it really disappeared long before that. The city we lived in was located by the ocean but, still, it is the feeling of sand on my tongue that I remember, the beach that crept slowly and steadily inland, into the houses. I remember how it crunched between my teeth. Everything got so dry; the heat caused the humidity to evaporate. In the end, it was as if the sun moved into the city, as if everything were just sun and sand.

I remember the fire. That we ran. Then I don't remember anything else, not until we met Marguerite.

I liked the house by the canal. I liked the boat that was on land. I liked that we were together all the time—Daddy, Marguerite, and I. But he said we had to leave; that as soon as the rain came, we would leave.

Afterward, I've thought about how he must have known the rain wouldn't come, that we would never leave the house, that we were stuck there beside the dried-up canal because, if we started walking, we wouldn't find water, and we wouldn't manage to carry as much as we needed. That was why it was better to stay put. I think that was his thinking.

Or maybe it was just a game. He often played games; he was the kind of father who played. There are many fathers who never play. I remember that it was my favorite thing, playing games with him.

I have thought so many times about what happened during the weeks we spent waiting, about why we never started walking, why we never tried to build something, a vehicle on wheels, perhaps, so we could take our water with us. Perhaps they really believed that it would start raining.

Or maybe they knew we were already lost and wanted to make our final days as nice as possible.

Or maybe their thirst made it impossible for them to think clearly, made them irrational, deprived them of the ability to find solutions, or, even worse, gave them delusions, hallucinations, led them into a reality that was no longer real, which was just Daddy's game.

I don't think so. I think they just wanted to make the last period as nice as possible.

And then the day came when it was too late. The containers were almost empty; just a little water remained, sloshing in the very bottom of one of them.

I remember that Daddy poured it out into bottles, that I asked what he was doing, that he wouldn't answer.

Then he packed the bottles into a knapsack along with two packages of dry crackers, the last we had. He put the knapsack on my back.

It's heavy, I said. Far too heavy.

He said it would be fine. He said I had to go find help, that he and Marguerite would wait here, and I must go out and find someone who could help us.

Then he accompanied me to the road. He said that I should walk north. If I lost my way, I should look at the sun. Think about the sun as the south, that I should turn away from it and walk in the opposite direction, always away from the sun. But the sun migrated too, so it wasn't so easy. In the morning, it should shine on my right cheek, he said, in the evening, on my left. And in the middle of the day, it should burn into my back.

Can you remember that? he asked.

My right cheek in the morning, my back all day long, my left cheek in the evening, I said.

Good, he said, clever girl, Lou. You can do this.

But why can't you come along, I asked.

Because we don't have enough water, he said.

But we can share, I said.

Because I sweat like a pig, he said, and will drink up all the water before you can say *moules-frites* with catsup.

I like *moules-frites* with catsup, I said.

I know, he said.

But why can't you go instead, I asked, or Marguerite.

Because you're small and light and need less water than we do, he said; that's why it's best if you are the one who goes looking for help.

Oh, yes, I said.

But that wasn't why. It was because he hoped that maybe there was a chance that someone would find me or I would find someone, because it was his last chance to save me.

He sent me away the way parents have sent away their children through the ages. There was a name for it before, *anchor baby*; they sent one of the children out first in hopes that the child could save them all but, most of all, in hopes that the child would be saved.

I left and I didn't cry because I imagined that I would just walk for a little while, and that he had made up a game for me. He said that a gnome was hiding behind every single lamp post along the road. They were shy, terribly shy, and hid every time human beings appeared. But if I were quick enough, if I hurried toward the lamp posts, running quietly toward them, I might catch sight of a gnome after all. And if I didn't manage it, all I had to do was try again at the next lamp post.

I'm not angry because he tricked me. He was just trying to save me.

He never said what I should do if I found help and I didn't ask.

I don't know how long I walked. I think it was just for one day, can't remember sleeping, I just remember the road and the gnomes, who I thought I caught sight of all the time but never managed to see properly, just like he'd said. They wore hats the same color as the dried grass. It wasn't strange, then, that it was difficult to get a good look at them. And I remember that not a single car passed, not a single one, and that I began to understand that this business of finding help wouldn't be as simple as I'd thought.

I drank the water. One bottle a day, Daddy had said. I drank two, he wasn't there, couldn't see me, couldn't be angry, so it didn't matter if I drank more. Besides, the knapsack was heavy, awfully heavy, and the more I drank the lighter it would be, I thought.

When the sun had wandered away from my right cheek, across my back, and was headed toward my left, a car finally came. It wasn't just the first car that day—it might have been the first car to pass in many days, I later thought. I was lucky, incredibly lucky, but I didn't know it at the time. When I was older, I taught myself to appreciate luck. I know that I've had a lot of it in spite of everything, that it's because of luck that I'm still alive, that I've met people who have seen *me* instead of just seeing themselves.

The car was moving fast. I raised my hand and waved, but it gave no sign of stopping, so I stood in the middle of the road. The brakes squealed.

A man got out. He yelled at me, said that he could have killed me, asked what I was doing out there all alone.

I said I needed help. I told him about Daddy and Marguerite, that they had no water, that they were at home in the house by the canal.

A woman also got out of the car. She asked the man what he was doing; she didn't look at me.

We must take her with us, the man said, and pointed at me.

The woman refused. They didn't have room, they didn't have food, they didn't have water.

I said I had my own water, my own crackers, that they didn't have to worry about me, and that they needn't take me with them, but they had to come with me to help Daddy and Marguerite.

The woman still didn't look at me.

We must take her with us, the man said.

No, I said.

No, the woman said.

She's going to die, the man said.

No, it's Daddy and Marguerite who are going to die, I said.

Finally, the woman looked at me.

Often that's all it takes. If you just look at a person properly, really look, you won't be able to stop yourself from helping them.

This is what she saw: a skinny, seven-year-old girl with a knapsack on her back that was far too big for her, with tangled hair, and clothes that hadn't been washed in weeks, with streaks of grime on her face, alone on a road in a landscape where nothing wanted to grow any longer.

Little one, she said, dear little one, and her lips were quivering.

Yes, I said, but we must help Daddy now.

They let me get into the car. They had two children of their own, a boy and a girl, both older than me. I got to sit by the window. The girl complained about how cramped it was in the middle; the woman told her to be quiet.

The car was cool. It had to be newer than any car I'd ever seen before because everything worked, even the air conditioning.

It's that way, I said and pointed behind me toward the sun. Daddy and Marguerite are back there.

The woman and the man exchanged glances, then she nodded. We'll see what we can do, and she turned the car around.

From the car, everything looked different. Everywhere it was the same. I told them about the canal; maybe they knew where the canal was. I told them about the road leading to the house, that it was narrow and that there were big trees growing along the roadside.

It's there, I said, no, there.

How far did you walk? the man asked.

Far, I said, I think it was far.

We kept driving, tried several of the roads I pointed at but never found the right one.

Finally, after a lot of time had passed, the man turned around to face me.

We'll search more in the morning, he said, when it gets light. Now, we must find a place to sleep.

Then the woman turned the car around.

I wanted to object, but I was so tired. I was just so tired. Besides, I trusted them.

Later, the woman, who wanted me to call her Mommy, said they regretted that they hadn't searched more, tried harder, but that they didn't even know if my father and Marguerite were real or just something I'd made up, that it got dark, that it was impossible to search anymore then. Besides, I was so lost, she used that word *lost*, but I was never able to identify with that. I never felt lost; I knew exactly what I was doing.

We drove for a while. I kept looking out the window. Everything was the same, but maybe I'd overlooked something, maybe I would catch sight of the road down to the house by the canal, after all, because maybe it was a little further down the road, maybe I hadn't walked as far as I thought.

Suddenly the car slowed down. Ahead of us was a roadblock.

Already, the woman said. I didn't think we would run into any until we got further north.

They must have moved it, the man said.

We drove closer, the car crawling down the road.

There's nobody there, the woman said.

I peered out the window, saw a shed. On a table lay a rifle.

There he is, the boy said.

A soldier was on his way up out of the ditch, struggling to do up his fly.

He was just peeing, I said.

Drive, the man said.

But don't we have to wait, the woman asked.

Just drive, he said. Drive!

She stomped on the accelerator. We flew past the shed, the soldier grabbed the rifle and ran after us, but the car was faster.

The boy and the girl laughed loudly—we can do it, we can do it, come on, Mom!

The solider never lifted the rifle to his shoulder. He merely gave us the finger and turned around.

Then we drove around a bend and couldn't see him anymore.

We got through, the man said.

Through what, I asked.

The first border, the man said. I didn't think we would manage it.

He and the woman looked at one another and smiled.

It wasn't until later that they explained to me that we couldn't go back, that we would never be able to get through the border checkpoint again, that we'd had this one chance because the soldier had to pee.

I remember that I objected, that I howled and screamed, that I just wanted my daddy. But it didn't help.

I don't know how long we kept driving, but one day the car stopped, the battery ran out of power, and we couldn't find a charging point anywhere. So, we had to walk. The weather had grown colder, autumn; one day it even rained. It rained but the drops falling from the sky didn't make me happy.

The woman who wanted me to call her Mommy said that I mustn't think about Daddy and Marguerite, but I was unable to think about anything else. Every single raindrop reminded me of them, of how they should have been here and felt the water too.

The drops were cold, made me shiver. I didn't like the rain.

We reached a refugee camp in northern Germany where we were given an old tent. There was ice-cold water but not much food. The camp was guarded by armed soldiers. I froze the entire winter. I remember that I was cold and hungry, that the girl and boy bickered with each other, but were nice to me. The woman always wanted me to sit on her lap. She wanted to comb my hair; I let her do it. She was kind. I liked her, but I never managed to call her Mommy.

During the day, she homeschooled us—taught me reading, writing, arithmetic. There were a few books in the camp. I read them again and again.

I remember the woman and man arguing; she wanted to leave, he wanted to stay. In the evenings, when they thought we were sleeping, they whispered to one another, hissing louder and louder.

We can't live like this, the woman said.

At least there's food here, the man said.

Not enough, she said, and for how long? Everything's falling apart, you see that certainly.

We're safe here, the man said, that's the most important thing.

I don't trust them, the woman said. We don't know what they're planning to do with us.

All winter long they argued. When spring came, she finally got her way.

We set out, migrating even further north, hitched a ride on a boat from Denmark, reached Kristiansand in Norway.

There we were put in yet another camp. A good camp—an old hotel—we were given two rooms. The adults stopped arguing. We could go wherever we wanted.

I started attending a proper school, learned Norwegian. The teachers praised me, said I was a quick learner. I learned to eat Norwegian food, too. Grains for every meal. Oatmeal for breakfast, bread for lunch, and pizza for dinner.

But everything got worse there, too, so gradually, so slowly that we didn't notice it from one day to the next, but when we thought back from time to time, remembered how it had been a year ago, two years ago, we understood that everything was changing. The fruit drink served with meals was suddenly only available on Saturdays, the sugar for our oatmeal disappeared, the bread became dry, the number of slices we were allotted each day was steadily reduced, we were given only one meatball each, and finally none. And the nice ladies who had worked at the camp were gradually replaced by soldiers.

We could still go wherever we wanted, and we saw that outside the camp everything was different also. The stores closed and outside those that were still open, people stood in lines; all day long they stood in lines, and they had started growing vegetables in their gardens. Everywhere people were trying to cultivate food; in the spring they fertilized the blossoms with pollen using feathers or paintbrushes. And they fought more and more often, in the lines, on the streets, everywhere.

And the weather . . . people were always talking about the weather. The rain would sometimes pour down hard and incessantly for months. The rivers flooded, washing away houses. Large land areas were under water; the wheat rotted in the fields. Then there were summers without a single raindrop. The fruit dried up on the trees, the grass turned yellow in the pastures, and the animals had to be slaughtered because there was no more hay to be found. I remember the snow; a winter the snowfall was so heavy that the whole world came to a halt. We huddled under blankets together in the hotel lounge in front of a fireplace that barely generated heat while we waited for the power to come back on.

The adults started arguing again. The woman wanted to leave, she wanted to move on, she wanted to find a place they could call their own. The man wanted the same thing, but he said they had to wait. They talked about permanent residency, about legal domicile, about forms and passports. They didn't appear to notice that everything was falling apart, that, not even here, in Norway, would they find anything that could be called a home.

We lived there for five years. My first childhood was with Mommy and Daddy and my little brother in the city that disappeared and, after that, with Daddy and Marguerite. These years at the hotel were my second childhood. I tried to think about the first as little as possible. It was simpler that way. My second childhood was, after all, not so bad. I got to attend school. I had two adults looking after me and two older siblings who also took care of me sometimes.

But then everything changed very quickly. One morning, we were awakened and told to pack our things. Soldiers stood at the exits making sure nobody escaped.

Five big buses drove up; we were ordered inside them.

There was one toilet on board. We were never allowed to leave the bus. Finally, the toilet clogged up. I remember how it stank, how the stench assaulted the senses. I also remember that everywhere along the road I saw wanderers—people starving, people who were thirsty.

They drove us all the way back, back to France.

When we were let off the bus, when I placed my feet on French soil again, I thought that now . . . now I will become an adult.

I was thirteen years old. I was tall for my age, almost fully developed. As my body matured, the idea matured in me that I could manage by myself, that the time had come, that I no longer wanted to burden the family that wasn't my own.

We lived on the road. The man and woman talked all the time about finding a place that was ours, about going north again, trying

Norway again, or perhaps Sweden, even though these countries were not good places to live anymore.

Then the woman fell ill. Pneumonia. We didn't know whether she would survive; there was no medicine. They crowded around her, father and children—the two children who called her Mommy.

We had sought refuge in an abandoned apartment in a deserted city. I remember standing in the doorway looking at them, the woman in bed and her loved ones. I remember that the children held her hands as her coughing ravaged her sick body, that they kept a bedside vigil.

They were a proper family; they were how a family should be. I had endless appreciation for them, but they weren't mine. It didn't feel right for me to join them at her bedside.

Besides, I knew I wanted something different from what they wanted, that sooner or later I would have to leave them. I had, perhaps, planned to wait, but I saw that this was the right moment—that they didn't need me, that they had enough on their hands. Besides, I knew that there was an element of uncertainty about my semi-presence in the family; I belonged and, then again, I didn't. I, the person I was, my feelings for them and their feelings for me were full of ambivalence.

I was someone with whom they had to share everything and now they had less of everything that could be shared than ever before. They would be spared my presence.

I left them that very night. I packed my few possessions in the knapsack Daddy had given me and tiptoed out of the apartment.

Why didn't I say goodbye? If I had said goodbye, they wouldn't have let me leave. Maybe they would even have convinced me to stay. And if I stayed, the ambivalence would grow—both theirs and my own. I didn't have any choice.

Ever since then, I have been wandering. I am not in a hurry. I have lived many places, for several years in some, but I will always be moving. Sooner or later, I will move on. Moving on will always, with time, prove to be the most sensible.

If you live in one place for too long, everything there will run out—the water, the plants, the animals. If one moves, one finds new resources.

This is how the world is now; it is best to keep moving.

I started my life by escaping. There has never been any place I could call my own. And the night I ran away from my family, from the woman who wanted to call herself my mommy, I decided that this is how I am. I am not someone who is always running away. I am someone who is always in movement.

EVA

While I was reading, Louise paced restlessly around the room, glancing constantly at the pages before me, trying to see where I was. When I finished and put the pages down on the table, she finally stopped.

"Do you understand now why I wanted to leave? Why I left you?" she asked.

I got to my feet.

"Louise."

I reached out my arms and put them around her. She let me embrace her. I could feel her tummy, a small, round ball against my own, and I noticed she was shaking.

"You left us because I got totally carried away with the baby things," I said softly.

"Yes," she said.

For a while we just stood there like that, with our arms around each other. She smelled of spruce and woodsmoke. Her cheek was smooth and soft against mine. Slowly her breathing calmed.

"Yes," she said, and released me carefully. "I left because you got carried away. But that was also why I came back. Because I have met someone who went nuts because I'm going to have a baby."

"I am very pleased to be allowed to go nuts," I said.

She nodded. "But afterward, when the baby comes . . ."

I stepped back, leaned against the kitchen table.

"You wrote that everything runs out," I said slowly. "That if you live somewhere for too long, everything will run out in the end."

"Yes?"

"But you were starving in the forest?"

"That was because I stayed out there—because I was unable to leave you and Isa."

She picked up her cup, walked over to the sink and poured out the rest of her tea.

"But you don't know how long you might have had to walk before you found something to eat or someone who could help you," I said.

"No, but I know that I would have found it in the end. The way I found the two of you."

She put down her cup with a thump.

"Everything is different with a child," I said.

"Children aren't more safe here than anywhere else," Louise said. "Nobody is safe anywhere."

"Here, at least, we have a door we can lock."

"A door? A door isn't worth a thing."

"But where do you want to go, really," I murmured. "Where will you stop finally?"

She shrugged. "I don't want to stop . . . well, maybe for extended periods like this winter, but not for good."

A sleeping bundle on the rawness of the ground, in the rain and the wind, soiled diapers, a toddling two-year-old on the road in the scorching heat, legs far too short, having to walk four steps for each adult step.

"That's no life," I said. "You are going to have a baby. That's no life to offer a baby."

"But you think this is?" She threw out her arms.

"I don't understand you," I said and suddenly felt the tears welling up.

"Yes, you do," Louise said. "You understand me. That's why I came back."

CHAPTER 11

A MATTER OF NOURISHMENT

We skinned the dead foal and cut off its skull, but the natives didn't want horsemeat.

"What about us?" I asked Wilhelm.

He shook his head. "Do you want to eat this animal?"

"No, I don't eat horsemeat either."

"And especially not this."

"Especially not this."

I was so relieved that he agreed, that we were of the same mind. Even though the foal was now skinned, even though pieces of it looked completely ordinary—cuts of red meat marbled with yellow fat, glistening membranes of connective tissue, a young animal, probably quite tasty and tender—eating this meat would be like eating a fictive animal, a unicorn.

We took the skull and the hide with us back to the camp. That evening, we sat with it between us watching how the flies buzzed around the skull before slowly disappearing as the smoke from the fire filled the air. At first, neither of us were able to speak. I think we were both struggling with the same conflicting feelings.

"Yet another dead horse," Wilhelm said after a while.

"But we found them," I said and grasped his hand. "We know they exist."

"Dead horses are of no use." His eyes were black as he stared at the skull. "Poliakov already has a skull, a hide. The species already has a name. We didn't come here to collect more skulls."

"We have both the spring and the summer," I said. "The next time, we will succeed. The next time, we will manage to bring them in alive."

He didn't answer, didn't look at me, turned away from the skull and sucked on his pipe so the tobacco glowed.

"We'll try again tomorrow," I said. "And the next day. And the day after that."

Although I was as dejected as he was, the words pleased me because they meant that we would have to stay here, in Mongolia, for a long time.

We didn't head out again the next day as I had anticipated. Instead, Wilhelm spent almost a week on preparations. We rode out three times to observe the horses. They were grazing in the same place. He also had long conversations with the different chiefs. Personally, I could neither contribute knowledge about local conditions, as the chiefs could, nor about the capture of live wild animals in general, which was Wolff's forte. I, therefore, predominantly sat with them as they made plans, nodding seriously or with a smile according to what seemed appropriate at any given moment.

Wilhelm concluded, after this period, that it would be impossible to capture live adult horses. They are too fast, too timid. They have an unrivalled ability to avoid predators—an advantage for them, a vital necessity—but a great disadvantage for us.

We observed how the lead stallion often stayed at a certain distance from the herd where he functioned as a guard for the others. At the first sign of danger, he would quickly join them. They then gathered in a formation with one of the year-old stallions taking the lead, the mares surrounding the youngest foals in the middle, and the lead stallion at the rear. If one of the youngest foals was unable to keep up, the stallion would herd it so it stayed with the group. The horses' behavior was designed to keep watch over the youngest, but Wilhelm still believed that it was the foals we should try to capture. All of his former wildlife capture experience led him to conclude that it was our only chance.

So, one day, we set out again, this time with an even larger hunting party. The youngest chief did not come along. I felt bad for him but was, nonetheless, relieved. The two others, who clearly had a better understanding of the mission, arrived with five men each and five additional horses. They were big, magnificent animals. Previously, they would certainly have impressed me, but now my immediate impression was that they were somewhat boring and ordinary compared to the takhis we were trying to capture.

We waited out of sight while the wild horses were drinking from the river, then we followed them cautiously. We came from the north with the wind in our faces as they moved away from the river. Here, the newborns lay down to rest while the other horses grazed around them.

Then we spotted our opportunity. On the signal, the entire hunting party leapt into motion as we shouted and roared at the wild horses. They jumped to attention, confused, immediately terrified, and started galloping south. They ran close to the river, which was the lowest point in the landscape, racing away at a breakneck pace over stones and grass, black silhouettes against the sun.

We followed in hot pursuit. Again, I fell behind but not so far behind that I couldn't see everything that happened. The takhis disappeared in a cloud of dust with the Mongols galloping behind them. The wild horses ran for their lives, the Mongols for wool ribbons and silver coins. A creature running for its life has a wholly different kind of momentum than one running merely to address a more superficial need and, although the Mongols' horses were larger and stronger, they couldn't overtake the wild horses.

We continued to chase them all the same. I don't know how long the pursuit continued or how far into the steppes we traveled. We rode and rode after the cloud of dust and then it changed character; something distinct stood out in the distance—small, fragile bodies.

It was the foals. They could no longer keep up with the adult horses. The two smallest and probably youngest were left behind all alone.

Finally, one of them stopped. It was a small stallion.

We stormed toward the foal. I dug my heels into the flanks of my own horse and was able to catch up with the others. The foal stood without moving while we formed a circle around him, his nostrils flaring, his flanks collapsing and swelling, collapsing, and swelling, he was completely exhausted, and so frightened that he was shaking.

The chief raised the *urga* carefully and placed the noose around the foal's neck. He did not resist.

The youngest of the hunters cheered and I also felt a flicker of joy. Joy, but mostly protectiveness. Because he, the very first live Przewalsky foal ever captured in the world, was so terribly small.

We led the foal to the river, but he turned away.

"He hasn't started drinking water yet," Wilhelm said.

Every single one of the cans of evaporated milk we'd brought from Petersburg had frozen and exploded, and the milk we hadn't consumed while it was still frozen and could be stored, had long since been destroyed by the heat. We had, therefore, acquired three goats and today had prepared ourselves by bringing along milk in a nursing bottle. The hope was that the foal, when we came back, would nurse directly from the goats' teats if the goat stood on a bale of straw at the right height. I had done this before with animals in the zoological garden and the hope was that, after a few days, we would manage to teach it to drink milk from a bottle.

However, it refused the bottle.

"We'll try again later," Wilhelm said.

He was concerned, as was I. We shared this feeling like two parents at the bedside of a sick child.

The ride back progressed slowly. The foal allowed itself to be led but quickly became tired. The little stallion stopped more and more often, lay down on the ground and closed its eyes.

We surrounded him as we waited, eleven men on big horses, around a tiny little foal, an infant.

He didn't move.

"What should we do?" I whispered to Wilhelm.

The minutes ticked by. The sun was warmer than ever before, already a foretaste of the Mongolian summer heat I had heard so much about. I felt a drop of sweat run from the bridge of my nose down my cheek.

"We must do something," I said.

"You look at me as if I have the answer," Wilhelm barked. "Catching a wild animal always involves a risk."

He said it with an affected harshness, I thought, as if he were trying to convince himself more than me.

"I know," I said gently. "I know."

The chief stared at us as expressionless as ever.

Then he jumped down off his horse, called a couple of his men, said a few words, and, together, they lifted the foal up onto the back of his horse, which was the largest of all of them.

We transported the foal carefully all the way back to the camp. Sometimes it moved and we would let it down onto the ground. It would walk a few meters, then just lie down on the ground, and we would have to lift it onto the back of the horse again.

When we finally reached the camp, it was dark. For the last time, the Mongols lowered the foal onto the ground. There it remained, lying down, moving from time to time, but still it refused to drink from the bottle. Wilhelm quickly milked one of the goats, placed the pail in front of the foal, and helped it to its feet.

It lowered its head toward the milk, sniffed it.

"Come on," Wilhelm said quietly.

The little stallion stuck his snout down into the pail but didn't drink.

"He needs something to suck on," I said.

I extended my forefinger and middle finger, dipped them in the milk and the foal took them in his mouth and started sucking. It was almost painful, but the feeling filled me with joy because, when the foal sucked on my fingers, it also drank some of the milk, and that was all that mattered.

The night passed. We took turns sitting with the animal. It remained standing on four legs and in the early morning lay down and slept again, which we presumed was its natural rhythm. But the foal slept for a long time, longer than we liked, and we both ended up pacing and watching over it in hopes that it would awaken.

When he finally opened his eyes, he was unable to clamber onto his feet, struggled against the weight of his own body. He placed his front hooves on the ground, pulled himself up, but could not manage to pull up his hindquarters and collapsed, tried again, stood for a moment on his front legs and collapsed onto the ground.

The foal now refused to drink milk even though we put the pail out, and I tried with my fingers again. It poked them with its snout before turning away.

Then it emitted some strange sounds, as if it were being strangled.

"What is that?" I turned to Wilhelm.

He didn't answer, just stared at the animal. It continued emitting these half-strangled moans.

The stallion was ill. The milk we tried to give him ran out again from his nose. His breathing rattled, he swayed and collapsed, pulled himself onto his feet, collapsed again.

Soon, he was unable to get up at all, just lay limply on the ground between us, its eyes half open, its gaze remote and body warm.

I sat down, took its head into my lap and, even though he was a wild animal that normally would have run away, he just lay there. I stroked his head, speaking to him softly.

"You must drink," I said. "You must eat."

I dipped my fingers in the milk, tried to stick them into his mouth. The foal sniffed them briefly, took hold, barely, but there was no strength there any longer, no energy for sucking.

I remained seated like this, completely still, feeling the weight of the animal's head in my lap, stroking his coat with my fingers, his soft ears. The calmer the foal became, the more anxious I was about moving, as if my movements might destroy something or other, kill him.

Wilhelm had the opposite reaction. He trotted back and forth, sighed, cursed, wanted to talk all the time, to try to reassure me.

"That's how it is," he kept saying. "It can be difficult to keep them alive. He's our first. We must think of him as an object of research. Through him, we can learn what we should do differently next time, with the next foal we capture and the next one after that."

"Are you trying to reassure me or yourself?" I murmured.

He didn't reply.

"It could be pneumonia," he said. "Or it's the milk. Yes, the goat's milk probably made him sick. We can try horse's milk, instead. We should have thought of that—of course, he would have tolerated horse milk better. Next time, we will have a few domesticated mares standing by. Maybe we will take them with us out on the hunt. Yes, I think so, we must have them there, standing by. They will need a few days to get used to one another. The mares must accept the foals as their offspring, after all, and the foals must think of the tame mares as their mothers, but I think it can work, I really think it can work."

That's how he talked, that's how he walked, faster and faster in a circle around us, while the foal breathed more and more slowly.

KARIN

While yesterday we drove south, now we set our course in the opposite direction. We drive with the icy winter sun against the rear window of the car. Kilometer after kilometer, advancing slowly. Jochi is constantly adjusting the mirror, apparently blinded by the rays of the sun. The heater is running at full blast, but cold air still seeps in from the ground, penetrating the car's undercarriage and the soles of our shoes. I try moving my toes in my hiking boots, but it doesn't help.

I cling to the binoculars. White, white, white. The sun is, at least, helping us a little. It creates shapes. Brings out contrasts, shadows crossing the ground from birds in the sky, exaggerated contours of low-growing bushes, blue patches against all the white, on the northern slopes of hills and mountains. I lower the binoculars for a moment. Discover my face in the side mirror. The binoculars have left marks around my eyes. Like a panda. No, pandas are cute. I look more like a skull.

I constantly keep thinking I see them. The horses become an optical illusion, like an oasis in the desert, a fata morgana, palm trees, bubbling water. Shadows and snow drifts become horses, all

281

the snowbanks and mounds. I start to get a headache. I want to smoke a cigarette but refrain from smoking out of consideration for Jochi.

The noises made by the car are erratic. The body creaks over every single hollow. The sound of the motor under duress becomes monotonous after a while, a kind of silence.

"They will be fine," I say.

"Yes. We will find them soon," he says.

We keep going.

"Yes, we'll find them soon," he says.

We keep going.

"They're made to tolerate this," I say after an hour. "For sure, we'll find them before lunch."

He nods. "We're going to be surprised at how well they are doing."

But it is only when the sun sinks low in the sky that I think I see them. Vague shadows at the bottom of a hollow, unlike all other shadows and nuances on the steppes. Or is it just another optical illusion?

"Wait," I say.

I press the binoculars against my eyes, adjust the focus.

Perhaps it's just bushes. In some places out here, the authorities have tried planting trees—short, mountain birches that cling stubbornly to the sunniest hollows, sheltered from the wind. Fragile baby trees with branches like skinny arms against the sky. They are still far too small to be able to determine whether the experiment was a success. But something is lying under the trees.

"Drive over there," I point.

Jochi changes directions. He puts the car into second, drives forward slowly.

As we approach, I have to keep adjusting the focus, adapting the binoculars and my gaze. The mounds of snow grow. Become mounds of sandy-yellow coats partially covered with snow. Their fur sticks up through the snow like dried grass.

They are lying there, all of them.

Horses aren't supposed to lie down. Not like this. Not without one of them standing guard.

But, then, one of them gets up. Must have heard the car and is lumbering heavily. I recognize her. It is Praha. Praha, the strong one.

Then, a short distance to the right, by himself, always by himself, Hamburg gets up.

I lower the binoculars, don't need them any longer, notice that my breath leaves my chest in rapid puffs turning into large, white clouds in the air before me.

Jochi says nothing, just presses his foot on the accelerator.

He stops the car fifty meters away. We get out, the wind at our backs. It carries the scent of humans and the scent of the hay we have on the flatbed.

Sydney gets up, followed by Askania Nova, and the foal Halle. They shake off snow, their movements sluggish. Snorts, whinnies softly, as if to make his presence known. I answer them.

"It's us. It's only us."

They walk slowly toward me, toward the hay they can smell, and now I can finally see them properly. The cold has taken its toll on them, especially Sydney. He has big frostbite wounds on his legs and under his belly like a mangy alley cat.

Some of them have yet to stand, but soon they will tear away from the white snowy surface and become live animals.

"There, there," I say softly. "You're going to be fed now."

I turn toward Jochi.

"We have to unload the hay."

"But, Karin," he says.

"Yes?"

"Paris isn't here. Neither is Woburn."

"Yes, they are," I say. "They're just still lying on the ground."

They have to be here. They have to be with the herd. A harem always stays together; they take care of each other.

While Jochi puts out the hay for the horses, I walk in a large circle around them, my eyes searching through the hollow. A neck, a head, an ear, something sticking up out of the snow like a sign.

But I find nothing. The snow is an unbroken surface, like an impossibly huge sheet of drawing paper.

I walk in a larger circle. Jochi has unloaded the feed; he also starts walking. We circle outward, farther and farther away from the horses and each other.

I see a hare footprint, embroidery amidst all the white and almost invisible etchings in the snow—markings left by birds. But no dents from horse hooves, no deep holes.

Then I hear Jochi shout.

"Karin!"

I run. In some places the snow is deep. My feet sink down. I become short of breath, my heart pounds, and my throat burns.

I see Jochi bend down, then squat. Then he starts digging with his hands, pushing the snow away as if he were a dog, creating a snow spray around him.

I reach him and squat beside him. The cold penetrates my mittens, burning. But we keep digging.

It is Woburn.

He is alive.

The foal's eyes are half open, his gaze distant. I take off my mittens and lay my hand against his flank. I can still feel heat inside there.

We dig him out. Jochi runs to get more hay and sticks some in the foal's muzzle. It sniffs at it and then eats.

Jochi drives the car up. We pull Woburn onto his feet; he sways. I support his hindquarters. Under the soft, thick winter coat he is just skin and bones. I can suddenly smell the strong odor of horse; it breaks through the white scent of snow.

"It's fine," I whisper the whole time. "It's fine, everything's fine now."

We push Woburn up onto the flatbed, where he collapses. Then we cover him up with blankets and tarps and drive back to the station.

When we arrive, we can't get him on his feet. He is half asleep, sliding in and out of consciousness. Agi, Mathias, and a couple of the others arrive. They lift Woburn onto a tarp attached to poles and carry him into the kitchen.

Carrying a wild horse into the house of a human being . . . I try not to think about what we are doing. How it violates the laws of nature.

Jochi does not take his eyes off me the whole time.

"They weren't ready," he says.

"He will survive," I say.

"We released them too soon." His voice is flat.

"They would have been fine had it not been for the storm."

"Winter brings storms. We should have waited a year. We should have given them a year. They have waited for one hundred years to be free; they would have managed one more year."

"*I told you so*," I say. "Now you can say it, *I told you so*. But we don't know if it was too early. It could have happened next year, too. And it can happen again."

I can see that he wants to say something else, that he is still furious. But Woburn makes a faint noise and we both bend over him.

The hours pass. Woburn disappears, comes back, disappears. Gradually, I feel his body getting warmer. We try to give him water. He doesn't want to drink. Just turns his head away.

I doze on the floor beside the foal while the hours go by. I don't even go outside to smoke. I can hear his breathing is rapid and strained. I venture to reach out one hand, stroking his coat gently.

"There, there, there."

I have to get him hydrated, but I don't know how. I have neither a catheter nor a probe. This is not a clinic. I never thought we would have to treat them the way we would a domesticated horse.

If his fever goes down, he will want to drink again. We have to get him warm, keep him warm. I hope that this is all it will take.

I keep trying to get him to drink. He swallows some liquid. It seems to help.

Mathias comes in early the next morning. I have barely slept.

"Here," he says handing me a cup of coffee.

I shake my head.

"I would prefer it in the thermos."

"Are you going out again?" he asks and puts the cup down on the table. "Are you going to look for Paris?"

"Yes . . . but I don't know if I can leave Woburn."

He hesitates.

"I'm here," he says.

"Yes?"

"I can stay with him."

I shake my head. "I don't think that's a good idea."

He lifts his hand, scratches his head a bit while considering.

"I must be able to manage it," he says gravely. "Just tell me what to do, then I can manage it, certainly?"

He straightens up, looks at me with an unusual gravity.

Yes, he can manage it, certainly.

"The foal has to drink," I say. "You have to keep trying to get him to drink, constantly."

His eyes light up. "I'll try."

"Don't try. You *must* get him to drink."

Now he is suddenly full of self-confidence. "Relax. I can do it." He lifts the cup of coffee off the table. "And now I am going to pour this into a thermos for you. You look as if you could use the caffeine."

"Fine," I say. "Thank you."

"My pleasure, Karin. Get going."

He opens a cupboard, looking for a thermos.

"Mathias," I say.

"Yes?" he stops midmovement.

"I didn't know the horses had become so important to you," I say.

"I know," he says. "You thought I was here for the fun of it."

"Not for the fun of it," I say.

"No, because of the drugs," he says. "To get away from using."

"Yes? That was why you came along?"

"But that's not why I stayed."

"My impression was that you thought what I'm doing is meaningless," I say, and a lump immediately forms in my throat.

Meaningless, it is perhaps meaningless.

"What?" he says.

"That it's lunacy to put your entire life on hold, invest everything, both money and career, to save a few horses."

"You haven't put your life on hold," he says. "Your life is here now."

"You know what I mean."

"No, I don't."

"What's the point of saving Przewalsky's horse?" I am speaking loudly, my voice almost shrill. "The takhis are one of ten million species on earth, a species that does not contribute anything. Why should we invest time and resources on saving a horse that has no utility value whatsoever?"

"You're asking me?" He smiles. "You haven't talked about anything but horses since I was a little boy."

Yet another day out in the field. Yet another day of searching. Agi sets out in one direction, Jochi and I in another. We have agreed to try to cover a large area around the place where we found the horses.

I drive first, while Jochi is responsible for the binoculars. But I am unable to concentrate on driving. I keep thinking I spot a mound of snow, a shaggy lump, something that could be Paris.

"There?" I point.

Jochi swivels, readjusts the focus, trying to see what I am pointing at.

"Nothing," he says.

A little later I point again. "What about over there?"

"No," he says. "Sorry."

"That over there, then. That mound. Isn't the shape of it a bit strange?"

He lowers the binoculars and lets them rest on his lap.

"I think you should stop the car."

"What?"

"I think it would be better if we changed places."

He says it without anger, without irony.

Then he puts the binoculars on the dashboard, opens the car door, and walks around to the other side. Hesitantly, I unbuckle my seatbelt and do as he says.

I become calmer when I can look for myself, when I am holding the binoculars.

Even though it doesn't help, because Paris is gone.

Yet another day we drive until nightfall. On the way home, we stop to check on the horses. They haven't moved away from the hay. We put out even more in the hope that they will stay together in the same place for one more day.

"We must come back and see them tomorrow," I say.

"What about Paris?" Jochi asks.

"We must search for her as well."

"But do you think . . ."

"We must search."

"If she isn't with the herd . . . that means that . . ."

I spin around to face him. "Don't you think we have to search?"

He keeps his eyes fixed on the snow in front of us, both hands on the steering wheel, driving with calm concentration.

"She would have been with the herd. If she were alive, she would have been with the herd. There are no solitary mares."

"Maybe she lost them."

"Karin . . ."

I don't reply but leave the binoculars in my lap. It's too dark to see anything anyway.

We drive back in silence. Yet another evening, I come home frozen and stiff in my body after all the hours spent sitting in the car.

But on this evening, Mathias greets me on the stairs. He reaches out for me the way he did when he was a child.

"Sorry, Karin," he says softly.

"What? What do you mean?"

"I lost Woburn."

EVA

We didn't talk anymore about staying or leaving; we talked about the winter, about the darkness, about the rain. But most of all, we talked about the baby that was growing and the spring.

The spring . . . *the spring*—it had become a word reverberating in our heads. It was a matter of getting through this winter, through this pregnancy, a matter of rationing the hay so it would last for the animals, and the food so it would last for us.

Spring, summer, and autumn are the seasons of change. Winter is stasis. And, during this winter, things were at even more of a standstill than in any preceding winter. It rained, grew darker, the precipitation colder; one morning we awoke to frost on the ground and a thin layer of ice on the mud puddles. In the course of the day, sleet began to fall, which became rain again in the evening. The frost came a few more times, but it never became properly white.

We went into hibernation. Stayed inside, for the most part, close to the stove in the kitchen. It was the greediest among us; we fed the fire constantly. Never before had we had a winter without electricity. I thought about heat when I woke up and when I went to bed. Firewood became a job; we stacked damp wood against the walls inside and in the cowshed. The wood barely had time to dry before we threw it into the firebox; heat was the constant focus of our attention. If the fire died, the house became uninhabitable. I would have given my right hand for electricity.

The nature of the winter is without change, just a monotone of grays and browns; nothing grows, nothing surprises. The only thing that changed this winter was Louise. I thought I could see her belly grow from day to day. Cell by cell, they divided and divided again, invisible changes from one minute to the next, inside there, in darkness, becoming externally visible. Her tummy began to bulge; I noticed it especially in the evenings. Her body became like mine when I released my abdomen, when I pressed it out. Isa had a hollow in there that never was filled completely. If I stood in front of the mirror and looked at myself, I always, automatically, held in my stomach, forcing my body to assume a figure that differed from my actual shape. The belly of a woman is actually a curve, not a straight line.

Once her baby belly had started to grow, it went quickly. Soon Louise became round; she dressed in soft garments, all sharp edges disappeared, her cheeks became softer, her upper arms plumper, a thin layer of subcutaneous fat spread throughout her whole body in preparation for what lay ahead. She didn't want to take more food than we allowed ourselves, but the food she was given she ate with the appetite of a wolf. I remember how I had felt when I was carrying Isa. I viewed food differently than before, noticed all the details of what I ate, the texture, analyzed the odors. I had to eat something before getting out of bed in the morning. I would pass out on the bedroom floor if I hadn't first eaten the packed lunch I prepared the evening before. I even woke up during the night to eat. It had still been possible to get hold of bananas at the time. I ate the sweet, slightly nauseating fruit constantly, probably four a day, and had at least one on my nightstand, which I would peel ravenously and munch in the dark. I needed food, I remember. The doctor said I needed it. I didn't gain more weight than I should have, but the pregnancy sucked the calories out of me.

Louise should have eaten more. I tried to give her a little of my own food. We still had some vegetables left and I willingly sacrificed my portion, but she always pushed them back across the table.

Also, her movements changed. She grew softer, slower, almost sluggish. Balanced, I thought. She unconsciously adjusted her rhythm for the sake of the baby so it would be calmer in there. I imagined that it must feel safer to lie beneath a slowly beating heart than to listen to a body in a state of hypervigilance. It was as if she just knew how to do this, as if she thrived in her pregnant body and understood the condition. I had never felt that way. The time during and after my pregnancy had been, first and foremost, informed by uncertainty. There were times when I wished I could have another child just to have the chance to feel that I knew what I was doing.

One day, right after Christmas, I went out to the wild horses. I usually checked on all the animals every single day, but it had been a few days since I'd walked down to see them. It had been raining so hard that I hadn't done anything outdoors except what was absolutely necessary. And it did not stop. The raindrops plummeted from the sky as if someone were standing up there and chasing them down to us, but Nike and Puma were not bothered by the precipitation. Their winter coats were thick; the drops rolled off them as they stood chewing with their heads bowed toward the ground.

The few nights of frost hadn't killed all the grass. In some places it was still green, but muted, as if a thin, gray film had been drawn across the landscape. Lacking in nutrients, I thought, they would have to get by on these small tufts. It could not possibly be enough.

I walked over to the fence. Puma was standing closest to me, Nike a few meters away, both sideways, the full profile of their bodies facing me. Maybe it was the short hiatus I had had away from them that enabled me to now see the change. They had grown horribly thin.

The foal was growing, drank almost no milk any longer but was wholly dependent on grass to survive, but he wasn't getting enough. Puma and Nike were not eating enough either; they would soon be just skin and bones. And they would need to draw from the reserves they had built up during the summer for many months.

I turned and walked quickly back to the farm. To the barn, to the bales of hay inside.

I didn't say anything to the others about feeding the horses. I didn't have to justify this to anyone, I thought, owed them no explanation because perhaps the horses would come in handy; maybe I could get them to pull a plough in the spring. It was said that they could not be tamed, but I could still try; that was a reason to keep them—that they could be of use to us.

I thought I had managed to keep my feeding them a secret, but the third time I went to bring hay to the horses, Isa was standing there waiting.

At first, she didn't say anything; didn't even say hello. She just stared at me with narrowed eyes. I continued unloading hay. If she wasn't going to say something, I wouldn't say anything, either. I didn't have to explain myself to her. She was only fourteen years old. Finally, she apparently couldn't bear the silence any longer.

"How long have you been doing this?" she asked.

"They don't get much," I said.

"I thought the idea was that they would be self-sufficient. That that was why we let them live, because they can manage on their own."

"But they can't."

"No?"

"No."

"I thought it seemed like suddenly the hay was disappearing faster than before." Her voice shook slightly, as if she were struggling to speak calmly.

She thought . . . had she started keeping track of how much feed we had? How much food?

"You don't say," I said.

"I know how much we have, Mom. You're not the only one keeping track. I usually even keep an eye on the amount of water in the well."

"Water," I sniffed. "The well won't go dry. At least not with the way it's raining now."

"Not this year," she said. "But two years ago, when it was so dry, you adults talked about how the ground water could disappear. You remember that, don't you?"

"Yes," I said. "Of course, I remember that."

Again, her eyes narrowed. "You've already forgotten about it. You don't know what you're doing," she said softly.

"What did you say?"

"And now you're giving hay to the horses. Hay that should have gone to Apple and Micro."

"This is a judgment call and you must trust in my ability to make it," I said. "We still have a lot of hay."

"No. We only have enough to feed four large animals throughout the entire winter. Not six. I've worked it out."

"You've worked it out?" My breathing intensified. "What is this all about, really?"

She was second-guessing me. Was I to be held accountable by her? A child?

"I've been thinking we should get rid of Micro," I said suddenly and without thinking.

"What?!"

"She's old. Doesn't produce much milk. And we can use the meat."

"No!"

"Then there will be one less to share the feed with."

"You are going to keep giving the horses hay and put Micro down?"

Her eyes were huge and wide open. Her lower lip trembled the way it had always done, the way it had done when she was three years of age. Somehow, it gave me peace that she was herself again.

"We can take one of the calves, too," I said. "Better meat. Then there will only be four animals left, four, like you said."

"No," she repeated. "You can't."

She drew a breath, clearly reconsidering, raised her head and looked at me with an expression that told me she really was fighting back the tears.

"But it's better if you take one of the calves instead of Micro. If you are going to take any of them. The calves don't produce milk."

Her voice was fragile. She was still so young, hidden behind an adult façade. I took a step toward her. "Sweetie," I said, "we don't need to slaughter any of them yet. It's nice that you're staying on top of things, but you must believe me when I say that it will be fine."

She backed away. "I'm not your sweetie, don't you get it? I'm not your sweetie any longer."

"Isa . . ."

I thought she would scream, yell, or at least be sarcastic. But she just stared at me. She'd gained control over her lower lip and in her eyes was something I'd never seen before.

"If we let the horses die," I said, "all the work that has been done to rebuild the species will have been in vain."

"Do you think they would have done the same for you? Sacrificed their food for you? Do you think so?"

"Isa, you can't think like that."

"You can't decide what I am supposed to think."

I drove the pitchfork into the ground. All of a sudden, I was shaking.

"Out of all the wild animals we had, only these two horses are left," I said, with hard-won control over my voice. "And, of course, they would not sacrifice their food for us. Of course not—they're horses, not people. But if I sacrifice their lives so I can eat, then I am also just an animal. Do you understand that then we would also just be animals?"

"Yes," she said. "That's exactly what we are. Are you a complete idiot?"

Are you a complete idiot? There she was again, the child.

"I guess I am," I said.

I lifted the pitchfork again and turned toward the horses, tossing a little more hay over the fence.

"We'll take Micro. But not just yet," I said. "We'll be fine for a few more weeks. That way you'll have time to say goodbye."

"It's not time I need, Mom. It's the milk."

. . .

Isa didn't say a word about Micro in the days that followed. Not a word about the hay that was disappearing too quickly, or about our conversation. On the whole, she didn't talk to me much at all. I thought it was a new strategy. One of her new teenager strategies. The irony had been replaced by the silent treatment.

Toward Louise, she was nicer than ever. I would find the two of them together all the time, laughing about something or deep in conversation, and, more and more often, Isa sat resting a hand on her tummy, sensing the person growing inside there, guessing, is it a foot, an arm maybe, a little hand, or a shoulder. She laughed when the child suddenly kicked, smiled tenderly when it twisted away.

I remembered that I hadn't liked the way people would touch me when I was pregnant. That my tummy, which had previously been a private affair, was suddenly public property, no longer a part of me, but rather something independent and separate, as if the child already existed. Louise apparently felt differently. She liked that we touched her belly, said it was nice because the baby was ours as well.

Even though Isa didn't say a word about Micro, I put off slaughtering the cow. It was as if our conversation had never taken place, as if I'd never said anything about putting her down. We kept milking the cows every day, kept making cheese and butter from the milk, kept feeding all four of them, kept mucking out the cowshed. Instead I began cutting back the feed rations, giving all the animals a little less every day. I could still see no visible weight loss; the cows produced almost as much milk as before. They seemed to be fine. And if spring came early, I thought, if the grass sprouted quickly, we might actually be fine. We could keep all six.

But until then, we had to live through gray days, weeks during which the rain just poured down, a steady inundation. *Rain, rain, go away, come again some other day.* I used to sing that to Isa when she was a little girl. I no longer had anyone to sing to, but soon the baby would come, bringing with it the sun and the spring.

KARIN

M athias follows me. No matter what room I am in, he follows on my heels.

I pop outside to smoke a cigarette but don't escape there either. He comes and stands beside me. His hands tremble as he lights the cigarette. The flame from the lighter flickers in his face.

"Sorry, Karin, sorry."

"It wasn't your fault," I say.

"I couldn't get enough liquid into him. I didn't do as good a job at paying attention as I should have."

"It wasn't your fault," I repeat. "It was mine. I shouldn't have made it your responsibility."

"But then you're saying that it was my fault. Actually." His voice trembles.

"No," I say. "That's not what I'm saying."

I stub out my cigarette. Mathias is just an amateur; I shouldn't have left Woburn in his hands. It was like giving the responsibility for a baby to a five year old. Of course, it would go wrong. It would go wrong, and I knew it.

"I am the one who is a veterinarian," I say. "It was my responsibility."

"I held his head," Mathias says, as much to himself as to me. "I held his head in my hands. At first, he was breathing rapidly. Hoarsely. Like in the upper part of his lungs. Then his breathing slowed more and more."

He turns toward me again. "Do you think he was in pain? Do you think he was afraid?"

"It's nice that you stayed with him," I say.

"Right before he died," Mathias continues, "I thought he rallied. Suddenly he started moving a lot."

"Don't give it another thought. There's nothing we can do."

"But he was moving? Squirming, like."

"Cadaveric spasms," I say.

"What?"

"No doubt it was cadaveric spasms that caused him to squirm. You're not the first to misunderstand."

Mathias sits completely still. His head is bowed. I can't see his face. He clings to the cigarette but doesn't take a single puff. The ash grows longer and longer, resembling the tip of a cattail, until it breaks off and falls. When it hits the ground, it disintegrates, turning to dust.

"I think you should go inside and go to bed now," I say. "Get a good night's sleep."

He nods but shows no sign of moving.

"Mathias?"

Finally, he looks at me. His eyes are large and black.

"I'm not capable of taking care of anything, you know that? I'm not capable of taking care of a single living creature."

"Now, Mathias."

He looks at me pleadingly. Wants something from me.

You're not the one who's incapable of taking care of living creatures. It's me. Woburn was *my* responsibility.

"You looked after him," I say. "You did the best you could."

"Maybe if you'd been there . . ."

"We can't know that for sure. Maybe it was already too late when we found him."

"But . . ."

I stand. "We have to turn in now."

He nods and swallows. I go inside without saying another word. I said that it wasn't his fault—don't know what more I can say, what more he wants to hear.

The next morning, Jochi and I lift Woburn back up onto the flatbed. I can't bear to drive, give the car keys to Jochi. He sits behind the wheel, starts the engine.

"Where do you want to go?"

"I don't know." I swallow. "Just drive somewhere. We can put him anywhere."

Foals will die; every single winter, foals freeze to death. It's a part of life out here. Woburn would have died anyway. I repeat this to myself. Woburn would have died anyway. It was neither Mathias's fault nor mine.

Jochi puts the car in gear and starts to drive. We follow the route inland toward the watering holes; the car meets little resistance. There are tire ruts in the ground. The snow that fell during the storm has almost disappeared. I don't know what happened to it. Blown away, sculpted into drifts, melted. Or, perhaps, the steppes basically eat the snow. They eat snow the way they eat living creatures.

Just before we reach the watering holes, Jochi suddenly downshifts and turns abruptly north.

"Probably best to stay away from the water," he says.

"The watering holes are frozen over anyway," I say.

"Yes . . . but still. To be on the safe side."

Unnecessary, completely unnecessary. The carcass would not remain there long enough to contaminate the water source. Everywhere there are hungry animals and birds ready to descend on dead meat. Everywhere on the steppes there are more or less half-consumed meals.

Jochi drives into the pass between the two tall peaks where the horses often grazed during the summertime. There he stops.

We pull the tarp holding Woburn down from the flatbed. The foal hits the ground with a thud.

Together we tease the tarp loose from his body, pulling it out between us. It lies in a heap beside Woburn. A huge, military-green sheet. We stand on opposite ends of it and fold it in two. Now it is small enough for us to lift it.

We fold it again. And again.

Neither of us pause.

We meet in the middle, creating sharp folds.

The plastic scraping of the tarp is the only sound to be heard. The act of folding is like a little ritual, the only death ritual a horse can receive out here.

Finally, the tarp can't be folded anymore.

Jochi puts the tarp on the trailer. Then he turns to the horse. We stand side-by-side with just half a meter between us.

Woburn is lying with his head at a strange angle, his eyes half open. I don't want to look at him but can't stop myself. Now that the life has slipped out of his body, it's as if the foal has become even thinner. Just bones and a pouch of skin. There can't be much left here for the scavengers.

Little Woburn, good, little Woburn.

I jump when Jochi places a hand on my shoulder.

"How are you, Karin?"

How are you, how are you. Always the same phrase. But the gentleness of his voice makes my stomach ache.

I try to reply, smile bravely, but my voice fails me.

"I'm fine," I manage to say finally.

He turns toward me and strokes my cheek with a mittened hand.

"Karin?"

I twist away, but fail to disentangle myself completely. His hand remains on my shoulder. It moves a bit; the mitten creates a faint, squeaky sound against the fabric of my down jacket. Despite the layers of down in both the mitten and the jacket, I can feel his fingers deep inside, that he is holding on to me tightly.

Suddenly, I don't want him to take it away. I want him to put his arms around me so I can lean against him, just lean against him for a short while.

And then he does just that, he pulls me carefully toward him.

We are both upholstered. Down jackets and quilted trousers, thick fur hats with earflaps and mittens designed for arctic expeditions. The only visible bare skin is our faces. I feel his nose as it glances across my cheek; it is freezing, like a dog's. When I hug him, it's his hat I press up against, but all the same, he is inside.

He holds me, I hold him. The lump in my throat disappears. His face is so close.

What will happen now?

Nothing can happen. Nothing should happen.

Abruptly I release him. I think he releases me at the same moment. "Shall we drive back?" he asks.

We don't talk to each other for the rest of the day. He stays outside, working on something, I don't know what. For my own part I have a lot to do in the office.

He turns in early. Doesn't say good night.

I close the door to my room also, but don't get into bed, just sit there on top of it. The embrace has left an imprint of a quilted jacket and a cold cheek on my body.

Get it together, Karin.

Quilted jacket, mittens, a cold cheek. My arms around Jochi. The embrace becomes more than an embrace, becomes clothes disappearing, hands against my back, against my bottom and thighs, his lips on my breasts, my mouth around his member.

It was just a hug. He was consoling me. He did not mean anything more by it.

Woburn is dead. Paris is gone. I must think of them. How I can prevent further fatalities? That's what matters.

Woburn and Paris.

Then I hear footsteps outside my door. Soft, cautious.

Immediately, I become aware of how I am sitting. The stiffness of my body. And I notice that I'm wet. My breathing is heavy.

He doesn't knock, just opens the door.

"Hi," he says.

"Hi," I say.

Should I remain seated? Or get up?

If I stand up, will he take it as an invitation?

He must notice how breathless I am? See how red my cheeks are?

I remain seated, just scoot over a few inches on the bed, barely perceptible.

It is an invitation. But it need not be.

Well, he takes it as an invitation because then he sits down beside me.

Are there codes, I wonder, are the codes here different from at home? Are there ways of doing this in Mongolia that are different from where I come from?

There aren't.

Everything is just as simple. And just as difficult.

I move my hand. It comes to rest on the bed between us. He moves his own, too.

We are a man and a woman, a girl and a boy. We are ageless. We do what girls and boys have done throughout all of time.

Again, he moves his hand. Closer to mine.

A landslide falls through me, vast and powerful. My hand just lies there next to his.

Then he finally takes it.

I don't dare, I don't dare, I don't dare.

He lifts my hand all the way to his mouth. I can feel his breath against my skin, across the tiny hairs on the back of my hand. Then he presses his lips against it.

When his lips do this to such an innocent part of my body.

He undresses me.

I undress him.

We stand facing each other, naked.

301

He is more beautiful than I am—younger, stronger.

Usually I don't think about my body. I am strong and quick, slender, but not skinny. I have a body that collaborates, that afflicts me with little pain. I have heard other women my age complaining about physical ailments, muscle aches, stiff knees, hormones run amok. I have never had such problems. I have just functioned. I functioned on the farm in Thorenc, where often I had to do a lot of heavy lifting. I functioned when I was pregnant, gave birth without great difficulty, the breastfeeding went easily. Now, standing stark naked on the cold floor, I suddenly see myself. The overly mature body, where gravity has long since taken its toll, where my skin has started to loosen. And my breasts, which were once larger than average, of which I was proud, if I ever thought about them, I now see them as well, how they have lost layers of fat, lost everything that made them round and soft, how just the most essential and least erotic parts of them are left: mammary glands and flesh.

"You're so lovely," he says. "I've always thought you were lovely."

"Lovely for my age?" I say.

"Just lovely," he says. "Ever since the first time I saw you I've thought so."

He strokes my abdomen, runs his hands down the sides of my torso, the part called the flank on horse, but which on humans has no ordinary name. His hands are eyes and I see myself through him. Yes, I'm lovely. Breasts, hips, genitalia, all soft curves, nothing drawn using a ruler, everything with a compass.

We lie down on the bed. This is so good. I'd forgotten that it could be so good. Everything is simple, I'm simple, I'm just a body. All I can think and say is—not because I'm a believer, but because it is what people often say when they are in this state, this simplest version of themselves—*oh my God, oh my God, oh my God.*

CHAPTER 12

AN EXCEEDINGLY
LARGE CAPTURE

The very next day after we'd lost the foal, Wilhelm began working on implementing his new plan. With the help of the two eldest chiefs, he acquired five robust, tame mares, each of which had plenty of milk. Then he told the nomads that he would give them a certain amount as a reward for every single foal they brought in.

He went out looking with them, bringing along a suitable mare, while I stayed behind at the camp. That was where I was the most useful—keeping things clean and organized. And neither Wilhelm nor I needed say a word about my inadequate riding skills. I was just a tag-along nobody needed, clumsy and slow.

My thoughts kept returning to the first foal.

The first foal; we never named him, but I always thought of him like that. I was unable to forget the feeling of his coat beneath my fingers, the warm head in my lap, how the cold slowly replaced life, the stiffness that arrived gradually, the finality of it. I was repeatedly thrown back to the moment when I absorbed the fact of its death. Because hope lingered as long as warmth remained in the body, comprehension of the finality did not come immediately, but it grew inexorably along with the cold and rigor mortis.

It is nighttime. I have spent the past few hours looking through my notes. Reliving the time in Mongolia forces me to also remember what I have sought to repress. The foal's rigor mortis is one such thing; I don't want to remember, but when I forced myself to write about it, it struck me that although the memory hasn't been foremost in my mind, it has been in me the whole time, like something physical, a pressure where he lay in my lap, in my fingertips that I ran gently through his mane, a discomfort. My memories of Wilhelm are also something physical. He is still a part of me even when I'm not thinking about him, when I have control over my feelings, our actions are present inside me and I wonder whether Flaubert wasn't mistaken. You can be the master over your feelings, but actions can still occur purely on an impulse, controlled by the body, by something deeply fundamental in our physique, more than by the heart.

I was reminded of how difficult it is to control these impulse-driven actions. When Wilhelm was going out to search for the horses again, I struggled against the desire to embrace him, but the eldest chief and his people stood around us staring with their usual inscrutability and I was able to control myself.

"Be careful," I said in French, the language of love.

He nodded. "When I come back, it will be with a foal for us."

That was the first night I'd slept alone since we left Petersburg, the first night in a long time when he wasn't lying close to me, and it was the first time I became intensely aware of the imprint his body had made on my own. I lay awake for a long time, eyes wide open. I listened for sounds that I knew weren't there. His breathing, his small movements in the bed. The feeling of estrangement was acute. I missed him the way a child misses his mother, a wife misses her husband.

My life was here; the tent was my home, the river my source of food, the stars pressing down through the dark night's thinly spun fabric were what illuminated my mind. And now I would soon be leaving Mongolia.

But did it have to be that way? Wasn't Mongolia, as much as it was a place, also a feeling? Couldn't Wilhelm and I continue like this forever, visiting new countries all the time, searching for unknown species? Our life could be one long expedition. I could be his travel companion for the rest of our lives.

Clinging tightly to these hopeful thoughts, I fell asleep, alone, curled up like a bear in its lair.

Surprisingly, Wilhelm returned the next day and was in such a hurry and so electrified that, for a moment, everything else vanished. He and the other hunters rode hollering and laughing into the camp right after sunset. He jumped off his horse and came toward me holding out his arms.

"A successful capture. Just one day and we did it!"

I had to hold up the lantern to get a good look at the new foal. It was older and larger than the first, reared its head backward, whinnied energetically, and flared its nostrils.

"It walked all the way by itself," Wilhelm said. "Didn't lie down once."

He looked at it proudly, as if it were a young son who had recently performed an important athletic feat.

Wilhelm led the foal into the paddock and released it.

Then he nodded toward me.

"Come."

We had placed a mare that had lost her foal during delivery in an adjacent paddock. The foal quickly discovered her and went over to the fence. The mare was a bit slower, but soon she also approached. The moment of truth. If she showed an interest in the foal, there was hope.

And quite right, she was a calm sort, taking her time as she walked all the way up to the fence and sniffed at the foal.

We gave them a little time to become acquainted, then, after a couple of hours, we took the chance of opening the gate between the paddocks. The foal trotted boldly straight over to the mare, seemed to think that she was *his* already. She studied him for a while, perhaps thinking, this one doesn't really look like mine, but allowed him to find her teats all the same. She had lost a foal of her own. I know of mares that have tried to kidnap the foals of other horses in desperation over their own childlessness. Maybe she was one of these who really wanted and needed to be a mother.

For the first twelve hours following this promising introduction, we did not leave their side, watching for the tiniest change in the foal that might be a sign of illness or that the milk didn't agree with him. But the foal was every bit as lively, running back and forth in the paddock with its new mother, swishing its golden tail so it rippled through the air.

"It's working," Wilhelm said. "It is actually working."

I nodded, but I was unable to smile because the new foal reminded me of the last one, the first one, and taking pleasure in the new one felt immediately wrong.

He elbowed me in my side.

"Why so serious, Alexandrovich? Look at him!"

The foal skipped to the far end of the paddock, stopped for a moment, turned around, shook his head, and dashed off in the other direction, as if happy to be alive, happy to be able to run.

"Yes, look at him," I said, but failed to summon any feeling of joy.

That evening, Wilhelm wanted us to open a bottle of vodka we'd brought with us all the way from Petersburg. He raised his glass toward me in a toast.

"Do you remember what I said about an object of investigation," he said. "It didn't die in vain, the first foal. Now we know how to proceed."

I raised my glass in response but was unable to return his smile. For the first time during the entire period we'd spent together, our feelings parted company. I could not comprehend how this could be so easy for him.

He became serious. "It will fade," he said. "The more foals we manage to capture, the more successful the expedition, the more these memories will fade into the background."

"I understand that," I said, and wondered for a moment if he also meant the memories of us.

I sat in silence, incapable of pushing aside my sadness and, at the same time, aware that I was naïve. I had worked with living creatures for the entirety of my adult life. I'd lost many; I knew perfectly well that the road leading one healthy and energetic animal all the way to Europe's zoological gardens and menageries was often strewn with many cadavers. But I could still feel the weight of the dead foal in my lap.

"Misha?"

Wilhelm stroked my hand.

"You're right," he said. "I've allowed myself to become callous. I apologize. We won't forget the dead foal."

I lifted my head and looked into his eyes.

"You are a good person," he continued. "The more I get to know you, the greater is my respect for you. I need someone like you. I've always needed someone like you but didn't understand it until we met."

Will you want to continue, I wanted to ask. Will you also need me later, after Mongolia? But I never asked the question—not because I feared the answer, but because I didn't dare take the chance that he would ask me the same.

Sometimes time can move slowly, just as sluggishly as a caravan in heavy snow, sometimes as quickly as a fleeing wild horse.

In the weeks that followed, the time raced by.

Wilhelm went out with the nomads on two more occasions, but soon we had so much to do at the camp that both of us had to stay there. The chiefs operated very well on their own. They came back with a foal, then another, and these new foals quickly became attached to the mares we had chosen as wet nurses. I greatly appreciated that Wilhelm no longer disappeared on the hunts but, instead, stayed at the camp with me. The few times he went out, I missed him intensely and was unable to think about anything but how things would be when we returned home. But as soon as he came back and was with me again, I was able to put aside my worries. We never talked about the future.

The nomads proved to be extremely competitive and the hunting expeditions became a kind of sport. They came back with the horses satisfied and left us with even greater satisfaction, their pockets full of silver, tea, and wool ribbons for their wives. After the first three foals had been captured, the hunters disappeared for a while. Then suddenly they appeared again and told us they had found another herd and that they had also discovered the trail of a third.

Several of the natives had clearly developed a taste for this endeavor or, perhaps, more so for the payment, because the hunting party soon increased in size. They would be gone for a few days and return with two foals. Subsequently, they disappeared again, this time returning with three, two of which were one year olds—stronger and more viable specimens, who needed neither a wet nurse nor extra follow-up.

We had built a paddock for the horses just a few meters from the opening of our tent. I awoke to the sound of snorting and whinnying, fell asleep to the sound of their hooves pounding against the ground.

We soon had more foals than we had ever dared hope we would manage to capture and far more foals than we actually needed. Still the nomads continued hunting. Wilhelm tried saying politely that it was enough, that we had what we needed, but they didn't stop until Wilhelm one day showed them the chest of wool ribbons and silver coins. It was almost empty. Finally, it appeared they understood because the next day, fortunately, they did not return with more foals.

That evening, we both stood beside the paddock. We had hired several helpers who assisted in the work with the foals. Three of them were now underway with the task of introducing the three latest arrivals to their foster mothers.

Wilhelm looked at the horses and shook his head.

"We have captured too many. The trip back is going to be completely different from what we had planned. The number of animals . . . both the foals and their foster mothers . . . I just don't understand how we will do it."

"But what do you want to do? Is it possible to release some of them?"

"Release them? We have captured Przewalsky foals and you want to let them go?"

"But the Duke of Bedford only ordered six horses; what do you think he will have to say about this? He probably should be informed of our situation . . ."

"It's more than one week's journey to the closest telegram office. Contacting him would be too difficult."

"And we should leave well before the autumn?"

He nodded.

"We'll just have to take all of them with us."

We left Kobdo on a morning in July.

I walked slowly around on the round patch of flattened, dead grass where our tent had been pitched and took in the sight of the multitude of creatures we were supposed to bring with us.

When we left Petersburg, the expedition included only the two of us; nobody paid attention to us and neither was there any reason why they should. Now I knew that, no matter where we went, everyone would turn around and look at our caravan.

The thirty foals were not alone. Many of them trotted side-by-side with their foster mothers. Beyond this, our party included fourteen camels, each of them heavily loaded with cargo. In addition to this, fourteen of the nomads with whom we had become acquainted over the past few months (all of whom had given the impression of being particularly solid and reliable) came along as herdsmen, guards, and crew, and each of them, of course, had their own magnificent horse. The young chief had accepted the commission. It seemed he had finally understood our objective and, even though he was sparing with his smiles, from his satisfied expression, I could tell that this was a kind of restitution. In addition to the wild and tame horses, we had a number of domestic animals that would provide food during the journey— cows, sheep, and goats.

The caravan produced a deafening uproar of whinnying, snorting, and neighing. Animal bodies were everywhere.

From two men to this. I grew dizzy and, in a brief flash, hope came to me. We had created all of this; if we could achieve this, we could certainly achieve anything?

I walked away from our former tent site and then stood still for a moment, taking in the sensation of Mongolian soil under my feet.

Then I swung up onto my own horse and turned toward Wilhelm.

"Are you ready?" he asked.

I couldn't bring myself to speak but I think he must have seen how moved I was because he came riding toward me, positioning his horse next to mine, and said softly so only I could hear— though he could have shouted it because nobody else there understood French—

"You and I, Misha. We are invincible."

"Yes," I said. "Invincible."

EVA

The rain was relentless. As it continued to pour down, the monotonous drone of raindrops became a pervasive background noise for everything we did, for all of our conversations.

Then one night I awoke and noticed that something was different. I felt disoriented and lay in the darkness for a long time trying to pinpoint what had changed.

It was quiet.

I went over to the window and looked out. A yellow half-moon hung above the trees, middescent. The Big Dipper lit up the sky. I wanted to shout with joy into the quiet night. It was impossible to sleep. I shoved my feet into my shoes and quickly got dressed. Everything I did produced a loud, clear sound. During these past weeks, when everything had been erased by the rain, I had apparently forgotten how many small sounds were found in the world.

Outside, the air was clear and mild, like a spring night, even though it was only February. The moon disappeared, the sky darkened, and the stars gained even greater clarity.

The night sky was completely different now; no lights from the earth challenged all the tiny suns out there. The Milky Way lived up to its name; the stars shone so brightly and were so numerous that the sky was more white than black as the galaxy poured through it. I leaned my head back as far as I could and watched the stars until the myriad of lights began to move, approaching me, and the earth.

A day of sunshine. A day of Isa singing as she ran across the yard and finally smiled at me the way only she can smile. A day of tea on the doorstep and warmth on my face. A day where we could put the wood out on a huge tarp secure in the knowledge that it would be completely dry by the time evening came; a day when the beads of water covering every surface shrank and disappeared; a day when the temperature finally rose and the air emitted the scent of everything that was to come.

But I didn't receive yet another night of stars. I didn't have the chance to show Isa the yellow sliver of a moon or stand beneath the sky looking at the Milky Way with Louise because, when evening came, the wind picked up pulling with it a gray wall of clouds. The pink light of the sunset disappeared as quickly as if someone had flicked a light switch.

I knew about wind like this. I recognized the velocity with which it arrived, the cold that suddenly slid in across the landscape, which gave me frostbite in my fingers when I tried to work. Now work was all that mattered. Everything had to be carried inside; everything had to be secured, closed, battened down. Once a wind like this had blown away our picnic table. We found it the next day thirty meters away from where it had been, broken lengthwise neatly in two as if a giant had used it for karate practice. The giant was the wind, the weather, the monster that the earth increasingly proved itself to be.

We were indoors when the first drops of water began hammering on the roof. We sat in silence before the stove. I'd told Isa to do her homework, that she shouldn't worry about the wind—if we always allowed ourselves to be stopped by the weather, we would never accomplish anything—but her gaze kept sliding toward the window where the raindrops were hitting harder and harder.

"What if it breaks," she said suddenly. "What if the windowpane breaks."

"We know that it won't," I said.

"Not yet, no," she said. "But one day. One day the windowpanes won't be able to take any more. They will give in. I would prefer not to be here on the day when that happens."

"Look here," I pointed at her notebook. "Aren't you supposed to be studying probability theory?"

"What's the point if the window breaks?"

"You can calculate the probability of that actually happening."

"Yuck," Isa said.

Louise smiled above the mending she had in her lap.

I was glad I was able to joke, that I managed to conceal my true feelings. I used to measure rainfall like this with Isa, the number of millimeters that fell. We made math problems out of it, saved the records. But with time, I stopped taking the initiative. I couldn't bear to talk about precipitation any more than was absolutely necessary.

None of us said another word. The two of them worked on their respective projects, but I couldn't concentrate, could not rid myself of the image of the windowpane shattering under the force of the rain, of glass fragments bursting into the room, water everywhere, on Louise's mending, on Isa's homework, on her sloppy handwriting, smudging it across the paper.

I stood up, noticing that a few drops had seeped in beneath one of the weather strips. I grabbed the dish towel, rolled it up, and lay it down along the sill. I could feel the porous, old woodworking under my fingers, the paint that was peeling, how rotten the rubber was. I didn't have any more paint, any more silicon, any new weather stripping to replace the old.

The candle stump had also almost burnt down. I had molded new candles from old wax remnants, but we would soon have burned all these as well. Soon we would have to sit in darkness in the evenings.

I blew out the candle, said good night, and all three of us went to bed.

It was impossible to sleep. Downpours like this allowed me no peace. I would not be able to calm down until it let up and I could assess the extent of the damage. And then I suddenly thought of the cellar door; had I remembered to close it properly?

So, yet again, on this night, I got out of bed. On yet another night, I got dressed in the dark and this time I didn't have the help of the moon. And now I wasn't standing out in the yard; now I was running, wading through water.

I was wearing my raincoat, rain pants, and boots, but, even so, the water soaked through. Ice-cold drops ran down my back, finding their way all the way down, over my hips, down my legs, into my boots; soon my feet were sloshing in water.

One of the flashlights still had a working battery. I turned it on for a moment. The stairs into the cellar had become a brook; the water ran in torrents, pooling down by the cellar door. There was more water than ever before. Yes, it was closed, but I knew it didn't help, not in the long run. The water would find its way inside, not just through the tiny cracks around the doorframe, but also through the foundation.

I couldn't open the door to the cellar to check because then I would let in even more water. I just had to trust that the rice, wheat, and vegetables were stored far enough above the floor to be out of harm's way. We had picked everything up off the floor; certainly the water couldn't rise all the way up there. It mustn't rise that far.

I opened the door to the cowshed. Apple turned toward me, lowed softly, and squirmed restlessly. Water was dripping from the ceiling in several places. I shone the flashlight beam upward to see where, so we could try to seal it again when the rain abated.

Just to be sure, I went into the barn. It was the newest building on The Farmstead and always made me feel safe. There were no rotting boards or deteriorating materials here. But the force of the rain that was falling now had vanquished the roof of the barn. Here, too, brooks were flowing, minicatastrophes. I couldn't hear my own breathing in the insane uproar produced by the rain, but could tell that I was breathing hard.

Rain was dripping on the haybales.

For a moment, I froze.

Rotten hay. If the hay got ruined, I might just as well slaughter all the animals one by one. I should have thought of that yesterday when I was running around trying to prepare the farm for the onslaught of water. But I had never before seen anything like this; never before had the rain dripped through the roof here in the barn. It was safe. It was usually safe.

I rushed to find a couple of large tarps and covered the hay with them. Maybe it was already too late, but I had to try, at least. While I was working, I tried not to think, tried not to picture the creatures being nourished by the water in there, who had begun their slow, incessant work where what was intended as nourishment for my animals would end up nothing more than nourishment for the earth, as fertilizer.

KARIN

Afterward, when everything is over. When there is no longer any God or anything beautiful. When we are just two sweaty, smelly bodies. When he runs his fingers over my body and again says I'm lovely. Then I am incapable of answering.

He falls asleep almost immediately. Makes himself at home in the bed as if it were his.

I turn over, trying to find a place for myself. He has wrapped his arms around me. His left arm is trapped beneath the weight of my torso. I twist my body to free it.

He remains lying on his back, one arm resting above his head. He breathes with his mouth half open. There is something ageless about him as there often is about people when they are asleep. It's easy to see how he was as a child. Smooth, innocent. And how he will look as an old man. Sunken cheeks, dark circles under his eyes. How he will look when he dies.

I turn away.

It is too hot. I throw off the duvet.

My body is clammy, and the air cools it.

But soon it is too cold.

I pull the duvet over me again.

Only one duvet to be shared by two. He should at least have gone to get his own before he fell asleep.

Just one mattress to be shared by two as well.

There's not really room for two people in this bed. I won't be able to sleep.

We are two adults, after all. Two adults can't sleep squashed together like this.

And what about tomorrow morning? Will he wake up here, too?

Must I awaken and see his face beside mine, feel his breath?

And when evening comes, will he come back again? Feel that he has the right to sleep here now? That he also owns this bed? Will he sleep here every single night from now on? Will I always be obliged to lie like this in the dark, clammy and cramped?

I sit up.

He is just a man. A male animal. I am a female animal. The two of us, out here, not so strange that something happened in the end. I was fooled by my own drives, my own instincts.

I reach out a hand. Poke him.

"Jochi?"

He squirms.

"Wake up," I say.

I lie in the middle of the bed. The duvet is no longer too warm.

It's better like this.

I don't even turn on the light, am simply relieved to be alone. Relieved that it is over.

I sleep alone in the dark.

I sleep in the darkness of war, blackout curtain darkness. It swallows me.

Woburn and Paris, their stiff, dead bodies lie on dry, yellow grass.

In the grove are three wild horses—a foal, a mare, and a stallion.

Mommy runs across the tennis court.

A ball descends, falling toward red sand.

My scarf is stained red from the blood of the horses.

You said there weren't any bombs here. I want to sleep.

A scarf around my neck, pink. Crocheted by Mommy. A Christmas present.

Blood on the scarf.

You said there weren't bombs here. I want to sleep.

Mommy puts the scarf around my neck. She is the one who crocheted it.

We go out into the hallway, Mommy first, quick, quick, I follow her, more slowly. The doors to the other rooms are opened.

You said there weren't any bombs here.

The servants of the household leave their rooms. Nobody says anything, they just hurry toward the first floor. A steady stream of footsteps. No stragglers.

I want to sleep.

Mommy pulls me behind her. We follow the footsteps through the big building where the servants live, down the stairs. Out the door. Across the courtyard, past the hunting lodge.

The booming comes closer. We run faster. Mommy tugs me. Her steps are rhythmic against the ground. She marches at a run, in step with all the others headed in the same direction, toward the safety of the bunkers.

We continue past the shooting range. The lake behind it glitters in the darkness, past the tennis court, behind it lies the forest.

A flash of light shatters the darkness. A bang. Even closer than before. Mommy pulls at me, but I stop short. Because now I hear screaming. It sounds like human screams. It sounds like humans.

I can discern them between the trees, whinnying, terrified. Back and forth, fenced in, no chance to escape.

"The horses are going to be hit, Mommy."

"We don't have time."

"The bombs will hit them. We have to open the gate."

But Mommy has me firmly in her grasp, dragging me along, squeezing my hand tightly. I try tearing away, but she is stronger.

Others push us forward. Hurry up, to the bunker, hurry. A man jostles against Mommy, she stumbles and falls, and at that moment my hand slips out of hers.

The horses scream.

I run.

Into the forest, between the trees. I survey my surroundings but can no longer see the horses. Then I hear them neighing, braying.

I'm coming, I whisper.

I keep running. Through the forest. Have to reach the paddock, find the horses, open the gate, so they can get away.

The bombs are falling, crashing around me, the flashing of bombs lights up the forest, the falling bombs blind me over and over again. I lose my night vision, recover it, lose it anew.

At last I can see them. Their pale coats between the trees, silver with sweat. They throw their heads back and forth. Their eyes are crazed. I hear them neighing, terrified and shrill.

I run toward them holding one hand out in front of me toward the gate, preparing to open it. But at that moment, another bomb shoots through the air hitting the forest directly before me. I see the horses screaming, but I can't hear them. I scream, but all sounds are swallowed up by the booming.

I reach the gate. My fingers tremble against the loop of hemp rope.

They are both lying on the ground. Wheat-colored coats splattered with blood. Black blood in the dark night. I squat down beside them, lay my hands on the wounds, trying to stop the blood that is pumping out of the big bodies. Tear off my scarf, want to stop the bleeding. But there's too much. Everything turns black.

Mommy calls me. Karin! Karin!

I'm here Mommy. I'm with the horses.

At that moment, another bomb drops.

Like a gigantic ball it hits the red, freshly raked sand of the tennis court. Sand sprays out in all directions.

I press my scarf against the blood. The pink scarf against all the black.

The tennis ball falls, again and again.

The sand sprays in all directions.

The booming tears me to pieces.

Mom, I'm here!

But now the night is silent. And she doesn't answer.

EVA

The rain relented. The water hadn't risen more than halfway up to the lowest shelf in the cellar and left the vegetables, rice, and wheat in peace. I removed the tarps from the haybales and tried not to think any more about the water I'd seen running down between the yellow straws, that the hay perhaps was rotting from the inside out, that we maybe had even less feed than we thought. But before that happened, before I spread the hay across the floor with the pitchfork and discovered that portions of it were inedible, we discovered we'd been visited by another kind of vermin.

I was on my way out of the barn when I heard Isa calling.

"Mommy? Louise? Mommy?"

She was sobbing. I put down the milk pail and ran out to her. She was standing by the cellar stairs, her arms reaching toward me.

"Someone was in there," she sobbed. "Someone has been in the larder."

"Who was it?" I asked. "Did they take anything?"

Without waiting for a reply, I ran down the stairs.

The potato bin was empty; that was the first thing I saw. Just a few, dirt-covered tubers lay on the bottom almost hidden under dry dust.

The bags of rice were gone, the canned goods we'd been saving for Isa's birthday were gone, the dried meat, too.

My gaze searched for something, anything; there had to be something left here.

Isa had come down. She stood quietly beside me.

"They took everything," she said. "Even the string of dried sliced apples I'd hung up. They cut them down and took them."

Then she put a hand on her stomach.

"I'm hungry, Mommy. I'm hungry."

Einar, I thought. There weren't many other people who knew about us. Could it have been him? Einar, have you stolen from your own child?!

At that moment, Louise came down the stairs, her bulky body cumbersome, her movements arduous, as she placed one foot carefully in front of the other, twisting her entire torso with each step.

She took one look at the empty shelves and understood immediately what had happened.

"Who?" she said.

"I think perhaps you know," I said. Suddenly I realized I was angry.

"What?" Louise said.

"You told someone that you're staying here. That we have food. That we still have food."

"What are you talking about?"

"You told someone that the cellar was full. When you took off."

"Who did I supposedly tell?"

"Mom, you're out of line," Isa said.

"I don't know who," I said. "Neither do I know where you went when you disappeared. Or who you were with. Maybe you were with Einar?!"

"Mother!"

Neither of them said another word; they both just stared at me. I turned away, my throat thickening as the tears threatened. Shit. Shit. I'd been in control. We would have been fine. We would have.

And I'm still in control; it's a matter of taking control. A ridiculous sentence flashed through my mind, something from an old American movie or song: It ain't over till it's over.

I walked quickly up the stairs and into the kitchen. There, in the drawer where Louise had put it after Einar's visit, I found the bolt gun. I stored knives there as well and now I took all of it with me, along with an empty bucket. Then I went out into the cowshed, over to Micro and stopped.

Isa and Louise followed behind me.

"Mommy?" Isa said, breathless, her voice tearful.

The huge animal moved slowly, bent over the hay, took a mouthful. I held the bolt gun, sticky and solid, in my right hand.

Louise moved behind me.

"Eva, are you sure about this."

I didn't answer. *Sure,* I wasn't sure about anything, the only thing I knew was that I was hungry, that Isa was hungry, Louise, the baby she was carrying.

The meat and entrails from Micro would potentially last a long time; she was old, the meat would be tough, but it was food all the same. And we could clean the intestines and use them for sausages.

But I had never slaughtered a cow alone before; Richard used to help me. She was so big, would she panic? And the blood, all the blood. She had to be bled, the blood had to be drained immediately. And then the meat. The quartering. The enormous amounts that would have to be dried, salted, boiled. It would take days, maybe weeks. The smell of meat, the metallic scent of red beef. Standing with my arms submerged up to my elbows in blood, smelling of meat and blood myself.

Suddenly Micro moved. She senses what I'm thinking; sees that I'm standing here with the gun . . . but no, she just bows her head over the hay again, takes another mouthful. Chews.

I walked back toward the exit. Isa and Louise followed me.

"Mommy, thanks," Isa said. "We don't need to slaughter her. It's better if she's alive. Thanks, Mommy."

But she fell silent when I stopped by the goats. They liked to keep warm, stayed indoors now during the winter. The kids were almost full grown, but were just as playful and affectionate as before. I open the door leading into them.

"No," Isa said.

Then I took hold of one of them. Isa had named them all. I never remembered which was which.

"Come on," I said calmly.

I had several ropes hanging in the cowshed. I tied one of them around its neck.

It followed me without resistance, leaping playfully across the floor.

I led the kid out into the yard, over to a corner by the barn. High up on the wall I had mounted a few hooks for this purpose. Isa was crying now. I could hear her begging me to stop. Louise, too.

I said they had to be quiet, so the goat wouldn't be frightened. We live on a farm, I said. You know how things work. I told Isa to pull herself together. She'd helped out with slaughtering many times before. I asked her to stop her foolishness.

Then I took hold of the goat, placed it between my legs holding its neck with my left hand, the bolt gun with my right. I placed muzzle against the middle of its forehead without measuring precisely, angled the gun so it would shoot downward and not hit me.

Isa screamed.

I told her to shut up.

Then I pulled the trigger.

The shot produced an ear-piercing bang. The goat collapsed.

Isa turned around and ran away.

Only Louise stayed put. She was pale.

I put down the gun, took the knife out of the sheath, twisted the goat's neck, it was limp and heavy, moved it into position, stuck the knife into the left side of its neck and slit its throat straight across, until the blood from the aorta began gushing out. I quickly placed the bucket underneath, we had to save the blood too.

Louise's face was as white as chalk.

"You aren't going to pass out," I said. "Don't tell me you're going to faint."

She didn't reply, just breathed heavily through her nose.

"Help me," I said. "Come on now."

When the worst of the blood had stopped gushing, I tied a rope around each of its hooves. Together we hung up the goat, head down. Louise kept turning away from what we were doing, small spasms jerked through her body; she was on the verge of vomiting.

I could have asked her to leave. I knew she wouldn't abandon me until I said she could go, but I didn't want to be alone. And I wanted her to see everything.

I had her help me skin the carcass, keeping her by my side as I sliced open the hide from the inside of the thigh.

"It's important to hold the edge of the blade against the hide instead of the meat," I said.

"And then you can keep pulling. Come here, look at this, like that, yes. Down along the abdomen, on the outside of the thighs, forelegs, use the knife here, like that and here you can just pull."

Then I went to get the saw from the toolshed and sawed the head off the goat. Bone meal, chunks of flesh, fur and blood stuck to the saw blade.

The head fell to the ground with a soft thump.

Louise bent over her big belly and threw up.

We kept working for several hours. First the entrails had to be removed. I cut through the membrane lining of the animal's body carefully so I didn't puncture the bladder, then I opened the abdominal cavity, stuck in my arms. The animal was warm; now the intestines slithered out of the body. I'd retrieved the slaughtering vats from the shed, positioning them to catch the intestines as they slid out. We would need them, had to eat everything. I cut away the heart, lungs, kidneys, and liver and removed the rest of the throat.

Finally, I brought out buckets of water and cleaned the animal thoroughly, then washed and dried the knife with care so it wouldn't rust.

I was rusty myself. It had been a long time since I had slaughtered anything. But I would have to get used to it. Louise and Isa would have to get used to it. If we were going to survive until spring, we would have to do it again.

CHAPTER 13

AN ANIMAL FROM
THE WORST OF MY
NIGHTMARES

nvincible, Wilhelm had said—you and I are invincible. But the words paled a bit more with each passing day. The caravan advanced slowly, moving through sand, through soil, between short trees clinging to the ground, through grass so dry that it would all disappear in a flash should anyone be careless with the matchsticks. It felt as if we were locked inside a pot with a lid on top; everything was boiling and immobilized simultaneously. There was nothing but the back of the horse, the heat, the small sips from the tepid water in the bottle and our eternally slow forward movement. Birds sailed above us—eagles, and falcons; we must have appeared so small and sluggish to them. The caravan barely moved and was so small that the steppes threatened to swallow it.

Then evening came. We found a site suitable for resting, for the tame and wild animals and for the humans leading them, where the grass grew tall and the ground was not too hard or full of stones. The nomads took us from watering hole to watering hole; they knew all of them. It was always with a feeling of anxiety that I said goodbye to a water source in the morning. I never fully trusted that I would actually see water again. But then another evening would come, and the nomads would have miraculously led us to yet another small mirror of life in the middle of the endless, stony flatland.

When the heat finally released its grip in the evening, the temperature plummeted abruptly. We lit a fire and roasted meat over the flames, but the air quickly cooled, and we had to seek refuge under pelts and carpets. I longed to curl up against Wilhelm's body, seek out warmth with him, but didn't dare, couldn't take the risk of someone seeing us. We slept side-by-side with the nomads on the ground. Maintaining the nomads' respect was increasingly important. They had to trust our orders, trust that we knew what we were doing. We couldn't afford to lose a single man, risk someone giving up. But it became increasingly difficult to uphold credibility. It was as if the apprehension seeped out of the ground beneath us as we rode, rising like gas from the soil that we inhaled and, the more deeply we breathed, the stronger it became. Wilhelm and I almost stopped talking altogether, and if we did, our conversations were only about how far we had traveled the past week, since sunrise, or perhaps just in the past sixty minutes.

Slowly, I thought constantly. I hate this slowness. I noticed every meter of our journey, every centimeter. But we couldn't push, couldn't force, couldn't go too fast, wear anyone out, neither humans nor animals, they all relied on our consideration, of how attentive we were to the needs of the foals. We kept our eyes on them at all times—on their movements, their contact with the foster mothers, their rest breaks, their nursing, how much they ate and drank, assessing whether they were old enough to eat grass and drink water.

They were the only thing I looked at throughout my waking hours. I gauged and assessed every single step they took, and I noticed that Wilhelm did the same.

They had been wrested from their native home, from their real mothers, from their herd, and no matter how painstakingly we watched over them, how much we did to try and meet their needs, nothing could compensate for that. The further we traveled away from the foals' natural habitat, the clearer it became that these horses were different from others. Their survival up to now had been based on fear, on an oversensitivity to their surroundings. They were timid and skittish, reacting to the tiniest of movements or sounds. Every single change was a strain and one by one they perished.

The youngest of them all, number seven, was never accepted by the foster mother. We were unable to induce her to take nourishment; she wouldn't drink from a bucket. She became more and more lethargic, and finally she collapsed and refused to get up again.

A big and strong male, number 24, suddenly fell ill after he suffered a leg injury in a fight with another horse. The wound became infected; he limped and soon he was no longer able to walk.

Number 13, a tan-colored female foal well into her second year, suddenly became seriously ill and refused to eat.

Number 21 lost its foster mother when the latter, who turned out to be far too wild, got into a fight with another mare and suffered an injury that couldn't be healed.

Number 18.

Number 5.

Number 14.

Whenever we lost one of the foals, we had no choice but to leave it behind for the scavengers. One would think I would grow accustomed to leaving a dead foal behind on the steppes, but it just became more and more difficult. The third time we left a foal behind—the dead body lying awkwardly twisted on the ground, inert, cold, and hard, the coat already losing some of its resilience, the birds circling dangerously close—an image flashed through my mind of not only this one horse, but of *all* the foals we had lost. They weren't lying alone as we had left them, one by one, but stacked on top of each other in a huge pile on the ground. In this pile, one could no longer see which hooves belonged to which animal, which head belonged to which body. It was just one large animal—a dead animal with forelegs and hind legs, hooves, ears, tails, flanks, bellies, necks and hocks, heads, eyes, eyes, eyes.

I started dreaming about this monster animal. Every time we lost another foal, the monster grew. And soon it was moving, making faint, moaning sounds, moving a hind foot, squirming, opening an eye. It got to its feet and stood there, swaying from side to side, slurping with all its tongues, howling like alley cats fighting at night. I couldn't see which of the many mouths created the sound or where it came from, but it grew louder and louder. I tried running away from the monster, but the sounds followed me, piercing through my brain, making me tremble with fear, and awaken with an intense feeling of shame.

Eventually, I was afraid to fall asleep. Instead I sat on the back of my horse and dozed—became distracted, unfocused, becoming negligent in my care of the foals—and we lost even more.

One evening when Wilhelm and I had pulled the fur bedcovers over us and laid down to sleep, I was so anxious about what sleep would bring that I had to say something.

"Is it always like this?" I asked.

"What do you mean?" he said.

"You've been on so many expeditions. How do you become accustomed to it?"

"To losing animals?"

"Yes, to losing animals. Especially foals."

"I don't know if I will ever become accustomed to it, not really."

"I dream about them, you know."

"I know. I hear you talking in your sleep."

"If we hadn't brought them with us, they would still be alive."

"You don't know that for sure."

"But it's the expedition that's killing them."

"But the expedition prevents them from being exposed to *other* injuries, from being attacked by wolves, from hunger and thirst, from being hunted by the natives."

"Meager consolation."

"When we finally arrive, they will live more safely than ever before. We will be able to protect them."

"We're not protecting them now."

"We're doing everything we can."

"It's not enough."

I wrenched away from him. His calm, reassuring voice chafed at me and the ground was so hard, the air so cold, always forcing its way through the gap between the fur bedcovers and the ground. I was tired of sleeping outdoors, tired of nature, even the star-filled sky.

"Have I told you about my Laplanders?" Wilhelm asked quietly.

I didn't answer, felt only how a sigh escaped between my lips.

"Misha?"

"No . . . no, you haven't told me about them. But I read about them . . . the story also reached the Russian newspapers."

"I had actually only ordered reindeer," Wilhelm said, "but an entire family came along with them."

"I'm tired," I said, and squirmed yet again on my hard bed.

"The story isn't long," he said.

I didn't answer and he must have read my silence as consent.

"The ship from Lapland arrived in Hamburg in September 1874," he began. "The sight awaiting me on deck was enchanting. Three small men dressed in furs from head to toe stood straddle-legged together with the reindeer, a little woman with a child in her arms, and a four-year-old girl hiding right behind them. They had very round heads, flat noses, and the color of their skin was a dirty-yellow. On the other hand, they were nice and small, their hands and feet like those of a child, and all were dressed in identical outfits."

"Where are you going with this?"

He moved closer to me so he could speak even more softly; his voice was gentle, just beside my ear.

"These small people were not exactly beautiful, not according to our definition of beauty, but they were so untouched by civilization, so naïvely innocent and good that it was like they were from another world."

"Or like animals?"

"No." He hesitated a bit. "Not like animals."

Then he continued, just as gently and reassuringly: "I understood immediately that these six people would be a huge success in Germany. My men and I led them all safely onto land and set them up outdoors near our property. The exhibition was a huge success from the first day."

"That's a strange idea," I said. "Exhibiting people."

"Why is that? The Laplanders were not aware that they were on display and they thrived splendidly in their new habitat. As a result, they behaved exactly as they presumably would have done in their native environment. Soon, all of Hamburg came to see this miniature Lapland and, unperturbed, the objects of attention simply continued with their work. They pitched their tents as they had always done, they repaired their tools, their sleds, and their clothing, all of which were made of natural materials. And, of course, they also took care of the animals. It was particularly fascinating to watch them as they milked the reindeer and this was a popular attraction. The six small friends must have found it odd that they received so much attention—they were just living their lives the way they had always done."

"I think the whole thing sounds odd."

He was quiet for a moment, lying with his face half turned away from me. It was impossible to understand what he was thinking.

"I grew very attached to them," he said finally, and was more introspective now. "As with many of the animals I have captured, they awoke a unique kind of love in me."

"What happened to them then?" I asked.

"They went home as satisfied as when they arrived."

"And you?"

"What do you mean?"

"Were you satisfied?"

"No . . . no, I guess I wasn't. I missed them, especially the eldest of the three men. He became a friend to me."

He spoke the last words with a special warmth.

"Why are you telling me about this? And about this friend?"

My voice was sharp.

"I didn't intend actually to tell you about *him*," Wilhelm said.

"No? You didn't?"

"My point is just . . . it all came about by chance and at a time when we really needed it. The number of bookings to the enterprise had diminished. Sudan's fantastic abundance of animals was being drastically depleted due to both hunting and war. This exhibition, the money we earned on it, was just what we needed. And the Laplanders had no idea about any of it. They never suffered any distress."

"Not even your friend? When he had to leave you?"

Wilhelm squirmed.

"I think it was worse for me than for him."

"And so, you continued?"

"What do you mean?"

"I've seen photographs of these exhibitions. Of Hottentots and Indians."

"I understood quickly that an opportunity lay therein."

"For revenues?"

"Yes, for revenues. When I sent another expedition to Sudan, I requested that human beings also be brought back. It was a great success. After that we welcomed a group of Eskimos. Then Somalis. Then Indians and Hottentots, yes."

"And did you make more 'little friends'?"

"No, no I didn't. I had my people handle all contact with the natives. And then the first letter from you arrived. It had been so long since I had personally been out in the field, and I understood that this could be exactly what I needed. I am a wildlife capture specialist. It's easier to bid animals farewell, after all."

Farewell . . . he was the first of the two of us to speak that word. I wish it had been me, that I was the one who had taken the lead, who had decided the final act for our expedition.

When I finally fell asleep, the monster creature was there again, the animal of shame. It howled at me with all of its heads, enormous and ugly and, at the very top, among the many horseheads, I caught a glimpse of a human face. It was his head, as if he were the true brain of this animal. He smiled so his eyes sparkled, and his mouth twisted in pleasure.

KARIN

Unable to sleep. Unable to wake up. Unable to breathe. The ceiling light is a large, glowing globe. A tennis ball, a bomb.

I close my eyes. Open them again.

Hear the horses screaming.

With a sob, I jerk myself awake.

Sit up in my bed. There's a pressure in my chest. I breathe faster and faster, but it doesn't help.

The horses are screaming.

My horses are still out there. I must get them back.

At long last, I manage to put my feet on the floor.

I splash cold water in my face. Get it together, Karin.

I dress with trembling hands. Pull yourself together.

I drive quickly, ploughing across the steppe. The snow sprays around the tires. Now and then, the wheels spin, but I force the car through every single obstacle.

I've asked to drive the Land Cruiser alone. Jochi is riding with Agi. He didn't question it.

The horses are in the same place we left them. I count. Yes, they're there, all five of them. Fortunately, they are all standing. We have filled up five ten-liter containers with water, have brought a drinking trough. We unload it and fill it with water from the containers. The horses jostle each other as they crowd around the trough. They stick their muzzles into the water, slurping as they drink.

There is still some hay left. Now we gather it and load it onto the flatbed. Then we lure them back to the station—with a trail of hay, we lead them and they follow. Step-by-step. Infinitely slow progress.

Sydney is always the last. He moves heavily and stiffly, limping, first on one leg, then on the other.

It is Praha who leads them at all times. Praha.

Hamburg accompanies the herd. He walks at a distance but still closer than he has ever been before. He seems unaffected by the winter, by everything that has happened. It seems, in fact, as if he has grown even larger and more powerful. Ready to take over. But it's too soon. Sydney must get better. It's too soon to replace the lead stallion. I need Sydney. And he has no visible injuries; the stiffness in his hindquarters is probably just because he was lying on the ground. He probably just needs some tender loving care. He will recover.

The horses stop from time to time, remain in the same place for several hours. I try calling them but it's as if they no longer respond to my voice. Or maybe they don't have the strength to respond. I drive back and get carrots and apples. Each time they show signs of settling down, I pull out the incentives.

I reach out my hands toward the horses.

"Come on. Please come."

"Not so close," Jochi says.

But I don't listen to him.

"Come, just come."

We don't arrive until evening. We lead them all the way into the paddock but leave the gate open so the harem can come and go as they please. Only Hamburg is isolated.

With stiff fingers, I loop the rope that holds the gate in place over the fence post. I stand alone there after the others have gone inside, faint with exhaustion, but I know I will be unable to sleep.

I stare at my five horses.

When they first arrived here, there seemed to be so many of them. I remember how the dust rose around them when they ran across the plains. That they were a storm of tails, hooves, and golden bodies. Now they are small despite their winter coats.

They must survive. Until the spring, until the cold releases its grip. You have to survive, do you hear me? Until more horses arrive.

The plan is ten. But ten isn't enough; I realize that now. We need twelve. Twelve plus the five I already have. And with the foal Praha is carrying that will make eighteen.

If I lose any next winter, the loss won't be as visible, as evident. Three out of eighteen is less than three out of eight.

No, I can't think like that. Every single one of them counts just as much. And I still have only these five.

I walk over to Sydney holding a carrot out to him over the fence. He lifts his head, half interested. Chews slowly.

Sydney. You must wake up. Become yourself again. Please.

I have to force myself to look at him. The heavy, sluggish movements, the frostbite injuries that are healing far too slowly.

I take a couple of steps away, my chest pounding.

It's madness, this here, the entire project. All the odds are against me—the finances, the hard winters, even the horses themselves. Because even if I succeed, even if the herd grows, even if this one herd becomes many herds, five hundred specimens, strong enough to manage without human assistance, there will always be an inherent danger in the horses themselves. In their genes. There are only thirteen of them. Are thirteen specimens enough to build an entire species? To make it stronger? More resistant to disease? To create a species that will survive in the long term?

Suddenly Praha neighs. The mare approaches me, sticks her head over the fence. Praha is as she has always been; Orlitsa's blood is running in her veins. She is strong and calm, her coat without frost injuries. I give her a carrot and it disappears into her hungry jaws.

"There you go," I say. "Good girl, Praha, good girl, Praha."

I save the last carrot. It dangles from the bunch of greens as I leave the harem and go over to Hamburg's paddock.

He is standing with his muzzle in the hay and I call to him. The minute he hears my voice he comes to me.

He gulps down the carrot. Hamburg is a survivor. I understand that I can trust him. If he is the lead stallion and Praha the lead mare, the herd will potentially survive.

I know what will be necessary. I must allow Hamburg to do what Hamburg knows how to do. The horses must work this out on their own.

Sorry, Sydney, sorry.

Slowly I walk over to the gate keeping Hamburg fenced in. With stiff movements, I open it.

Then I walk over to the harem. Open the gate there as well.

Then I leave them, moving away quickly without looking back.

EVA

I never got used to the color. More and more often, I found myself vomiting over the work, vomiting over my red hands.

The quality of our days had changed now. We took care of the animals that remained. Otherwise, our time was spent pickling, salting, and smoking meat. Only half of the hay we had left was edible. It was a choice between either the bolt gun and the knife or allowing the animals to starve to death. The death I gave them was, after all, quicker and more compassionate than starving.

We slaughtered only a few of the hens; most of them still laid eggs. But I put down both of the calves, the goats, and the pig, Boeing. I had been saving him for a party, saving him because I thought that, one day, we would have something to celebrate. He didn't understand what was happening when I shot him, grunting contentedly up to the very end.

Afterward, I went out to the horses taking a shovel with me, thinking I would turn over the soil outside the enclosed pasture, see if it could be cultivated, if I could perhaps start planning for the growing season. But I didn't have the strength for the job, just sat down on the ground, feeling the moisture soak through my rain pants. My neck ached, my hands shook. I will never rest again, I thought. Before I could take breaks for a week or two; I could slow down the work for short periods during the year. Now it was no longer like that. I couldn't rest for one single day, for one single night.

After awhile, Isa came out. Without saying a word, she sat down beside me.

"You'll get wet if you sit here like that," I said. "And cold. You can get sick."

"I don't care if I get sick," she said.

"You should care."

Death was closer now, she knew that. A couple of years ago, there was a doctor here in Heiane, and a year ago, it had still been possible to buy medicine on the quay. If she were to fall ill now, contract pneumonia, we wouldn't be able to get hold of any antibiotics.

"You don't care whether *you* catch a cold either," she said.

"Yes, I do," I said. "I'm going to stand up now, move around again."

But I stayed where I was. So did she. Her face was partly hidden by the shade of the hood on her rain jacket, but, all the same, I could see that her eyes were red. Water dripped off the brim, a curtain of rain in front of her face.

"Are you still giving the horses hay?" she asked.

I didn't reply. Couldn't bear to argue, not now.

"Mom?"

"You won't understand my thinking, no matter what I say. You've obviously made up your mind not to understand."

"But I want you to explain anyway."

"There are still many of us," I tried. "But there are so few horses. And now, who knows whether there are any others that have been taken care of." Isa drew a breath shakily. She tried to say something but failed, drew yet another breath.

"You're angry with me," I said. "I can understand that you're angry."

"No, Mommy," she said.

She pulled the hood off her head. Let the rain fall on her hair and face, didn't seem to care, just stared at me with a gaze I couldn't read.

"I'm not angry," she said. "I was angry, I've been angry. But now I feel sorry for you."

I could feel the water soaking through my rain pants; I was getting gradually wetter. The air temperature was just above freezing; the ground was cold as ice. I could get a bladder infection from sitting like this, so could Isa. The infection could spread to the kidneys. There was no medicine available. Isa could get sick and there was no medicine.

I looked around me. The dim rainy light was just as gray as the landscape. It was late March, but spring hadn't come. Still nothing was growing.

At that moment, a shadow appeared at the edge of the forest moving slightly back and forth. I heard him snort but didn't need the sound to understand who it was. Rimfaxe had returned.

Rimfaxe, the horse ridden by the Norse god Natt, who released darkness over the earth.

I glanced at Nike and understood why he was here. Even though spring had not arrived, she had already begun her summer. She was in heat again and Rimfaxe was ready. He took what he could get. It made no difference to him that Nike was another species; his genes would win out regardless.

I got to my feet, but Rimfaxe was already heading toward her. She noticed him and whinnied, lasciviously, I thought.

They stood on opposite sides of the fence. He stretched his head and neck toward her; she turned her hindquarters toward him.

"No," I said.

Neither of them reacted.

"Git," I said.

But he pushed his head between the rotten fence boards; it was just a matter of time before he would manage to break through.

"That's enough now."

I walked over to him and picked up the shovel I had thrown down on the ground. "Enough, do you hear me?"

I brandished it like a weapon.

"Git out! Damn horny devil!"

"Mommy!" Isa called, half shocked, half afraid.

"Git!"

I took a step toward him, waving the shovel.

But nothing made any impression on the large animal. He just stared at me. His nostrils flared slightly, he snorted faintly, then he redirected his attention toward Nike.

I was at his side in two bounds. Yet again I raised the shovel. I made no attempt to be careful and drove the blade straight into his flank.

"Get lost!"

He neighed, finally he neighed as if he were responding, but it was not the answer I wanted, because he was still trying to get to Nike.

"Mommy! What are you doing?"

I didn't answer, just pushed the shovel blade even harder into Rim-faxe's flank.

"Mommy!"

It was a scream now, but she didn't dare come any closer.

"I have to chase him off, Isa."

"But you're tormenting him!"

She came over to me, took hold of my arm. Her thin, sinewy arms gripped me tightly.

"That damn horse has to get out of here, don't you see!" I shouted.

"No!"

She hung on. Her fingers dug into my forearm.

At that moment, Rimfaxe twisted his body hard toward one side. I had time to see his ears flattening. Then, in one quick and firm movement, he braced himself, lifted both legs, and kicked backward.

Isa screamed.

I thought he'd hit her, that she was screaming because she'd been kicked. Everything else disappeared for a moment. Isa, my child, injured; for a split second, I saw her lying there, the blood running, eyes closed, saw myself picking her up, running off with her. But then I noticed the pain. Because she wasn't the one he'd kicked. I fell. And everything went black.

. . .

In and out of darkness. Isa sobbing. Louise and Isa lugging me back to the farm. I hear a voice mumbling, my own, incoherent speech, the horse, I wanted to say, stop the stallion. Drops are dribbling from my head, dripping onto my clothes, red drops, even more blood. A washcloth on my forehead. Mommy, Mommy, can you hear me. I am lying down again, damp fabric against my face. I am so thirsty. They give me drops of water, the glass knocks against my teeth, it's not enough. I must lift my chin to be able to drink, my arms and legs are throbbing, no, my head is throbbing, a hole, stinging, dry lips, dry throat, I raise a hand, manage to raise it, feel something tight around my forehead, big swatches of fabric, wisps of hair sticking out, dried blood, a metallic scent, like after a slaughter.

KARIN

I avoid the horses. Can't bear to watch what lies ahead. I keep myself busy with paperwork indoors, at my desk, but am so tired that I keep falling asleep over the documents.

Only at night am I awake. I avoid my bed, too. It's better to sleep with my head resting on my arms at my desk.

Every day, Jochi and Mathias fill me in on what has happened. Whatever happens is what is meant to happen. What I meant should happen. What always happens.

Sydney and Hamburg fight. Every day they wrestle with one another. Biting and snapping.

Sydney puts up more of a fight than I'd anticipated. I start to hope that he will manage to hold his own. But then he slowly founders, becomes weaker, more debilitated. Loses heart.

One day, it's Hamburg who is standing by the harem and Sydney is walking by himself.

It's done. There's no going back.

But everything is still not as it should be because Praha doesn't want to submit to Hamburg. She ignores him. Praha is carrying Sydney's child. That's why she remains loyal to him and will continue to do so until after the foal is born. Horses are predictable, after all. I am familiar with the parameters, know the rules, know what's in their nature.

But there are other rules that I don't understand. I don't know what's in *my* nature. Animals don't become lovers; animals become mates. Jochi has mounted me and I have, strictly speaking, mounted him. We should, perhaps, be mates now. But nothing has changed. Nothing, except for the looks he gives me. Nothing, except for all the times he touches me tentatively when he believes nobody is watching. Nothing, except that I look away, duck away from his touch, or just carefully avoid it.

After a while, he stops touching me. Then he stops looking at me. He starts moving quickly and doggedly. Slamming doors, rolling his eyes. Sighing over the things I say.

Is it true that once two people have had sex they can't go back to having a platonic relationship?

How will we manage to work together now?

I avoid Jochi and I try to avoid Mathias. It's not easy. He's there all the time. Following me. Asking questions and digging for information about the horses, says he wants to learn. I don't understand why. It disrupts the work. I can't have further disruptions now.

One evening, I am obliged to go down to his tent. He has borrowed a book of mine and I want it back.

"Come in." He answers as soon as I knock.

"Hi," I say.

"Oh, it's you," he says and his eyes narrow as he smiles cautiously. "Yes?"

Was he expecting somebody else?

The tent is neat; he has always, even in his worst periods, been good about keeping his things organized and neat. At least I managed to teach him that. He is lying in bed. It's dark in the tent. He's not reading but not sleeping either, apparently. Has still not put on his pajamas.

"Were you about to turn in?" I ask.

"No," he says and sits up.

"How are you?"

I say it because it's the kind of thing one says. To be polite. But then he sits up quickly, lights the oil lamp on the table, and reads something more into the question.

"I guess I'm fine," he says, and it looks like he has something he needs to get off his chest. As if there were a *but* at the end of his sentence. *I guess I'm fine, but . . .*

"Good," I say quickly. "That's good."

"Yes."

He looks at me. Clearly, he thinks I ought to have something more to say.

"How long are you planning to stay?" I ask.

"What?"

"Here. How long are you planning to stay in Mongolia?"

He squirms. "I hadn't really thought about it."

"I see."

"Have you?"

"Have I what?"

"Have you thought about it? Do you think I should leave?"

"Not at all. It would just be nice to know how long you're staying."

As I speak the words, I understand how important this question is to me. I must know when he is leaving. I must know when Jochi is leaving, too. It must be possible to organize the work here differently. There needn't be two of us here at all times.

"And what about you?" Mathias asks suddenly.

"What?"

"How are you?"

"Well," I laugh, "I'm fine of course."

"Are you still upset about the horses we lost?"

"No. It's okay."

But he doesn't seem to believe me because then he gets up and throws out his arms.

"Give me a hug, then."

"Why?"

He stays where he is, holding out his arms, and I have no choice but to accept the hug.

"Night, Karin," he says while his arms are around me.

"Night," I say.

The hug lasts for a long time, the way Mathias's hugs always do.

"See you tomorrow," I say and wriggle free from his embrace.

"Yes," he says. "As per usual."

I turn around and leave. On the way back, I remember I forgot to ask for the book, but it's too late to go back now. Besides, Jochi is walking down the path toward me. We say hello. He asks if I've been to see Mathias.

"Yes," I reply. "Why do you ask?"

"Is he doing okay?"

"Yes . . . yes, he's fine."

Good God, must people really ask each other that question so often?

"Are you sure?"

"Yes," I say. "Of course, I'm sure."

CHAPTER 14

A PECULIAR SHIFT

When we arrived in Moscow in April, we had been traveling for eight months. After the slow passage on foot over the steppes, the desert, and the mountains, and, subsequently, by boat down the Ob River on the final leg of the journey from Biysk, we made good time by train. But the speed was of little consequence because the traveling conditions were actually worse. The horses were packed together in cramped cars and we lost even more.

The caravan was now quite a deplorable sight. Out of the thirty foals we left Mongolia with, only sixteen remained, and the number of tame animals had been decimated to a fraction of the original count. The foster mothers were no longer with us; the foals had no need for their milk. We had replaced many assistants along the way and the herd was much smaller. We were sunburned and thin, our bodies covered with scars and bruises. We looked like savages.

In Moscow, the animals rested in a guarded paddock while Wilhelm and I checked into a hotel for the night. It was my first encounter with a proper bed in many months. For a while, I was able to suppress all my worries, taking pleasure in the scent of the bedding, and I cheered when I saw a filled bathtub awaiting me. While I bathed, Wilhelm cut off my hair and beard. Then we switched places and I did the same for him. The bathwater was soon full of my dark hair and his blonder locks. They bobbed on the surface, mingling, until they slowly sank to the bottom.

I had never cut anyone's hair before and took my time, fussing with the curve above his ears to make it as even as possible.

"It doesn't matter," he said.

"No," I said.

But I kept trimming with the same meticulous touch.

"The water's getting cold," he said and smiled.

"Sorry," I said. "I'm almost done."

When he was finally allowed to emerge, the hair in the bathwater stuck to his skin. I picked up the jug from the bathwater basin and poured clean water over him.

"Brrr," he said.

"My apologies," I said and handed him a towel.

Afterward, we stood in front of a large mirror with a silver frame that hung on the wall of the bathroom.

"It appears you're better with the scissors than I am," I said. "In spite of my exertions."

He looked at his reflection in the mirror. "It looks splendid."

"Far more uneven than mine, unfortunately."

"No. We both look splendid."

We took out the shaving kit and then we both shaved, covering our cheeks with shaving cream simultaneously, drawing the razor across our cheeks in the same slow movement.

"Are you shaving off everything?" I asked.

"Yes, everything."

"Even the moustache?"

"Even the moustache."

Once our faces were clean-shaven, we picked up our towels and dried our faces. I blinked at my own reflection and rubbed the smooth skin on my cheeks with one hand, suddenly feeling the chill in the air.

"Been a long time," I said.

"Does it feel good?" he asked.

"I don't know."

"You look good. You've always looked good."

For a brief moment, I didn't fear the homecoming.

Night came, what would be our final night together. We reveled in clean bedding, play-wrestling, and laughing with one another like children, stroking each other's freshly shaven, smooth faces and embracing again and again. But in every moment, I could feel the tears welling up. In every moment, there was sorrow behind our playfulness, and neither of us said a word about what lay ahead.

The final train trip from Moscow was one I knew well. When I looked out at the landscape that became more and more like home, with the serfs' small houses and open fields soon ready to be sown, it was impossible to keep my fear at bay. Wilhelm sat across from me, almost unrecognizable without his long hair and overgrown beard, deeply immersed in his own thoughts. Our eyes did not meet on a single occasion.

I tried starting a conversation several times, but he replied only in monosyllables.

We finally reached Petersburg and went straight to the zoological garden. I'd sent word to my mother that we were on our way but didn't give an exact time of our arrival so she hadn't come to meet me, neither at the station nor the zoo. Maybe I should have let her, maybe she was sick with longing, but I had too much on my mind. I didn't have the strength to deal with her as well.

The horses were going to rest for a few days in the paddock before Wilhelm continued with them on to Western Europe—first by train, then on the highway. They were all emaciated and tired. I immediately ordered a diet of carrots, crimped oats, and boiled bran mash.

When they were settled in, we stood beside the paddock looking at them.

"You have to choose the two you want," Wilhelm said.

I looked at one horse after another, our foals. I'd tried to avoid thinking about it, that out of the sixteen that remained, only two would stay behind here with me. I was reminded of the great difficulties my mother's cousin Betty had had in choosing Aleksej and Jelena from all nine children, and that she so clearly had never been fully comfortable with the decision she had made.

"Can't it wait?"

"You've been waiting for months already."

"This evening or tomorrow, it makes no difference."

"You're not stupid, Mikhail," Wilhelm said.

I turned toward him, suddenly saw that he was irritated.

"No, I'm not stupid. I just don't understand why it has to happen right away. Nothing has to happen today."

"Just choose two horses."

"We can wait."

"No. I don't want to wait," he said. "It's better to do it quickly. It will be painful regardless. Best to get it over with, the sooner the better."

I turned toward Wilhelm and tried to summon an impulse resembling clarity of purpose.

"I would like to be able to think about it for a day or two. If that's not a problem for you."

I used the hard, formal Russian *you*. To this day I don't understand why, and I saw that Wilhelm was nonplussed, though he quickly recovered his composure.

"This is not a choice," he said slowly. "It's simple. You will take number 17 and number 26. They were both a year old when we captured them. They're robust, have shown no signs of distress in the course of the journey. There shouldn't be any doubt."

I glanced toward the two horses he mentioned—number 17 was a stallion, number 26 a mare. Indeed, both were healthy and strong and among the largest in the herd. Number 17 would potentially be a good leader for a harem; number 26 would potentially give birth to many healthy offspring.

I turned away and shrugged, not daring to meet Wilhelm's eyes.

"That's that, then," he said. "It is absolutely the most sensible."

"How nice that you chose for me," I said.

"What?"

"How nice that you made that choice for me. You know much more about all this than I do, although I have worked in this zoological garden my entire life and was even the one who initiated our entire expedition. But still, it makes sense that you, Wilhelm Wolff, should decide."

"But my dear, Mikhail."

"There's nothing to discuss. Seventeen and 26 can stay here. You take the others." I turned and left the horses. "I have to find a carriage. It's time for me to go home to Mother."

"Fine," he said. "That's done, then. And your mother is, I would dare say, eagerly awaiting your homecoming."

Then we fell silent. Hard, angry retorts rushed through my head, but I managed to hold myself in check.

When the carriage drove up in front of the main entrance to the zoological garden a short time later, we still hadn't spoken a word.

"Are you coming?" I asked. "Will you accompany me?"

To my dismay my voice cracked like an insecure little boy.

He didn't move, just stood there stiffly without looking at me.

"I think I will find an inn instead," he said.

"But there's no point in that. Mother will be happy to have you."

"She will be even happier to have you all to herself."

The coachman stared at us impatiently.

"At least get into the carriage with me," I said. "We'll drive into the city together."

He climbed in hesitantly behind me and closed the door.

Once inside, we sat facing each other. It's over now, I thought, it's over already—the expedition, our friendship. I'm not even home yet and it's over.

"What about tomorrow?" I asked. "And the days the horses will need to recuperate. Will you be staying at an inn all that time?"

"The Duke of Bedford has been generous," he said. "He sent even more money. Besides, now I have an overview of the remaining expenses. I can pay for lodging the final nights without difficulty."

"No, of course, that will be much more comfortable."

Wilhelm instructed the coachman to stop at Grivtsova Lane and gave my hand a quick squeeze goodbye. He didn't expect an answer, just said that he would drive on to a suitable establishment. I had recommended several.

I closed the door to the carriage behind me and looked up at the house on the street of my childhood. It looked exactly the same as when I'd left it a year and a half ago. The daylight was fading and there was light in the parlor windows. I knocked on the door, the servant opened, and I heard my mother's running footsteps on the stairs. She is so light on her feet, I thought; she was at my side in a heartbeat. Then she put her arms around me without concern for the looks of the people around us.

"Misha, mishenka."

She felt tiny in my arms, a head shorter than me, but she embraced me with all her strength.

"Mother," I said, and held her just as tightly.

Then she released me, grasped my upper arms with her hands, and sort of patted me into place.

"Let's look at you, look at you . . ."

She looked me up and down, her eyes shining.

"You are the same, aren't you, you are the same? Mikhail Alexandrovich?"

"I'm, at least, still your son," I said.

Then she laughed, tears spilling out of her eyes, and she had to hug me one more time.

She didn't serve hen in white sauce on this evening, but veal in red wine prepared in the French manner, and I understood that both she and the cook had pulled out all the stops. Still, the food had no taste; it was like eating paper. And when afterward I was lying alone in my bed in my old bedroom, which was exactly the same as it had always been, it became impossible to stave off my discomfort. A feather fluttered up when I turned over and floated toward my face, tickling. I wiped my cheek with one hand to brush it away but the sensation remained, itching and prickling. There must be something wrong with the pillow, I thought; there were big holes in it and now it was leaking feathers, the down seeping out, fluttering over me, forcing its way into my nose, my mouth, down my throat. I threw the pillow onto the floor, the wool blanket as well, and lay there in the middle of the big bed. There I curled up into a ball, pulling my knees all the way up under my chin. I bowed my head and bit my hand to muffle the sound of the overpowering, wild sobs that shuddered like spasms through my body.

KARIN

The horses are shedding their winter coat. It falls off in huge, hairy heaps. It lies on the melting, rotting snow like perplexed dust mice. The horses rub up against each other with evident pleasure to shed their coats more quickly. They enjoy having the itchy spots scratched.

I can bear to be with them again, now.

The herd still stays close to the station. They are given hay and water every day, the water enriched with vitamins. But when the grass begins to sprout, they venture farther away from the paddock, a few more steps with every passing day. Soon they've reached the closest watering holes. They are living like last year, before the cold came. Almost the same, except the hierarchy has changed. It is Hamburg who is the leader now. He is the one who approaches the mares constantly, sniffing their urine, assessing whether they are ready. And they move into position for him; let him carry on. All of them except Praha, who is heavy and big and walks by herself, while she waits for her foal.

It's going to work, I think. They've accepted Hamburg. And Praha will also accept him once the foal arrives.

I seldom eat with the others. I wolf down meals at the counter before dashing outside again. But one day, Mathias has made *khorkhog*, a meat and vegetable stew. I can't resist sitting down at the table.

"Good," Jochi says, and nods.

"Thanks," Mathias says.

I chew on a piece of mutton. It is quite tender after stewing for several hours on the stove.

"Did you put hot stones in it, too?" Jochi asks.

"I dropped the stones," Mathias says.

"It's still good," Jochi says.

"What do you think, Karin?" Mathias asks.

"What do you mean?"

"Of the food."

"Good," I say. "I said so."

"No. You didn't say anything."

"Sorry. It's good. Tastes the way it's supposed to. Like meat and vegetables that have been simmering for a long time. Not too spicy."

"But *khorkhog* isn't supposed to be so spicy," Mathias says.

"Do you prefer it spicy?" Jochi asks.

"No. Not at all."

Both have stopped chewing and are just staring at me.

"It's good, I said."

They start eating again. Nobody says anything for a while. Then Jochi starts talking to Mathias, just to him, without looking at me. Mathias answers. And *he* looks only at Jochi.

"Halle has grown," Jochi says.

"You think so?" Mathias says.

"Yes," Jochi says. "She looks strong. Will do well, that one."

"Good," Mathias says.

"And that she's a mare," Jochi continues, "a mare and not a stallion, that's good, too. We will be able to keep her."

Mathias is immediately serious.

"What is it?" I ask.

"Are you thinking about Woburn?" Jochi asks.

Mathias nods.

"Try not to think about it," Jochi says, offering him a smile of encouragement.

Consoling.

As if it's Mathias who needs consoling about Woburn's death.

As if either of them is in need of consolation.

It's Woburn who's dead. We're alive.

I quickly finish the rest of my stew. It really doesn't have much flavor. I wished Mathias would prepare something other than Mongolian food now that he's finally decided to take responsibility for the cooking. I've been fed up with Mongolian food for a good while now. Meat and potato stews. Every possible kind of gravy. And yogurt. I'm sick to death of yogurt.

I stand up, pick up my plate and glass, and put them in the sink.

Then I go outside. Light a cigarette and get into the car. I drive with one hand on the wheel, following the tire ruts inward through the valley so rapidly that the car jumps.

It's been going on for a while. Jochi and Mathias talk to each other a great deal, but very little with me. Mathias hangs his head, Jochi consoles him. Sometimes he even touches him; I've seen it, the way men do, gripping his upper arm with one hand.

I keep driving. Stub out the cigarette on the floor. Stay in third gear, putting pressure on the motor, still can't see the horses. They must have moved even further away today.

I grow hot, my back sweaty. The light fades. I shift into fourth. The car thuds against the ground squealing metallically. The small of my back aches. I tense all the muscles in my body.

I don't see them until I reach the watering hole. I stop and get out of the car, feeling my heart pounding, the stiffness in all my joints.

The wild horses bow their heads toward the water and drink, then turn and start walking up the hillside. Hamburg and the harem stay together. But Praha walks alone a hundred meters away.

I can't see Sydney. I must find him afterward. If he recovers, his health restored, he may have many good years ahead of him. I can try mating him with one of the horses I'll bring in from France. It's only a month until they arrive. Then everything will start over again, for me, for Sydney. All we have to do is wait.

The grass is a bright, verdigris green. It grows in patterns, like running water, down along the hillside where the soil has the most moisture. The horses move upward. There's enough to eat here and enough to drink. They can stay here for a long time.

But Praha is outside the herd. It is even more obvious than before. The harem moves farther and farther away from her. Praha, who has developed udders, who is approaching her due date, walks all by herself.

If she found her way back to Sydney. . . . If she started again with him and the new foal. . . . But it won't happen. Praha is a part of Hamburg's herd. She recognizes the strongest. It's her foal that is the problem. Sydney's foal. It's in the way.

I move closer to Praha. The mare raises her head and glances at me before lowering her head toward the grass again. Her stomach is huge. Inside there is the foal protected by the mother's body. The foal that belongs to the wrong stallion.

Will you take care of your child, Praha?

Will you be as good a mother as you have been before?

Up until the birth, Praha will be alone. And when the foal arrives, nobody will be protecting it. Maybe not even the mother.

I can't interfere. I shouldn't interfere.

But both Praha and the foal need me. They need me here all the time. It doesn't help that I'm in the camp and come here in the daytime. I must be *here*. Move here for these weeks.

I hurry toward the car. If I'm quick, I will have time to pack a tent and provisions and get back before sundown.

EVA

A strong light in the room. Isa was there, standing by the window. She'd just opened the curtains, but then she hurried to my side.

"Mommy, are you awake? Mommy?"

She sat down on a chair beside my bed, lifted her hand and stroked my forehead. Her face was riddled with anxiety, but there was something else there, as well, something I had only seen in brief flashes with the animals—an all-consuming compassion, the kind of caring that makes one forget about oneself.

"Can you talk? Say something, Mommy."

"I can talk," I said, my voice hoarse.

She laughed with relief. "Yes. You can talk."

She picked up a washcloth from a wash basin, wrung the water out of it, and wiped my face carefully. The water was lukewarm, room temperature; it had been in the basin for a long time. And the feeling of the cloth against my face, the rough, damp terrycloth, reminded me that she had done this before, sat like this and washed me.

You take care of them, you wash them, you feed them, you watch over them, listen to the rhythm of their breathing, put your own needs aside twenty-four hours a day for their sake. But one day, the

359

roles change; one day, the child becomes the adult. The child is the one who takes care of you, washes, feeds, watches over, listens to the rhythm of your breathing.

But not now. That wasn't how it was supposed to be, not for many years yet; she was only fourteen. I had to get out of bed.

I sat up in bed. A cutting pain shot through my head, the room rocked.

"The animals." I said. "The milking."

"We've got it, Mommy," Isa said. "We've got it."

I fell back onto the pillow, had no choice, and again she wiped my forehead with the damp washcloth. It seemed cooler now.

A concussion, it was just a concussion. The horse had kicked me in the jaw. Isa and Louise had tried to patch up the wound, but I should have had stitches. I would always have an ugly scar at the bottom of my cheek and my face was a little crooked, as if my chin sagged on the left side of my face.

Slowly, I healed. The room no longer started spinning when I sat up on the edge of the bed. I managed to make it to the outhouse on my own. One morning, I even managed to lean against Apple's flank and milk her calmly. On my way back to bed, I saw that the budding apple trees were about to blossom. I stopped, touched one of them carefully. It would soon be time to pollenate, carefully brushing the pollen off every single blossom, allowing it to dry for two days, and then brushing the blossoms with pollen anew. I usually used Isa's old paintbrush, but there were almost no remaining bristles on the brush. I should come up with another solution now; I had to try to make one, maybe out of animal hair. I had heard that the bristles of a badger were suitable for shaving brushes; perhaps they would work for paintbrushes too. But it had been a long time since I had seen a badger, didn't know whether there were badgers here any longer. And finding a badger, hunting for one, no, there had to be another way. This, that nothing could be acquired any longer, neither paintbrushes nor fruit. All I had was myself. As if there had ever been any doubt that there was nobody else—no help, no higher power, no God. All I had was myself.

My head pounded. I felt dizzy, but I couldn't go back to bed. I had already stayed in bed for too long, had lost count of the number of days, had lost track of the food, of the hay.

I turned around, walked across the yard, and down the stairs to the cellar. It took a little while for my eyes to adjust to the darkness. Then the walls emerged. I glimpsed faint blotches, salt stains, and saw that the floor was damp. I walked over to a shelf. There was our food, our meat. I lifted a jar of canned tongue. I had never canned meat before, just hoped we'd done it right, that the meat was still good. I stood holding the jar in my hand, couldn't bring myself to open it to check, held it for a moment up to my nose, and immediately I could smell the rancid odor of meat gone bad. I quickly put the jar down again. Then I checked a smoke-cured ham that hung from the ceiling. I didn't need much light to be able to see that it was moldy.

I inspected more jars; checked a couple of sausages. Some of the food was edible, but portions of it were ruined. We should slaughter one more animal, another animal. But what good would it do if the meat rotted or if we were robbed again? Somebody knew about us; somebody was watching. It could happen again at any time. And it didn't help that I was here. It didn't help that I kept working on the farm, that I ploughed, sowed, slaughtered.

I left without saying where I was going, took the main road, didn't worry about anyone seeing me, just had to get down there as quickly as possible. Now and then, I stuck my hand in my pocket where I had put the bolt gun. The metal was cold against my fingers. I had just brought it as a precaution, would only use it if they didn't want to accept the deal.

There was a fork in the road—one direction would bring you to the main road while the other led to the harbor and Heiane city center. I stopped there for a moment. How easy it would have been to keep walking, take the main road headed north. Leave everything behind. Just me and the road, nobody to answer to, nobody to take care of.

I turned and walked toward the harbor.

It was a sunny day and the clouds floated buoyantly in the sky. The water was dead calm, not a sound to be heard, not a seagull in sight.

I gazed at the empty houses in the village. I thought I smelled chimney smoke but couldn't tell which house it might be coming from.

All the same, I knew I wasn't alone; that there was someone here, someone watching who came and went.

I heard him before I saw him, the sound of footsteps on wet asphalt echoed between the white wooden houses.

I straightened up, preparing myself.

He appeared at the end of one of the dead ends leading to some of the village's most beautiful cottages. Those with an ocean view and a swimming pool, those located so close to the ocean that it now threatened to swallow them.

It was Peter, Einar's friend, Peter.

He walked all the way over to me, nodding almost imperceptibly. He looked sober. His gaze was clear, but his eyes were red.

I gave him a once over. He was big and heavy, but I was quicker. I could run away from him if necessary, I thought, but then caught myself. I wasn't here to run away from them.

"You've been through the wringer, I see," he said and pointed at the bruises on my face.

"I need food. And hay for my animals," I said without explaining. "And I need to know who is still here and if someone can help me."

At that moment, yet another man appeared on the road ahead. Slow movements, powerful work hands. It was the fisherman. Did he live here in Heiane now? Had he been living here all along? Was he one of them, that kind of man after all?

The fisherman approached, went to stand beside Peter, looking me up and down.

"You can come home with us," he said.

"Yes," I said. "Fine."

Don't hesitate, don't show any signs of uncertainty, just go with them voluntarily.

We walked without saying a word. I put my hand in my pocket, but maybe they saw it; maybe they understood I was carrying a firearm. I took my hand out again quickly, could still feel the faint pressure of the pistol against my thigh.

We reached the end of the road where the cottage with an annex was located. A number of the windowpanes on the glassed-in veranda were broken. The swimming pool was full of brown rainwater and dead leaves were floating on the surface.

Peter held the door open for me with a gentlemanly arm gesture.

"Welcome."

The fisherman grinned.

"Thanks," I said, as if I hadn't noticed the game.

We went into the living room. The embers in a huge fireplace in the corner were glowing faintly. That kind of fireplace was mostly for decoration, didn't generate much heat, they probably had to feed it around the clock to reap any benefits from it. They had to work, even people like them had to work now; stealing from others was no longer enough, there was hardly anyone left to steal from.

It had been many weeks since the robbery. If they were the culprits, they would probably not have much left, but perhaps something. They must have something. I looked around trying to detect signs of our food. Whatever that might be. Suddenly, I felt foolish. A scabby potato from last year would still be nothing more than a potato.

My hands and feet were tingling. I suddenly realized how cold I was; the raw air had settled into my body during the time I'd been outside. Here, inside, the air was warm. I was so tired, my head pounded, and I wanted to be done with this. I had nothing, but for them, I had something. A body, a woman's body. Even though it was worn out and looked older than it was, they probably didn't care.

Peter pointed at the couch.

"Have a seat."

It wasn't a question.

"And take off your jacket. It's nice and warm in here, don't you think? You don't need to keep your jacket on here."

I sat down but left my jacket on. "I'm still cold," I said.

Peter sat down beside me. "Poor thing."

I could smell him, a surprisingly faint body odor. He was thinner. I wondered how his skin would feel, if he was dirty, if he had any infectious diseases.

"You have food?" I asked.

"Are you hungry?" Peter asked.

"Yes," I said. "We're running low after the winter."

I wasn't stupid, I hadn't wandered thoughtlessly straight into the lion's den. I was just doing what I had known all along would be necessary. What women have done throughout the ages when their hunger became unbearable. I was selling the only thing I had to sell.

"We have food," Peter said. "At least, since it's you who's asking so politely."

Then he lifted his arm and lay it behind me.

I knew exactly what was going to happen. The knowledge of what was coming was hereditary, a biological history, even though I'd never done this kind of thing before. He would put his arm around me, pull me close, move a hand down onto my thigh, kiss me. I would turn my head away, so he understood that this was not something I really wanted to do, but had to do; this would excite him, not greatly, but enough so he would take hold of me and lay me down on the couch. Then he would quickly undo his trousers, pull them down to his thighs, expose himself, while simultaneously bragging about his own member, maybe say something about the size to hide the shyness he suddenly felt about his penis wobbling foolishly between us. Then he would pull down my pants, too; he wouldn't take the time to look at my breasts—what was important now was to finish the job. He would penetrate me without bothering to find a comfortable position. He would accept my turning my face away, wanting only to get it over with, moan and empty himself. Then he would, without saying a word, nod to the fisherman. He would perhaps come even more quickly; he would sense how his decency melted away with each thrust. Afterward, they would both be ashamed and, to hide this, they would exchange lewd comments, talk about how *fucking great it was to get some pussy again.*

Then they would give me what I'd asked for. They wouldn't call it a sale, but they had to give me something, because if they didn't give me anything, it would be rape and then the shame would be worse. Maybe they would give me more than I'd asked for, maybe even offer me some hay. And I would be numb and warm; the numbness would remain in my body for a long time, maybe forever, and grow worse every time I came here, every time the transaction was made. But it made no difference as long as they stayed away from us and from the farm, as long as they stayed away from Isa and my animals, from Louise and the baby that would soon be born.

His arm lay behind me and I was ready.

But at that moment, I heard footsteps on the stairs. Einar came into the room, his face startled when he saw Peter's arm around me.

"What's going on here?"

Peter stood up. Was about to say something, perhaps apologize, but Einar beat him to it.

"Aren't you going to offer her something?"

Peter nodded, hurried toward a door to what I assumed was the kitchen.

Einar turned to the fisherman.

"You have something to do in the kitchen, too, don't you?"

He nodded quickly and left the room as well.

I wanted to stand, but then Einar sat down beside me. He stroked my face gently with one finger. I forced myself not to pull away.

"What has happened?" he asked.

"I want my food back," I said softly. "And I want you guys to stay away from us."

He behaved as if he hadn't heard me, but calmly removed his hand. I noticed a bandage on his other arm. There had been a cut there before, undressed and dirty. I reached out my hand and touched him; there was nothing gentle about my touch. He slumped and whimpered.

Then I noticed his fingers. His hand was red and swollen.

"It's crazy, right," he said. "I've robbed probably fifty doctor's offices and pharmacies. We've lived off that for years. But I can't get hold of a single package of something that actually works."

Then I saw that his eyes were glassy with fever. And that he was sober. I couldn't remember the last time he'd been sober.

"I'm sorry about the cellar," he said. "That's about as low as a person can stoop, isn't it? Stealing food from your own daughter."

"She's not yours," I said. "You can't call yourself a parent if you've never been there."

"Come on, Eva. You never let me try."

"I never let you try because I knew you wouldn't manage it."

He found nothing else to say, just stared at me in frustration, exhaling through his nose.

"I thought you'd all left," he said.

"So, that's why you came in the middle of the night? That was why you broke in as quietly as you could?"

"Okay, I'd hoped that you'd left, then."

"You've never showed up quietly before."

"I didn't want to wake you. Especially not her, the one who's living with you."

"Louise."

"Crazy lady."

"She is the kind who does what she has to do," I said and got to my feet.

I stood over him, feeling the weight of the pistol in my pocket. But I knew I didn't really need it. He'd shrunk. All I needed to do was kick him in the arm in the infected wound—he would collapse and give up.

"I want our food back. And I want you all to stay away from the farm. Stay away from Isa and the animals, Louise and the baby, when it is born."

"I really hoped you had left," he mumbled.

"I'm sure you did. You hoped that we would give up. That there would be yet another abandoned farm you could rob."

"No," he raised his head and looked at me. "Leaving is not giving up. Staying is giving up."

His gaze was completely open, and I thought I recognized something of the person he had once been. The person I'd thought he might become if I just took good enough care of him.

He stood up. Suddenly he smiled weakly, almost beseechingly.

"I'm the kind to stay," he said. "But you . . . I hoped you were the kind to leave. You and Isa. You can do it. You're able to think the way it's necessary to think. You can see what's required, picture it, while all I manage to do is what I've always done. And when there's nothing left to steal, it's over for me. And, anyway, it will be over for me long before that."

He held out his arm. I could smell the stench of rotting flesh.

CHAPTER 15

AN UNAVOIDABLE
FAREWELL

I got up early the next morning after a sleepless night, barely picked at my breakfast, and wanted to hurry back to the horses in hopes that Wilhelm would be there. We just had to talk, I thought, it should be possible to clean the wound, bandage it, and move on?

Mother was still smiling at me.

"Have a little more tea, here, and maybe another hard-boiled egg?"

But I couldn't stomach much.

"Have a nice day," she said when I got up from the table.

"Thank you."

She accompanied me out into the hallway. I noticed she was wearing a shawl I'd never seen before over her shoulders.

"Is that new?"

"You've always been good about noticing such things."

"It's nice."

Again, it struck me that she looked contented and that her contentedness was not due to my homecoming, but rather something that already existed inside her. The day before, when we had embraced, she was without question genuinely happy to see me again, but nothing of what I had feared—the tears, the clinging embrace—had come to pass. While I sat in the carriage on the way to the zoo, the image of her smiling face above the new shawl was still imprinted on my retina and there was something about this image that compounded my uneasiness.

I worked intensively with the keepers all morning, trying to teach them as much as I could about the needs of the horses. It was necessary to separate some of the stallions from the rest of the herd. They were now old enough that they were starting to act on the instinct to assert themselves as the leader and we couldn't risk losing any of them to aggression and fighting.

Afterward, I went into the zoological garden to discuss the new construction projects with a carpenter. Beside the camel's pen, I wanted to set up a pretty little space for the horses. A stable was to be built with a roof resting on four beams, the construction like that of a traditional stall, and a beautiful rose-painted hay manger. The stable would be centrally located in the park so the horses could be viewed from three different angles. There would also be only a fence between them and the public and, since the area where the horses would be was relatively small, the public would have many possibilities for studying them at close hand.

The director of the zoo came to call later. He shook my hand and thanked me heartily for his efforts. He was the picture of sheer joy. He even claimed ownership of the expedition; I noticed that he referred to it as *ours*, as if he had also made the entire trip to Mongolia and back.

Shortly thereafter, Poliakov, whom I'd summoned by messenger, arrived as well. He had immediately jumped into a carriage and driven as quickly as possible from the Zoological Institute. I accompanied him to the paddock and showed him the horses.

He gaped so widely that the entire row of his brown teeth was visible.

"Look, there they are, there they really are," he said. Then he turned to face me. "Imagine. You really did it."

I nodded. It was only now, in meeting with Poliakov's irrepressible grin, that it sunk in that I had actually achieved my dream. No, I'd completely surpassed it. There were not two horses grazing here, but sixteen, and here I stood, a world traveler come home again, every bit as rugged and tanned as the heroes of my childhood. And, if that weren't enough, Poliakov informed me that he had just had a conversation with none other than the Geographic Society and they wanted me to give a lecture there on both the expedition and the horses.

"It will be a full house," he said. "Everyone has been talking about you, you see. Everyone wants to know as much as possible, both about you and the journey. And about the horses, of course."

I nodded, aware that I should be happy, that had I ever had a type of destination for my life's journey, the podium in the great auditorium of the Geographic Society was as close to it as it was possible to get. But the thought incited no enthusiasm in me, no feelings whatsoever.

I kept a frenetic lookout for Wilhelm. Again and again, I thought I spotted him on the walking paths of the zoo or outside the wooden building that housed my office. But all I saw were shadows of him, copies that each time proved to be somebody else.

As the hours passed, I grew more and more frustrated. I was unable to focus my thoughts on anything but him and soon, a dim, nascent rage began smoldering inside me.

Wasn't our friendship worth more?

I'd promised Mother that I would be home early. It hadn't occurred to me that he wouldn't show up in the course of the day, and when I left work, I was still perplexed.

I left a handwritten note for him on my desk and gave word to all the keepers to be sure that he received it.

Sir Wolff,

I understand that you have a need to rest after the journey and hope you have found suitable lodgings, perhaps at one of the establishments I suggested? Please leave word about where I can find you so I can contact you should something happen to any of the horses.

You are most welcome to call on my mother and me this evening. Mother would certainly be delighted to see you again (she asked about you several times yesterday). It would also be useful to discuss the road ahead. My questions are many. How long are you planning to stay here in Petersburg? What preparations do you think we should make for the upcoming trip with the horses? Would you like me to accompany you on parts of the journey?

I sat looking at the last sentence for a long time. Finally, I asked the questions that had been on my mind for so long. Writing them down was so easy. Could it really be so simple? Without thinking, while the courage from the words my pen had formulated was still aflame inside me, I signed the letter, put it in an envelope and left the room. Then I went straight home.

While dinner was being prepared, I held watch from the windows facing the street, in hopes of hearing a carriage stop there or hear his footsteps walking toward the front door. I was certain he would come; for a few hours, I actually believed he would come. But the minutes passed, the hours faded away, and finally Mother had to ask the servant to clear away the additional place setting.

"I am so sorry about the bother," I said to Mother.

"All the more for us," she said.

Mother did her best to eat up the food, but I was unable to get much of anything down.

After the meal, I retired to my study where I sat watching the clock. Nine, nine-thirty, ten. It was impossible to sit still. I couldn't bear to stay indoors, knew that it would be pointless to try to sleep, so I donned my hat and coat and went out into the spring evening light.

I strolled for several hours, although strolled would imply the leisure of a Sunday afternoon walk. No, I rushed, almost ran through the streets at such a pace I felt myself breathing hard and noticed dampness forming on my back and under the brim of my hat.

First, I walked the full length of the Katarina Canal from north to south. The air here was damp, as usual; a cold gust blew up from the still winter-cold water, but it did not disturb me. I looked for him constantly and, whenever I passed a hotel or an inn, I peeked inside hoping that he perhaps was staying there and would be just on his way out. But, of course, I didn't see him; such coincidences are most likely to occur in literature, seldom in real life, at least, not in mine.

As I wandered, I began to dislike my own city. Petersburg is a city that swallows people like a pike in the darkness of the sea, with sharp, greedy teeth that snap up everything in its path. The city's orderly architecture, duly planned by its founder and namesake, summons a feeling of alienation.

The walls of the buildings loomed around me growing taller, darker, the streets narrower, the smell of the canals more putrid. I felt that, for the first time, I saw the city for what it actually was, really *saw* it. I didn't belong here; none of these people really belonged here, not just in a figurative sense, but also literally. The city was so young that we could all consider ourselves outsiders. Peter the Great had wanted to create a European capital to connect Russia to Europe, but this had only created a distance between us and the city. We were Russians, each and every one of us, placed in a European city in the middle of a swamp wilderness, where previously there had been nothing but wasteland, in a city eternally at war with the water, where the buildings, no matter how solidly they were constructed, in the end had to surrender because the water drilled its way in, tiny droplets, until floors and walls were slowly broken down, disintegrated, and collapsed.

Wilhelm had compared our friendship to drops of water and maybe he had been right. We were just a building in a rainy, swamp wilderness.

The next morning, I arrived at work earlier than usual. First, I went to check on the horses. They had everything they needed; the keepers were caring for them as instructed. I asked one of them if they'd seen Wilhelm. He nodded and said he'd come just after I'd left and that he had then stayed to work with the horses the entire evening.

"Did he receive my letter?" I asked. "Did you make sure to give him the letter?"

Yes, of course, he had received the letter.

I hurried to my office, the key at the ready long before I arrived, holding it up in front of me as if I were pointing with it, and stuck it into the lock before I'd stopped in front of the door. I was shaking so hard that it took me a minute to unlock it.

The room was empty, well, not empty, but I didn't find a letter. Nothing lying on the desk or on the bureau; the sideboard beneath the window was also empty.

I sat down in my chair feeling so horribly heavy, my behind pressed against the seat cushion, my feet motionless upon the floor. I picked up a sheet of paper, dipped the pen in the inkwell, and wanted to write yet another letter, but no words appeared on the paper.

I tried again, the nub of the pen scraping in the silence, and managed to write one single word—two small, black letters on the cotton-white paper: *We*

He arrived finally in the afternoon, just before the zoological garden closed to the public. He went directly to the horses' paddock without stopping by my office. It was one of the keepers who let me know he had arrived.

I put on my hat and coat and went to find him. A biting April wind blew through the park; a few guests were leaving, a guard rattled his keys impatiently. I rounded a corner and Wilhelm came walking toward me, his coattails flapping, his face hidden under the brim of his hat. He was listing a bit as he walked, I thought, calling to mind a heeling vessel. I stopped. To my right was the area where the two horses would be; the carpenters had worked quickly, they'd already raised the roof on the structure, but had now left for the day.

Wilhelm walked over to me, reached out his hand, sort of business-like.

Beside us, the brown bear paced restlessly in its cage.

"Kovrov."

How long it had been since he had spoken my surname, so long that it sounded strange coming out of his mouth, strange and hard, like the sharp creaking of a thick, frozen crust of ice on a lake.

"Wolff," I said.

I wanted to hold his hand longer, but he released mine at once.

"I just wanted to inform you that I will be traveling tomorrow," he said.

Tomorrow. A word that meant nothing, a word that dissolved, became individual sounds, just sounds without meaning, the kind animals make.

"So, that's all?" I asked. "Did you receive my letter?"

The brown bear walked around and around in a circle inside the cage, its paws silent against the ground.

"We're home now," Wilhelm said, his eyes on the bear.

"And?"

"We're home and other rules apply here."

"You said we were invincible," I said and stared at him. I hoped my gaze would induce him to turn his head to face me, to *see* me.

"And we were. But we can never win against the rules we have inside us."

His head was still turned toward the bear, but his eyes weren't following its movements; they were just staring blankly into space.

"You mean that we are like animals? That these rules are inherent to our species?"

He nodded slowly. "Yes, perhaps that's what I mean. It lies in our disposition, our genetic makeup."

"No, Wilhelm. Human beings are more complicated than that. The sordidness you spoke of . . . which manifests. I've never experienced anything sordid."

"Now you're lying," he said. "I know you have felt the same thing."

374

He lifted his arms, wrapping them around his torso as if he were hugging himself and, finally, he turned to face me.

"I must take care of myself, Kovrov."

"Mikhail. My name is Mikhail."

"It's Kovrov now."

He rocked from side to side, his eyes shiny, on the verge of tears. He pained me greatly, while rage mounted inside me.

"We can travel together," I said in a voice that barely carried. "We can just keep traveling."

"I am leaving tomorrow," he said. "Perhaps I am not the master of my feelings, but I am the master of my actions. And I hope my feelings will follow suit."

"No!"

He stared at me beseechingly. "Please don't make this more difficult than it has to be."

Then he turned and left me. He walked down the path to the exit, his back as round and closed as a snail shell.

KARIN

I pack rapidly, not wanting to leave Praha alone out there any longer than necessary. Provisions for a week. If I need more, I can ask Agi to bring it when he comes by on his daily rounds.

Both Jochi and Mathias circle me as I pack, but they say nothing. It's only when I'm ready to go that Mathias comes over to me.

"Well, this is a neat solution," he says.

His voice is sharp.

"I don't dare leave her alone out there; not now that she's about to give birth."

"I've understood that."

"You should be pleased about it. You've been so down about Woburn."

He looks away. Are his eyes shiny? Is he about to cry? Why in the world is he about to cry?

But luckily, he pulls himself together again.

"What about the station?" he asks. "And Jochi?"

"He has things under control here. I'm needed more out there. And he has you, too."

"What do you mean?"

"The two of you have become such good friends."

"Yes. Anything wrong with that?"

"Not at all."

"Karin, I don't think you can take off. In just a few weeks, you're going to pick up the new harem in Thorenc."

"He can handle things just fine by himself," I say.

"What about Agi? Wasn't the whole point of hiring a ranger so that he would supervise the day-to-day?"

I suddenly notice that Mathias's cheeks have turned red; his eyes are narrower and his lips pursed. He looks old. His face is haggard even though he's only thirty-four. Old and angry.

"What are you getting at?" I ask.

"What I'm getting at?"

He rolls a cigarette, his hands trembling slightly.

"Do you know why I came here with you, Karin?"

"Yes."

"No, you don't know."

"Do we have to do this now? It's not a good time . . ."

"It never is."

I sigh. "It's not like I can save you. It's not like you can keep expecting me to save you for the rest of your life."

His lower lip trembles the way it did when he was a child. He's an adult, tired and, at the same time, new to the world.

"The rest of my life," he says. "No, not the rest of my life."

"I have to go," I say.

"You always do," he says.

"Knock it off."

He doesn't answer. I stand waiting. Must say something more. Was too hard on him. No need to come down so hard on him. My anger could drive him away. Out onto the streets.

"I just meant that . . ."

"I know what you meant," he says.

And we are in Mongolia now, not Berlin.

"Bye, Karin. Go to your horses now," he says.

"Yes. Bye."

Fortunately, he says no more.

I wave to him when I leave. He lifts a hand and waves back. He didn't have to. If he were really upset, he wouldn't have waved.

Agi comes along on his moped, helps me pitch the tent a few hundred meters away from the horses. I am glad he speaks so little English. And that I speak so little Mongolian. At least one person I'll be spared having to talk to all the time.

"Bye, then," I say.

"Yes, bye-bye," he says.

I watch him drive away. The sound disappears first, swallowed up by the steppes. The last sign that he's been here is the dust rising into the air in his wake.

Three days pass, quiet days. Finally, I sleep well. Too well. Just want to sleep all the time.

On the third afternoon, I sit down in a camp chair outside the tent and try to read. I've brought along some research articles, but I am unable to make sense out of the sentences, become drowsy. Yawn loudly holding one hand over my mouth even though there's nobody there. The sun sinks toward the horizon. I keep an eye on Praha, watching to see whether she leaves the herd, tries to run away. Foaling always takes place at sunrise or sunset. But she is with the others.

I try to read again, start the same sentence over and over. Eventually, I give up. Maybe I need glasses; maybe I've grown farsighted. Most people my age have long since started wearing reading glasses. Most people *my age . . . my age . . .* as if age were something I owned, and maybe it is. In French, one uses the term *j'ai* about one's age: one *has* a certain number of years. I prefer it to the German and English "to be": I *am* fifty-eight years. I *have* fifty-eight years is better. Yes, the years are something one owns, not something one is.

It is also said that age is just a feeling, but that's foolishness. Age is wholly real. My body is aging daily. The cells die. I am just as mortal as everything else, as the grass under the camp chair, as the horses grazing a few hundred meters away from me. And there is no such thing as a soul. Neither the horses nor I have a soul. We have electrical signals, nerve pathways, hormones. All of it disappears when we die. Death always occurs when the brain stops functioning. It's the only way to die, the same for all the animals in the world, whether they are called *Homo sapiens* or *Equus przewalskii poliakov*. It's just a matter of getting as much done as possible before the brain's electrical signals stop.

The horses must have time to procreate.

And, fortunately, they do what they can. The mares lift their tails. Hamburg sniffs them. Soon they will be ready.

Sydney is keeping his distance. He hasn't fought with Hamburg for many days. He is still limping, but not so much that I must consider putting him down.

In between the harem and Sydney, Praha is grazing. Alone.

The next morning, I wake up early, think I hear a sound, unzip the tent flap, and look out. A pale moon is still shining in the sky. A full moon. Foals are often born at a full moon.

The sun has just extended its first tapered rays across the steppes. The harem walks over to the watering hole as usual, drinks as usual. Hamburg is not among them but will soon appear from behind a hill and join the herd.

Sydney has found his own little puddle a short distance away. He stays there.

But Praha isn't walking to either of these water sources. She is no-where in sight.

I wait. Nothing happens.

I can't sit still, start walking in circles around the tent, around the harem.

I look at the valley, at the mountains; there are many places to disappear here, ridges and curves in the landscape, many places where she may have hidden.

I don't want to go looking for her, know that I shouldn't look for her, know that Praha will manage on her own.

Still, I find it impossible to sit down. I keep walking, looking for the mare continuously.

And, finally, she appears—a slender form, slinking back, wandering toward the watering hole, paying no heed to me or the horses, heading straight toward the water.

She's alone.

I walk closer. The mare is thin, almost skinny. Her belly has disappeared.

"Where's your foal, Praha?" I ask softly. "Where is your foal?"

But Praha isn't listening. She is a wild horse, of course she's not listening.

"Dammit, Praha. Dammit!"

She pricks up her ears, sensing my anger.

Take it easy, Karin, calm down.

I turn to Hamburg. He had also been off by himself. He came from the same direction as Praha.

I walk toward him. He is darker than the others, but his coat still doesn't hide the traces of blood. Dried, dark-brown blood running down his neck and leg.

I hadn't seen it. Why hadn't I seen it? If I had seen it the minute he came back, there might still have been time.

I run away from the horses, in the direction of the hill they both came from.

At that moment, I hear the sound of a car. I don't care, just keep running.

It might not be too late. Just because Praha has come back alone doesn't necessarily mean anything.

The car keeps driving to the tent, stops, the door opens. It is Jochi.

"Karin?"

"Not now," I shout to him.

"You have to come."

"Not now!"

But I stop. Even from a distance I can see that he is worried. That something has happened.

I turn and walk a few steps toward him. He runs in my direction, breathing hard by the time he reaches me.

"Mathias," he says. "Mathias has disappeared." The words come in spurts. "He ran off last night. His bag is gone, the most important of his things. I thought maybe that . . . I thought he might have gone into the city, that his kind . . . run away when things get difficult . . . that he's gone to find some . . . to try . . . that he's going to . . ."

His kind.

Once a junkie, always a junkie.

"We must look for him," he says. "We must go into the city and find him."

There was no need for me to be so hard on him.

But he waved. He waved when I left.

"No," I say. "Praha has foaled."

"Now?"

"Last night."

Jochi suddenly starts paying attention to the horses. He looks at each of them one at a time.

"But, where is it? Where's the foal?"

"I don't know."

I start walking.

He hesitates, looks at me. I understand what he's thinking, that I am putting the foal before Mathias. What kind of mother am I who prefers another child, another species, to her own offspring?

But he doesn't know how many times I've searched for Mathias. He doesn't know about all the hours, all the nights I have wandered the streets. The bags of drugs I've found in my son's pockets, the money he has stolen from me. This time I must choose differently.

"Mathias will manage," I say. "He has always managed. I must find the foal. You have to help me."

. . .

We search in silence. Again we search. It's as if this year has been all about searching out here, as if it were but a continuation of my previous life.

We walk together. Without a word, we scan every inch of the landscape. Lift the binoculars. Look. Adjust the focus. Squint. Lower them again. Keep walking.

He is the one who finally finds it. He raises his hand and points at something fifty meters away from us.

"There."

We run.

It is half buried in dust, almost invisible, only the dark patches of blood are visible.

I sink to my knees. Carefully, I dig it out, can feel that the body is already cold. I run my hands over its tiny chest.

"The ribs are broken."

I remove my fingers. The unpleasantness of touching something dead. I don't want to touch it any more than necessary.

Jochi squats down beside me. He, too, runs his hands over the foal's chest. He grimaces.

"Hamburg," he says. "Hamburg did it. He kicked the foal to death."

"It could just as easily have been the birth."

"But the blood on Hamburg's coat? He had blood on his leg when he came back."

"He could have gone over and sniffed at the placenta."

Jochi shakes his head. Stands up abruptly.

"I'm sure it was him," he says. "Damn stupid animal."

The man who never swears.

"We don't know for sure that it was him," I say. "Maybe it was the birth. Maybe the foal broke its ribs during delivery."

. . .

When we return to the horses, Praha is the first one I see. No grief, no expression of loss. She has already joined the herd, is standing amongst them. She has accepted Hamburg as the leader.

There are only five in the harem, but the fittest have survived. Darwin in practice. I wish that Darwin were wrong.

I turn away, notice Jochi looking at me searchingly.

"What do you want to do now?" he asks.

I feel a weight on my chest. Don't want to, don't want to go down that road again. But it is perhaps my fault; it has certainly always been my fault. That is why I am condemned to search.

"Now I am going to find Mathias."

EVA

As soon as I entered the yard, I heard the screams. The window to Louise's room was open and I recognized the sounds immediately. Too early, far too early, I thought.

"Isa!"

I ran into the house. In one bound, she was at my side, red in the face and hugging me tightly in a way I couldn't remember her having done since she was a child.

"Mommy . . ."

I let her hold me, crying her eyes out. I murmured into her hair, *sweetie, little one*. She was in there somewhere, the girl she had been, and although everything changed, something would always be the same.

Then I heard Louise again. A low rumbling, as if it came from a place in her body disconnected from the voice, until it increased in volume, gradually intensifying into a wordless scream.

"How long has she been in labor?" I asked.

"Since breakfast," Isa said. "Where have you been?"

"How far apart are they?"

"What?"

"The contractions?"

"I have no idea. But you just disappeared. Why did you just leave? I thought you had left for good. I thought it was because I said I felt sorry for you. I've been so afraid."

"Sorry."

I stroked her hair. "It will be fine," I said. "It will all be fine."

She nodded, sniffed, dried her tears. Then we walked into Louise's room together.

She was standing with her feet on the floor and her upper body leaning over the bed. Her elbows rested on the mattress and her head was hidden in her hands. The scream faded away, the contraction passed; she lifted her head and noticed me. Her eyes were distant, dazed with pain, she said my name, but nothing else. There was scarcely room for relief in her.

She tried to stand up, swayed slightly on her feet.

"Should I lie down?" she asked. "Or stand? I don't know what to do, how to do this."

"You must wait," I said. "And you must figure out how you can best withstand the waiting."

I seldom thought about Isa's birth, thought I had forgotten it. But now every single detail came back to me; everything had been precisely stored, memories wrapped up in tissue paper. The all-pervasive pain, all the hours that melted into one, that felt never-ending.

"Let me have a look," I said. "I must try and see how far you've come."

I helped her into bed; she lifted her hips obediently, let me pull off her underpants. They were stained with mucus and blood.

All the animals I have delivered . . . but this was, nonetheless, different. My only reference was Isa, my own body. Then, I was on the inside, consumed by pain; now I was the one who would attend the birth, be the helper, and I didn't know what was required.

Centimeters, I thought suddenly, I remembered centimeters.

Louise's dilation was dark and still small.

"It's going to be a while longer," I said.

"But how long?" she asked. "How long must I wait?"

"Until you are fully dilated. Ten centimeters."

"But *when* will I be fully dilated?"

"I don't know."

She laughed, a mere croak.

"You can't give me an exact time, in other words."

Then I remember what the midwife who delivered Isa had said.

"With every contraction you are a little closer."

"No comfort in that, either," Louise said, "if you don't know the total number of contractions."

We laughed—all three of us—a brief, reassuring laughter, and then Louise shrank into herself again as another wave of pain washed over her.

I turned to Isa. "Get a clock, please."

She nodded, clearly relieved to have been assigned a task.

I sat with Louise. She had closed her eyes, lying on her back, and yet another roar rumbled through her, but weaker this time. I saw how her body tensed as it reached its climax and relaxed as she rode it out.

She opened her eyes.

"That one wasn't as bad, luckily."

"The strongest ones are often the most effective," I said.

"You are really bad at reassurance," she said.

Isa returned with my alarm clock.

"I want you to pay attention to how often they come," I said. "Can you do that?"

Isa nodded eagerly.

"Write it down," I said, to give her even more to do. "Then at least we'll know where we are."

She ran out of the room again to find a paper and pencil. I washed my hands and turned to face Louise.

"I must check inside you. Is that okay?"

"Do I have any choice?"

I stuck my fingers into the dark opening, fumbled around. Both soft and hard, bone and flesh. I pushed my fingers all the way inside, then they hit something. It was the baby's head, slippery beneath my fingers, impossible to get hold of and it still hadn't descended enough. I pushed a bit and could feel that it gave way, like a ball.

"It's the head," I said. "I can feel the head. But it's still too far inside you, I don't think it has reached the pelvic floor. You must walk. I remember walking helped. The baby has to descend further down. We have to allow gravity to do its job."

So, the hours of walking begin, arm in arm, from the bedroom through the hallway, into the kitchen, to the living room, back to the bedroom again. Isa kept track, writing down the minutes and seconds.

4:45, 4:52, 5:03, 5:09, 5:13, 5:22, 5:35, 5:40.

I thought the contractions were too far apart, too irregular, and, at the same time, I could see how Louise was slowly losing her strength.

She leaned more and more of her weight on me, dragging her feet, until finally I led her into the bedroom and helped her lie down on the bed.

"I feel queasy," she said.

"Find a bucket," I said to Isa.

She returned a few seconds later, tossed the washrag onto the floor, and handed me the bucket. Louise was in the middle of another contraction. When it subsided, she leaned over the red plastic bucket and vomited.

"Why is this happening? Is something wrong?" she sobbed.

"It's because of the pain," I said. "It's the pain that makes you throw up."

"I haven't done anything but vomit the past few months. Dammit all," she said.

"Yeah," I said. "Dammit all."

Yet again, the pain took hold of her. Even stronger than the last. She writhed, wept, working against the pain instead of with it.

"You have to breathe," I said.

"I can't," she howled. "I don't want to do this. I want to get away, do you hear me, I can't do this."

I stuck my fingers inside her again. Now the baby's head had moved farther down and it no longer gave way when I pushed it.

"You're getting there," I said. "It's going slowly, but you're getting there."

Isa had sat down on a chair with the clock in one hand and the pencil in the other. Her eyes were large and round.

"Look at me," I said to Louise. "Look at me and we'll breathe together. You have to breathe through the contractions."

"I can't do it."

"One . . . two . . . three . . . you're doing great, Louise . . . you're doing great."

"Don't leave," she said.

"No," I said. "Of course, I won't leave."

"I mean it," she sobbed. "I need you."

"It will be over soon," I said.

But it wasn't over. It was just the beginning.

Her water broke. It was a strange color, not shiny the way I remember mine had been, but with a faint green tinge.

I didn't say anything to the others. I remembered that I'd read about discolored amniotic fluid. The baby had become stressed and defecated inside; the color came from the feces. It wasn't dangerous, necessarily, but could give both the mother and baby an infection.

For a long while, I pretended not to notice that Louise was feverish. I said nothing to Isa, but at one point when she came over and gently stroked Louise's cheek, she gave a sudden start.

"She's burning up," she whispered to me.

"There's nothing we can do about it," I said. "You must keep on writing down the time."

9:38, 9:42, 9:45.

"Louise, Louise," I whispered to her between contractions. "You're doing great, do you hear me, you're doing great, you can do this."

But she didn't reply, consumed by fever and pain. And I still couldn't see the head.

. . .

Gradually, the sounds she was making changed. Something deeper invaded them, something almost compressed, and she was gripped by panic.

I washed my hands again, didn't know how many times I had washed them. Then I stuck my fingers inside her. I probed around and, for a moment, I thought maybe I could get hold of the baby, but it was impossible, the head was as slippery and smooth as a stone in a river.

"It's pressing," she screamed. "I have to push. I can't help it."

"No," I said. "No, you can't push. It's too early. The head hasn't descended. You have to resist."

11:15, 11:17, 11:18.

"I can't."

"You must, Louise."

Isa was on her feet now. She'd forgotten about the clock, dropped the pencil.

"Mommy?"

But I had no time for her. I took Louise's hand, squeezed it, tried to get her to look into my eyes.

"You must wait, do you hear me? You must wait, it's too soon."

She responded with another half-strangled scream.

"I can't do it. You must do something," she sobbed in the brief respite between two contractions.

"You have to get up again," I said. "You have to walk. The baby has to descend all the way."

"No, no, I can't bear it."

"You must."

I took hold of her, hauled her out of bed, got Isa to help me support her. Louise screamed and shook. The contractions were constant, arriving without cease.

We stood together—all three of us—Louise in the middle wearing just a T-shirt, burning up, dripping with sweat, a single, loud scream. Isa and I stood on either side holding her up, just holding her.

. . .

I didn't know how many minutes had passed, how many contractions, but the sounds Louise was making became deeper and deeper. She was no longer able to refrain from pushing, her legs trembled beneath her, and again we helped her back into bed.

I leaned over her, hoping to see the little head down there, ready to arrive. But it still hadn't descended far enough, the baby was sort of stuck against the mouth of the uterus.

"Is it ready?" Louise whispered.

"Almost," I said.

I hesitated for a moment, then I climbed onto the bed, squatting beside her, all the while cursing the human body, the malediction upon women, our two legs. When the great ape rose to stand upright on two legs, its hips became narrower, but all the same, the large head of the human baby was supposed to descend through the far too narrow birth canal and all the way out.

I saw myself from the outside as I stuck my fingers inside her, as if I knew what I was doing, as I stuck my fingers inside her and she howled even more loudly. This was worse than everything else—that I disturbed her down there was more painful than anything else, and I saw the bleeding. Blood.

Soft flesh, the head was banging up against soft flesh. I pushed, tugged at the flesh, shut everything else out, Louise's screams, Isa's laments: *no, Mommy, what are you doing, no.* I could feel only the baby's head, so warm, far too warm, the warmth of a fever, her own or its own, slippery against my fingers, and the flesh that I tried to push, force aside, to make room for the head.

Louise screamed, no, no, no, no more.

But I tried again, stuck in my fingers, thinking now I'm injuring it, remembered the fontanelle, the soft spot on an infant's skull.

And then it was as if the mouth of the uterus gave way, as if the head made it past an edge in there, it slid toward me, the mucus-covered scalp, downward, and finally I could take out my hands.

"Now you can push, Louise, do you hear me? You have to push now. The baby is in position and you are fully dilated."

But Louise was out cold, only the whites of her eyes were visible. I picked up a washcloth, sprinkled water in her face.

"Louise! I can see the baby now! I see it! You can push, Louise, are you listening? Now you have to push. Your baby is ready."

Then she was back. Another contraction gripped her body.

"You have to push," I said.

She nodded weakly and then she began. I held her stomach, gauging the spasms.

"Now," I said. "Chin on your chest, come on."

We cheered her on, Isa and I, we cheered and counted. Relax. Push. You're doing great, you're doing great, Louise.

But the baby wouldn't come out. It was as if she were holding back. Exhausted, terrified, as if she had nothing more to give.

"I can't do it," she sobbed finally. "Please."

I lay on top of her, tried to place my own weight on her, pushing together with her.

"You must," I said.

"No, no."

"Listen to me. Your baby has a fever. Your baby is not well. You have to push for your baby."

She made a slight head movement. Her eyes cleared as the contraction expanded inside her.

"You have to push for your baby," I repeated.

And finally, she was back. Her gaze held mine, the screams vanished. All that remained was the task at hand.

"You can do it," I said, my face against hers. "We can see your child now. We can see the baby. You can do it."

My voice was calm. I didn't understand how it could be so calm.

Isa stood beside the bed clinging to the headboard so tightly that her knuckles turned white. "Now it's coming, now it's coming."

Louise finally pushed the way she should, again and again, the contractions arrived one after the next without interruption—she *became* the birthing itself.

I moved, preparing myself. And then, suddenly, it slipped out. Louise released one final, wordless scream and there he was.

The head in my hands, whole, the large head and the body that followed, the tiny, fragile body.

But something was not right. An absence of sound, no, an expectation of sound that was instead filled with silence.

Because he didn't cry. His face was gray, his skull sort of compressed and lopsided. I leaned over him, feeling my way, took hold of his forehead, bent the little head back.

"What is it," Louise said, and leaned forward to see. "Why isn't it crying? Isn't it supposed to cry?"

Without thinking I grasped the tiny feet and held him upside down, he was slick with blood and mucous, but I held him tightly, tightly, and shook.

And suddenly a sound came, a cough.

I lay him on his side on the bed, he coughed again, the tiny body did what it needed to do. And then he cried, a frail bleating, just as he should.

"It's a boy," I said. "You had a boy and he is lovely."

"He's so lovely, Louise," Isa said and sobbed. "He is so very lovely."

I laid him on Louise's breast. She stroked his cheek, his soft shoulders with two careful fingers. Then she said the same thing I remember I said when Isa was born, the same thing I remember thinking.

"Hi," she said. And she gazed at him with recognition in her eyes. That's how it had been for me, too. That's maybe how it is for all mothers—an all-consuming wonder and a clear recognition of something familiar at the very same time. "Hi, little one. It's you. There you are."

Afterward, when we had cleaned up the baby and dressed him in the smallest baby clothes, which were still a little too big, Louise laid him carefully in Isa's arms, who accepted him with trembling hands.

"How do I do this?"

"You can manage it," Louise said. "Just watch his head."

Isa sat completely still, looking at him and slowly became more confident, dared to relax the hold of her right arm and cradle him in the nook of her left arm, while she held his hand gently with her index finger.

"He's holding on." She smiled.

"They do that." I said.

I sat watching my daughter and the baby. The little boy clinging to her finger.

Yes, they hold on, I thought. Teeny-tiny hands gripping our adult fingers. Chubby fists clinging to your hands when they take their first steps. Anxious baby hands that slip into yours when the world threatens. They hold on tight, until one day they let go.

And then there's someone holding *them* because their hand has become the adult hand. In this way, the hands are the links between humans, and anyone who can't experience holding another human being, or being held, has not really lived.

Isa had released me now. She stood alone, the way human beings do, in the years between the separation from parents one hasn't chosen and the connection to people one will call a family—maybe the loneliest period of life. But, fortunately, it didn't last long. One day before too long, Isa will take hold of someone who is a stranger to me, someone she will call *her own*; and, eventually, she will also have a little one— someone who will cling to her, the way she clung to me.

No.

No. Because as long as we lived here, Isa would never meet this person. As long as we lived here, she would always be alone. As long as we lived here, this empty period between childhood and adulthood where one has nobody to turn to—this would be her whole life.

THE STORY OF MY VOYAGE TO MONGOLIA
AND WHAT I FOUND THERE

CHAPTER 16

A SENSIBLE DECISION

May came and went. June as well. This was the period of Petersburg's white nights, during which young people wandered outdoors all night long, but it was not the color white that I associated with these months but rather a deep, dirty-gray darkness.

I received a lot of attention for my expedition and was asked to give countless lectures to the great surprise and enthusiasm of the director. I delivered all of them without a sign of nervousness, but rather with a slight remoteness and lassitude that my listeners, judging by the applause, did not appear to notice.

The only thing that held a touch of something meaningful to me was the work with the animals. The zoological garden had been neglected during my absence. The director was, above all, a paperwork person. His world consisted of numbers. If absolutely necessary, he might notice if the park was busy or quiet, although I suspected that it wasn't the people he heard, but the jingling from their purses. He did not, however, take notice of rust on a fence, a board in need of replacement, or a loose shingle. He paid even less attention to the animals, failing to notice if the brown bear's coat lacked sheen or his eyes had acquired a look of something drained and desperate.

394

And luckily, I had the horses. Naming them gave me joy. As their sole parent, it was only right and reasonable and, after having pondered the matter for a while, I decided on Dolly and Stiva. Not because these were my favorite Tolstoy characters—I actually had greater sympathy for Levin—nor because I knew the visitors of the zoological garden loved such literary references, but because Anna Karenina's brother Stiva and his wife Dolly had become the parents of many children, and also, quite simply because I thought the names suited the two chosen ones. I thought that they were a little bit like Dolly and Stiva: simple souls. *She* was fertile and *he* had a large appetite for the opposite sex.

The summer worked its way forward, emerging slowly from the light-green budding of spring, transitioning through its vibrant-green culmination, and fading into a tawny brown with the faint scent of old age. Nature rolls onward steadily, independent of everything else; the changing of the seasons cannot be halted. Regardless of whether everything else is completely backwards, upside down, or if one has been turned inside out, the change of the seasons will always arrive, and following their changes, come changes in oneself. Because it is really true that time heals all wounds and, therefore, nature's changes—which are actually not changes at all, but a cycle, the same things happening over and over again—will also change a human being's inner life. This cycle in nature was an inviolable rule, I thought. Nothing can change the march of the seasons: autumn leading to winter, winter to spring. I clung to the rules of the seasons and also thought about the regulations that existed for me, of Wilhelm's rules. I trusted him more than anyone else and, therefore, precisely therefore, I should accept his ordinances. But I just didn't have it in me.

I wrote to him all summer long. My first attempts at correspondence were filled with hard words, with irony, pain, as much against him as against the world. There was something wrong with our world, I wrote, a world that forbade beauty. There was something wrong with him, who ran away from happiness.

I wrote to him, but I never sent the letters. Instead, I tore them to pieces and threw them in the fireplace. Subsequently, I tried to compose friendly letters, polite, informal, but these made me so unwell, so queasy that every time I'd finished writing the letter, I found myself compelled to lie down. It was as if every single word I wrote about him and about us pushed me closer to an abyss.

I spent long days at the zoo, not arriving home until late in the evening to have supper with Mother. I always looked forward to ending my day with these tranquil meals. They were bright spots in an otherwise barren darkness. Here, I could openly speak my mind about the Great Alexander III—a vulgar boor, who dressed exclusively in rough military jackets and often showed his strength by bending pokers and breaking decks of cards in two with his bare hands—and listen to my mother's wise observations about him: *we must fight back our doubts, we must adapt, he knows what he is doing, he is the tsar, after all.* I appreciated the meals we shared, but gradually, as the weeks passed, I became increasingly uncertain as to whether the same could be said for her. She was constantly fidgeting on her chair, pushing her food around on her plate, and always seemed to want to end the meal at the first opportunity. Initially, I thought it was of no significance—a bad day, a difficult week—but with time I noticed that her restlessness grew worse.

One evening, I finally summoned my courage and asked her gently whether something was bothering her.

"No," she said curtly. "Absolutely nothing."

"But ever since I returned," I said, "I've had the impression that you are not quite well."

"I feel better than ever before."

"Brilliant. Nothing is more brilliant than that. You also look extremely well. It's as if you were younger than before."

"Thank you. That's kind of you." She spoke without sincerity.

We ate in silence. She took a bite, but chewing appeared to be a struggle. Suddenly she put down her fork and summoned her strength.

"There's something I have to tell you," she said.

"Yes?"

"Although I have a good life, although I am perhaps young for my age, it does not necessarily mean that my life is the same as it always has been . . . that things can't change, that in my life, even though I'm an older woman, important changes can't occur."

She spoke quickly and with intensity.

"No? No, I understand that."

I, too, put down my fork. Eating was suddenly impossible.

"No, Misha, you understand very little," she said.

"But I'm trying to understand. I really am." I could hear the shrillness in my voice.

"Imagine, I am absolutely not convinced that you are," she said, her words soft and well-mannered. "You wander around in your own fog, work all day until late in the evening, talk only about the horses, about the zoo, about the animals, yes, as you have always done . . . and I appreciated it before, but since you've come home, I've been thinking that . . . I've been thinking that this must change."

"What . . . What is *this* that must be changed?"

"I don't know how to say this in an appropriate and sensitive manner, Mikhail. I don't know if an appropriate and sensitive manner exists."

An appropriate and sensitive manner . . . for what? She was going to tell me something and was presenting it as if she were reading a book, a story. A horror story.

"A short time after you left on your expedition, I was introduced to a widower my age," Mother said.

"I see."

A widower, a widower, I didn't want to hear about any widower.

"Our first meeting occurred purely by accident," she continued. "It was a coincidence, he helped me one day when I stumbled on the street."

"An accident. You say that as if it's a justification." I was unable to hold back the words.

She ignored me.

"Then we met one another again. He was invited to the Rostov's—you know, they always receive visitors on Tuesdays. His wife used to come before but, now that she is gone, he has taken her place."

"Mother, I really don't need to hear the details."

"I just want you to know that I never went looking for this. I didn't try to find him, and he didn't try to find me."

"No. That's fine. You need not explain yourself any further."

"While you were away, we spent time together constantly. I really enjoyed his company."

"How pleasant for you, unbelievably pleasant. I'm happy for you."

She ignored my sarcasm, reached out her hand and laid it on mine. I felt like tearing it out of her grasp but sat there as if paralyzed.

"I never imagined that it would be this way," she continued. "I imagined you would be the one to come home and tell me about a marriage proposal, that you would find a girl, that it would be you who moved on."

"You know that I avoided meeting girls because of you. I have stayed here all this time because of you."

"But, Misha, that's not true."

Then I finally managed to snatch back my hand. I laid it in my lap with the other, folding them tightly.

She drew a breath, preparing herself for the rest of what she had to say. "He has asked me to marry him. Right before you came home, he proposed."

"Did he, now. And how did you reply?"

Then the tears welled up in her eyes. "But Mikhail . . . my Misha . . . of course, I said yes."

I stood up, wanting to throw the china dishes against the wall, fling the carafe of wine at the mirror, see it shatter, see the wine dripping, trickling down the light-green wallpaper onto the carpet on the floor, where it would leave stains that never disappeared.

"I asked him to wait to announce our engagement until I'd spoken with you," Mother continued softly but insistently. "He has been patient for a long time. . . . I can't let him wait this way forever. We will be married soon. It will be a simple ceremony, of course, we are old. We don't need a wedding that resembles what I had with your father."

"There's nothing here that resembles what you had with father."

"Mikhail." Now she stared at me severely. "You are a good son, you always have been, but you don't know anything about this, nor about what I had with your father."

I clutched the chair I had been sitting on, holding the chairback with both hands. I felt dizzy.

"I will, of course, move in with him," she said. "As soon as we are married. He lives in a lovely house with a big garden. Think about it, how nice it will be, to be able to walk in the garden every single day instead of being locked up in this apartment."

"Locked up? So that's what you think of your life here?"

She answered, her voice was gentle now, "Don't you?"

I was mute, like an animal, as if someone had suddenly deprived me of speech and the only thing that would come out if I were to try to express myself would be guttural sounds.

"My idea," Mother said, and now there was no anger to be discerned in her voice, "my idea was that you would find yourself a girl. That you would get married and have children, preferably at a young age, that you wouldn't start as late in life as your father and I did. And when that didn't happen, when you continued to live here, my conscience began gnawing at me. I didn't want to be the one who stood in your way."

She paused for a moment, stood up, waving away the maidservant who had poked her head in hoping to clear the table.

"Then you started talking about the horses. Your enthusiasm was so great, much greater than for anything else. At first, I didn't know what to make of your expedition. It jarred with my image of you, of your future. And my own. Beyond this, of course, my greatest wish and hope was threatened: a grandchild, a descendant, someone to carry on the family name."

"But why did you want me to leave, then? You were the one who said that the die was cast," I managed to mutter.

"I thought you'd understood."

"I noticed that your enthusiasm for Wilhelm grew, especially after the murder of the tsar. But, beyond that, I have clearly not *understood* anything at all."

She paid no heed to my irritation and just kept talking with the same affability and kindness.

"My doubts disappeared on the Katarina Canal that evening, that's correct. They disappeared when I understood what an absolutely splendid individual Wolff is. But it was not first and foremost due to him, it was due to you, that I understood who you are, that it wasn't a family that would make you happy, but a friendship. That you belonged out there in a wild and barren landscape in the company of someone like him."

"Stop," I said. "Please, will you just stop."

I turned away from her, sensing my tears like a clutching spasm in my diaphragm, like a stinging pain in my throat and chest, which made it impossible to breathe. Consolation. I wanted to be held by her, sit on her lap, cry in her arms, *Mommy, Mommy, Mommy*.

But no consolation, no lap can save a grown man; he can only save himself.

Our actions, Wolff said, are all we can control, and he was right. I had to trust him. It was perhaps the only way out of my grief.

I took two deep breaths before I recovered my voice, terrified of bursting into tears when I spoke: "I appreciate that you have tried to love me for who I am. That you now, as always, have been more concerned about my welfare than your own . . . but your idea about me with a woman and about you in your old age, surrounded by grandchildren, that is an idea you should hold on to. The expedition was my adventure; it was perhaps something I needed to do before settling down. But now, I'm ready. I will find a wife and I would like to hear your recommendations."

I thought she would smile, express relief, but she just looked at me sadly.

"But, Misha," she said. "Didn't you hear what I said? That is no longer what I want for you."

"I heard what you said," I said.

"But then I don't understand . . ."

"It is perhaps not what you want for me any longer, but it is what *I* want."

Five days later, a Tuesday, I accompanied Mother to Rostov's home. The hostess wished me a warm welcome. They expressed joy about my finally paying them a visit, the same enthusiasm they were also quick to display when Mother's cousin Betsy arrived a bit later along with Aleksej and Jelena. Apparently, they were not in the habit of frequenting this home on Tuesdays either, and for that reason, it was "particularly pleasant" that we all chose to spend our evening there. Mother and Betsy smiled at each other. Betsy's smile was radiant, like that of a winner, though in Mother I sensed something forced.

I had several conversations with Jelena in the course of the visit, though always in the presence of the others; Mother and Betsy, in particular, were scrupulous about hovering nearby. She spoke with admiration of my expedition, was accommodating, and her gaze was direct. At one moment, she dropped her handkerchief on the floor and when I bent over to pick it up, she said I could keep it.

Two days later, I donned my white French suit and a straw hat. The strict geometry of the paths in the Summer Garden greeted me. Here everything was straight-lined and well organized. The marble statues were arranged with millimetric precision. The gods and heroes of antiquity, which I usually associated with chaos and passion, had been tamed here and reduced to ornamentation.

I found Jelena in the midst of a gaggle of girls. I lifted my hat and greeted them all, but her in particular. The others immediately began strolling just a tad more quickly, while she slowed her pace. They did this so naturally, so smoothly, that I understood that experience lay behind it, that this was something they'd done many times before, this was something young people did, a game everyone knew how to play except me.

But the game was easy to understand. I felt neither apprehension nor nervousness about the rules.

We walked on alone, just the two of us, Jelena and me. For the first time we were one-on-one. Our conversation flowed lightly and effortlessly. There were a number of customary phrases to be spoken; we asked each other questions, she asked me more than I did her. Her comments were expressive of her youth, but I couldn't very well criticize her for that.

We conversed for a long time. I noticed Jelena's nervousness, but I believe that my sedate manner calmed her because I was fully composed. There was not a trace of the nervousness I have understood that young people have on rendezvous of this nature in me, and I smoothly concluded our conversation by stating that I looked forward to spending more time with her.

For an instant, I envied her the blushing cheeks she displayed when I proposed a time for our next meeting. But her hands were clammy and trembling when she grasped mine and my envy was quickly replaced by compassion.

That afternoon, I went home and started the work of writing my story. I no longer had *him* in my thoughts when I wrote and now the words flowed from my pen. By imagining a reader other than Wilhelm for my notes, a neutral third party, it became possible for me to write about us and about the horses without the pen feeling like a suicidal weapon in my hand.

It has taken me four weeks to get it all down on paper and, in the meantime, the yellow leaves on the trees have shriveled and lost their life. Soon they will fall to the ground lightly and begin decomposing. My painful feelings are in a similar fashion also in the process of losing their weight. I thought I was writing the story of the wild horses, but it was actually my own story I put down on paper. I thought I was writing for another reader, but the only reader this account will ever have will be me. In the way drops of fresh water clean a wound, the work on my story has purified me. With every sentence I have composed, every letter I have scratched out onto the page, I have come closer to a recognition of what should and will be my future.

Tomorrow the horses' section in the park will be ready. It will be every bit as colorful and florid in its ornamentation as I wished, and I am convinced that the public will adore this new addition to the zoological garden. The city's newspapers have already dedicated many column inches to Dolly and Stiva, and long lines of visitors eager to see the new arrivals are anticipated.

I am particularly looking forward to showing Jelena the wild horses. I think she will be both thrilled about the horses and proud of me. Maybe I can even let her stay after closing time, if Cousin Betsy will permit it. Maybe she and I can stroll unaccompanied up to the horses and maybe it will be with the horses as my witnesses that I will ask the all-important question.

I know what I have lost. Never again will I feel an intense joy flooding through me; such luminous wildness belongs to days gone by. My movements are more weighted now. But with such weight comes wisdom and reflection. For the first time in my life, I can say I truly feel like an adult. I am ready for what must come, and I clear away my pen and notes in the knowledge that I will do the right thing.

KARIN

N ight has fallen by the time I reach Ulaanbaatar. The bedlam of
the city traffic can still be heard. A steady drone, so strange after
the silence of Hustai.

I park on a side street adjacent to Sükhbaatar Plaza. He must be
here. I am sure he will be easy to find, that he wants to be found. I
prepare myself for the sight of him, sitting with his head bowed and
nodding against his chest. I won't talk until I reach his side to make
sure he doesn't run away. But then, when I am standing one meter
away, I will say his name. Dispassionately, not despairingly. He will
look up at me, bleary eyed. He will grin and say *Hi, Karin. Well, here
we are again.* Maybe he will say sorry. *Sorry. Just a tiny relapse. You
know, that's how it goes. Once a junkie, always a junkie. You can take
the drugs out of the boy but can't take the boy out of the drugs.*

I've never understood what he means by that. Neither why he continues to refer to himself as a boy. He is a man well over the age
of thirty. There's nothing boyish about him, except for his assumed
boyishness.

I stride across the plaza. The city is quiet. No bars or restaurants
are open. I don't understand how he has managed to score drugs. In
a foreign country, a foreign culture, in a language he doesn't under-

stand. But his kind always manages it. They read codes. Recognize each other. I am sure he has gotten hold of something without great difficulty. Maybe opium. That's probably the thing here. Or simply heroin. No reason why they shouldn't have heroin in Mongolia, just like everywhere else. It is, after all, one of the world's largest export items. And Mongolia is closer to Afghanistan than Germany is.

I reach the end of the plaza but still can't see him. A couple of elderly men are sitting on a bench dozing. Nobody else.

He should have been here. He should have been easy to find.

I start walking, take one street at a time around the plaza, expecting to see that hunched figure on a stairway, in a courtyard, on a construction site.

But he's not anywhere.

I keep walking.

Here, there's only asphalt and stone, a hardness that starts beneath the soles of the feet and travels upward all the way to the neck. I miss dirt and grass, a soft walking surface that allows the body to sway gently, that gives something back.

I hate the rock surfaces the city is made of, want to get away from here, but must allow the city to swallow me.

The streets become completely deserted, completely silent. I turn a corner, come upon a stone stairway. I shouldn't sit, but I sink down all the same. I look at the time, 3:47. I have been walking all night without eating or drinking.

I cradle my head in my hands. I just want to sleep, to rest, but must keep going. He, my son, is in this city. He couldn't have gone somewhere else?

The car is cold and damp. Keys in the ignition.

I keep both hands on the wheel and try to picture him.

He tosses his things quickly into a bag. He leaves the tent, leaves the camp. Continues toward the main road.

Hitchhikes to the city.

He wants to get away. From the horses. From Mongolia. From me.

I have always wanted for him to be his own person. That he would *want* to get away from me, because that's what children do. Becoming an adult means leaving one's parents. I just wanted him to be like all the other children.

Perhaps he is finally doing what I want? Perhaps he never did hitchhike into the city?

I wrench the steering wheel hard to the left. Step on the gas, drive out onto the highway, out of the city. Toward the airport.

He is lying on a bench in the departure hall sleeping with his cheek on his carry-on bag. Beside him, unattended and sort of trusting, is his knapsack. It looks barely half full. In a year, he hasn't acquired any more possessions than those he arrived with. Things have never been important to him.

He is fast asleep.

I stand in front of him hoping he will wake up, but nothing happens.

Finally, I must go over to him. Still he doesn't react. I lift one hand. Should I rumple his hair? Stroke his cheek?

I take hold of the sleeve of his jacket and tug it gently. Say his name softly.

He squirms but doesn't wake up. I say it again, more loudly now.

Finally, his eyes flutter open. He notices me and sits up.

"Hi."

He has indentations on his cheek from the bag, but otherwise seems alert and clearheaded. He shows no sign of being surprised that I showed up here and scoots over a bit on the bench, making room for me.

"Have you been looking for me in the city?" he asks.

"I didn't know where to look," I say.

"You looked for me the way you're used to looking for me?"

"Yes."

"It's been years since the last time. Since the last time you went looking for me."

"It has been a few years, yes."

"Were you angry?"

"No. I've never been angry."

"Yes, you have, Karin. You've been furious. So furious that you stopped looking."

I don't reply.

He continues. "You never wanted to have children. Then I came along and that was hard enough. All alone with a little boy. You probably thought it would be easier with time, when I got older. You looked forward to it. But then it just got worse. And you thought even more about how you never even wanted me, really."

No, I think. That's not how it was.

"I wanted children," I say.

"Don't lie," he says harshly.

"Anyway, it was nice when you arrived," I say.

"There were also a lot of things that weren't so nice," he says.

"Some things," I say.

"And it hasn't always been nice to have you for a mother."

"I know," I say.

We sit in silence. He fiddles with the strap on his bag. I pull out a lighter and cigarettes, offer him one, but he shakes his head. I struggle with the lighter as I try to light my own. My hands are shaking hard, but I pull myself together and manage it finally.

"When's your flight?" I ask.

"Quarter past six."

I peer at the departure board hanging in the middle of the hall.

"The flight to Moscow?"

"Yes."

"Aeroflot? Good luck," I attempt a smile.

"Thanks," he says but doesn't return the smile.

We fall silent again. I finish my cigarette but there's no ashtray in sight, so I put the butt inside the cigarette pack. I can smell the sour stench of it and hastily shove the package into my pocket.

Around us, the airport is waking up. A cleaner walks past pushing a cleaning trolley. A waiter is rattling dishes, about to open the café.

Two uniform-clad women walk toward the check-in counters and start preparing for a departure.

"Why are you leaving?" I ask.

"Why did I come to begin with?" he answers.

"Because you wanted to get away."

"Yes. Because I wanted to get away. But that wasn't the main reason."

"Because you had to."

"No, Karin. I just wanted the same thing I've always wanted."

He leans forward, resting his elbows on his knees, speaking softly without looking at me: "I remember when I was little, I would hold out my arms to you and wish that you would take me in your arms, hug me. But often I couldn't reach you. You were too far away, didn't take my hands . . . and now . . ." He pauses momentarily, bowing his head even more, so it is impossible to see his face. "I still can't reach you. . . . We can spend a whole day together, talk pretty easily, but I am still standing with my hands outstretched toward something that is just a bit too far away."

"Mathias," I say, "I know that I haven't always . . ."

He interrupts me. "I've always thought it was vital to reach you. That I had to keep trying. Just as I always thought that it was because I did something wrong when I was little, when you wouldn't hold me, that I was the one standing too far away. But that wasn't how it was. It's not how it is."

He stands up, picks up his bag, throws it over his shoulder, runs a hand through his hair. He looks awake now, the marks on his cheek are almost gone. Handsome, he is handsome, a beautiful man, a bit tousled, the type of man many women like.

"Goodbye, Karin."

He lifts his palm in my direction. His fingers splay like thin branches. I stand up. We are standing two steps away from each other.

"Yes," I say. "Yes. Goodbye."

Mathias had always been so easy to console. I just had to give him my breast. He was an easy baby. And so beautiful that I couldn't take my eyes off of him.

I turn away. A family passes on their way to the check-in counter. They have two young boys who are play-fighting, the eldest chasing the youngest. The parents scold them mechanically. As the youngest boy runs away from his brother, he is howling. It is a howl that could tip either way, toward tears or laughter. Then he drops his suitcase, a miniature copy of an adult suitcase with a picture of Mickey Mouse on the front. The handle falls toward the floor with a metallic click that is enhanced by the echo in the departure hall. The boy walks a few more meters, and then it's as if he understands that he no longer has his suitcase. He turns around, dashes back, and picks it up. Suddenly, his older brother is all over him, jumping around him, hugging him fiercely, wrestling with him. They both yell. The youngest laughs. But it is a laughter right on the edge, under pressure, because it's too much; the little boy will soon burst into tears.

I look at Mathias again. Lift my hand, the way he did. It feels like a strange imitation of his gesture. Doesn't he have to go? Doesn't he have to leave now? He must go before the boy with the suitcase starts bawling. Before the sound of his crying pierces through the walls, back and forth, back and forth. Before the sound triggers other frequencies, causing the fluorescent lights to buzz, sending vibrations into the walls, up to the ceiling, into the building structure, the framework, until the beams shudder, break.

"Bye, now," I say again.

He nods. "Bye."

He takes a few steps away, then he turns to face me, looking at me with a gaze I don't understand, neither anger nor sorrow, something else entirely.

At that moment, the boy starts to cry, a shrill screeching sound. The fluorescent lights buzz.

Don't go, please, don't go.

One step. I can manage to take one step.

"Mathias," I say.

And another.

"Wait."

He turns around.

"Yes, Karin, what is it?"

The boy sobs, the father tries to console him, but it doesn't help. The vibrations spread through the floor, proliferating.

Mathias just looks at me. He still has the same expression on his face.

Then he turns toward the departure board.

Boarding. The word flashes at us.

"Nothing. It wasn't anything," I say.

The vibration of the fluorescent lights buzzes fiercely in my ears. The boy must stop crying now. He must stop crying.

Mathias looks at me one last time. "Go back to your horses."

I nod.

Again, he turns away from me.

Then he leaves.

I think I notice a slight tremor in his shoulders but can't be sure. He doesn't look back. Not when he checks in, not when he goes through the gate and disappears.

EVA

For several weeks, he was all there was. No other points of reference existed but the baby—his smell, sounds, the silence when he was asleep. Louise recovered quickly, didn't complain about the stitches I'd had to give her, or the sleepless nights, or the mild mastitis that came and went. There was no sign that what the baby had been through had affected him. He was like all infants—just as beautiful, just as difficult, just as incomprehensible, just as familiar, and unfamiliar.

He cried as he should. The wan sound of his crying infiltrated everything and carried a stillness with it, a calm like no other.

He quickly gained weight, his cheeks became chubby, and he was given a name, David, after Louise's father.

I thought time stood still for a few weeks, but the only thing that doesn't change is that everything changes. Everything around us moved and grew, just like him.

Louise picked him up with an innate assurance. She lay him on her breast without hesitation; she quieted his sobs confidently and resolutely.

One bright, warm spring evening, she was sitting on the stairs when I returned from my evening stint in the cowshed. She was nursing him.

I could hear him swallowing and the soft sniffling sounds of exertion and well-being.

I sat down beside her, allowing myself to be infected by the calm.

"When I had Isa, I floundered for a long time," I said.

"Floundered?"

"Couldn't do anything right, was afraid to offer her my breast, afraid to take her away, afraid to pick her up, afraid to put her down, afraid when she cried, afraid when she was quiet, too."

"It's just a baby," Louise said.

"That's what I mean," I said. "For you it's just a baby."

She bent toward David for a moment, stroking his forehead carefully with one finger. The child had fallen asleep at her breast. Now she disengaged his mouth gently.

"I think he's ready now," she said.

"Yes," I said. "He's ready."

Anne believed that the last thing the earth needed was more people and the last thing children needed was to be born given the way the world is now. Maybe I would meet Anne again. I wanted to try to find her. I wanted her to meet Isa and David. Two children of our world.

David snorted gently in his sleep, twisted his head slightly, the corners of his mouth stretching outward into a smiling grimace. I couldn't find a single thing wrong with either him or Isa, and neither anything wrong with having had them. They belonged here. It was up to me to give them a life.

There was a light breeze. Banks of clouds filled the sky. The sky rose high above us, lofty and boundless. Puma and Nike were grazing at the foot of the paddock, slowly chewing the light-green grass of spring; the blades reached toward them as if asking to be eaten. And outside the fence, the meadows lay ready for the horses. They had an entire summer ahead of them.

I had asked Isa to come with me. Louise was resting in the house. David had cried a lot the night before; perhaps he'd had a growth spurt or maybe he'd sensed that we were packing, that the atmosphere in the house had changed, was hectic and excited.

I didn't want anyone else here with me now anyway.

Isa walked all the way up to the fence, stopping when we reached the horses. They lumbered toward us, watching me expectantly. My wild horses; they would have disappeared had human beings not intervened. If a Russian and a German had not once upon a time traveled to Mongolia and captured the animal everyone believed to be extinct, if the staff of zoological gardens and nature reserves all over the world hadn't taken care of them and rebuilt the species, if a German veterinarian had not, in the 1990s, returned them to the country of their origin and invested her life in making the species strong and independent.

"I don't have anything for you today," I said and held out my empty hands.

They continued to stare at me and suddenly I thought of Hans, the horse that could count. I wanted to say something to Nike and Puma, a few final words, but didn't know what. The horses didn't understand my words, anyway, and they would probably also forget the sound of my voice.

A noise came from the grove—the sound of branches breaking under the hooves of a heavy animal. A shadow was moving around in there. Rimfaxe was waiting—the horse who pulls the darkness across the sky. He just did what he had to do; he sought out the company of others. He was searching for a herd.

Rimfaxe was the kind who survived, a winner. He wasn't particular, but easy to please and he would never find a mare. Horses like him, they ate whatever they found. They took pleasure in simple things like fresh air and clean water, they lived according to their surroundings instead of themselves, adapting their lives. Those able to form connections despite differences would always survive. I could only hope that I was like him. That Isa was like him.

I walked over to the gate and turned toward my daughter. She nodded.

Then I lifted the rope end that held it shut, the hemp rough against my fingers.

But suddenly I stopped, my movement suspended. Just stood there, suddenly feeling dizzy, it was as if something were stepping on me, walking over me, like hooves on my chest. I swayed.

"Mommy?"

Isa came over, laying a hand on my shoulder.

"Mommy, are you okay?"

"I don't know if I can do this."

She looked at me, her eyes immediately wide with disappointment. "But you don't want to, after all?"

"Yes, I want to, sweetie. I want to go."

"Then I don't understand . . ."

I nodded quickly. "I'll do it now. I'll do it."

Finally, I placed my hand on the dark woodwork and pulled the gate toward me.

The hinges creaked. The horses twitched their ears in the direction of the sound before bending once more toward the spring grass.

It was open. It was done. But the horses didn't see the exit. Maybe it would take hours for them to discover that they could go wherever they wanted, maybe days. They would stand this way for a long time, heads bowed toward the ground, constantly eating, until perhaps they noticed the grass outside, that it was suddenly also available to them, and walked through the gate.

I could have used my voice. I could have lured them out, but chose not to. They would have to find the way on their own.

Instead, I turned around and started walking. I looked over at Isa, my daughter, who was walking beside me, half a head taller than me. Her hand brushed against mine, but she didn't take it.

We left the horses there. I let them work it out for themselves. They will figure it out in time, I thought. It will just have to take the time it takes.

POSTSCRIPT

Petersburg, June 1890

I've been awake all night long perusing all my old notes, sitting on the floor of my study with the papers all around me, sheets of paper filled with tiny, dense handwriting. I haven't managed to keep them organized, been so busy reading that I forgot to put them in a neat pile but, instead, spread them around me in the shape of a fan.

I can see that, toward the end of my writing period, I assumed that my text would not be of value to anyone but myself. On that point, it could be that I was mistaken. Because now that there are scarcely any wild horses left in Mongolia whatsoever, since the people who took part in the three great expeditions made in recent years have captured or killed the majority, it would certainly be of interest to many to read about the first expedition and the origin of some of the horses found in the European zoological gardens today. But in order for my account to be worth reading, some substantial editing is in order.

That is not, however, why I feel compelled to write again. I thought my story was over, but that's not the case. My story will last for as long as I'm alive and for as long as he, Wilhelm, exists, and it will last as long as our horses and their descendants are grazing on the grassy plains of this planet.

The pen trembles in my hand. I am unable to keep from splattering ink on the paper. From the open window, I can hear the sound of a city coming to life, hooves against the cobblestones. The sound of running, young feet, perhaps a courier, passes by. From the kitchen comes the sound of pots and pans banging; they have started preparing breakfast. And from the bedroom, I can hear Jelena singing softly to little Darja, our youngest, to wake her. I try to hold on to the sounds, but they fade away. It's as if I am standing outside the entryway to my own life and then, slowly at first, then faster and faster, walk away.

Wilhelm came back today. I was just going to open the door to my office to air it out a bit—the day was unusually warm—and, suddenly, there he was, standing two steps away from me.

He tipped his hat.

"Good day, Mikhail Alexandrovich Kovrov."

"Wolff?"

"Yes," he said. "It's me."

I froze where I stood.

"Wilhelm? No . . ."

"Did you think I wouldn't come?"

"No . . . no . . ."

"But you summoned me."

"Yes."

"And here I am."

Here he was.

He stood with his hands hanging at his sides, neither forthcoming nor dismissive, just two steps away from me.

"I've traveled far," he said. "For many days and nights."

I walked toward him; he reached out his hands and I grasped them in my own. For a while, I just held them. But it wasn't enough. I had to move yet another step closer, so I released his hands, took hold of his shoulders, and pulled him to me.

His cheek was rough against my lips, his lips warm when I kissed them as well.

"It's really you, you came, you're alive, you're here."

"Yes," he said. "Yes, I'm here. I received your letter. I left immediately."

I gasped into the fabric of his coat, which smelled like wool and tobacco and *him*, and he murmured my name.

"Misha, Misha."

When I married Jelena, I was convinced that I'd achieved a state of equilibrium, that everything I'd been through was a kind of purification, that I had come to terms with my pain, and that now I was ready to meet the rest of my life as a blank slate.

The years passed, and I tried as hard as I could to live according to my decisions, to follow the rules I knew to be embedded inside me. I let Herbert Spencer's concept of *survival of the fittest* guide me. I was *the fittest*; I had it in me, if only I made the right choices. At the same time, I did everything I could to ensure that the horses would survive, that their bloodline would continue. During the first years, they suffered and it was my fault. The stallion hadn't wanted to copulate, the mare never conceived. It was when I finally allowed them to move about freely in the large paddock that he finally became interested. Still, a year passed, then two, without any results and I started wondering whether the names I'd given them were a curse because Tolstoy's Stiva was a man with a huge appetite for the opposite sex, but the appetite wasn't directed toward his own Dolly, but instead toward a long string of mistresses.

Late in the autumn of the past year, I understood, however, that Dolly was finally in foal. I thought I would be happy, but instead I cried. I sat up in my office crying all night long for nights on end.

When the foaling commenced—when Dolly's udder began leaking and she started walking restlessly around the paddock, sweating, lying down, getting to her feet again, scraping the ground with her forehooves—it was as though I became infected with her restlessness.

I was neither able to find rest, to sit, to stand. I just wandered back and forth along the fence of her paddock and monitored every one of her movements.

Had she been a tame horse, I would have approached her, tried to help her, wiped her down with a damp cloth, bandaged her tail, given her a stall of dust-free bedding. But she is wild and all I could do was wait with her.

When her water finally broke, a liter of red liquid poured out of her. She lay down and the bearing-down phase started. I stood as if paralyzed and watched her give birth, the contractions shuddering through her body, each one more powerful than the last. I watched the time—the minutes passed, a quarter of an hour, twenty minutes, but still the foal hadn't emerged.

Then, suddenly a small hoof came into view. Then another. Dolly lay on the ground, her entire large body struggling. Soon the muzzle would appear, soon . . .

But it did not appear. The contractions continued. Dolly moaned loudly. She continued for almost a half hour; it shouldn't take so long.

Stiva stood far away from her grazing calmly, as if he didn't realize what was going on, like all men, exiled to the hallway, chain smoking, or even further away, socializing with other men, a drink in hand, while life's greatest miracle unfolds without any need for them.

Dolly was alone; all she had was me. I couldn't bear to stand on the outside of the paddock any longer.

I opened the gate, went over to her cautiously, and squatted down. She looked at me with eyes pleading for help.

I carefully took hold of the foal's forelegs and pulled them gently. I tried to find the rhythm, to pull in time with her contractions.

Finally, the muzzle appeared. I wiped the amniotic membranes off the muzzle and nostrils.

Now only the final phase remained.

"Come on," I whispered. "You can do this."

We worked together, she and I, contraction by contraction.

I talked to her calmly the whole time.

"We can do this, love. I'm here, I'm here."

Then finally, in two short thrusts, the foal emerged, slimy, slippery, and healthy. I saw immediately that it was a stallion and my chest swelled with joy. A tiny stallion, the zoological garden's very first own takhi!

Both the foal and the mother remained lying on the ground and I retreated tentatively, not wanting to disturb. The umbilical cord would break by itself when she stood up, the afterbirth she also disposed of without my assistance. There was nothing more that I could do.

Even so, I had such a deep desire to do something. I ended up circling the horses' paddock, walking faster and faster as the enthusiasm bubbled inside me, my eyes constantly on the mare, the stallion, and the foal. There had been two of them and suddenly there were three. A brand-new creature on this earth, created from almost nothing. Life's great miracle, I thought. The miracle of life!

Abruptly, I changed course and walked straight to my office. When I got there, I sat down at my desk, and picked up a pen and sheet of paper. Then I composed a letter to Wilhelm requesting that he come immediately, telling him that Dolly had finally foaled, that I could think of a thousand reasons in the world for why he would neglect to respond to my invitation, but that none of the arguments won out against this one: we had finally produced a foal.

And now he was here.

I held his hand and pulled him after me into my office, where I closed the door hard behind us and, to be on the safe side, hung up a sign I seldom use bearing the words *Do Not Disturb*. I then sat him down in the chair in front of my desk.

"Sit, dear friend."

I stood in the middle of the room for a moment, wondering whether I should sit down behind my desk, but it felt wrong, as if he then became a subordinate, so instead I sat *on* the desktop right beside him. I sat looking down at him and he up at me and his eyes sparkled even more than I remembered.

"You haven't changed," I said.

"I'm older," he said. "I'm a weary, skinny, middle-aged man, my body full of cuts and scars, the state of my soul is not much better."

"I think you look good," I said. "You've always looked good."

It was the exultant joy of the reunion that was guiding my body when I lifted my hand and stroked his face. I felt the coarseness of the skin on his warm face beneath my fingertips, the rough stubble of his beard.

"You haven't changed, either," he said.

Then he lifted *his* hand and placed it on the back of my neck and pulled me toward him. We embraced the way we'd done so many times before, an embrace not intended for the eyes of others.

I know that what I am writing now can never be read by others. I know that I must hide these notes, or maybe burn them, that Jelena must never find them, nor any of the other people in this house.

Yet, write I must, and as I move my pen across the paper, I relive my reunion with Wilhelm.

We knew that the moment we left my office, we would lose what constituted *us*, that in the presence of other people, *we* didn't really exist. For that reason, we stayed in the office for a long time. For that reason, I drew the curtains. For that reason, I ignored all other interruptions shouting *just go away and come back tomorrow* and *read the sign* to anyone who knocked on the door. For that reason, we dared not let go of one another.

Our embrace lasted for hours. He was the way I remembered him, yet different, the feeling of that which was him was even stronger. The experience of him offered a kind of clarity, a transparency, as if everything that had happened since we'd said farewell was obscured by a mist—like the frost that forms above the canals in the winter—and it was a mist to which I knew I never again wanted to return.

Afterward, we lay beside one another. I whispered words into his hair, words I've never said to anyone before, everything I'd been thinking throughout all these years, but never dared to express, and he responded with the same words, at least as strong as my own, and this made me cry. Cry with much needed sobs, as loudly as only a grown man can sob.

When no more tears, passion, ardor, or want remained inside me, when we finally left the office, driven out by hunger and thirst, the zoological garden had long since closed for the day.

"I have the key," I said. "We need not leave just yet. You must see the foal."

I took him with me down the path headed west.

"This wasn't here before," he said.

"No, we had it built three years ago."

"And what about the area beside the camel?"

"The horses weren't happy there."

"I can imagine."

"The camel was also suffering. He died shortly after you left."

"That doesn't surprise me."

I laced my fingers through his and led him through the dwindling light. Finally, we reached the horses.

He went over to the fence and lay his hands on it.

"How nicely accommodated they are now."

I had had a large paddock built; we had expanded the zoological garden to accommodate them. I'd tried to convince the director that we had to give all the animals equally spacious living quarters, that it would be good for them, but also wise on our part, perhaps even financially beneficial, because happy animals are also good breeders. He promised to think about it.

Dolly and Stiva noticed me and trotted toward us.

"I don't have any oats today, dear friends," I said. "Sorry."

"It was sensible of you to choose those two," Wilhelm said.

"You're the one who chose," I said.

"Yes," he said. "Yes, I'm sorry about that."

"You needn't be."

"No. I'm not sorry about them. I'm sorry about how everything turned out."

At that moment, we heard something moving in the grass and Wilhelm jumped. His eyes widened when the foal, which had been lying on the ground hidden in the tall grass, suddenly got to its feet.

"There he is! Or maybe it's a she?"

"His name is Levin. A young stallion."

The foal ran toward Dolly in the singular fashion only children of all species run—a bit unsteadily, awkwardly, and absolutely happy.

"He appears healthy."

"Completely healthy, so far. But I watch over him as if he were my own."

"He is, after all."

"Yes, he is."

Wilhelm turned to face me.

"He's not just mine," I said.

Wilhelm smiled.

Then we just stood there silently, together, while the foal ran around and around in the enclosed pasture and its parents grazed in their quiet manner.

MATHIAS

Mongolia, 2019

We fly into the sunrise above the Gobi Desert. I haven't slept a wink, haven't room to stretch out my legs. I have a window seat and spend the time looking out. The sand is at first tinted pink by the sun, then it becomes gradually more yellowish in hue while the sky transitions from gray to blue. Blue, exactly as I remember it.

I wonder how it would have been if Karin had been with me on the plane. If my mother sat beside me while the Aeroflot rig from Moscow rumbled through the turbulence vortexes above the Gobi Desert. She had never been skittish, would probably have raised a knowing eyebrow the way she so often did, and grinned at the tightness of my grip on the armrests. And she would have thought I was fussy when I wrinkled my nose at the food served by Aeroflot.

Karin isn't here. But Sarah is with me and she also grins when my face turns ashen from the turbulence. She is much more of a globetrotter than I have ever been. She has done the things I've understood you're supposed to do when you are young: backpacked through the East, studied in Australia, gone rafting in Norway. Mongolia has always been the only thing I've had, the only exotic experience I could boast about when she showed photographs and videos from her trips. Now she will also have Mongolia. And I'm glad she's with me.

Besides, I think Karin would have liked it. Although she didn't exactly take to the grandmother role with zest and zeal, she did think it was nice we had Sarah.

The landing at Genghis Khan airport is every bit as crude and rough as the flight has been. The plane shakes, I hold on for dear life; for a moment, I'm afraid something will happen to the urn, that the door to the overhead luggage compartments will pop open, that the lid will fall off, and the ash will be scattered through the air inside the airplane. It would undeniably have been quite a story but wasn't exactly the plan for the trip.

I remind myself that the urn has a screw-on top, is made of metal and cannot be broken, and that the luggage compartments are, without doubt, closed properly, even on Aeroflot.

The brakes squeal but still the plane is traveling too fast.

"You know that landing is the most dangerous part?" Sarah says.

"Yes," I say. "Thanks, I did know that in fact."

Finally, the plane slows down and we stop.

I wonder about when I became such a coward. It must have come with age. Sarah is twenty-six years old. When I was twenty-six, I wasn't afraid of anything. I was too busy to be afraid. Busy finding cash for the next fix, the only thing in my head. And I had nothing to lose either, really. He who has little to lose has little to fear, it's said. Quite true.

It was only after I'd stopped using, after Mongolia, after I was given the right to start seeing Sarah, that fear crept into me.

Every time Sarah has been out traveling, she has had to call home to me much more often than to those she calls her parents, even though they deserve her calls much more than I do.

Relax, Mathias, she would say. I can take care of myself.

Stay away from everything, I would say, and everyone, and, for God's sake, watch your drink.

Then she would laugh at me. Don't you think I know that? Do you think I haven't learned a thing?

She's so easygoing, it's as if everything rolls off her. She doesn't hang on to things, doesn't get stuck. She could have been stuck in a lot of things. The nights when she cried and cried but wasn't picked up because her mother was only semiconscious, lying on the floor of the living room, far away on her own high. The soaking wet diapers, her behind full of sores, excrement on the floor, syringe needles in the corners. And hungry, she must have been hungry a lot, my child. We didn't even manage to feed her.

Every time I think about it, I just want to weep.

But Sarah is sitting beside me, strong and cool, has a denim jacket and those trousers with short, wide legs that young people are wearing today. Her backpack on the floor is full of schoolbooks. Soon, she will be taking her final exam in biology. She is so smart that she has already secured a job for the autumn, even though she has spent every Friday of the past few months organizing school strikes. I've popped down to see her a couple of times; she usually stands in the front row, her voice is loud and clear, impossible to ignore, now as back then.

She never seemed to stop crying. I've heard there's a difference between babies. Some give up when nobody comforts them, some resign themselves to it; they don't believe an adult will ever pick them up again, they learn that there is nobody with whom they can form a connection, that they have only themselves. But Sarah didn't give up. She wailed the way only babies can. It penetrated to the marrow, that wailing, and penetrated the walls. Luckily, the walls were thin in our building. The neighbors reported it. And reported it again. And again. Sarah still hadn't given up.

Finally, someone picked her up. Finally, there was someone who changed her diapers and fed her at last, and not a moment too soon for her. She came to someone who was there for her, with whom she could form a connection, and let her be a child. I owe her parents, her real parents, absolutely everything. I try to tell them so each time we meet. Sarah has mentioned that maybe it can be a bit too much. I will keep saying it anyway. I can't help myself.

A driver picks us up at the airport. He is holding a sign with our names on it. It feels a bit like being the director of a multinational company, except that we have traveled in tourist class and the car is a dusty Toyota Land Cruiser full of dents.

Behind us we see the city. It has grown—apartment buildings and high-rises are emerging everywhere—but we aren't headed there. We drive away from the center of town, directly west toward Hustai.

Neither of us sleeps. Sarah sits wide-eyed by the window. Gone is the sophisticated globetrotter; now she is just an eager tourist.

"Look there, and there, so many animals, there are animals everywhere, and the tents, imagine, they still really live there and so immense, so immense and empty."

"I did tell you it was big."

"But not *so* big."

"Four times the size of Germany."

"That's huge."

Being here is also huge. I get the urge to reach out my hand, take hold of hers, say something about how pleased I am that she came with me, but don't dare.

The roads have been upgraded over the past twenty-five years, thank heavens—it was sorely needed. But when we turn off the main road and drive into the park, it still reminds me of the old days. Full of bumps. The driver slows down, but it doesn't help much. Again, I start worrying about the urn in my bag. The lid that might come loose, the ash that could spill all over my clothes.

Hustai National Park, a large sign welcomes us. The park now has its own logo—round, with horses on it, of course. It must have come after Karin's time.

"Will we get to see them today?" Sarah asks. "Can we see the horses today?"

"Tomorrow," I say. "We'll go out to the watering hole before breakfast. They'll be there then."

"What time?"

"Half past four."

"Half past four?!"

"Do you want to see horses or not?"

"Fine . . . half past four."

"And that's when we're going to do it?"

"Yes. That's when we'll do it."

We drive on into the valley. The new station is located closer to the main road than the old one was—a large wooden building with solar cells on the pitched roof with some twenty tents on the plain in front of it. We get out of the car; three Chinese tourists pass us on the way to a visitors' center. Inside, you can see both an exhibition and a film about the national park and the horses. I have read about it on the park's website. Tourism is the main source of income. The area has been given national park status, has become something the country is proud of and no longer depends on foreign donations or sponsors for its operations. The park is run and owned by Mongols now.

At that moment, a smiling man in his thirties comes toward us.

"Mathias?"

He takes my hand. "Tim, *the manager*."

"Hi," I say. "Nice to finally meet you."

After all the emails we've exchanged, I feel like I already know him. I know he is happy we're here, that Karin is a kind of legend in these parts.

He shows us to our tent. It is spacious, outfitted with beds decorated with painted flowers, closets in orange and blue, soft carpets, and clean bedding. The mattresses emit the unmistakable scent of sheep's wool. On the table, is a thermos containing hot water for tea, of course.

Everything is just as it was before. And Sarah reacts just as I had hoped.

"Wow! This is over-the-top awesome!"

"I know, right?"

She sits on the bed, runs her hands over the duvet, is silent. She is just as clean as the white sheets, the skin on her face, on her throat, arms and hands is smooth, no scars, no blemishes.

I can't come up with anything that is wrong with her, not a single thing.

For my own part, I am nothing but scars, wounds. Dirt . . . for so many years I was dirty. Layers of filth covered my body, dust from the street plastered by sweat to my throat, behind my ears, in every single crease in my flesh, my teeth full of cavities.

I remember my hands. Always a little swollen and red, don't know why they got like that, must have been the drugs maybe, yellow nicotine stains on my fingertips, small cuts and sores, dirt under my fingernails, grime between my fingers, streaks of it along the blood vessels in the palms of my hands. And the stench. I stank, always noticed that people turned their backs when they met me.

It's easy to forget that I don't smell any longer, that my hands look quite ordinary—except for the scars. But many of them, probably most of them, come from my job, from carpentry work. And it's easy to forget that I don't stink of sweat or filth any more than anyone else. I take a shower every day, baths too, quite often, but that doesn't always change how I feel.

"Are you sure you don't mind sharing a tent?" I ask. "We can have separate tents. Tim said it wasn't a problem. There will be no charge."

Her face breaks open into a smile.

"Are we supposed to like, lie here alone then, tonight. In the middle of the steppes in a huge tent. How dark does it get here? I bet it gets pretty dark. And you've said there are wolves here."

"The camp is fenced in. They never come here."

"Still."

"Fine . . . ," I say. "Fine. We'll share the tent . . . then there will be room for even more Chinese tourists. And the park will earn even more money."

"China makes the world go 'round," she says.

I have to turn away, so she won't see that my eyes are shiny. Just because my daughter wants to share a tent with me.

When the alarm on my mobile phone rings, I don't know where I am, or why I set it for 4:30 a.m. It is evening in Europe, morning here; I've lost all sense of time. Then I smell the scent of sheep's wool and come to.

I switch on the flashlight and go over to Sarah, shaking her gently. She wakes up with a start and sits up.

"Is it time?"

"Yes, it's time."

She yawns, runs one hand across her face.

"I feel pretty good. No jet lag. Probably because it's not night yet in my body."

"It will be worse later today."

"You're really comforting."

"I know. It's always been my forte."

The jet lag gives my body a strange lightness, almost like being a little stoned. I like it. Since I quit everything, I search for things that can give me something resembling a high. I like the feeling of the chemistry at work in my body, hormones and whatever else, am happy to discover it's possible to find something like it from natural causes.

Tim stands waiting by the car looking unbothered by the hour; this is just a normal morning for him.

"Good morning," he says. "Tired?"

I nod. It looks as if he likes it, likes that the tourists are not as bright and chipper in the morning as he is, maybe even a kind of meager consolation for his having to turn in at 9:00 p.m. every single night.

"We'll be fine," Sarah says.

. . .

429

MAJA LUNDE

Day breaks as we drive inland in the direction of the old research station. The landscape is how I remember it, how it was when I came here at the same time of year all those many years ago. It's as I remember it, but still, not quite.

"It's dry," I say and point at the grass.

"Not much rain in the spring," Tim says. "The rainy season has started coming in autumn instead."

"Why's that?"

He shrugs, as if it is of no consequence. "Global warming."

"What does that have to do with it?"

"It's part of it. Less grass. Fewer animals."

Tim is clearly not the kind of guy to create drama.

We drive past the station. It's still a bright blue, but the windows are dark.

"Why did you move?" I ask.

"More practical," he says.

Then we drive in silence.

I knew this landscape so well, was out here almost every day for one year. Still, there is a lot that I've forgotten. Forgotten, really forgotten; it doesn't come back because I'm here again, either. My memory is shit, my brain full of holes. I remember the grass, I remember the marmots that always darted across the road. They're here now, too. Sarah squeals every time she sees one.

"They're so cute, oh my God, so cute! And so many of them, they're everywhere!"

"I told you."

"I thought you were exaggerating."

But I don't remember every single hill, valley, and summit in the landscape. I don't remember where the road leads inland toward the watering holes. I don't remember how many birds there are, or how often you see carcasses on the landscape. My memories of Mongolia are predominantly a feeling, the feeling of Karin, my mother.

We keep driving inland following tire ruts. Behind us the sky to the east grows steadily brighter.

430

We approach the watering holes and suddenly Sarah shouts, "There they are!"

Because there, on the slope where a brook is flowing and the grass grows greener and taller than elsewhere, are the horses.

"How beautiful! And so many of them!"

Yes, there are many of them. I count quickly; there must be at least three different harems and a couple groups of stallions.

They were all born here. Tim told me that the park hasn't imported horses from Europe since 2000.

I count twenty-one horses, but that's just a fraction of all the horses living in Hustai now. Three hundred twenty horses in all. And fifteen hundred in the world. From thirteen to fifteen hundred—over a hundred times more.

You did it, Karin, I think.

Nonetheless, I know she wouldn't be satisfied. There's a difference between three hundred twenty horses and the five hundred horses she aspired to. She would not have trusted that the population would survive, that there were enough of them.

And then she would, no doubt, have been frustrated about the losses. Last year, ninety-one horses died. There were foals that didn't make it, stallions that killed other stallions.

They are still dependent on the help of humans, on rangers who chase away wolves, chase away herds of tame horses so they don't mate with the takhis, dependent on the saltlicks they put out, on the birthing assistance the mares receive sometimes, on the monitoring carried out by humans at all times, keeping track of who mates with who, and the efforts to avoid inbreeding.

But progress is being made, Karin. You should have seen it.

Tim waits in the car while Sarah and I walk toward the horses.

We don't stop until we are one hundred meters away. We aren't permitted to come any closer.

I open the bag I have brought with me and remove the urn. The lid is screwed on tightly; not a trace of ash can be seen on the outside.

Suddenly, I feel repulsion. This is Karin's incinerated body—her arms and legs, her hair, her ears, and eyes. I'm suddenly afraid of getting the ash on me, of soiling my clothes, and regret the entire idea. I don't know if she would have liked it either; probably she would have thought it was a pretty meaningless idea. But most of the ash is from the coffin. There is a kind of comfort in that. And it is carbon anyway, all of it. Both the coffin and Karin are nothing but carbon now. Besides, she's dead. Completely gone. It is my decision and I have decided that it is here that Karin will end her days.

"Where should we do it?" Sarah asks.

"I don't know." I look around.

Scattering ashes on the wind, it's called. But the morning is windless.

"Up there, maybe?" Sarah points at a small hill.

"There, yes," I say and am relieved that she's here. "That's a nice spot there."

She walks quickly up the hill ahead of me and I have difficulties keeping up with her. I hold the urn under my arm, squeezing it hard against my body, afraid of dropping it on the ground.

"There," I say, trying to hide the fact that I am out of breath. "Nice. This is nice."

She nods. "It's nice everywhere."

"She would have liked this, you know," I say.

Sarah grins and suddenly looks a lot like her grandmother.

"Are you sure?"

"No."

"Me, neither."

"But I guess we're doing this," I say.

"Yes," she says.

And suddenly I see that her eyes are shiny.

"She was a cool lady," she says.

"Yes," I say. "She was. A pretty cool lady."

"She achieved all of this," Sarah says and throws out her arms.

"More than most people," I say.

Can someone be a lousy mother and still a good person? I don't know. I just know that I will never forgive myself for not being a better father. But then, I haven't rescued many horses. The only one I was given responsibility for died.

"Are you sad, Mathias?"

Sarah takes a step toward me, her eyes brimming with tears.

"No," I say. "No, it's fine. Or yes . . . I am sad, but not like I'm going to start crying or something. It's fine."

She nods. "Good."

I probably should cry. Should cry for Karin, my mother, whom I never called Mommy, for everything I still got from her, everything I cost her, for all the times she actually searched, yelled, tried to help me.

And the period after I got clean, after leaving here, was a pretty decent time. I visited her in Thorenc. Sometimes she called on me in Berlin, but never for more than two days. I understood eventually that *I* shouldn't stay more than two days in Thorenc, either. In two days, we had time to talk about the place, operations, the horses. I told her things about my job and about Sarah. We could look at photographs. But after two days, it came to an end because at that point the conversations could lead to other things, things neither of us wanted to talk about. We learned to stop in time.

I wasn't with her when she died. She had apparently passed away in her sleep at home; she was lucky that way. Lived in her own tiny house on the property in Thorenc, had nothing to do with operations any longer, but was up and about every single day. A woman fit for fight, always was, I guess that's what Sarah means when she says *cool*.

I'm not crying now, but I have cried over Karin. I have cried over Mommy. When I left Mongolia . . . the entire flight, I just cried and cried. Finally, a stewardess sat down beside me, offered me tissues and cup of tea. I cried because I had lost my mother. And because I had never had a proper Mommy. I cried because I'd repeated all her mistakes, just in another way. I cried because I was born with a disposition poorly suited for having Karin as a mother. It might have been different if I'd been a calm and reserved child, if I'd been more like her. Maybe I could have gotten more from her then, maybe she would have been able to give me what I needed if I had needed something different. And I cried for all the shit I knew she'd experienced during the war when she lost her mother, because maybe that's where it all began. Or maybe not? I cried because I would never have an answer to that question either, because I would never ask.

I continued to cry in the weeks that followed—while I found myself a place to live, while I applied for an apprenticeship with a carpenter, while I contacted Child Services to ask whether I could have one final chance to qualify for visitation rights with Sarah.

It wasn't until *that* was approved that I stopped crying. She was five years old and the most wonderful human being I'd ever met.

"Shall we do it, then?" I say and unscrew the lid on the urn.

"Yes," Sarah says.

I stand for a moment holding it in my hands, trying not to smell the odor of ash rising out of the urn.

Then I pour the ash out onto the ground, trying to spread it evenly across a patch of land in front of us on the slope facing the horses. I shake the urn to make sure I've emptied it.

"Bye," I say.

"Bye, Grandmother," Sarah says.

The ash settles on the grass, gray against the green.

What do you do with an empty urn? I forgot to ask about that, too. I stand there holding it, then I put the lid back on.

"We'll just have to take it back with us," I say.

"Yes," Sarah says.

Her lower lip is trembling. Suddenly she puts both arms around me and hugs me. I am unable to hug her back because then I would drop the urn. Her hair smells faintly of the freshly laundered pillowcase she slept on. Her chest heaves with three silent sobs and I can't refrain from comforting her.

434

I drop the urn on the ground. Apparently, I forgot to screw the lid on all the way, it pops off and disappears between two stones on the ground.

"The lid," I say.

"It doesn't matter," Sarah says.

I pull her against me, holding her tightly. My eyes are stinging fiercely and my throat burning.

"It doesn't matter," she repeats, and I don't know if she's talking about the lid or the tears. "It's going to be all right, Daddy. It will be all right."

THE END

A NOTE FROM THE TRANSLATOR

The process of translating *The Last Wild Horses*, Maja Lunde's masterful third book on the theme of climate change, has been a uniquely pleasurable experience. It is a gift to have the opportunity to translate several works by the same author, and I have had the good fortune to accompany Lunde on the journey these books entail. In the course of this journey, I have worked my way into a familiarity with Lunde's writing style, and as such, with time, the translation work has been afforded with greater certitude in addressing the author's literary choices.

Many years ago, I was involved in a translation project with the Norwegian poet Sigurd Helseth, in the context of which he suggested to me that one of the inherent values of translation lies in the introduction of "new"—as in "foreign"—constructs and their adherent concepts into another culture. This is absolutely the case for Lunde's literary project. In my work on the translations, I have been obliged to develop various means of stretching and subverting what is permitted in the English language so as to convey the poetic rhythms and cadences of Maja Lunde's prose. While for the translator the underlying question of this endeavor becomes, What else might language be? the larger implication of that question translates into, What else might *we* be? What other worlds might we envision? This question informs her novels as a whole, both with respect to the grim, dystopian scenarios Lunde creates and the characters who find themselves obliged to dig deep for courage they'd never dreamed they possessed and extract the means to rally onward, often in the face of seemingly impossible odds.

A NOTE FROM THE TRANSLATOR

While the worlds depicted in *The Last Wild Horses* are richly drawn, there is a leanness to the prose that speaks to a particular Norwegian mindset, in the sense of an almost minimalist, to-the-bone attunement with the natural world. This finds expression in the role and depiction of the exterior landscape in each of the stories. No mere backdrop for human endeavor, the environment here has the status of a protagonist in its own right, one who is sometimes benevolent, sometimes evasive, sometimes loud, and even violent, and always uncompromising in its summons. Each of the characters finds themselves struggling in different ways to respond to that summons and manifest their idealistic visions, a struggle that pits them against their own inner flaws and personal limitations. This is clearly epitomized by the story set in nineteenth-century Russia about the zoologist Mikhail, who is reluctantly launched out of the comfort and safety of a dream world into the realization of those dreams, on an expedition demanding the sacrifice of creature comforts, and inevitably enabling him to redefine who he is as a human being, the kind of man he wants to be.

To the extent that we take climate change seriously, it behooves us to take our cue from this, even as it demands an about-face, a turning away from much of what we have felt to be life's necessities. In this sense, the process of translating Lunde's work is imbued with a significance that underscores the message of the work itself: if we are interested in saving the planet, we must stretch and challenge the conventions of our thinking in innovative ways. Beyond the informative value that lies in learning about the history and fate of the beautiful, wild horses around which the novel revolves, and the sheer enjoyment of reading about their impact on the respective characters' lives, the stories of *The Last Wild Horses* inspire the reader to think beyond what appears given, to discern and rescue whatever at-risk "wild horses" they might find in their immediate surroundings or on distant horizons. The novel invites the reader to ask, quite simply, what other worlds might be.

Diane Oatley

ACKNOWLEDGEMENTS

I will begin by thanking all those who have taken the time to read drafts, answer questions, and think aloud with me in the course of my work on this novel: biologist Anne Sverdrup-Thygeson, horse expert Margreth Olin, Mongolia expert Benedikte Victoria Lindskog, biologist Dag O. Hessen, hydrologist Lena Merete Tallaksen, farmer Live Johnsrud, Russian translator Marit Bjerkeng, biologist Petra Kaczensky, and zoologist Petter Bøckman. I would also extend my gratitude to Therese Lindström and her colleagues at Nordens Ark for their warm welcome and to Ingunn Skjerve Løken and Simen Løken at Sjøsætra for teaching me how to milk a cow. I would also like to thank Heidrun Reisæter, who accompanied me to St. Petersburg, and Peter Kozyrev, who showed us the many sides of the city, and I must also thank the horse veterinarian Kristin Olstad for her invaluable assistance and unending patience. A large thank-you to the staff at the Hustai National Park and the International Takhi Group in Mongolia, who welcomed me with open arms and shared their knowledge, particularly biologist Usukhjargal Dorj, Programme Manager Jamiyandorj Batsukh, and Project Coordinator Munkhtuya Byamba.

A special thank you goes to the entire staff at Aschehoug and Oslo Literary Agency, especially my indefatigable agent Annette Orre, who takes such good care of my novels all over the world. and my wise editor Nora Campbell, who has accompanied me and this book throughout the entire process, even all the way to Mongolia.

ACKNOWLEDGEMENTS

Last, but not least, I must thank all the people who throughout the course of the past two centuries have done their part to ensure that the Takhis still exist on this planet. This story is also theirs.

Oslo, August 2019
Maja Lunde

SOURCES OF INSPIRATION

I have utilised many sources in my work on *The Last Wild Horses*. Mikhail and Wilhelm's story is in part inspired by the wild animal merchant and zoo pioneer Carl Hagenbeck's story of his life *Beasts and Men* (1912). Karin's story draws inspiration from Piet Wit and Inge Bouman's book about their longstanding work with Takhis: *The Tale of the Przewalski's Horse: Coming Home to Mongolia* (KNNV Publishing, 2006) and the documentary films *Wild Horses Return to China* (Clive Copeman, Natural History New Zealand Ltd & Xinjiang Television China, 2010) and *The Takh Back to Mongolia* (Micaela van Rijckevorsel, Stichting Arte et Cetera, 2006). Lee Boyd & Katherine A. Houpt's (eds.) exacting collation of research articles *Przewalski's Horse, the History and Biology of an Endangered Species* (State University of New York Press, 1994) also merits mention, as it has been a solid source of reference for my work on all three stories. However, I must emphasise that even though *The Last Wild Horses* tells the story of an actual species and humankind's endeavours to ensure that species' conservation, the book is wholly and fully a novel, in which all the main characters and the majority of the events are either fictional or coloured by my imagination.

Other important sources of inspiration

Acton, Edward (1995). *Russia, the Tsarist and Soviet Legacy.* Longman.
Andersen, Reidar & Steinøien, Hans K. (2018). *Arten som forandret alt*. J. M. Stenersens forlag.

European Environment Agency (2016). *Climate change, impacts and vulnerability in Europe.*

Harari, Yuval Noah (2016). *Sapiens.* Cappelen Damm.

Hessen, Dag O. (2017). *Vi. Samarbeid – fra celle til samfunn.* Cappelen Damm.

Kolbert, Elizabeth (2015). *Den sjette utryddelsen* [*The Sixth Extinction: An Unnatural History*]. Mime Forlag.

Kaczensky, P., Walzer, C. & Steinhauer-Burkart, B. (2004). *Great Gobi B.* Eco Nature Edition.

Lindén, Lena M. (2014). *Med näbbar och klor, Nordens Ark och kampen för hotade djur.* Votum.

Norwegian Environment Agency. *Klima i Norge 2100*, NCCS report, no. 2/2015.

Przewalski, Nikolai (1879). *Mongolia, the Tangut Country.* Sampson, Low, Marston, Searle & Rivington.

Przewalski, Nikolai (1879). *From Kulja, Across the Tian Shan to LobNor.* Sampson, Low, Marston, Searle & Rivington.

Sebag Montefiore, Simon (2017). *Romanov.* Cappelen Damm.

van Rijckevorsel, Micaela (2006). *The Takh Back to Mongolia* (documentary), Stichting Arte et Cetera.

Seymour, John (2010). *Den nye komplette håndbog i selvforsyning.* Gyldendal.

Smetania, Katerina (2006). *Russland og russere.* Orion.

Steinhauer-Burkart, Bern (2014). *Hustai Nuruu National Park*, Eco Nature Edition.

The following works are cited or referred to in the novel:

Aristoteles [Aristotle] (2013). *Den nikomakiske etikk* [*Nicomachean Ethics*].Vidarforlaget.

Flaubert, Gustave (1980). *The Letters of Gustave Flaubert: 1857-1880.* Belknap Press of Harvard University Press.

Hagenbeck, Carl (1912) *Beasts and Men.* Longmans, Green, and Co.

Shakespeare, William (1996). *Richard III.* Oktober Forlag.

Spencer, Herbert (1864) *The Principles of Biology.* Williams and Norgate.